# Small Things

by

## Joe DeRouen

Small Things Press

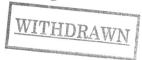

Visit Joe's website at www.JoeDeRouen.com

First Printing: December 2012

ISBN 978-0-615-73771-3

Cover by Renée Barratt, thecovercounts.com

Author photo by Jasmine Teramura

FIRST EDITION

Printed in the USA

\* \* \*

Small Things Press | www.SmallThingsPress.com

*For my wife Andee and my son Fletcher, without whom this book most likely would still have been possible, but not nearly as rewarding*

## Acknowledgements

I'd like to thank everyone who contributed to helping make this novel happen, including Andee DeRouen, Bruce Diamond, Jason Warner, Jennifer Kuzbury, Annie Sturdivant Coppock, Jessica Rotich, LaDonna Elston Meredith, all the folks associated with NaNoWriMo, Rod Serling, Ken Grimwood, Charles de Lint, and my high school Junior English teacher, Mr. Snowden, who was the first person to encourage me and tell me I had talent.

Special thanks also go to Lisa Lauenberg, Jeffery and Tasha Derouen, Judy SoRelle, Pan Sticksel, Rebecca McFarland, Joe Reynolds, Phil and Melissa Rhoads, Jesse and Kristie Floyd, the real Zoom Beezie, Dave Doohan, Burgundy Wisrock-Eckert, Steven Jasiczek, Douglas Smith, Kristen Scissons, David and Shelley Darling, Paul and Ruth SoRelle, Melissa Jordan, and Vanessa Wages.

# Small Things

# Chapter 1

**Summer, 1975**

SOMEONE HAD been following him ever since he returned home. The hint of movement outside the window, just beyond his line of sight, or the sense that someone had quickly stepped behind a building or a tree mere seconds before he turned around; nothing concrete to prove his suspicions, but someone had been there, of that he was dead certain.

Even this morning, getting ready for his best friend's funeral, he'd felt a pair of eyes following him as he climbed into the back of his dad's station wagon. He hoped that whoever it was hadn't followed them to the church.

Lost in his thoughts, he could almost forget Tanner's death, if only for a moment. Breathing deeply, he forced himself to take stock of his surroundings.

Shawn Spencer sat with his parents inside the Immaculate Conception Roman Catholic Church of Carthage - a hot, stifling building that he had only visited a handful of times before. They occupied the third pew from the front, just behind Tanner's family. The air inside the church was stuffy and the seats were hard and uncomfortable, and Shawn tried desperately to tune out the droning voice of the priest whom Tanner's family had chosen to lead the service.

When he closed his eyes, he could still see Tanner dressed up in his Sunday best, his mouth molded into an unnatural smile and his skin a color in death that it had never been in life. It just wasn't Tanner. And he hated those clothes they'd put him in. If he was going to have to spend eternity underground, couldn't they at least have picked out more comfortable clothes?

Tanner had drowned just three days ago. The two had been inseparable since the middle of fourth grade, and he couldn't quite grasp the thought of life without his best friend.

"Shawn," whispered his father, the word coming out in a choke, "we're pretty much done here, unless you want to go up and say goodbye one last time. I think it's about time to go to the cemetery for the burial."

Shawn's stomach clenched at his father's words, and he looked across the rows of wooden pews to the coffin where his best friend lay in his uncomfortable suit. A quiet murmuring chatter danced among the mourners, pleasantries exchanged about what a good boy Tanner had been, how the family had endured more than their share of tragedies over the years, and why it was perfectly understandable that Tanner's sister was having a hard time coping with her loss. Shawn just wanted them all to shut up. He needed this day to be over. More than anything, he desperately needed his friend back.

He snuck another glance toward the entrance to the church – nothing – then watched as the other mourners filed past the coffin, some pausing to say a prayer or to drop something in the casket, others rushing past without so much as a glance. Two of Tanner's cousins paid their respects, followed by a teacher from school, and finally a blonde-haired man in a trench coat. *A strange choice of dress for a hot summer morning,* thought Shawn, but then the procession began to slow, and he knew it was his turn.

And there it was again. The hairs on the back of his neck prickled, and the flash of something dark, something that shouldn't be there, opposite Tanner's coffin and across the hall, outside the heavy wooden doors that hung open exposing the church to the rest of the world. He clenched his teeth and moved forward, ignoring his racing heart.

He didn't want to say goodbye, didn't even know how, but he knew he had to do it. Moving closer to the box of burnished wood, he noticed Tanner's sister putting something inside the coffin. He caught her eye and she blushed, her cheeks turning a shade of crimson to match her long, red hair and freckles, as she pushed a pair of tortoiseshell glasses further up the bridge of her nose.

"Hi Shawn," Jenny smiled shyly. "Mom said it was okay to put something in with Tanner. You can too, if you want."

"Like what?" Shawn asked, confused, his eyes darting between the girl and the doorway beyond the church. "What would he need, now that he's… well, you know…"

"Yeah, I do know," said Jenny, her emerald green eyes welling up with tears. "Sorry," she sniffled. "Well, Mom put in a poem, Grandma put in a bible, and Dad put in a few of Tanner's favorite comics. I put in his Galahad doll."

Action figure, he silently corrected her. Girls.

He studied the eight-inch plastic knight lying atop Tanner's cold body: The Mego figure's armor had a small split and was missing his helmet and visor, though at least he still had his sword and shield. That in itself was amazing considering how many adventures Tanner and Shawn had put their figures through over the years.

Shawn's Ivanhoe was in a similar state of disrepair, having long ago lost his weapons and both of his boots. Though they didn't really play with them anymore, both he and Tanner still had their figures proudly displayed on bookshelves in their rooms.

His eyes swept the rest of the offerings: there was the bible and the comics, along with some photos, Mrs. McGee's poem, a little silver cross, and an old mason jar of change. Shawn stared at the jar, thinking for a moment that it was the same one they had found earlier in the summer, but of course that couldn't be the case. He knew Tanner had been saving money for a new bicycle, so maybe his parents had included the jar along with the rest of the offerings.

"Jenny, I don't have anything to put with him," Shawn apologized, firmly positioning his back to the door lest he be compelled to look again. And then he remembered the nickel.

Earlier in the summer, just two weeks before the start of summer vacation, Shawn and Tanner had finally managed to get into the old Spencer house on Randolph Street. The huge three-story spread, abandoned for years, had fueled their imagination for as long as he could remember. After all, it was Shawn's birthright: Charles Spencer, the last known occupant of the house, had been Shawn's great-great uncle. And that's where they'd found the nickel.

"Well, I guess I do have something after all," reasoned Shawn, reaching into his pocket. Bypassing his pocketknife and two pieces of Bazooka bubble gum, he pulled out an old Buffalo nickel. "Think this'll do?"

"Couldn't hurt," Jenny smiled, adjusting her glasses. Taking the nickel from Shawn's outstretched palm, she blanched as she noticed a wet stain of blood on the coin. "Hey, did you hurt yourself?"

Looking to his bleeding thumb, he thought he'd probably pricked it on the old pocketknife when digging around for the nickel. "My pocketknife. I guess I need to get rid of that thing," he shrugged, sucking the blood from his finger. "Sorry about that."

Answering his shrug with one of her own, Jenny returned the nickel before slowly walking away to rejoin her parents. "I'm not sure what he could buy with a nickel, though," she called over her shoulder, giving Shawn a half-hearted wave.

"I'll miss you, buddy," said Shawn, flicking the coin into the air toward Tanner's coffin. The coin landed on Galahad's head, bounced once, rolled down the toy's torso, and finally settled between his legs and the dead boy's hand. "I'm sorry I wasn't there," he whispered, turning away from the coffin to follow Jenny back into the world of the living.

# Chapter 2

SHAWN HAD only been to one other funeral before this one, and that had been eight years ago. Today's events brought back a flash of memory; the sight of rosy-pink skin turned blue, and a body that should have been breathing...

He shook his head, pushing back the memory. Shawn wasn't looking forward to going to Tanner's house any more than he was the ceremony itself, but that's exactly where he found himself less than thirty minutes after they'd lowered his best friend into the ground. He'd seen no sign of his follower between the church and the house, so maybe it was his imagination after all.

The McGee house was filled with all the same people who had been at the church and the cemetery. They drifted in and out, new people inexplicably arriving to take the place of anyone who left. Shawn consoled his misery with another tiny ham and cheese sandwich from the huge buffet table in the dining room and tried to stay out of everyone's way.

The table was filled to the edge with all kinds of cheese and lunch meats, three baked hams, four pies, and just about every kind of casserole you could imagine. Shawn was contemplating a huge piece of cherry pie when someone tapped him on the shoulder.

Shawn whirled in panic, knocking over a glass of iced tea someone had carelessly left on the table into a half-eaten cherry pie. His eyes big and his heart racing, he blushed as he saw it was only Jenny.

"Hey Shawn," she said, a cup of lemonade in one hand and the program from the funeral in the other. She still wore the depressing black dress she'd had on at the cemetery, but her long red hair was pulled back into a ponytail. Jenny smiled as she straightened her glasses. "Can we talk?"

"Umm, sure," answered Shawn, doing his best to ignore the mess as the tea soaked into the fruit-filled pastry. "I guess so."

"I'm sure you've heard by now that I'm totally nuts," she forced a smile as she led Shawn from the dining room and out the door to the back porch.

"Well, yeah, I guess I have," answered Shawn, sitting down on one of the lawn chairs that adorned the small deck. He forced himself to suck down a huge gulp of air and exhaled slowly. He didn't like being out here, at the mercy of whoever had been following him.

"Well, I'm not. And I need your help. Did they tell you what happened?"

"At the lake, you mean?"

"Yes, dummy, at the lake. What did you think I meant?" She smiled, taking a seat beside him.

"Well, dad told me that Tanner drowned at the lake, and that you found him. There doesn't seem to be much else to tell."

"But that's not what happened!" Jenny argued. "A monster got him, Shawn, a huge, black monster. And I know how that sounds, but it's true. I didn't even have time to say anything, or do anything, before it rose up out of the water and grabbed him. Then it shook him and growled at him, and it pulled him under." Fresh tears glistened on her cheeks. "And then it killed him. It murdered my brother. And I need your help to find it."

"Jenny! I can't help you find it, because it doesn't exist. There wasn't any monster. Monsters don't exist." At least that's what he'd always believed. "Tanner..."

"Tanner was murdered, Shawn!" Jenny sobbed, jumping out of her chair. "He was murdered. Don't you get it? Don't you want to find out what really happened?"

"Jenny, I'm sorry. I really am. Jesus, he was my best friend! But I just don't believe…"

"You're wrong," she said, stifling her tears. "And I'm going to prove it."

# Chapter 3

SHAWN PUSHED the kickstand into place, sliding off his Schwinn at the lake that had stolen his best friend's life. He stood at the far end of the water, beside the little dam and spillway that kept the lake from flooding. A putrid stench wafted up from the water, filling his nostrils and causing his eyes to burn. The lake had turned. It was that time of year.

The smell stood out in contrast to the beauty of the stately oak trees that framed the other side of the lake and the sounds of nature all around him. The lake was beautiful and ugly at the same time. His senses worked against each other; smell causing the boy to hold his breath, while sight and hearing drew his attention to the placid waters and the birds calling to their brethren in the trees beyond.

His parents had seemed confused and a little concerned by his need to bike out to the lake alone just an hour after the memorial. From the moment he found out that Tanner had died, Shawn knew that he would eventually be driven to visit this place, the last place on Earth where Tanner's feet would ever tread. He wasn't sure if it was morbid curiosity or an attempt to find closure after the funeral, but he needed to see the spot where his best friend's life had ended, stalker be damned. Besides, he hadn't seen or sensed hide nor hair of whoever had been following him since the funeral. Whoever it was seemed to be gone, if he had ever existed in the first place.

Shawn and Tanner had spent many summers fishing in the very spot where Shawn now stood. He knew he could never again cast out a line or reel in a bluegill without seeing his friend's head bobbing under the water, lungs filling with liquid, arms and legs floating lifelessly just beneath the surface.

Bending low to the ground, Shawn scooped up a handful of rocks. One by one, he threw them into the lake, watching as they broke the surface to disappear below. Was that how it had been with Tanner?

He still didn't understand why Tanner had drowned. They'd been fishing together countless times over the years, and his friend had proven to be both surefooted and a skilled fisherman. They both knew the lake was filled with sinkholes and had been warned countless times not to swim near the dam, so why on earth would Tanner have ventured out into the water? The lake was filled with catfish, bluegill, bass, and croppy, and he'd never caught anything that weighed more than about fifteen pounds at the most, so there was just no way that a fish could have pulled him under.

None of this made any sense, and he supposed that he'd never really know exactly what had happened at the lake that day, why his friend had been taken from him before they were even out of high school. He almost wished he could make himself believe in monsters. At least then he'd have something to blame. Shawn shook his head at his own foolishness and let the last stone fall from his fingers. It was time to go home.

The rest of the day passed in a blur. Shawn spent time reading and watching television, trying to relax. Still no sign of whoever had been following him, and he'd all but managed to put it out of his mind. He flipped through some of the comics his Grandfather had bought him at the airport, but couldn't get into them, nor could he interest himself in the old "Ma and Pa Kettle" movie that was running on channel 11.

Shawn stared at himself in the mirror and wished not for the first time that he had been at the lake with Tanner and Jenny. He studied his light blue eyes, hating himself. He and Tanner had been blood brothers; they had vowed to always protect each other and, when it really mattered, he'd failed. Tanner was gone, and it had happened while he was over a thousand miles away.

Wiping away tears, Shawn turned from the mirror and flopped down on the bed, thinking of the last day he had spent with the best friend he ever had.

\* \* \*

"Come on Shawn… it's a tradition!" said Tanner, holding out his hand. Tanner was shorter than Shawn by at least three inches, but what he lacked in size he made up in both girth and bravado. Where Shawn was tall and lean, Tanner was short and pudgy, with dark unkempt hair that caused his freckles to stand out by contrast. Tanner may not have been the strongest or most athletic kid in school, but he'd never met a dare he wouldn't take or a kid he wouldn't dare, and he intended to see that Shawn followed in his footsteps.

Shawn and Tanner sat at a picnic table in the Carthage Jaycee Park, picking at the remains of the hot dogs they had bought at the Tastee Freez just half an hour earlier. There were a few younger kids playing on the slides and merry-go-round, and a girl they recognized as being a few grades behind them sitting on a swing across from the picnic area, but mostly the park was deserted. It was almost two in the afternoon on the fifth day of summer vacation, just two days before Shawn would leave for Texas, and most of their classmates were off playing baseball or swimming at the public pool across the street.

Shawn eyed the knife nervously, knowing what was coming next. Every year since they became blood brothers, they'd started out the summer by renewing their pact. Tanner always said that this would keep the bond strong, but he suspected that the boy just enjoyed watching him squirm.

"We're already blood brothers. Do we really have to do this again?"

"Hey, I've already cut myself," Tanner held up a bloody thumb. "You don't want me to bleed to death, do you?"

"No, I guess we wouldn't want that," Shawn sighed.

Quickly snatching the knife from Tanner, not giving himself time to think about it, he pricked the pad of his thumb. "Ouch!" A droplet of blood rose to the surface of the skin, like a ruby shining brightly in the hot summer sun.

"Blood brothers for another year," Tanner announced triumphantly, pressing his thumb to Shawn's. They held their thumbs together for a few seconds to let the blood mingle and then pulled back, Tanner sucking his thumb to stop the bleeding, Shawn wrapping his in the napkin from his hot dog.

"So what now, brother of mine?" Shawn wondered aloud. Wiping the knife on his napkin before passing it back to Tanner, he added, "Maybe we should finally take Jenny to the pool and just get it over with?"

"But what fun is that?" asked Tanner, "I have a better idea. Let's finally do it. Let's break into the old house."

A puzzled look passed over Shawn's face, almost as if he had woken from a trance. Shaking his head to clear the cobwebs, he said, "You know, I actually had a dream about the house last night…"

"An omen if there ever was one!"

"We're going to get in trouble," argued Shawn, half-heartedly.

"C'mon," said Tanner, swallowing the last of his hot dog, "You know you want to do it. You've wanted to as long as I can remember. C'mon, I dare you."

Shawn smiled and spun his yo-yo down to the ground, then jerked the string, sending it climbing back up again to land in his hand. Tanner's dares were famous in their small mid-western farming town, and had resulted in more than one of their classmates ending up with broken arms, lost bicycles, or furious parents.

But Shawn just couldn't say no to Tanner. Besides, the older boy was right: Shawn had wanted to go inside the old, abandoned house ever since he was told that the previous owner had been his great-grandfather's brother. Charles Spencer had apparently disappeared without a word to anyone over 25 years ago, leaving the house abandoned.

Why no one had ever claimed the house or at least the land it was on was a mystery to Shawn. His father had said there was some sort of dispute about the ownership, and that the taxes had been paid far in advance, and as far as anyone knew the man – probably long dead now – still legally owned the property.

"Well?" asked Tanner, getting up from the picnic table to retrieve his bike. "It's either this or teach my sister to swim, which isn't exactly on my top ten list of things I want to do this summer. So how about it? Jenny can wait until later for the swimming lessons."

Shawn thought about the old house that had brought so much mystery and speculation into their lives, and decided it was time to finally find out what Great-Great-Uncle Charles had left behind.

"I'm in," he said tentatively. What harm could it do? Rising from the table, he joined Tanner beside their bicycles. "It's now or never, I guess, so let's go!"

\* \* \*

A knock on his bedroom door pulled Shawn back to reality. He rolled off the bed to his feet just as his mother appeared in the doorway.

"You've been in here for hours," smiled Ellen Spencer, her blonde hair and blue eyes a reflection of Shawn's own. Dressed in a long red and white checkered flannel nightgown, she held out a steaming mug of hot cocoa to her son. "Dad and I are getting ready to turn in and wanted to make sure you're okay, and I made this for you to help you sleep."

"I'm okay," Shawn said, taking the offered cup from his mother as she leaned in to give him a kiss on the cheek. "I was just thinking about Tanner."

"It'll get better in time. Say, do you want to go back to Arkansas and spend the rest of your summer with your Grandparents? They'd love to have you back. They were really sad about Tanner, you know, and about you having to come back early."

"No, Mom," answered Shawn, thinking of Jenny and her frantic pleas for help. He'd help her, alright, just not in the way that she imagined. "I miss them too, but there's always next year. I'd rather just stay home. Besides, I promised someone I'd teach them how to swim."

# Chapter 4

SHAWN AWOKE with a start, knocking the empty cocoa mug off the nightstand. He jumped as the cup shattered against the floor, then spun around to look out the window, coming face-to-face with a pair of glowing red eyes. He blinked once, and it was gone. There was nothing there save the stars. Had he been dreaming?

Samson, however, sensed something as well. The old tom stood staring at the window from his spot at the foot of Shawn's bed, his hackles raised and a low throaty growl coming from deep inside his chest. The stalker was real after all. He shook his head violently, not daring to believe it was true.

Pale moonlight filtered around the old weeping willow outside of his window and in through the curtains, illuminating the little clock he kept beside his bed: it was almost five in the morning. Willing his heart to stop beating jackhammers against his chest, Shawn reached out to click on his lamp. It had to have been a dream. Stretching to pet the orange and white tabby, Shawn picked up the cat he'd had since he was seven years old and stroked his short coat of orange and white fur.

"Shawn," yelled a voice from the hallway, "Shawn, are you okay? I heard a noise." His father, hair tousled and in his pajamas, stood in the doorway.

"Sorry, Dad," Shawn apologized, setting Samson down on the ground. "I had a bad dream, I guess. Don't worry, I'll clean up the mug."

"You scared the beejeesus out of us," breathed Henry Spencer, sucking in air as he reached out to touch his son's shoulder. "I was halfway down the hall before I was even awake. Are you sure you're okay?"

"Positive, Dad," Shawn lied. "I don't even remember what the dream was about."

"Okay, then. I'm going back to bed. And don't worry about the cup. You can clean it up in the morning."

"Are you sure you're okay?" asked his mother, gliding into the room to give him a hug. "I'll clean that up right now."

"Don't worry about it, Mom, I can handle it," said Shawn, embarrassed. "I made the mess, I'll clean it up."

"All right, honey," she answered, concern still in her eyes. "You can sleep late tomorrow, if you want. I know you've had a rough day."

"I'm okay, Mom. Just a bad dream, that's all. Once I get back to bed I'll be fine."

He watched as his mother left the room, closing the door behind her. He felt like a little kid again, being comforted by his mother after waking up screaming from the nightmares he'd suffered on and off for a year half his lifetime ago.

But this hadn't been a nightmare, no matter what he wanted to believe. He was almost positive of that. Something – a rustling, scratching, creaking sound – had come from the window, waking him in an instant. And he'd seen those eyes, like a vampire from one of those old movies that Tanner had loved so much.

It was probably just a squirrel or something, he tried to tell himself. Or maybe, as his father always used to joke when Shawn was little and thought he'd heard noises under the bed, it was just the early bird trying to get the jump on the worms.

Sighing, he knelt down to pick up the shattered pieces of the mug. He'd been thinking about his and Tanner's sojourn into the old Spencer house before he fell asleep, so maybe he'd just given himself an old-fashioned case of the creeps. Or maybe, regardless of what his gut was telling him, it really had been a dream after all.

Shards of the mug in hand, Shawn walked lightly through the hallway, past the living room and into the kitchen where he flicked on the wall switch over the breakfast nook. Light flooded the room and Shawn spied Samson just a few feet behind him. The big house cat slunk to the corner of the room and hunkered down in front of his food bowl, mewling plaintively. Stepping over the cat, he found the trashcan under the sink and dumped the sharp remains of the mug into the trash before filling Samson's bowl with fresh Friskies.

Shawn looked at the clock that hung on the wall above the telephone. It was just a few minutes past five now, and the faint light of the morning was starting to seep in through the curtained window. Making his way to the refrigerator, he poured himself a glass of water from the pitcher his mother always kept chilled in the icebox. That's the only way you can stand to drink Carthage water, thought Shawn: ice cold. And even then, once a year or so, the lake turned and forced everyone to boil the now-brownish water before drinking or using it for cooking.

Thinking about the lake brought the image of Tanner in his church clothes unbidden to mind again, lying there not looking anything at all like the boy he'd known. Shaking his head, Shawn tried but failed to dispel the image from his thoughts.

Everyone said that he had slipped and hit his head before drowning, but Tanner had been an excellent swimmer as well as sure on his feet. What had so distracted him that he hadn't paid attention to where he was walking? And, damn it, why hadn't they taught Jenny to swim so she could have at least tried to save him?

But he didn't blame Jenny for not saving Tanner. She had wanted to learn to swim, but they kept putting it off, always having more important things to do. If anything, it was their fault that they hadn't done the deed before he left for Texas. It was too late to save Tanner, but he could at least keep his promise to teach his best friend's sister how to swim.

In three quick gulps Shawn downed his water. Clicking off the kitchen light, he carefully craned his neck to peer out through the window above the sink. Nothing. It had to have been a dream, Shawn repeated to himself as he walked back to his bedroom, leaving Samson to his breakfast.

\* \* \*

And outside, something watched. Hiding behind the old willow tree, the thing spied Shawn reentering his bedroom, turning out the light, and clambering back into bed. It watched as the fifteen-year-old boy glanced out the window, his eyes briefly settling on its own before moving on. Finally, the boy pulled the covers up to his chin, rolled over, and lay still.

There would be other chances, the creature knew. It would have time. And, besides, there was always the girl...

# Chapter 5

JENNY ROLLED over, her bright pink bedspread tangling under her exposed feet. Still asleep, she instinctively pulled at the covers, inadvertently exposing more of her bare legs to the cool morning air.

Slowly, silently, the creature let itself through her open window and dropped without a sound to the carpeted floor below. Its eyes darting this way and that, the small, dark thing took in its surroundings.

The room was painted pink. The bedspread was pink, as were the sheets. The trashcan that rested beside the open window was pink. Even the carpet was pink. Disgusted, the creature made a noise in the back of its throat like something halfway between a growl and a hiss, causing the girl to roll over in her sleep, finally pulling the blanket out from under her and back around her exposed feet. The beast wondered how all the pretty pink would look when drenched in the meat's blood.

Moving like a cat, soft as a strangled scream, the pitch black beast slowly sidled across Jenny's room, finally sliding under her bed. It was looking for something, and wouldn't leave until it found it, or had at least feasted on the steaming entrails of the teenage girl lying fast asleep on the bed, wrapped in the ugly pink bedspread like a caterpillar.

Aside from a naked Barbie doll, a copy of Dynamite magazine and a single pink tennis shoe, the beast found nothing. Growling melodically to itself, it glided across the room to the bookshelf against the far wall, where it carefully began to remove and look through various *Nancy Drew* books, *The Wind in the Willows, Alice in Wonderland, The Hobbit, The Three Musketeers, Dandelion Wine, Something Wicked This Way Comes,*

*Flowers for Algernon*, a book on Latin, and three tomes on world mythology.

Again the girl stirred, forcing the creature to temporarily abandon its hunt and meld into the shadows. Jenny mumbled something in her sleep, yawned, and then stretched before finally rolling onto her stomach, asleep again.

The beast scurried back to the bookshelf, methodically taking books from the wooden stand, flipping through each in turn before casually discarding them into an ever-growing pile in the middle of the room. It would find what it sought sooner or later, or at least enjoy making the meat pay for wasting its time.

# Chapter 6

IT WAS NEARLY seven in the morning now, and Shawn still couldn't sleep. Letting out a long sigh, exhausted from the previous day's activities but inexplicably still wide awake, he sat up, dislodging the cat that lay curled up at his feet. Samson yawned, stretched, and fell back asleep, kneading the covers with his paws. *Wish I could do that,* thought Shawn, envious of the cat's ability to nod off almost at will.

Turning toward the window, shading his eyes against the early morning sun, he scanned the yard for intruders. Nothing. More than likely, no one had actually been there last night. Jenny had probably just spooked him with all her talk of death and monsters and he'd let his imagination get the better of him. Tanner would get a big kick out of it when he told...

He shook his head, mentally chastising himself. Tanner wouldn't get a big kick out of anything, because Tanner was dead. It still hadn't sunk in that Tanner was really gone. He kept wanting to call him, to tell him something, to make plans for the rest of the summer. It just didn't seem real. He had to remind himself that he'd never see his best friend again.

They'd had so many plans, dreams that now would never come true. They had talked for hours about saving up to buy a car once Shawn turned sixteen, Tanner getting it Monday and Wednesday and him Tuesday and Thursday, and alternating the weekends.

After high school, they were going to backpack through Europe. Tanner's ancestors were Irish, and he wanted nothing more than to visit Ireland. Shawn was okay with that, and figured Ireland was as good a place as any to start their journey. He wanted to see the world, explore everything that the globe had to offer, and could think of no better way to do it than with his best friend at his side.

Everything they planned, the car, the trip, their futures: it was gone. Sure, Shawn would still learn to drive and eventually buy his own car, and he may even visit Europe someday, but it just wouldn't be the same without Tanner. He felt a familiar ache in his chest, the same hollow feeling he'd felt last night at the funeral, but forced himself to roll out of bed because he knew if he didn't he was likely to just lie around all day feeling sorry for himself.

Rifling through his drawers for a pair of shorts and a t-shirt, he felt more alone than he had in years. Clean clothes in hand, he quietly made his way to the bathroom and toward a hot shower before heading over to Jenny's house for her swimming lesson.

\* \* \*

*"Fuck!"* rasped the creature, the first sound it had uttered since letting itself into the meat's bedroom. Jenny slept fitfully through the thing's tantrum, stirring but never fully waking. It almost wished that she had. It was always more fun when they were awake, like her brother had been. All in good time, the old man had told the creature. There'd be plenty of time for eating later. But the hunger ached cold and deep in the thing's belly, and it knew it couldn't wait much longer.

The beast went through every book and record album on the bookshelf, turning every page and looking in every sleeve, but found nothing. Then it searched through the closet and went through all the drawers and cabinets in the room, throwing all of the girl's clothing on top of the growing pile of books and records once it was satisfied that what it was looking for wasn't there. It even forced itself to open and look through the little wooden (at least it wasn't pink!) hope chest at the foot of the girl's bed, but still it found nothing. Nothing! Wherever the object was, it wasn't here. It could tell that she'd held it, though, or at least been close to it. It could smell it on her, and smelling the meat made it hungry for her blood.

Lost in thought, the creature absentmindedly withdrew a pair of white cotton panties from the pile of belongings in the middle of the floor. Bringing them to its face, it inhaled deeply. A happy gurgle escaped its throat: the girl had already gone through menstruation. Meat tasted *so* much better when it had ripened. Biting a jagged hole in the crotch, the beast giggled before tossing the underwear back into the pile. It quivered in anticipation as it moved closer to the meat in the happy pink bed, finally ready to give into its desires and feast.

* * *

Shawn let himself out the front door, careful to shoo Samson away from the great wide open that the cat so desperately longed for. It was early – seven thirty in the morning – but he wanted to talk to Jenny. Today was Saturday and the pool stayed open until six, so he could start her swimming lessons whenever she wanted.

Riding his Schwinn down Augusta and past his neighbors' houses, taking bites from an apple he had cadged from the kitchen, Shawn quickly found himself on the town square. Following the sidewalk around the square and toward Main Street, he passed Men's Firestone, Newsland, and the Carthage Townhouse restaurant, but of course none of them were open this early. This is the time of day that he best enjoyed the town, before everyone else was awake and working and before the summer heat settled down on the little city. He had the air and the sun and the trees all to himself, sharing only with the birds and whatever other animals were out foraging for food, joining Shawn in an early morning breakfast.

Whizzing past Sherrick's Drugstore, the thought suddenly occurred to him – what if Jenny was still asleep? He didn't want to wake her, especially after the argument they'd had yesterday afternoon after the funeral, and he certainly didn't want to bother her parents. He probably should have waited until later in the day. Just because he couldn't sleep late didn't mean that anyone else had that problem.

Still, he rode onward, past the Ben Franklin five and dime and finally out of the square and on to the brick cobbled Main Street. If Jenny wasn't awake, he reasoned, he'd just leave and come back later. He could peek in her window before knocking. Sure, he risked being labeled a Peeping Tom for the rest of his life, but at least he could avoid dealing with a cranky Jenny McGee.

Enjoying his ride in solitude, Shawn allowed his thoughts to once again drift back to Tanner, and their adventure in the house.

\* \* \*

It had taken them less than ten minutes to bicycle across town ("across town" didn't mean much in a town the size of Carthage, Illinois, population 3,620 and falling) and back to Tanner's house to pick up the older boy's backpack. The boy insisted on bringing it along, filling it with a handful of items that might assist them in their quest.

Strapping the ancient green canvas bag to his back, Tanner climbed on to his bicycle with Shawn in tow. They quickly peddled their way to the old house, stashing their bikes behind the weather-worn and half-collapsed garage adjacent to the towering, three-story house. Bolstered by their ride, the boys were pumped up with excitement and anxious to began their exploration.

The house was surrounded by a huge stone and wrought-iron fence, standing at least five feet tall, with gates in front and beside the garage. Both entrances boasted an ornate and regal looking five-pointed star surrounded by a circle, welded into the iron that made up most of each gate.

The house itself was awe-inspiring: the Victorian manor stretched up a huge three stories, seemingly reaching through the clouds in an attempt to snatch the sun down from the cobalt blue sky above. The house had once been painted white, though only peeling bits and pieces of the original coat remained anywhere on the building. Dark satin-green shutters and massive white columns and gables completed the ensemble, giving the house an eerie look of foreboding. A long, spired chimney broke through the roof on the east side of the third floor, like a periscope sent up by a cautious sea captain to keep an eye on the world at large.

"I bet we can get in through the cellar," said Tanner, peering through the locked gate. "I mean, it's around back, and no one should be able to see us from the road. It's better than going in the front door."

"Just how long have you been planning this?"

"Ever since you told me that the house was a family heirloom."

"Hey, look," Interrupted Shawn, pointing to the south side of the yard. The last time he had seen the house the fence was intact, but today the gate facing Randolph had collapsed in on itself. He moved to investigate.

"Hey, no!" whispered Tanner, grabbing his friend's arm. "Someone might see you. C'mon, give me a boost."

Throwing his backpack over the fence, he used Shawn's intertwined fingers as a starting point, then huffed and puffed his way over the fence before finally landing with a thump on the other side. Shawn quickly followed, exhibiting a natural grace that his best friend lacked, landing without noise on the other side of the fence.

"So, come on already," Tanner grumbled. He walked purposefully around the East side of the house, toward the old storm cellar door.

"No time like the present," said Shawn, resigned to whatever adventure lay beyond.

The two boys stood before the cellar door, staring at the old rusted padlock that stood between them and their imagined discoveries. Uncharacteristically, Tanner began to develop cold feet the second that Shawn knelt down to examine the rotting entryway.

"I don't know, Shawn, maybe we shouldn't..." he mumbled, the crowbar he had taken from the backpack just minutes ago dangling limply from his hand. Staring at the cellar door, he added, "It might be dangerous."

"Dangerous?" asked Shawn, confused by Tanner's abrupt change of heart. "Since when have you been worried about danger?"

"Maybe we should just go back to the park."

"C'mon, Tanner. What would Zoom Beezie do?"

Tanner just stared at him, uncomprehending. Zoom Beezie was the super hero they had created in fifth grade, back when they were both convinced they would someday be famous comic book creators. He couldn't even remember where the goofy name had come from, but they'd managed to fill two entire spiral notebooks with his adventures before moving on to other things. He had a hard time believing that Tanner had already forgotten the bravest hero in the universe, Zoom Beezie.

"Oh for crying out – give me your crowbar!" Shawn rose to his feet as he snatched the tool from his friend's unresisting hands, the heft of its weight heavy in his own. He glared menacingly at the lock, thumping the crowbar into his palm, ready to force his way inside.

It took Shawn less than a minute to snap the old padlock, swinging the warped and weather scarred cellar door wide open. "Are you ready?"

Tanner stared down into the musty, dank depths of darkness below, then whispered, "We really need to get out of here before it's too late."

"Too late for what?" Shawn asked, wrapping his fingers around Tanner's wrist to pull him forward. The two friends slowly walked down the crumbling concrete stairs. Spiders and cockroaches scurried from under their feet as they motored down the steps, finally reaching the dirt floor below.

Shaking his head, blinking his eyes, Tanner looked confused. "I'm sorry I wussed out there for a minute. Just a case of the willies, I guess."

"Well, maybe you were right. We can't get very far if we can't see."

"I just happen to have a pair of flashlights in my big bag of tricks," said Tanner, removing two green Coleman's from his canvas backpack.

Shawn looked around the room. Despite the daylight pouring in from above, he couldn't find the walls of the cellar past the thick darkness that threatened to engulf them. He gratefully accepted the flashlight.

"You really thought this through, didn't you?" He said, clicking on the Coleman. The room opened up around him as Tanner's light joined his own. The two boys moved their beams in arcs across the room, trying to get a feel for what lay around them.

"I've been thinking about this for a long time," said Tanner, taking his first good look around the dark, moldy cellar, pointing out a rotting pile of firewood and a rusty metal axe lying beside it, "ever since your dad first told us about the house's history."

Still moving his beam around the room, trying to find a set of stairs that would lead up and into the house, Shawn chuckled, "Yeah, well, me too."

The cellar was covered in an incredibly thick coating of dust and cobwebs, and a rusty furnace rested against the far south wall. A tiny slit of a window stood high on the west wall, but the view was obscured by both a thick layer of grime that coated the glass from the inside and a thick patch of weeds and ivy that grew up and over the window from the outside. The dust on the floor was undisturbed, which probably meant that the two boys were the first to walk the floor in a very long time.

"Here's the way in," Shawn whispered, shining his beam up a set of rickety wooden stairs that ended at a rotting oak door.

"Well, let's…"

"Shit!" Shawn yelped, jumping back as an enormous black rat shot out from beneath the stairs toward his feet. At the last second, it veered off and ran up the concrete stairs and out into the light of day.

"Scared of a mouse?" smirked Tanner, back to his old self. He pulled the cellar door closed behind them. "We almost forgot this. Wouldn't want anyone to see us snooping around, would we?"

"Did you see the size of that thing?" said Shawn, his face an ashen white.

"And there are probably plenty more where that came from," grinned Tanner, holding the flashlight beneath his chin. "Oh no, oh no, the rats are coming to get us…"

"Shut up, McGee," Shawn countered, giving his friend a quick punch in the arm. "Okay, let's get this show on the road."

"All right then," answered Tanner, rubbing his shoulder. This time he took the lead, slowly climbing the wooden steps, ever closer to the interior of the house.

* * *

Shawn was almost to Tanner's house when he noticed Tillie Young, the head cafeteria cook at his school, out in front of her house watering roses.

"Hi, Mrs. Young," Shawn called out, trying to act casual. He didn't want her to see him peeking into Jenny's window.

"Why hello, Shawn," the short, dark-haired woman smiled as she leaned over to water the plants. Tillie Young was in her late fifties, plump as a Christmas goose, and cooked the best meatloaf that Shawn had ever tasted. "Good morning. What are you doing up so early?"

"Just ridin' my bike," Shawn replied, a little too earnestly. He slowed his bicycle to a halt, leaning his foot against the ground to hold it steady.

"Well, you'd better not get into any trouble!" Mrs. Young said, waggling her finger at him. "For goodness sake, Shawn, I'm just teasing you," she smiled, her face softening at the boy's horrified expression. "You know, I was so sorry to hear about Tanner. I know what good friends you two were. I'll miss seeing him in my cafeteria."

"Thanks, Mrs. Young," Shawn said, an idea forming in his head. "I was just on my way to his house to see if I could do any of his chores or anything."

"How thoughtful of you!" she chimed. "What a good boy you are. Take care of yourself, and please tell Tanner's family that they're all in my prayers."

"I will. Thanks again, Mrs. Young!" Shawn called over his shoulder, already peddling away.

# Chapter 7

THE CREATURE slowly licked the girl's feet, a raspy gurgle escaping its mouth. Jenny McGee mumbled something in her sleep, turning over before pulling her feet back under the covers. Undaunted, the beast gently peeled back the blanket, exposing the sleeping girl beneath. The teenager, dressed in pink cotton pajamas, hugged her pillow tightly against her body as goose pimples prickled to life on her legs.

The girl smelled so good it could almost taste her. It imagined her warm, rich blood sliding into its mouth, down its throat and into its stomach as the meat's life slowly drained from her body. But where oh where to begin? Should it start at the top, perhaps, sucking her pretty green eyes out of their sockets, then slicing open her tender pink neck with its needle-sharp teeth, or maybe in the middle, taking slow, sweet bites out of her budding young breasts, then gutting her while she was still alive?

The beast trailed its thorny tongue between the girl's toes in anticipation, slowly, ever so slowly, in and out, licking and sucking. This time, it decided, it would start at the bottom and work its way up, taking in every little bit of her, not stopping until its hunger was fully sated. Slowly, tantalizingly, the beast drew its sharp talons across the girl's ankle, gently breaking the skin and bringing a thin line of blood up to the surface. Its long, sinewy tongue trailed up from Jenny's toes to her ankle, lapping greedily at the blood, craving it, needing it, wanting more.

And suddenly the girl was awake, screaming at the top of her lungs, kicking out hard against the monster's ebony face. The beast stumbled back, startled, surprised to feel the warmth of its own blood trickling down its mouth. And then, before it could even react, it heard the crunch of gravel beneath running feet from outside, quickly approaching the open window.

* * *

Shawn parked his bicycle in the driveway behind the McGee's red Chevy pick-up, looking around to make sure that Mrs. Young had finished watering her roses. He couldn't believe he was doing this. But, as Tanner would have said, there's no turning back now.

Grimacing at the noise his sneakers made on the gravel beneath his feet, Shawn imagined his face on the front page of the weekly Carthage Journal-Pilot newspaper, the headline screaming, "Peeping Tom Arrested Just One Day After Best Friend's Funeral." It wasn't a pretty thought. He willed his feet to crunch just a little softer as he crab-walked around the side of the house.

And then he was at Tanner's window, his mission to check on Jenny's sleep status forgotten. Looking through the glass and into the room beyond, he was struck by how little had changed since he'd last been inside. All of Tanner's action figures (save Galahad) were carefully lined up across the top of his bookshelf, comics, magazines, and dog-eared paperbacks filling three of the shelves beneath. His old school notebooks, along with a few board games and a broken Walkie Talkie that Tanner had been promising his mother he'd throw away for at least the last two years, took up most of the bottom shelf. He could almost imagine his friend asleep in his bed, snoring loudly under the covers, eking out all that he could from an extra ten or fifteen minutes of sleep. But of course he wasn't asleep; he was gone forever. He was dead.

Sobered by his thoughts, Shawn tore his eyes from Tanner's room. This was going to take some serious getting used to, and he wasn't at all sure that he ever would - or could - accept that his best friend was truly dead. Shaking his head, Shawn quickly made his way past Tanner's window and around to the back of the house.

He heard a scream from inside the house that stopped him dead in his tracks. Jenny! Forgetting all thoughts of stealth, moving quickly into a sprint, he whipped around the corner just in time to see a wiry black ball of teeth and claws propel itself from Jenny's window straight into his face.

Shawn instinctively raised his arms as the animal crashed into him, protecting his face and eyes from the creature's attack. Sharp claws dug into the boy's forearms as teeth gnashed out, opening a deep jagged cut from his left wrist to his elbow. He stumbled backward, flailing his arms before him, falling flat on his back.

And then, as suddenly as it had begun, it was over. Shawn scanned the yard for the animal that had attacked him but found nothing. It was gone. Scrambling to his feet, Shawn felt light-headed and thought he might pass out. He looked down - blood was everywhere, his white t-shirt now a dark wet shade of red, and his arms and hands wore a series of cuts and deep scratches.

"Shawn, is that you?" quivered Jenny, leaning out the window. Slipping her glasses onto her face, she gasped at Shawn's condition. "God, are you okay?"

"I heard you yell, and then this... thing, I guess it was a cat or something...jumped out of your window and almost clawed my eyes out," Shawn said, desperately wanting to believe that his attacker was nothing more than a crazed alley cat. "When did you get a cat?"

"It wasn't a cat, Shawn," she answered, looking as if she might throw up. "It was the monster from the lake. And it came to kill me, just like it did Tanner."

"Jenny!" shouted a voice from inside the house. Paul McGee threw open the door to his daughter's room and barreled into view. "Jenny, are you alright?" asked the tall, burly security guard, his bright green eyes wide with fright.

"Yeah, I think so, I…"

"Jenny, what did that boy do to you?" her father growled, moving quickly toward the window.

"God, Dad! No! It was the monster from the lake. It attacked me, and it almost killed Shawn."

"No, it wasn't," Shawn interrupted, leaning against the window sill to steady his shaking legs. It wouldn't help for Jenny's parents to think that they were both nuts. "It was a feral cat or a coon or something. I heard Jenny yell and came around the side of the house and it jumped out and attacked me. That's what happened."

"Shawn!" shouted Jenny, "It was the monster. It had to be."

"Then why wasn't it as big as you said?" Shawn countered, mentally willing her to shut up. "That thing couldn't have been more fifteen or twenty pounds, tops."

"Shawn," sighed Mr. McGee, moving to the window. The big man looked as if he'd aged a hundred years in the last few days. "Why don't you come on in and we'll get you cleaned up. Then we can sit down and figure out what's going on."

Shawn and Jenny sat at the McGee dining room table as Jenny's mother, a nurse at Carthage Memorial Hospital, bandaged the boy's wounds. The cuts weren't as bad as they looked – shallow scratches and abrasions, mostly, save for the one long gash running about three inches down his forearm.

"Well, the good news is that you won't need stitches," Jenny's mother assured him. "As long as you take care of your arm, you should be okay. But that thing might have had rabies. It's a shame it got away. You might want to see a doctor, just to be on the safe side."

"Abby," Jenny's father started, not giving Shawn a chance to reply. "They'll both be fine. I want to find out exactly what happened. Shawn, why on Earth were you over here so early, and on the day after... after I buried my son?"

"I wanted to see if Jenny still wanted to learn to swim," he answered, mentally kicking himself. What if Jenny's father talked to Mrs. Young across the street? Still, it was probably better to go with the truth. "Tanner and I had promised to teach her this summer and since Tanner... well, you know..."

"There," interjected Abby, putting the final touches on Shawn's bandage. "All better. Remind me to give you some gauze and tape before you go. Your mom will have to change the bandages once a day until the cuts close up and start to heal."

"Go on, boy," said McGee, ignoring his wife as she fussed over their dead son's best friend.

"Well, that's about it, really. I couldn't sleep last night and didn't realize how early it was. Otherwise I would have called first, or waited until after lunch."

"When I saw you there and with her room such a mess you have no idea the thoughts that went through my head..."

"Dad!" interrupted Jenny, her face growing red as she glared across the table at her father. "He saved my life! If Shawn hadn't heard me yell when he did, the monster might have killed me."

"Jenny," said Abby, shaking her head, "we've been over this too many times now. A monster didn't kill your brother: he drowned. And whatever attacked you was probably just a wild animal like Shawn said. Things sometime look funny in the dark."

"Mom, it couldn't have been..." She felt Shawn's hand squeeze hers under the table. His touch seemed to be saying, *not now*. Jenny grew silent. "Who knows, maybe it was just an animal after all."

Her mother suddenly leaned across the table to kiss Jenny's cheek. "We'll get through this, I promise," she said, "and I think you should take Shawn up on his swimming lessons, no matter," she paused then to glance at her husband, "what your father thinks."

"Fair enough," grumbled the big security guard. "I know when I'm beaten. Abby, why don't you fix us all some breakfast? And Jenny, go get out of those pajamas and put some clothes on. We don't run around half-naked in front of company in this house."

"Okay Dad," she acquiesced, rising from the table as her mother bustled off to the kitchen. "Be back in a few minutes."

With his daughter out of the room and his wife making breakfast, McGee turned his attention back to Shawn. "So, son, aside from the swimming lessons, what exactly *are* your intentions with my little girl?"

"What do you mean, Mr. McGee?"

The older man sighed. "Shawn, we're all going through a lot right now. I know you miss Tanner. I don't even know..." he faltered for a moment, looking like he wasn't sure what to saw next. "I just want you to be careful with Jenny, okay? She's hurting too. I don't think right now is necessarily the best time for her to start hanging out with boys, and certainly not with her dead brother's best friend."

"But that's not what-" he stammered, his face turning red.

"I know you mean well," Paul McGee interrupted, "but every time she sees you, every time any of us see you, it's just a reminder of Tanner and what we've lost. Just... stay away for a while, okay? Jenny can have her swimming lesson, but after that... just stay away."

# Chapter 8

"WHY DOESN'T anyone believe me?" Jenny complained aloud to her empty bedroom, as Harry Chapin's *Cat's in the Cradle* streamed from the radio on her nightstand. She carefully separated her clothes, books, and records into little piles, putting away each in turn. I get straight A's in school. I've never gotten into trouble. I don't fight, steal, drink, smoke, or do drugs. I go to church. I've never, not even once, lied to my parents. So why won't they believe me?

And then there was Shawn. She hadn't thought he believed her, but his squeezing her hand under the table gave her hope. At least until she came back from getting dressed. He wouldn't meet her gaze throughout breakfast, and left immediately after he'd gulped down his bacon, eggs, toast, and half a glass of orange juice. Even her mother picked up on the strange vibe that seemed to surround the breakfast table, but when she asked her dad if he'd noticed anything weird he just shrugged and walked away.

She finally called Shawn about an hour after breakfast, but her father never managed to pick up on her hints to leave the room and so she hadn't been able to talk as openly as she would have liked. When she asked him why he'd left so quickly after breakfast, he mumbled something unintelligible and quickly changed the subject.

He had, however, agreed to come over after lunch, to begin her long-promised swimming lessons. Learning to swim was the last thing on Jenny's mind at the moment, but at least they could use the time to talk. The monster had killed her brother and then come after her the morning after his funeral. Jenny didn't want to believe in monsters –

she'd thought that she was too old for that – but she knew what she'd seen, and now she'd seen it twice.

The monster had been bigger when it killed her brother, but she knew that both creatures were one and the same - she had looked into its eyes both times and seen the raw, evil hatred smoldering just beneath the surface. She'd never forget those flaming red eyes as long as she lived.

Lost in thought, putting away her things as she pondered the mystery of the monster, Jenny's focus snapped instantly back to the present. A small gasp escaped her lips as she looked down to the piece of clothing that she held in her hand: a ruined pair of white cotton panties. A hole had been ripped through the crotch, as if by a wild animal searching for something to eat. Suddenly feeling claustrophobic, she backed away, dropping the underwear to the floor. The room spun around her as she fell to her knees and vomited everything she'd just eaten.

* * *

It was just past noon as Shawn knelt beside the ancient weeping willow outside his bedroom window, looking for evidence of his nighttime visitor. He'd convinced himself that it had been a dream, but now he wasn't so sure.

His stomach rumbled, despite having eaten two ham and cheese omelets, three pieces of buttered toast, and two full glasses of orange juice just a few hours ago at Jenny's house. Why was he so hungry? He took the last bite of the banana he'd grabbed from the kitchen, washing it down with a gulp of Royal Crown cola.

He still wasn't ready to believe Jenny's assertions that whatever had attacked her was a monster, but between that and whatever had been following him, he did have to admit that something was going on that he didn't fully understand. And it was too much of a coincidence that he'd heard noises outside of his window just an hour or two before the attack.

And yet he could find no evidence to support his growing suspicions. *This is stupid*, he thought. Circling around the tree, he was ready to give up when he noticed something unusual. Four long, jagged strips of white paint peelings lay in the grass beneath the window. His eyes moved quickly to the window sill, and there was his evidence - four matching gouges raked deep into the wood.

If whatever had been outside his window had also snuck into Jenny's room, what did it want? Why was it after them? And was it possible that what Jenny said was true, that this *thing* was also responsible for Tanner's death?

Anger surging through his body, he decided that there was only one way to find out. Full of questions and determined to get answers, the boy made to stand but instead doubled over in pain. The bottle of RC cola fell from his hand, splashing on his shoes and spilling into the grass. Clutching his left arm, the world spinning around him, he stumbled to one knee. The gash on his arm felt as if it were on fire, his vision blurring with tears. He reached out to steady himself against the old tree, and then, just like that, the pain was gone.

He peeled back the bandages from his left arm. He wasn't sure what he expected to find, but everything looked normal. If anything, the cut looked like it was healing faster than it had any right to - the skin was already starting to mend, and the swelling around the gash was nearly gone.

Shawn sat still for a long minute as he tried to put the incident out of his mind. With this going on and what Mr. McGee said to him at breakfast, he didn't even know which way was up. He should have been at Jenny's over half an hour ago, but was nervous about facing her father. Shawn had no intention of doing anything to hurt Jenny, and wished her father could see that.

Finally he rose, stretched, swung one leg over his Schwinn and began peddling toward Jenny's house. Halfway there, as he rode by the county seat courthouse on the town square, he nearly ran into the blonde man with the trench coat from Tanner's funeral. Turning to apologize, he was confused to find that he was already gone.

* * *

The little black creature licked its lips in hungry anticipation. It crouched in the shadows of the courthouse, behind the huge rock where Abraham Lincoln once stood, watching its prey. It could pounce now, take him from his bicycle and snap his neck before he even knew what was happening. But that would be too easy.

It had watched the meat leave his house and then let itself in through his window, searching the room. It hadn't found anything, though it could smell the object on the clothing the boy had worn the night before. Its Master told it to leave everything where it was, but hadn't explicitly said that it couldn't add something to the room. It left the boy a present in the back of his closet, buried at the bottom of an old box full of toys. It was unfortunate that the meat probably wouldn't live long enough to find the gift.

The beast felt a prickly tingle begin to take form in the middle of its forehead, between its eyes and somewhere deep in its brain. He knew that the old man was watching again, willing it to follow the meat, to find that which its Master so desperately craved. Afterward, once the object had been recovered, the beast would eat again. It rejoiced at the thought, slinking off from shadow to shadow, following the meat away from the grassy yard and toward his eventual death.

* * *

Jenny paced back and forth on the sidewalk in front of her house. She had her swimsuit on beneath her clothes and had been waiting for Shawn for nearly an hour. Her mother made her promise not to call him, but this was getting ridiculous. Looking down at her Mickey Mouse watch, she noted the time: ten after three, and he was supposed to show up by two-thirty.

The pool closed at six but that really wasn't her concern – she desperately needed to find out whether he believed her about the monster.

And that's when the thought struck her: *maybe he's not coming. Maybe he's decided I'm too much trouble and thinks I'm crazy, just like everyone else in this stupid town.*

Jenny sighed with relief as she finally saw Shawn careening down the street on his bicycle, waving and calling her name as he coasted to a stop at the edge of the driveway.

"Hey Jenny," he said breathlessly, stepping off his bicycle. "Sorry I'm late."

"Don't worry about it," she lied, absently playing with the stem of her glasses. Why didn't she want him to know how long she'd been waiting? She rolled her eyes in frustration. Maybe she shouldn't have agreed to this after all.

"Well, anyway, I was thinking about all this."

"And," Jenny asked, "What did you decide?"

"I believe you," he said simply.

"Thank you!" Jenny smiled, her misgivings forgotten. Running up to Shawn she threw her arms around his neck, hugging him tight.

"Hey, hey, it's all right!" he said, embarrassed, pushing her away. His eyes kept darting toward the front door. "No need to get all huggy and stuff."

"Sorry," she mumbled, trying in vain to hide her rapidly reddening face. She straightened her glasses again, then let herself speak, "It's just that no one would listen. You have no idea what that's been like or how hard it's been. You have no idea at all."

* * *

It was Shawn's turn to feel embarrassed. Why had he pushed her away like that? What was Mr. McGee going to do, shoot him? Shaking his head, he closed some of the distance between them, reaching out to take Jenny's hand.

"I'm sorry," he said, meaning it. "I'm sorry that I didn't believe you. But...something strange has been happening. Something has been following me. And when I was getting ready to come over here, I remembered that I'd had a visitor of my own last night."

"Following you? Oh, Shawn," Jenny gasped, "Don't tell me it came to your house too!"

"All I know is that something has been stalking me ever since I flew home for Tanner's funeral. And then last night I woke up around four in the morning, sure that I'd heard something outside. I looked out the window, but couldn't see anything."

"But that could've been just about anything at all!"

"Let me finish," he continued, "This afternoon I decided to look around outside. I found these weird little scratch marks on the house under the window, and I know they weren't there before. So something was definitely there last night. Thank God I don't sleep with my windows open."

"Yeah, yeah," Jenny grinned, "I've learned my lesson already, so give it a rest, okay? We need to find out what this thing is before it kills somebody else."

"You're right, we do," agreed Shawn. "So get your bike. We need to at least make an appearance at the pool. Then we'll go over to the park and figure out what we're going to do."

* * *

Hiding under an old blue Buick parked just up the road from Jenny's house, the creature watched as the teenagers rode away on their bicycles. It would wait until they were alone at the park and then take them both together. Finally, when it had its Master's prize, it would begin to play with them, slowly ripping apart their bodies and feeding on the sweet meat inside...

# Chapter 9

THE BLAZING summer sun beat down on the Carthage Public Pool, making the concrete walkway hot to the touch, scorching young feet as they danced and ran to get into the cooling, chlorine-blue water. Shawn and Jenny had been in the pool for close to an hour, and the fifteen-year-old girl was finally starting to get the hang of floating.

"You're doing great," encouraged Shawn, watching Jenny float on her back in the kiddie section. She wore a two-piece yellow bathing suit and had her long red hair tied behind her head in a pony tail, and Shawn was trying desperately not to notice how good she looked. He'd never thought of her as anything more than Tanner's little sister, and felt almost guilty for enjoying spending time with her.

The pool was packed today, even for a Saturday, and Shawn recognized almost everyone present. There was Judy SoRelle, who was in the same grade as Jenny, throwing an orange inflatable ball back and forth with her best friend Pan Sticksel, while little Tasha DeRouen and her father Wayne played in the kiddie section.

Two juniors from the high school - the Meredith twins, Nik and Lexi - stopped by to say hello and to tell Jenny how sorry they were about Tanner before swimming off to compete in an impromptu game of Marco Polo.

As soon as the twins were gone, however, a pair of bullies Shawn knew all too well made a beeline for him and Jenny.

"Shawnie's got a girlfriend," laughed Mike Jackson, a tall, pockmarked teenager from Shawn's school, "Shawnie's got a girlfriend. First comes love, second comes marriage, and then comes Shawnie with a baby carriage!"

Rusty Boyer, a chubby, brown-haired bully dressed in black trunks sporting sewn-on orange flames, swam over to high-five Shawn's tormenter. Shawn had been enduring the abuse ever since he and Jenny arrived at the pool, and he wanted nothing more than for them to just go away and leave them alone.

"Just ignore them," sighed Jenny, casting a withering glance toward the two annoying boys.

"Aw, we're just having some fun!" claimed Jackson, as he and his friend swam to the far end of the pool to pester a pair of fourth-graders trying to find the courage to jump off the diving board.

"You never did tell me," said Shawn, doing his best to ignore the stares from the other kids in the pool, "why didn't you ever learn to swim?"

Jenny's reply was drowned out by the shrill whistle of the lifeguard, a sun-darkened teenager with surfer-blonde hair. "All right, kids!" the nineteen year-old smirked, not much more than a kid himself. "Break time for Toby. Try not to drown yourselves while I'm gone, okay? Be back in five."

Shawn rolled his eyes, watching as the lifeguard strutted away. "What a dork. I know his brother, and the doofus just got this job because his Dad plays golf with the pool manager."

"You'd asked why I never learned to swim," said Jenny, picking up the conversation where it had dropped off. "Well, good question! For one thing, I wear glasses, and I'm practically blind as a bat without them. My parents could never afford contacts," she looked embarrassed, "and I'm not sure you can wear them in the pool to begin with. I just hate not being able to see."

"And that's it?"

"No, that's not it. I actually tried to learn to swim once, before I had to get glasses. I was six, I think, and Tanner had just learned the year before. So Mom signed me up for lessons, but I was a little scared.

"Anyway," she continued, "the instructor didn't have much patience with me, and so one day, after everyone else was swimming and I wasn't, he decided to throw me in and hold me under until I learned. The thing is, though, I didn't. I just freaked out, and they had to call my Mom to come pick me up early. And I guess I've kind of been scared of it ever since. "

"Jesus, Jenny, that's awful! They should have fired that guy!"

"They did," Jenny smirked.

"Remind me never to make you mad," Shawn joked just before a deep, searing pain wracked his body. His wounded arm spasmed uncontrollably, causing him to thrash around in the water like a fifteen-pound flounder caught on a fishing line.

His surroundings blinked in and out, and for a moment it was as if he were standing outside the pool, hiding behind a pile of concrete slabs, looking in through the surrounding fence. He could see himself gasping, taking in huge mouthfuls of water as his head went under. He saw Jenny on her feet, shouting at him, asking him what was wrong. Then everything went dark and the whole world spun around him, disappearing in a series of rapidly shuddering blinks.

Shawn woke up in the hospital, flat on his back, in the most uncomfortable bed he had ever had the misfortune to lie upon. Struggling with his thoughts, trying to remember where he was and how he got there, Shawn blinked once, then twice, and finally the room swam into focus. His mother and father were there, looking down at him.

Jenny was also there, her swimsuit abandoned in favor of a t-shirt and a pair of shorts. She sat in one of the standard-issue oversized hospital chairs, hugging her knees. Her still-wet hair had lost its pony tail and now hung in crimson ringlets around her face, and her cheeks were stained with tears.

"He's awake!" shouted his father, brow creased with worry. "Shawn, you scared the hell out of us."

"What happened?" mumbled Shawn. The last thing he remembered was watching Jenny float in the pool.

"Shawn, thank God!" Jenny sobbed, jumping out of her chair.

She took two steps toward the bed before stopping, her face red. Breathing deeply, she removed her glasses to wipe the tears from her face, and then began to clean the lenses with the tail of her shirt. She lowered herself back down into the oversized chair, looking lost and alone and as if she might start crying again.

"Shawn," whispered his mother, reaching out to take Shawn's hand. "We were worried sick about you. You've been out like a light for over an hour."

"What's wrong with me, Mom?" croaked Shawn, not sure if he really wanted to hear the answer. "Everything's pretty fuzzy."

"The doctors aren't really sure," answered his father, "but they think that you might have passed out from sunstroke. They're going to keep you overnight for observation. If you're still okay by tomorrow, and if the blood they took comes back okay, then you can probably come home in the morning."

"Jenny saved your life," added his mother. "You went under and no one could find the lifeguard. Jenny managed to grab hold of you and haul you out of the pool. By that time someone had called an ambulance, which is how you wound up here."

*What's happening to me?* He was starting to remember what had happened in the pool, the strange sensation of somehow watching himself from outside his body. Shaking his head, trying to clear the cobwebs, he turned his gaze toward Jenny but found that she was gone.

# Chapter 10

IT WAS NEARLY seven o'clock, and, at Shawn's insistence, his parents finally left the hospital. His mother wanted to stay but the doctor, thank God, didn't think it was necessary. Shawn finally feigned sleep in order to get his parents to leave. He didn't want to stay in the hospital but he needed time alone to think and to figure out what was happening.

Thinking about Jenny almost caused his heart to skip a beat. He wondered, not for the first time, why the girl had left the hospital room without even saying goodbye. He tried calling her, but her mother said that she had come straight home from the hospital and immediately gone to bed. Shawn hung up, feeling hurt, frustrated, and more alone than ever.

Flipping through the few channels that managed to show up on the hospital room's black and white television, the fifteen year-old watched a few minutes of *Hawaii Five-O* before realizing it was one that he'd already seen. Finding nothing else to hold his interest, he turned off the TV and decided to ring the nurse to ask for a snack.

Hospital food, he decided, wasn't any better than school food, Tillie Young's award-winning meatloaf notwithstanding, but for some reason he was ravenous. An hour earlier, a pretty blonde nurse named Vanessa had brought him a tray containing a withered-looking chicken breast, a serving of soggy green beans, a piece of bread, a bowl of red gelatin with bits of banana suspended within, and a little cup of orange juice.

He consumed the foul-tasting chicken in three bites, followed quickly by the bread and the weird gelatin dessert before devoting his full attention to the cup of juice. The drink, amazingly, was actually good, but when he'd asked for more he was told that the hospital cafeteria had closed for the night. Ah, life at good old Carthage Memorial.

Nurse Vanessa walked through the door, carrying a fresh pitcher of water. She glanced down at his dinner tray. "Wow, Shawn, don't they feed you at home?" she smiled, picking up the empty tray and replacing the old pitcher of water with the new one. "I guess you liked the chicken."

"Not really, but I was hungry," Shawn grumbled, wishing for the tenth time in as many minutes that he could have just gone home with his parents instead of spending the night at the hospital. "I'm still hungry, actually. Do you think I could get a snack?"

"We don't have much available outside of the cafeteria," she shrugged, "but I can bring you some saltine crackers, if you'd like."

"Anything, I'm starving," he said, as his stomach growled again.

"Just give me a few minutes and I'll be right back," Nurse Vanessa smiled.

Shawn tried to ignored the pangs of hunger rumbling through his stomach as he watched her walk out the door.

* * *

Jenny felt guilty about abandoning Shawn at the hospital, but she just couldn't take it anymore. Less than three full days after she watched helplessly as her brother was pulled under the depths of the lake, her brother's best friend had almost drowned as well. Just thinking about it made her nauseous.

Curled up on her bed, deep under the covers, Jenny felt small and alone as she tried in vain to hold back the tears she felt welling up in her eyes. *Damn it,* she thought, throwing back the covers and scrambling out of bed, *I will not cry again!*

She'd been crying ever since she'd walked home from the hospital. After explaining to her parents what had happened at the pool, she'd retreated to her bedroom and locked the door behind her. Ignoring her mother's pleas to come out for dinner and then, later, to return Shawn's phone calls, Jenny had spent the entire evening alone and miserable in her room. Jenny's father had driven down to the pool to retrieve their bicycles and Shawn's backpack, making her feel all the worse.

She was really starting to care about Shawn. She had loved her brother with all of her heart, and he had been murdered. And now she was falling for Tanner's best friend. Sure, she'd had a crush on him for years, but he'd never really noticed her, not until they talked after Tanner's funeral. But Jenny wasn't stupid: she'd seen how Shawn looked at her at the pool, and it had caused her heart to flutter like a butterfly doing loop-de-loops in her chest.

She'd always been shy and awkward around boys and had never really gone on a real date, much less had a boyfriend. Sure, she'd briefly "gone steady" with a boy in junior high and even let him kiss her behind the bleachers, but she'd quickly realized that Roger Barry had been much more interested in getting under her blouse than he ever had been in getting to know what was going on inside her head. She'd dumped him before the whole thing ever really got started, just three weeks into their relationship.

There were many things she still didn't know about Shawn, things like his favorite color or what books he liked to read, but she knew for certain what he wasn't: he was no Roger, and that in and of itself was a good start.

Jenny was just a few months younger than Shawn - he'd turn sixteen at the end of the summer, while she'd turn the same age in October. Because Shawn was born just before the school cut-off date, he had been almost a year younger than her brother and everyone else in their class. But, though he and Jenny were practically the same age, she knew he'd always looked at her as a little girl.

Maybe that was finally starting to change, but none of it would matter if they were both dead.

Slipping on her glasses, Jenny walked to the window to stare at the twinkling stars spinning high above her in the night sky. She held her breath for a moment, finally exhaling, as she made a decision. She knew that she would never – *could* never - stop missing her big brother, not even if she wanted to. But she also knew that he was dead, and she wanted to live. She wanted to finish school and then go to college; to travel and see what the world looked like outside of Carthage; to grow up, fall in love, get married, and maybe someday have kids of her own. And if she wanted to do all of these things, she knew she couldn't give up, and certainly couldn't spend the rest of her life hiding away in her bedroom, huddled under the covers like a frightened little bunny rabbit.

Unlocking her bedroom door, she walked through the now-dark hallway to the kitchen phone, finally ready to return Shawn's phone call.

"We're sorry," answered the recording in Jenny's ear, "but visitation and telephone hours are between 10 AM and 10 PM, Monday through Sunday. Please call back or come to visit during those hours."

Jenny looked at her Mickey Mouse watch: it was two minutes after ten. Setting the phone back in its cradle, she couldn't believe it. If she'd finished feeling sorry for herself just a few minutes earlier, she might have been able to talk to Shawn. As it was now, she'd have to wait until morning, unless…

Abruptly, a thought struck her: Shawn's room was on the south side of the hospital building, on the first floor, and the windows were easily accessible from outside. She'd heard her parents going to bed just a few minutes before she came out to use the phone. If she were careful and quiet, she could sneak out of the house and ride her bike across town to the hospital, tap on his window, and get to talk to him after all.

All thoughts of the monster forgotten, Jenny snuck out of the house through the garage and climbed on to her pink Huffy. She coasted out of the driveway, putting foot to pedal as soon as the bicycle's tires hit the brick road, making her way down the street and toward the hospital.

* * *

Shawn felt as though he were drowning again. Darkness surrounded him, and he had no idea where he was. The dim street lights, the glowing stars above him, even the old house that stood across the road; everything looked blurry and surreal. And something else was wrong: he was looking at the world from near-ground level, just a foot or two above the hard terrain at his feet.

His vision cleared in an instant and he settled into the new environment. He was standing across the street from the old Spencer house, the house that he and Tanner had broken into earlier in the summer.

An unseen voice vibrated in his head: *"Fetch, check on the girl. If she's alone, take her and be quick about it. And when you're done, go pay a visit to the boy."*

It was as though a snake had slithered through his head, leaving crumbling and broken scales wherever it touched. He nevertheless felt himself immediately acquiesce, and then he was off - running down Randolph Street, staying in the shadows, heading through the town square and toward Main, to kill Jenny McGee.

*No,* Shawn railed against his thoughts, *I don't want to kill Jenny!* But he couldn't stop running. He couldn't do anything but watch the scenery around him unfold; an unwilling participant in someone else's nightmare.

An image formed in his mind, like a memory or maybe a dream — he was sniffing a pair of Jenny's panties, suddenly and savagely biting through the crotch, tearing out a patch of the white cotton material with his teeth. He spat it across the room, desire conflicting with rage. His mouth salivated at the thought of Jenny's sweet, virginal flesh.

He scampered behind a mailbox, then under a truck. Always keeping to the shadows, he drew ever closer to Jenny and to the sweet meat that lay inside.

Shawn was awake again, bile rising in his throat as his arm throbbed with a sudden and painful heat. He knew that it was real, that it was all real, and hadn't been a dream. He wasn't sure how he knew it, but he knew that unless he did something Jenny was going to die tonight. He'd seen through the eyes of the monster, lived its life, felt its thoughts, and tasted its hunger. And even now the beast was racing in Jenny's direction, its twisted, sick heart intent on eating her alive.

Trying to calm his pounding heart, Shawn downed a cup of lukewarm water from the nightstand before scrambling out of bed to pull the hospital gown up and over his head in one quick jerk. Quickly donning the faded blue jeans and t-shirt his parents had brought for him and slipping his feet hurriedly into his old white sneakers, he stepped into the bathroom to look for anything that he might use as a weapon. He picked up an old plunger, though he doubted it would have even the slimmest chance of injuring the monster.

Shawn started through the door to the hallway but thought better of it. He couldn't afford to be stopped by a well-meaning doctor or nurse. Quickly unlatching the big window that filled the south side of his room, he pushed out the screen and quietly let it drop to the grass below. Climbing through the window, the teenager took off in a dead run across the driveway and toward Jenny's house.

He raced down South Adams, his legs pumping, all the while knowing there was no way he could make it in time. The monster was much closer to Jenny than he was, and it could run much faster. The girl was as good as dead.

Already exhausted and panting, he stopped in the middle of the road, frantically looking for anything, anyone, that could help him. Then he saw it: a big red motorcycle parked in the trailer park driveway just across the street. Closing the short distance in seconds, he knelt over to look at the ignition. Yes! The keys dangled from the motorcycle like an open invitation.

Not even pausing to think, Shawn raised the kickstand and quickly walked the Kawasaki backward and out of the driveway. He hurriedly turned the bike in the right direction and twisted the key: nothing. Cursing, he started to get off the motorcycle and resume his run, but then flashed back to his cousin's bike and the ride the boy had let him take last Christmas.

Turning the key again, trying to remember everything his cousin had showed him, he checked to make sure the bike was in neutral, then pulled the choke all the way out. Squeezing the clutch lever down with his left hand while pushing the start button with his right, he was rewarded with the hard thrumming noise of the motorcycle revving to life. It was the most beautiful sound he'd ever heard, at least on this night.

The door to one of the trailer's flung open and Shawn turned to see a blonde, long-haired hippie wearing nothing but white boxers and a ratty t-shirt running toward him. "What the holy fuck you doin', man? That's my bike!"

"Sorry," Shawn yelled back, "right now, I need it more than you do." Gunning the engine, he pushed down hard on the lever that controlled the gas. The Kawasaki almost shot out from under him as it screamed down and away from its angry owner.

\* \* \*

Just blocks from the meat's house, the fetch saw its prey slip out from the garage and jump on her bicycle, peddling furiously, heading toward the creature. It was on its own now that the old man had fallen asleep, and so it decided to play a little game. Amused and more than a little curious where the girl was headed, the fetch held back, deciding to toy with its prey before bringing her down and finally, mercifully, ending her life and feasting on her corpse. It blended into the shadows as the girl passed its hiding spot, then began to pace her, loping just a few yards behind, following the sweet smell of her sweat and the fear that lay beneath.

* * *

The cool night wind whipping through his hair, Shawn sped down South Adams at nearly seventy miles an hour. It had taken him a few minutes to remember how to shift gears, and he'd had a nervous moment when he'd thought the engine would blow out from cycling too fast, but his memory of the Honda served him well, and he'd so far managed not to destroy himself or anything else in his path.

Making a screeching left onto Locust Street, Shawn shot by a couple of older kids playing a game of midnight basketball at the Lincoln elementary school, then had to weave to avoid hitting a big golden retriever as it ran across the road, chasing after a wayward cat. The motorcycle skidded to the right, but he managed to regain control before careening into a ditch and once again picked up speed as he raced against time to save Jenny's life.

And then he was inside the monster's head again, darkness surrounding him as he slinked from shadow to shadow, stalking his prey. The monster was following Jenny, who was riding her bicycle. She was crossing the south side of the square, heading down North Adams and past the elementary school. Shawn was driving away from her! He'd driven down Locust because it was the quickest route to Jenny's house, but, because she'd left home, he was going to miss her entirely. And then the creature would have her.

Abruptly Shawn realized, I'm still on the motorcycle! Mentally willing his eyes to close, doing his best to ignore the creature's thoughts and emotions while fighting down his own panic, he concentrated on being back in his own body, on the cool night wind against his face, and the feeling of the vibrating Kawasaki beneath his legs, knowing that if it didn't happen in the next few seconds neither he nor Jenny were likely to survive the night.

And in an instant, he was back. Jerking his eyes open, Shawn squealed to a halt, nearly rolling the motorcycle on top of himself. The bike skidded, burning rubber, as Shawn tumbled from the seat to the concrete road below, flipping head over heels and landing hard on his tailbone. The motorcycle spun around once, twice, finally landing on its side fifteen feet away, the sickening clang of twisted metal ringing in the boy's ears.

\* \* \*

"*Jenn-eeey,*" squeaked the creature's raspy voice as the girl's bicycle turned away from the square and toward the hospital, "*Jenn-eeey.*" The fetch loped casually after the girl, running from one shadow to the next, excited and hungry, as it began to close the gap between them.

\* \* \*

*Oh God,* Jenny thought, her heart ballooning against her ribcage. *Oh God, oh God, oh God!* Risking a look back, she nearly ran her bicycle into a ditch but couldn't see a thing. She had heard the voice, though, mocking and cruel, and knew that it had to be the monster. Pushing past her cramping calves, peddling as hard as she could, she raced toward the hospital.

\* \* \*

"Come on, come on, come on!" yelled Shawn, as he tried to re-start the bike. Bruised and banged up but miraculously otherwise unharmed, he had managed to right the heavy Kawasaki but couldn't seem to get it running again. Something was broken, he knew, but if it could just get him down the road…

There! After what seemed like a thousand lifetimes, the motorcycle finally roared back to life, its engine racing and bucking beneath Shawn's weight. Slamming the bike into gear, he peeled down the road, back the way he had come, leaving nothing but smoke and rubber in his wake.

* * *

The fetch caught up to Jenny's bike in a matter of seconds. Letting loose with a heart-stopping howl, it leapt into the air, swatting her back tire with its heavy claws. The bike wavered then spun out of control. Both Jenny and the pink Huffy squealed as she headed straight for an old metal swing set that stood off the road, right in the middle of the Lincoln Elementary playground.

Jenny's bike crunched hard into one of the heavy steel posts, the front wheel rim cracking into pieces as the frame bent in a direction it was never meant to go. The girl sailed up and over the handlebars, flying through the air to crash into the graveled ground below. Landing on one knee, feeling the sharp, agonizing sensation of dozens of little jagged pieces of gravel pierce her skin, Jenny's breath was knocked out of her by the impact. She tumbled onto her back, gasping, unable to even scream.

"*Oh, Jenn-eeey,*" called the creature from the shadows, mocking, giggling maniacally at her fear, "*Jenn-eey...*"

Her chest convulsed as she drew in huge, greedy gasps of air, willing herself to breathe. Jenny spun around in the gravel, her knee on fire and her eyes blinded by tears, trying to get to her feet as she scanned the playground for the monster. Anything more than a few feet away was a blur. She reached up to adjust her glasses, but they were gone. Sobbing, desperate, she grabbed for one of the dangling swings, gasping as the canvas seat was yanked away by an unseen hand.

Weeping harder, hiccupping uncontrollably, Jenny again reached for the swing, and once more the chains squeaked as the seat swung out of her reach. Not wanting to believe it, thinking she might somehow be safe if she never actually saw the creature, Jenny nevertheless forced herself to raise her head and squint toward the top of the swing set. A blurry outline of black sat perched atop the frame, chain in hand, licking its dark, leathery lips in anticipation of its next meal.

\* \* \*

"Sweet Jesus," Shawn gasped. The school was in full view now, and he watched in horror from across the campus as Jenny slammed hard into the swing set. The furry little black creature – the *fetch* – scampered up the metal frame of the playground equipment with an agility and preternatural grace that he had never seen before in his life. He instinctively pulled the motorcycle hard to the left, jumping the ditch, ripping through grass and dirt, screaming across the campus toward Jenny.

\* \* \*

Licking its lips, preparing to pounce upon the girl, the fetch felt an electric rush of exhilaration course through its body as it pulled the swing out of the girl's reach for the second time. This is what it lived for - the hunt, the chase, and finally, when it had played with the meat until it tired of the game, the kill. Tonight it would feast, tearing deep into flesh, breaking bones. It would drink deep of the honeyed liquid that pumped so vibrantly through her body, gorging on the sweet meat that lay just below her all-too-fragile pink skin.

Sighing to itself, feeling the warm, wet release that always came just before the feast, the fetch ignored the low thrumming sound of an approaching engine. Launching itself gracefully from its perch, jumping straight up into the fresh night air, spinning in mid-flight, plunging down toward the meat, claws extended, the monster prepared to finally take the girl and dine upon her body.

\* \* \*

"*STOP!*" thought Shawn desperately at the fetch, attempting to open the conduit that he mysteriously shared with the monster. He forced himself to once again see through the eyes of the creature, to live in its skin, to command it to obey him as whoever was controlling the beast had done earlier.

Shawn's vision went hazy and he briefly thought he might lose control of the bike. But a moment later, skidding across gravel and almost to the swing set, he was back in his own head, looking across the playground and into the eyes of the beast. And he knew that he had failed. He watched in horror as the creature dove through the air, claws extended, falling noiselessly toward Jenny's body.

\* \* \*

*Stop,* whispered an unfamiliar voice inside the fetch's head. This had never happened before. Confused and afraid, the beast closed its eyes and curled up into a ball, bouncing harmlessly off the huddled form of the screaming girl below.

\* \* \*

*I'm not dead,* thought Jenny, as an aching agony shot through her damaged knee. *If I can still feel pain, then means I'm not dead.* Opening her eyes, grateful to be alive, Jenny's gaze met the scarlet eyes of her tormentor, a furry little ball of wiry hair, teeth, and claws, sitting stone cold still on top of her chest.

"Gahh!" she screamed, frantically pushing the beast away, scrambling backward. She was just a few feet from the monster when it's haunting red orbs turned toward her and blinked, slowly came out of its stupor. Hissing, baring its claws, the beast let out a blood-curdling yowl as it sprang into the air, launching itself at Jenny's face.

"Oh fuck!" she heard another voice yell. And then a huge motorcycle was barreling past her, radiating heat from its engine as it whooshed through the air, slamming violently into the creature seconds before it would have reached her throat. With the creature hanging precariously from the front fender, the bike slammed headlong into the heavy metal chain link fence that separated the school from the fire department next door. The bike momentarily seemed to come to a stop as it pinned the little monster between itself and the fence, grinding the creature hard against the rough metal links. It finally flipped over, coming down

with a huge crash on top of the creature and ripping the fence from its
steels posts in one fluid crunch.

* * *

Shawn propelled himself from the Kawasaki seconds before it
slammed into the fetch, violently knocking the monster back into the
chain link fence. Shawn sailed through the air, landing hard on his
shoulder before rolling to a low crouch. Ignoring the pain, Shawn
stared in shock as the motorcycle pushed against the fence, seemingly
driving of its own accord, holding the fetch between it and the metal.
Abruptly the bike flipped over, coming down with a thump on top of
the beast, gas pouring copiously from its ruptured tank.

"Shit!" he screamed, struggling to get to his feet. Jenny was hobbling toward him, oblivious to the impending disaster. Ignoring the
pricks of pain shooting through his body, time seemed to slow down
around him as he raced away from the motorcycle and toward the injured girl.

"Jenny, get down!"

He tackled her hard to the ground, rolling on top of her as the motorcycle exploded in a cacophony of sputters and shrieks behind them.
Fiery shards of metal and burning, fetid flesh rained down all around
the playground.

"Shawn?" she asked, her ashen face bleeding from a dozen little
cuts. "Oh God, Shawn," she screamed, flinging herself into his arms,
holding on for dear life.

And this time he didn't push her away. He pulled her closer, and
something in him finally broke. He collapsed against her, his tears joining hers, as the two teenagers cried in fear for themselves and each
other, then in grief for Tanner, and finally, joyfully, in sheer bliss over
simply being alive.

Emotionally drained, the two parted, and Shawn noticed for the
first time that Jenny wasn't wearing her glasses. Wiping the tears from
his own eyes, still holding her hand, he led Jenny over to the swing set

to retrieve her glasses. The left lens had been shattered but the right one remained unharmed. Releasing Jenny's hand, Shawn took the pair of glasses and slid them gently up and over the bridge of her nose.

"Thanks," she smiled shyly. "At least I can see now, sort of."

She turned to look at the fence, where the remains of the motorcycle sent thick clouds of smoke into the dark night sky. Moving closer to Shawn, she stopped cold as she noticed his bandage dangling uselessly from his left arm.

"My God, Shawn, your arm," she breathed. The boy was bruised and abraded from head to toe, but the gash he'd received this morning had all but vanished, leaving only the tiniest of pink scars in its wake. "It's all better. Shawn, it's completely healed."

# Chapter 11

THE OLD MAN awoke to a searing pain, as if someone had plunged a red-hot knife through his chest. Coughing and wheezing, he rolled out of bed. He reached out for his cane but missed and tumbled to the floor instead, his breath knocked out from him as he landed face first into the carpeting.

What was happening? He struggled to catch his breath, his body convulsing in time to some unseen rhythm, like a frantic marionette being jerked about by an epileptic puppeteer.

Finally, mercifully, the spasms subsided, as the old man's head lolled back, his mouth hanging open, taking in deep, ragged breaths of stale, recirculated air.

# Chapter 12

A DOZEN WHITE ROSES clenched tightly in his short, sausage-like fingers, Sheriff Fred Ruskin stood just inside the gates of the Moss Ridge Cemetery, trying to catch his breath. Tonight was the fifteenth anniversary of his family's death, and he was surprised to feel the warmth of tears cascading down his round face. He hadn't thought he had any tears left, having used them all up many years ago. But he supposed he'd always have more in reserve, to go along with the memories.

The memories always brought him back to this place, this precipice, daring him to jump, though today was worse than usual. For most of the last fifteen years, he'd felt as if he'd been living on borrowed time. Perhaps it was finally time to pay up, to cash in his chips and make the leap. But he knew that they'd never want him to give into that self-destructive impulse.

Sighing, Ruskin turned his gaze from the twin tombstones before him to the brass wind chimes that hung from the shepherd's hook he had planted between the two graves five years ago. The brass had tarnished, of course, but he could still see his reflection – sad gray eyes, set deep in a doughy face surrounded by thick, shaggy brown hair. If not for the face staring back at him, he wasn't sure if he'd believe that he still existed. Even with the proof right there in front of him, he still sometimes wondered.

He visited the cemetery at least once a week, but the anniversaries were always the hardest. He missed his family with a sharp ache that had refused to ease over time, instead growing deeper and more raw with every passing moment. It was his fault that his wife and daughter were dead, and he would never – could never – forgive himself.

It was why he tended to visit at night, he supposed. The darkness brought no other mourners, and so there was no one else to see his shame, and certainly no one to share his grief.

Lost in thought, Ruskin carefully brought the handful of roses to his nose, inhaling deeply. Nothing. The flowers had been freshly cut that morning, but his three-pack-a-day habit had all but destroyed his ability to smell or taste. Grief had slowly chipped away at the rest of his senses, so much so that he didn't even notice when a sharp thorn from one of the roses pricked his thumb. A trickle of blood rolled down the length of the stem before finally dropping to the soil below.

Tonight, like all the nights before, he carefully divided the twelve roses into two groups of six, kneeling down between the two graves to place half of the bouquet on each. All that separated him from his wife and daughter was six feet of earth and two wooden boxes, and he could almost imagine their hands thrusting up from the soil to take his simple offerings back with them to the grave.

Wiping his eyes with the back of his hand, Ruskin rose on creaking knees back to his feet. "I'm sorry," he whispered, fingering the pair of wedding rings that hung from a chain around his neck. Letting the chain fall back under his shirt, he turned away from the graves and headed back to the car.

Ruskin's police radio squawked from outside the gate, snapping him out of his reverie.

"Sheriff, we just got a report in of a stolen motorcycle and another of a disturbance at the Lincoln Elementary," said a loud female voice. "Tried to call you at home. What're you doing out so late?"

Christ, what was it with this town lately? He'd gotten more calls in the last week than in the previous dozen weeks combined. He hoped it wasn't another tragedy. His mind flashed back to Tanner McGee's pale, lifeless face as they pulled him out of the lake, and he shook himself, forcing the image from his thoughts.

Hurriedly running to the police car, he reached in through the open window for the transmitter but paused a moment before answering. "Okay, Bonnie," he finally wheezed, ignoring her question. "I'm on it. Radio Delacroix and have him meet me there."

"Will do, Sheriff. Over and out."

Ruskin climbed into the police car and lit a Winston, then leaned across the passenger's seat to remove a little silver flask of whisky from the glove compartment. Twisting the cap off, he threw back a long swallow, then replaced the lid and slid it back into the glove box, careful to conceal it beneath a yellowing sheaf of papers.

The flask was almost empty, and he reminded himself that he needed to fill it. It was going to be a long night. Hell, it already had been a long night, and things just seemed to be getting better and better. Resigning himself to the trip, Ruskin cranked up the black-and-white and headed for the school.

# Chapter 13

"OH SHIT!" groaned Shawn, his arm forgotten as he heard the shrill sound of police sirens approaching in the distance.

"What's wrong?" asked Jenny. "They have to believe us now, don't they? I mean, they can see for themselves."

"See what?" Shawn asked, nervously glancing down the street. "As far as I can tell, the monster was completely destroyed in the fire. We can't show them anything. And that motorcycle? The guy I stole it from didn't look too happy when I left."

"Hey, you kids!" yelled a gruff old voice from across the street. "What's going on over there? I just called the police, you stay where you are!"

"Jenny, we've got to go!" Shawn turned his attention to Jenny's bloodied knee. "Do you think you can run?"

"I think so," she said, looking unsure but willing to try.

"Then let's go!"

Shawn pulled her into a run, heading through the playground and toward the back of the school, leaving the shouts of the old man across the street and the growing whine of the police car sirens in their wake.

\* \* \*

"I told you," growled Jim Warner, a white-haired old man with watery-blue eyes, his blue robe pulled taut across a sunken chest and bony frame, "I heard a big explosion and looked out my window and saw the fire. Doreen said I should call the police, so I did."

"Did y'all see who it was?" asked Deputy Alan Delacroix in a slow Southern drawl. A tall, thin Cajun with unruly dark hair and a moustache to match, he was both excited and nervous, his eyes darting first to the fire, then to his boss, and finally to the old man who had called in the accident. He'd been with the county police for six years, ever since he'd moved to Carthage from Louisiana, but he'd never seen an accident like this before, much less one where the rider burned up in the crash.

"When I came out to watch the fire there were a couple of teenagers standing over by the playground. A boy and a girl, I think. They ran off when they saw me, and I think one of them left their bicycle."

"Probably just some kids who heard the commotion and came out to look, same as you did, Jim," explained Sheriff Ruskin, a burly man with shaggy brown hair who had appropriately enough earned the nickname 'Bear' early on in his career and had never quite been able to shake it. "I wouldn't worry about that."

"We had a report of a stolen motorcycle just down the street, by the hospital," continued the Sheriff, gesturing with thick sausage fingers, "and we think it was probably some kid stoned out of his gourd, out for a joyride through town."

"These kids today…" Delacroix shook his head, staring at the fire as it began to die out, "and their drugs. It's just such a shame. Why, when I was a kid…"

"I tell you, those teenagers were up to something," interrupted Warner, pulling his robe tight around his body.

"Jim, just go back to the house," advised Ruskin, clapping the man on the shoulder and nearly knocking him off his feet, "and leave this to the professionals. We'll check everything out and let you know what happened."

"Okay, okay," sighed the white-haired old man, as he turned to walk across the street back to his house. "Just be sure to let me know what happens, okay?"

"Will do," promised Ruskin, tugging a cigarette out from behind his ear, forgetting about Warner as soon as he was out of sight.

"Maybe we should wake up the boys," chuckled Delacroix with a Louisiana twang, looking over his shoulder at the fire department that stood less than a hundred yards away. "You know, if they could sleep through an explosion in their own back yard, I guarantee you they could sleep through anything..."

"The fire's dying out by itself, but, yeah, we should call it in," said Ruskin, striking a match and lighting his Winston. He walked over to the smoldering motorcycle. "And we'll call Doc Jenkins as well, though I suspect there won't be much to examine. There doesn't seem to be anything left of this kid but blood and charcoal."

"Want me to call it in, Bear?"

"No, I'll do it," the Sheriff said, sucking on his Winston as he bent over to pick at a piece of smoldering tire with his gun, "if you don't mind staying here until the Doc shows up. I'm going to drive over to the biker's house and take his statement, and then it's bedtime for this old grizzly. With all those missing cats and dogs everyone's been hollering about, the McGee boy drowning at the lake Wednesday, and that missing teacher over in Hamilton the night before... well, it's just been a long week, that's all."

"Understood, boss," answered Delacroix, for the first time noticing the bicycle that the old man told them about. "I'll just hang out with the boys and leave once the Doc shows up."

"I owe you one, Alan," smiled Ruskin, walking back to his car. "Coffee and doughnuts are on me tomorrow."

"I'll hold you to it," Delacroix called out as he knelt down to examine the pink bike. The front wheel rim was shattered, and the frame was bent almost in half. Some serious damage had been done here, and maybe the teenagers that the old man saw were involved after all.

Delacroix started to call out to his boss but looked up to see his car driving away, lights off and siren silent.

Glancing at his own car, wishing he were back in bed with his girl-friend, or at least home with his wife, the deputy decided that the bicycle could wait until morning. Besides, the boys at the fire department should be waking up now and over here in no time, with Doc Jenkins hopefully not too far behind.

Delacroix walked over to stare at the ruined motorcycle, shaking his head at the loss of a perfectly good ride. Maybe something could be salvaged, he thought, after it was released from the impound yard. The back fender, at least, still seemed to be in decent condition.

"*Fuck,*" rasped a voice from beneath the remains of the motorcycle, the pile of debris starting to shift and move.

Startled, the Cajun jumped back, instinctively reaching for his gun. Then he remembered that the weapon was back in the car, locked safely away in the vehicle's glove compartment. Hurriedly moving away from the motorcycle, hitting his shoulder hard against metal as he backed into the swing set, the deputy's face turned a pale shade of white, his heart thudding rapidly against his rib cage, as he watched a bloody and burned little creature pull itself free from the fiery wreckage.

"What the hell?" asked Delacroix, the stench burnt hair and flesh hitting him in the face. Stumbling over the broken pink bicycle, losing his footing, he fell over backward, landing flat on his back in the gravel.

"Mary mother of Jesus, help me!" screamed the deputy, frantically crawling backwards. He clutched the rosary hidden beneath his shirt. "Somebody help me!"

The fetch, bloody and broken and charred beyond all recognition, flung itself at the retreating peace officer in a frenzy of sharp claws and teeth, quickly slashing his jugular, killing him in an instant. And then with great hunger, and an even greater need, it began to gorge on his body, feeding with reckless abandon, growing slowly larger, leaving not even a single bone or strip of flesh behind.

\* \* \*

"Where are we going?" asked Jenny, pain shooting through her damaged knee. They'd been running for ten minutes, having traversed the tall weeds, dandelions, and unmowed grass behind the school, keeping their heads low in the event that anyone happened to be looking their way. In an attempt to avoid the road around the school, they'd crossed Augusta and continued through alleys and behind houses until they finally came to Wabash Avenue. Panting and out of breath, Jenny leaned against an old metal trash can behind someone's house and glared at Shawn.

"Okay, okay," Shawn whispered, pausing to catch his breath. "I think we should go back to the hospital. I left through the window so, if we're lucky, they won't even realize I was gone."

"What about me?" Jenny stood with her hand on her hips, squinting through her damaged glasses. A smile slowly spread across her face, haloed by bright light from the full moon hovering above.

"You have an idea?"

"I sure do," smiled Jenny, "though it'll involve lying to my parents."

"Are you sure you can do that?"

"Somehow I think I can," she announced with a mischievous grin. "Hey, it's about time. You see, up until now, I've always been a very good Catholic girl…"

Shawn held his tongue in check, deciding to keep the images that were running rampant through his head to himself.

"So here's what we do…" Jenny continued, formulating her plan.


Holding hands and moving as quietly as possible, Shawn and Jenny ducked from shadow to shadow, from car to car, slowly making their way across the parking lot.

Shawn nearly had a heart attack as he spied a police car driving away from them, heading past Locust and toward the school. It was then that he remembered the angry blonde guy in the boxer shorts who had confronted him less than forty-five minutes ago. The cops must have come to see him. He felt a pang of guilt over the ruined bike.

They finally reached the window, crouching just outside of Shawn's hospital room. The boy slowly raised his head to peer through the glass, sighing with relief that the room was still empty.

"Okay, the coast is clear. But we don't know yet whether or not they came in while I was gone."

"Now's as good a time as any to find out," said Jenny, smiling encouragement as she brushed an errant strand of long red hair from her eyes. "I'll wait here."

Shawn quickly scaled the window, ducking inside, as Jenny rose to push the screen back into place. Hurriedly changing from his street clothes into the ill-fitting hospital gown, he shimmied back into bed, wiped the cold night sweat from his brow, and reached for the call button just as the door opened.

"How's my favorite patient doing?" smiled Nurse Vanessa, shaking down a thermometer. "Nice to see you're back in bed. I thought maybe you'd run out on us."

"What do you mean?" he gasped, desperate to keep his trembling voice from betraying him.

"Just that I came in earlier and you were in the bathroom, or at least I assumed you were. The door was closed. Come to think of it," the nurse said, glancing over her shoulder at the bathroom door, "it still is."

"Trust me, you don't want to go in there," said Shawn, relieved. "I did us both a favor by closing the door."

"Nasty!" admonished the nurse, as she slid the thermometer under Shawn's tongue. "Don't tell me it was the hospital food?"

"Urk," was Shawn's reply, as the thermometer warmed in his mouth.

* * *

"Mr. McGee?" asked a trim oriental nurse with almond eyes as she spoke into a phone, tapping her fingers impatiently on her desk. Maya Wang had worked at the hospital for over two years but had yet to be able to transfer from the night shift. God, how she hated it! Nothing ever happened in the daytime because everyone saved it all up for the night, even in this sleepy little burg. "Mr. McGee," she nudged, giving the girl's father a chance to wake up.

Just a few minutes ago, a red haired teenager wearing a broken pair of glasses had hobbled through the emergency room door, crying. Her knee was scraped and bloody and her hands and arms were cut and bruised. Maya thought she recognized the girl as being in the same freshman class as her little sister, though she wasn't sure. The girl said she'd been in a bicycle accident - someone on a motorcycle had cut across her path and zoomed through the elementary school playground just down the road, taking a header into a chain link fence.

The girl, sitting across from Wang in one of the waiting rooms, had apparently swerved to avoid the biker and run straight into a swing set, bending up her bicycle and throwing herself from her ride. Not knowing what else to do and unable to help the rider, she'd hobbled down the street and shown up here, in Maya's life, interrupting Don Kirshner's Rock Concert on channel ten.

"I'm so sorry to wake you," the nurse said, twirling a long strand of straight black hair that tumbled from beneath her white nurse's cap, as the girl's father finally mumbled something unintelligible into the phone, "but your daughter's been involved in an accident. Oh no, Mr. McGee, other than a scraped knee and a few minor bumps and bruises she's perfectly fine."

"Well, apparently, she was riding her bicycle to the hospital to see another of our patients, even though it's well past visiting hours," she glared at the girl, shaking a finger at her, softening the admonishment with a quick smile, "and some lunatic on a motorcycle ran her off the road. She turned to avoid the driver but ran her bicycle into some playground equipment." Picking up the steaming cup of hot coffee she had poured just before the girl had walked up to her desk, she paused long enough to take a quick sip, enjoying the hot caffeinated buzz that coursed down her throat and through her system.

"Oh no, I promise, she's just fine," continued the nurse, rolling her eyes at Jenny. "No, nothing broken, the doctor has already examined her and treated her wounds. She's perfectly fine, just like I told you earlier. Oh no, sir, we'll just send you a bill, don't worry about a thing."

"All right, Mr. McGee," answered Maya, as she doodled on a prescription pad one of the doctors had inadvertently left behind, "yes, sir, I'll tell her. I'm going to let her go visit with her friend now, even though it's against hospital policy." She smiled again at Jenny, shrugging her shoulders as if to say, *well, rules were clearly made to be broken.*

"No, sir, I'm happy to do it, don't give it a moment's thought. All right, Mr. McGee, we'll see you in a few minutes," said the nurse, finally hanging up the phone.

"Boy, you're in trouble," joked Maya to Jenny, who rose from the chair to walk up to the young night nurse.

"Is my dad coming?" Jenny asked.

"As soon as he takes a shower and gets dressed, he says. So if you want to see your *boyfriend*," Maya teased, "you'd better get moving!"

"Thank you so much!" called Jenny as she disappeared down the hallway, toward room 117.

"Teenagers," sighed Maya, swiveling around in her seat to bring the little color television back to life. If she were lucky, she thought to herself, she'd still be able to catch Foghat's performance on the Rock Concert.

Quickly turning from the television, she stared with astonishment at absolutely nothing. Strange, she could have sworn she'd seen someone out of the corner of her eye – a man wearing a khaki-colored trench coat, approaching her desk – but nobody was there. That's it, she told herself, as she pushed the cooling cup of coffee across her desk and out of reach, no more caffeine for me. Sighing, she turned her attention to the television, oblivious to everything in the world but Foghat.

* * *

"So," said Jenny, sitting cross-legged at the foot of Shawn's bed, "how in the heck did you know that thing was after me?"

"It's a long story, and if your dad is coming I'm not sure we have time to talk about it right now." Shawn sat at the other end of the bed, his feet dangling off the side.

"We may not get another chance, at least for a while. I'm sure he's going to ground me, and we probably won't get to talk again until sometime next year," Jenny prodded, removing her glasses and inching closer to the sandy-haired teenager.

"Really? Are you serious?"

"Well, maybe not," grinned Jenny. "He's going to be upset, though, that's for sure. But I think I can talk my way out of getting grounded. So how did you know it was following me?"

"You're not going to believe this. I'm not even sure I do. But I think when it bit me it opened up some sort of weird psychic connection between us. I fell asleep tonight and had a dream – at least it seemed like a dream at the time – that I *was* the monster. I was standing across from the old Spencer house on Randolph Street watching, waiting for something. And then… I was following you…" Shawn faltered, feeling ashamed as he relived the emotions he felt while trapped inside the fetch's head.

"Shawn," Jenny prodded, squeezing Shawn's knee, "are you sure this wasn't a dream after all?"

Shawn had held back one important piece of information that he didn't want to share unless he absolutely had to. "Jenny," he started, laying his hand across hers, "that pile of your stuff that it made in your room. Did you put it all away?"

"Of course I did."

"Did you find a pair of... a pair of," Shawn stumbled, unable to make himself utter the word "panties." Embarrassed, he looked toward the door, hoping her father would show up and save him from having to tell Jenny what he had seen - but of course he didn't. Sighing, Shawn went on, "Okay, Jenny, did you find a white pair of underwear with a hole bitten through the crotch?"

Jenny's face went pale and she gasped, jerking her hand away from Shawn's. "Oh my God, Shawn!" she whispered, looking into his eyes. "Oh my God..."

"Jenny!" shouted Paul McGee, slamming open the door to room 117. His face was red with anger while his eyes betrayed fear and worry. "Jenny, are you okay?"

\* \* \*

Shawn still didn't know the answer to that question, and it had been nearly an hour since he'd heard it asked. Jenny's father had swept into the room, gathered up his daughter, ignoring her protests and refusing to listen to her explanations.

Shawn still sat in the middle of the hospital bed where they had left him, stunned by all that had transpired at the school yard. Not quite daring to believe that it was truly over, he wondered what the fetch wanted from them in the first place.

Once again, it felt like he hadn't eaten in days. His stomach grumbled, but he forced himself to ignore the hunger pangs deep in his belly. What was wrong with him? Why was he so hungry? He'd wolfed down the saltines the nurse brought him earlier as quickly as he'd gotten them, and he knew the chance of getting another snack this late was pretty much nonexistent.

Looking down at his arm, his insatiable appetite was all but forgotten as he finally noticed what Jenny had commented on as they stood together by the swing set. He was shocked to see that his wound had completely healed. He didn't even have a scar. He thought about the fetch, how he had watched it burn alive while trapped between the motorcycle and the chain-link fence that surrounded the school. But if Shawn could heal this quickly after the monster bit him...

Maybe it wasn't over yet after all.

# Chapter 14

RUSKIN STOOD alone at the accident site, looking up at the gray clouds that were beginning to form over Carthage, wondering for the fifth or sixth time this morning just where in the blue hell his deputy was. The coroner had come and gone from the accident scene, saying that there was nothing he could do. Despite the crimson tide of blood that covered everything from the chain link fence to the pebbles on the ground, the motorcycle no longer seemed to have a rider.

The Fire Marshall concurred, saying that his men hadn't found anything of substance except for the gutted and warped remains of the burned out Kawasaki. Even Doc Jenkins, an old wit who rarely let anyone else get a word in edgewise, had been puzzled and hadn't been able to offer Ruskin much to go on. The stench of roasted flesh was still fresh in the air, but, without a body, none of this made any sense. There was no way in hell that anyone could lose that amount of blood and leave the scene by any other means than a body bag.

He'd driven past the school on his way home last night, after he spoke with the blonde hippie who'd reported his motorcycle stolen and started this whole ball rolling. He resented the man, all the while knowing full well that it wasn't *his* fault that someone had stolen the bike. Still, Ruskin had enough to deal with, and he didn't need one more thing on his plate. And now he had the mysterious disappearance of his deputy to investigate as well.

He shouldn't have left Delacroix alone. He hadn't seen the man when he drove past the school after taking the hippie's statement, but just assumed that he was off somewhere taking a piss. The boys from the fire department were there by then, so he hadn't worried about it and instead just headed home to bed, thinking that everything was in good hands. But that had been nine hours ago and when his deputy hadn't kept their daily doughnut ritual – especially after Ruskin had offered to pay - he knew in his gut that something was wrong. Whatever Delacroix was (and the man was a lot of things, including a wife-beater and an adulterer) he wouldn't just abandon his black-and-white cruiser at the scene of an accident, and he would never, ever give up a free meal.

Still, he'd telephoned both the man's wife and his mistress, but neither had seen any trace of the deputy. Tellingly, both suggested that the Sheriff talk to the other, and neither seemed too concerned with the man's whereabouts. In fact, his wife seemed almost relieved. Maybe Delacroix's past had finally caught up to him and some sweet young thing whom he'd charmed into bed and later abandoned had told her boyfriend or husband and the man had caved in the back of the horny Cajun's head with a tire iron.

But that didn't make sense. Delacroix was a trained police officer, and there was no way that someone could have gotten the drop on him without a fight. And even then there would have been signs of a struggle – a ripped piece of clothing, hair, something – and there just weren't any. Other than blood – and there was a lot of that - there just wasn't any evidence.

Ruskin still intended to have the blood tested and typed, of course, because there was always the chance that some of the blood they'd found at the site of the accident was Delacroix's. Because Carthage didn't have its own lab, they would have to send it off to Quincy, and it could take weeks for the results. And what would a blood type tell him anyway? Delacroix was a Type O, the universal donor, so if the blood from the site also turned out to be Type O it really wouldn't prove a thing.

And that brought the Sheriff full circle. There were facts everywhere, but none of them seemed to add up. Taking out a little red notepad, he began to establish a timeline:

10:00 PM: Larry Diamond's Kawasaki was stolen from his home

10:15 PM: Thief crashes bike into chain link fence, destroying bike

10:20 PM: Report called in by Jim Warner

10:45 PM: Ruskin/Delacroix arrive on the scene

10:50 PM: Jim Warner reports seeing two teenagers by wreckage

The disappearance of his deputy notwithstanding, that was pretty much all Ruskin had. According to the nurse, the McGee girl had shown up just a little before eleven, but, according to the timeline he had just established, she must have seen the motorcycle and swerved to avoid it just minutes before the Kawasaki crashed into the fence. So why had it taken her nearly 45 minutes to make her way seven blocks to the hospital? Wang said her knee had been pretty banged up, and it was an uphill walk, but even hobbling it shouldn't have taken more than fifteen or twenty minutes, tops.

Ruskin still had no idea what was going on and where his deputy was but there were a whole lot of things that didn't quite add up, and the only one he could actually do anything about right now was the girl. Waving at the Fire Marshall and the workers that were loading up the remains of the crash from the night before, he forced his burly frame into the police cruiser and headed to the McGee house for the second time in less than a week, to question Paul and Abby McGee's only surviving child.

* * *

Sunday morning came early for Shawn. A new nurse, a plump old lady named Montgomery, had shown up in his room at eight o'clock sharp. She'd woken him from one of those dreams where you run around school in your underwear, unable to find the class for which you're already ten minutes late. Nurse Montgomery had taken the boy's temperature and blood pressure, given him a thorough if quick exam, and finally pronounced him fit as a fiddle and ready to be discharged. Of course, the final word on whether or not he would be going home today was the Doctor's, and, according to the old gray-haired RN, he wouldn't be making rounds until at least ten or eleven.

And so he was trapped in the sparse little hospital room for at least another two hours. Anxious to go home, he passed the time by flipping channels on the television before finally settling on *Rocky and Bullwinkle*. He'd seen all the episodes countless times before, but it was either that or the usual Sunday morning fare where television preachers tried to get you to call in and pledge money to their ministries. Having no money of consequence to give and no real inclination to give it had he had it in the first place, the boy decided that watching the squirrel and moose foil Boris and Natasha's plans for the umpteenth time was probably his best bet.

Curiously, he was no longer starving. He ate his meager breakfast of a scrambled egg, bacon, and an English muffin with grape jelly, washing it down with orange juice, and that seemed to fill him up just fine. He'd fallen asleep hungry and miserable and was glad that the hunger seemed to have passed sometime during the night.

As the first half of *Rocky and Bullwinkle* came to an end and the adventures of Sherman and Mr. Peabody and their "wayback machine" began, Shawn found himself thinking back to the previous night's events. He still had a lot of questions, but no clue whether or not he'd ever figure out the answers. It was all too easy for him to simply let last night's events fade from his mind and pretend that none of it had ever happened, especially with his arm having miraculously healed as though it had never been hurt in the first place. Even the cuts and bruises he suffered during last night's motorcycle ride had all but faded. But it did happen, all of it happened, and he was determined to find out why.

* * *

Ruskin stood outside the McGee house, knocking softly on the door. It was nearly nine now - at least an hour before the family would be going to church - so they had no excuse for avoiding him. He wanted to interview the girl as quickly as he could, to see if she knew anything or if he could poke any holes in her story, and then get back to the search for his deputy, stolen motorcycle be damned.

The Sheriff hadn't yet called in a report on Delacroix and wouldn't as long as he could track him down by Monday. It was embarrassing, losing one's deputy, and he was determined not to let the Mayor or anyone on the city council know anything about it unless he had absolutely no other choice. Cursing Delacroix and his propensity for skirt chasing (he was now almost certain that the man's disappearance would wind up having something to do with the deputy's insatiable taste for bedding other men's wives) he started to knock on the door a second time when it finally opened to reveal Abby McGee, dressed in a conservative black skirt and sporting a strand of pearls.

"Good morning, ma'am," greeted Ruskin, tipping his hat to the woman who'd just lost her son. He'd known the McGee family for over thirty years, well before he'd disgraced himself and the force in Chicago and subsequently moved to Carthage, tail between his legs, to accept the post of county Sheriff.

But in a town the size of this one, people tended to be a little more forgiving, especially if you were a former big city detective who had managed to convince the county that he was doing them a favor by accepting the role of Sheriff and the pittance of a salary that came with it. He was a big fish in a very small pond, but at least he was still working, still involved in enforcing the law, and that meant something to him.

"Good morning, Sheriff," said Abby, surprised to see him standing on her doorstep. "Can I do something for you? We're just about ready to leave for Mass."

"Well, ma'am, first of all, again, I'm sorry for your loss," he paused, "And I hate to bother you at a time like this…"

"I saw you at the church, you know," she interrupted, "standing in the back. You could have come up and said hello. You would have been welcome."

"I just wanted to pay my respects. I know how hard this is for you and Paul, losing a child," he paused, and the woman nodded, acknowledging his words and gesturing for him to continue, "and now is a rotten time to have to deal with this, but your daughter was involved in an accident last night up by Lincoln Elementary, and I'm here to take her statement."

"Abby," called a voice from inside the house, "who is it?"

"Paul, it's the Sheriff. He said he needs to talk to Jenny."

"It won't take more than ten or fifteen minutes, tops," interjected Ruskin, tipping his hat again as Paul McGee joined his wife at the door. "As I'm sure you know by now, there was a motorcycle accident at the school last night and apparently your daughter saw the whole thing. I just need to talk to her for a few minutes, get the time-line straight, and then I'll be out of your hair."

"Bear," said Paul, using the Sheriff's nickname, "can't this wait? She's still pretty shaken up over what happened last night, not to mention her brother's death, and I know you of all people know how it is."

"I'm afraid it can't, Paul," said the Sheriff, politely edging a foot into the door, looking past Paul and Abby and into their home. It was a nice house, very neat and tidy, decorated differently but otherwise just as he'd remembered. Paul McGee's parents had grown up here and Paul and his bride had moved in to the house shortly after his parents had died, right after Jenny had been born, around the time his own family had been taken from him. "I promise I'll be as quick as possible and do my dead level best not to shake her up too much."

"Mr. Ruskin, I really didn't see much of anything," explained Jenny, brushing red hair from her eyes as she sat beside her parents with the Sheriff in the den. "I'd just gone out to see my friend Shawn at the hospital – yes, Dad, I know it was a stupid thing to do, going out that late at night without telling anyone – and suddenly a motorcycle came out of nowhere and nearly ran me over. I swerved to avoid it and, the next thing I knew, I was flat on my back under the swing set and the motorcycle was on fire, tangled up in the fence."

"And did you see the driver?" asked the Sheriff, leaning toward Jenny. He tentatively sipped from a cup of coffee Abby had been kind enough to offer him, wishing that the woman had also been so inclined to include a generous shot of Irish whiskey in the steaming hot brew.

"If I did, I can't remember what he looked like. Everything happened so quickly, and now it's all just a blur."

Looking at his notes, the Sheriff said, "According to the time-line we've established, the wreck occurred at approximately 10:15 PM, and you arrived at the hospital nearly 45 minutes later. Even with an injured knee, it shouldn't have taken you more than ten minutes to walk that distance. Mind you, I'm not calling you a liar; I just want to find out exactly what happened so we can put this thing to rest."

"I don't really know, Mr. Ruskin," said the girl, looking him straight in the eye, almost daring him not to believe her. "I'd left my watch at home, so I wasn't exactly sure what time it was. And the fall really knocked the wind out of me, so I'm not even sure how long it took me to get on my feet. And once I did, I had to find my glasses, which had fallen off in the crash.

"I'm not sure how long it took me to find them. And even after I did, I had a hard time seeing because one of the lenses was broken. I didn't know what to do, so I just hobbled to the hospital and told them what happened and asked the nurse to call my parents."

Ruskin was disappointed. He wasn't sure what he'd expected, but the girl seemed to be telling the truth. Everything she said was entirely plausible and made perfect sense. And then he remembered something.

"Mr. Warner, who lives across the street from where the accident happened - well, he said he saw two teenagers standing out by the swing set, not just one. Jenny, can you explain that to me?"

The girl's face dropped for a second. The question had clearly thrown her, but she quickly recovered, shrugged, and said, "I don't know what to tell you, Mr. Ruskin. As far as I know, I was the only one there. But, then again, my glasses were broken and I don't see very well without them…" she let herself trail off, watching the Sheriff's reaction.

"Well, Mr. Warner is an old man and probably needs glasses himself," smiled Ruskin, letting her off the hook for now. He'd have plenty of time to tighten the slack and reel her in later. "Like you said, it was pretty dark, so who knows what he actually saw?"

"Can we wrap this up, Sheriff?" interrupted Paul, irritation evident in his voice. "My daughter's told you all that she knows. She made a mistake and she knows it, but she didn't break any laws that I'm aware of."

"I never said that she did, Paul. At any rate, I do think we're done here. And once again, I'm sorry for bothering you on a Sunday morning, and I'm so sorry for your loss."

Ruskin rose on creaky legs, shook hands with Jenny's father, and let himself out the front door, his mind for the moment only on the little silver flask of gin hidden in the glove compartment of his patrol car.

# Chapter 15

SOMEWHERE ELSE, deep in the woods just on the other side of the Carthage Lake, the fetch rested beneath an old oak tree, healing. It had eaten the man in the school yard, clothing, bones and all. That had helped make it bigger, made it stronger, but it was still in pain. Its life force still flickered like a match in a windstorm, threatening to go out. Its fur was still singed, falling off in places, and it was missing several claws on both hands as well as its left eye. But it knew it would survive, to kill again, to hunt, and to serve its master.

It had almost died in the attack, and it seethed with anger over the memory. It would kill the two teenagers, of course, but it would do so slowly, without mercy, and it would make their pain last a long, long time, far longer than its own pain had lasted. It would enjoy their struggles, gloriously feeding off their screams.

First, though, it had to find the object for the old man. Oh, how it hated its master, how it longed to tear out his throat. It was bound to the old man by a magic it could never understand, had been bound to him for as long as it could remember, and it had no choice but to do exactly what he ordered.

The fetch could almost remember a time Before, a time when it had been free to do what it wanted, to hunt where and when it chose, and to live life free of the old man's thoughts and whims. But try as it might, it could never press past the invisible constraints that seemed to cloud its mind, to access its memories and finally remember. Someday, though, someday, when the old man had what it wanted, when he no longer worded his orders quite so carefully, the slave would turn on the master and rip his still-beating heart from his chest, slowly eating it as the old man watched. And finally, it would be free. Someday soon, it would have its freedom, and its revenge.

Thinking about such things soothed the creature as it dug at the base of a tall oak tree, deep into the ground, covering itself with dirt and leaves and moss; hiding, healing, waiting.

# Chapter 16

FINALLY, JUST before noon, Shawn was allowed to leave the hospital. The doctor echoed Nurse Montgomery's assessment and pronounced him healthy and able to leave the confines of Carthage Memorial. No one really seemed to want to address the condition of his arm and he wasn't about to press the issue, happy to leave well enough alone and avoid being asked questions that he couldn't even begin to answer.

Celebrating his clean bill of health, his parents insisted on driving him across the bridge that spanned the Mississippi into Keokuk, Iowa, to treat him to lunch at Cassano's, his favorite pizza joint.

Though the food was delicious, he couldn't stop thinking about what had happened last night. It almost seemed like a bad dream, but he knew it had been all too real. That thing had tried to kill Jenny, would have killed her if whatever strange connection it shared with him hadn't kicked in.

His thoughts kept coming back to Jenny. They'd been friends for as long as he could remember, yet there were still so many things he didn't know about her. What was her favorite color, for instance? What kind of books did she like to read? What flavor ice cream did she like? He could guess at a couple of those, but didn't really know for certain. In fact, the only thing he really knew for sure was that, despite her father's objections, he wanted to know more.

Two hours after lunch, Shawn found himself wondering if it was safe to call her. Her father seemed to have developed an intense dislike for him since he'd showed up outside of Jenny's window yesterday morning, but who could blame him? He certainly hadn't made the best of impressions, but it would be nice if Jenny's dad were a little less suspicious of his motives. Was it because he wasn't Catholic? But that didn't make sense. According to Tanner, his mother only converted to Catholicism after marrying his father. He knew that what Mr. McGee said was probably true, that every time Jenny saw Shawn she thought of her brother. But was that necessarily a bad thing?

He wondered how Tanner would have felt about Shawn wanting to date his little sister. *He probably would have punched me in the face*, he thought, *but after he got used to the idea I really think he would have been okay with it.* A familiar lump rose in his throat as he realized that he'd never have the chance to find out.

Thinking about his friend caused his thoughts to once again drift back to the last day they'd spent together, exploring the old house on Randolph Street.

* * *

"Holy cow, Shawn, you've got to see all this!" exclaimed Tanner from the top of the cellar stairs. The older boy had taken the lead, rushing ahead of Shawn only to encounter another locked door, this one sporting a lock not nearly as rusted – and thus not as easily breakable – as the one that guarded the cellar from outside. Fortunately, much like the first lock, this one was no match for Tanner's reclaimed crowbar; with a hard twist on the long metal rod, he'd quickly shattered the lock with the glee of a kid busting a piñata on his birthday, then scampered up the stairs into darkness.

Shawn slowly climbed the old wooden stairs, listening to the low creak that sounded from his footsteps. He hoped the wood wouldn't collapse beneath him. But the stairs held strong and a moment later he joined his friend in the kitchen of the old house, a wave of suffocating humidity washing over them as they stepped deeper into its secrets.

The room was huge and echoed with their every footstep. An old cast iron stove stood against the north wall, next to a wooden pantry and a rusting metal icebox. The walls were covered with cabinets. Opening them revealed a small stack of plates, a handful of tarnished flatware, and maybe a half a dozen cups laden with dust and cobwebs. The floor was covered with tile, though it was difficult to discern the color or even a pattern through the thick layer of grime that had swallowed it whole.

Wiping sweat from his brow, Shawn pointed his flashlight through a door on the west wall that led from the kitchen into an enormous dining room. His beam fell upon a great wooden table surrounded by twelve chairs, every one of them covered in mildew and mold. A small crystal chandelier hung from the ceiling, completely encased in spider webs and dead flies trapped within. He noticed the floor there change from ceramic tile to a rich, dark wood as it crossed the threshold between the two rooms.

Tanner waved his own flashlight around the room, taking a cup out of the cabinet, holding it up to the light to examine it.

"Weird," he said, placing it on the white tiled kitchen counter. "Why's all of this stuff still here anyway? You'd think when your great-great-whatever moved away, he'd have taken some of this with him. "

Shawn shrugged. "Who knows? None of us ever knew much about good old great-great-uncle Charles. Or should that be great old good-good-uncle Charles?" he paused dramatically, sighing as the older boy cleared his throat and rolled his eyes at the lame joke.

"Some people just don't have a good sense of humor," Shawn glared. "Anyway, according to my dad's dad, he showed up here just after World War II, saying now that the war was over he wanted to settle down in Carthage. The guy buys this huge house, moves into it all alone, and then skips town a few years later. And, at least according to what my Grandpa remembers, no one ever heard from him again."

"Oh, sounds spooky!" Tanner grinned, getting into the mystery. "Maybe he died in here, you know, slipped on his soap in the shower and broke his neck or something, and his ghost has been roaming around ever since?"

"Yeah, right, and pigs have wings."

"Well, you never know, and … oh my God, Shawn, he's right behind you!"

"Shit!" Shawn yelped, the color draining out of his face as he spun around toward the old stove. The flashlight dropped from his hands to land on the tile floor with a dull clatter.

"Gotcha!" Tanner smirked, holding the flashlight under his chin while sticking his tongue out at his friend, "OooOooOoo, I'm coming to get you, Shawn Spencer, and I'm gonna eat your brains!"

His face red with embarrassment, Shawn bent over to retrieve the flashlight as he fought to slow the crazed woodpecker that was hammering in his chest as though it were trying to whittle a door through his ribcage. "Good one, dork," he muttered, rolling his eyes. "Come on, now. let's get this show on the road."

"Now you're finally speaking my language. Let's check out the rest of the house!" said Tanner, stepping toward the entrance to the dining room.

"Hold up, Tanner. Hey, look at this!" said Shawn, gesturing at a three foot wide by two foot tall panel set into the middle of the south wall. "I've never seen one of these in person before."

"What is it?"

"It's a dumbwaiter." Thumping the panel with the heel of his hand, he heard his knock echo inside as a thick cloud of dust plumed high into the air. "See, it's hollow inside."

"Okay… a dumb what?"

"It's something that old rich people used to use to transport food up and down the floors of a mansion. It's like a little elevator. The chef would cook the food and then put it inside the dumbwaiter and send it up to the floor above, where servants would remove it and bring it to whoever had asked for it. Then, when they were finished, they'd send the empty dishes back downstairs to the kitchen. I've read about them in books."

"Do you think you can get it open? There might be something good in there."

"I'll try," said Shawn, prying at the little panel. It opened with a soft pop, revealing a pair of worn brown ropes trailing down an empty shaft. "Well, it must be on another floor," the boy shrugged, staring into the dark space where the dumbwaiter used to be.

"Maybe it'll be upstairs? How do you make it work?"

"I think you pull these little ropes," answered Shawn, pointing at the pull cords threaded through the center of the shaft. He reached out to tug one and then the other, but neither would budge.

"I guess it's broken," shrugged Tanner. "Come on, let's go search the rest of the house."


"This is all just too weird," said Shawn, as he poked through the huge brick fireplace that covered the east wall of the living room.

They had explored almost all of the first floor, finding a second dining room, two bathrooms, a utility room, a little foyer that led to the porch outside, two sets of stairs, and two living areas. This place was huge! They stood now in the second living area, the larger of the two, and could see the front porch from the dusty and cracked stained glass windows that looked out into the world beyond.

"What's weird?" asked his friend absently, sitting on the dusty living room couch, leafing through a handful of old books he had found on a little wooden shelf that sat against the opposite wall. The couch looked to have once been white but was now a moldy color somewhere between green and brown. Shawn shuddered at the thought of even touching the rotting old thing and could barely fathom Tanner sitting there, casually flipping pages as though he were at home in front of the television doing his homework.

"The fireplace doesn't look like it's ever been used. I mean, sure, there's dust and bugs and stuff, but no logs or even the remains of logs, and no rack to hold them. There's a big star enclosed in a circle – like a pentagram - engraved into the floor where the rack should be. It's just weird."

"Hey, get a load of these books – there's one about witchcraft, one about faeries, two about South American mythology, and, hey, something right up your alley – *The Lord of the Rings*. Why did this guy leave all his books?"

"Tolkien?" asked Shawn, suddenly interested. He'd read all of the Tolkien books by the time he was twelve and enjoyed anything having to do with hobbits, wizards, and dragons, even if he didn't believe in any of them. Abandoning the fireplace, he moved carefully over the creaking wood floor to kneel in the dust beside Tanner.

"It's yours," said Tanner, handing the book over to Shawn.

"Very cool, and it's a first edition, too. Neat!"

"First edition?" asked the other boy, consternation spreading across his face. "Does that mean it might be worth something?"

"If it is, we'll sell it and split the money down the middle."

"Deal!" he agreed, slapping Shawn a high five.

"Find anything else?"

"Talk about weird," said Tanner, passing a small leather-bound journal to Shawn. "It has a little clasp and a keyhole like a diary, but the hole is rusty and besides the book is open anyway. Not that there's anything to see."

Shawn quickly thumbed through the book; the spine was creased and the cover was well worn, but the pages were all blank. Flipping the book closed, Shawn realized that the cover was empty as well, just as empty as the house now felt, save for the scattering of belongings that his relative had abandoned years ago. Disappointed, he dropped the book to the couch.

"Hey, here's something," said Tanner, holding up a worn, dog-eared book with the words *Mein Kampf* emblazoned in gold type across the cover. "Hitler's autobiography, I think, which is kind of creepy. What, do you have Nazis in your family tree?"

"Not that I know of," Shawn shrugged, rising to his feet. "So are there any other books?"

"There's one about carpentry, one about the life of Abraham Lincoln, three cookbooks, and one about farming," Tanner said, rising from the mildewed couch to continue their search. "Fun stuff, huh? But I think I'll keep the one about Lincoln and the Hitler one. They might come in handy for a book report or something somewhere down the road. But where did he hide all the really good stuff. Old books just don't cut it."

"Maybe there just isn't any 'really good stuff'," countered Shawn.

"Hey, we should have brought along my Ouija board," Tanner grinned, waggling his eyebrows. "Then we could just ask your Nazi uncle where he buried all the treasure."

"Your board worked so well last time," Shawn sighed, "and he wasn't a Nazi!"

"Yeah, yeah, that's what they all say," Tanner chuckled as he left the room with Shawn in tow, retracing their steps through the house to a creaky oak staircase by the kitchen, climbing the stairs to the second floor of the manor.

* * *

Sighing, Shawn rose to his feet from the bed he'd been sprawled across since coming home from Keokuk, deciding that if he was going to make the call, now was probably the best time to do it.

He'd only asked a girl out once before, and that hadn't exactly worked out so well. Her name had been Rebecca McFarland, a bookish, brown-haired girl who had just transferred into his freshman class from Warsaw. He'd noticed her in English class and had been impressed by some of the books she carried with her – Tolkien, Heinlein, Dick, Beagle – before even noticing her pretty brown eyes and beguiling smile.

It took him three weeks, but he'd finally found the courage to talk to her and had planned to ask her to an upcoming school dance. He'd made the mistake of approaching her one day in the cafeteria, with Mike Jackson and Rusty Bower, Shawn's tormentors since fourth grade, sitting just a table away. He'd asked her if she planned to go to the dance and when she said she wasn't sure, he casually suggested that they might go together.

Jackson and Bower pointed at Rebecca and began snickering, giving her the impression that they were in on some elaborate practical joke with Shawn and that his overtures were nothing more than a prank designed to make her the laughing stock of the school. Tears running down her cheeks, her face red with shame, she quickly fled from the room in a cacophony of jeers and laughs from Jackson and Boyer. He had never had the courage to approach her after that, and she had moved again at the end of the freshman year, this time to Missouri, without ever knowing that Shawn had really liked her and genuinely wanted to take her to the dance.

He'd always regretted never clearing the air between them and didn't want to be anything but straightforward and honest with Jenny. He just had to get past his fear of her father. Suddenly remembering that he actually had a reason to call Jenny independent of romance that even Mr. McGee couldn't disagree with, he grinned with relief; both his bicycle and his backpack were still at Jenny's house, where they'd been since her father had picked them up from the pool last night. Her father couldn't possibly argue with Shawn walking over to get his stuff.

He pumped his fist into the air in victory, preparing to go to the den and telephone his best friend's sister. And then an unrelated thought struck him; where was Samson? He hadn't seen the cat since he and his parents had returned from lunch, and he was suddenly worried. What if he'd gotten out? The last time that happened, he'd gotten into a fight with another tom down the street and ended up with twelve stitches in his left haunch.

"Samson!" Shawn called out. He expected to see the big orange and white tabby bound happily into view, but the room remained empty. Shrugging to himself, he decided that the cat was probably napping in some out of the way corner of the house. Momentarily pushing thoughts of Samson aside, he walked to the den to call Jenny.

* * *

Paul McGee found himself standing outside the door to his daughter's bedroom, trying to find the will to knock on the thin wooden door that separated them. A man of few words, he wasn't exactly sure how to start the talk he knew he needed to have with his daughter.

He'd been hard on Jenny since Tanner's death and he needed to somehow find the words to explain why, to express his feelings and open up to her. He needed to tell her the reason he'd been acting the way he had, something he hadn't even realized he'd been doing until his wife had finally pointed it out to him.

"Paul," she'd said, as they sat alone together in the living room. "Shawn's a good kid and I think he really cares about Jenny. You know he cared about Tanner, and would have done anything in the world for him. I just don't think you're being fair to him."

"He's trying to take advantage of our daughter," he'd responded, the words sounding hollow even as he said them. He desperately wanted to blame someone – anyone – for Tanner's death, but there was no one to blame. Paul was a devout Catholic and had always believed that if you lived a good life, said your prayers, and went to Mass, everything would turn out okay. But what kind of God takes a child from his father? He was questioning his faith now, questioning God, and taking the deep anger he felt at the loss of his son out on what was left of his family.

"I know it's not really about Shawn, or even Jenny, but she doesn't know that," Abby said. Laying a hand upon her husband's shoulder, she began to rub his neck. "You're a good man, Paul, and I love you with all of my heart, and so does Jenny. You just need to let her know what you're going through, let her know how you feel, before it's too late."

He'd been standing outside in the hallway for the last five minutes trying to put his thoughts into words, but they just wouldn't come. *Let her know how you feel*, Abby said, but that was easier said than done, especially when you weren't exactly sure how you felt in the first place. Taking a deep breath, knowing it was now or never, Paul crossed himself and then reached out to gently rap his knuckles against the closed door.

"Jenny," he called, pushing the door open a little so that he could crane his neck around the frame, "Jenny, can I come in for a minute?"

"Sure Dad," answered the girl, bringing her legs up onto the bed, hugging her knees close to her as she shifted toward the headboard to make room for her father.

"Jenny," he started, sitting beside her, "I miss your brother so much. I must walk by his room a thousand times a day, and I have to stop myself from looking in, to see if he's there."

"I know, Dad," Jenny said softly, "I miss him too." She pushed her glasses - her back-up pair, which sported a cheap black frame – toward the bridge of her nose.

"I don't know if I've ever told you this, but I lost my big sister Margaret around the time you were born, when Tanner was just a baby. And of course you know your Granddad died fighting in the Second World War…" he crossed himself again as he let his words trail off.

Jenny knew about her Grandfather, of course, and there was a grave at the cemetery with her Aunt Margaret's name on it, but she'd rarely heard her father even speak Margaret's name, much less mention anything about her death. She knew he came from a "big Irish family" with two brothers and two sisters, and she knew all about her other aunts and uncles but next to nothing about Margaret. She started to ask, but quickly grew silent when she sensed that it wasn't something he was ready to talk about.

"My father came from Ireland to the states nearly seven years before we went to war with Japan and Germany. That man loved America with a fierce passion and when the Japs bombed us in '41 he felt it was his God-given duty to protect the land that had brought him so much happiness. I was only five at the time and can barely remember him, but I still miss my old man. But even though he died young, he died when he should have."

"What do you mean?"

"He died before any of his sons and daughters. He died even before your Aunt Theresa was born. He missed her birth by less than a month, I think. But my point is that a parent should never outlive a child. It just isn't right. So if I'm over-protective of you, and I know that I sometimes am, it isn't because I don't trust you, or trust your judgment. It's because I lost my sister and my father, and now I'm grieving for your brother, and I can't even bear the thought of losing you..." Paul started to shake. He closed his eyes tight, keeping in the tears that were so desperately threatening to come out. "Jennifer Anne, I just can't lose you, too. It would be too much, much more than I could take, more than any father should have to take. I just can't do it."

A lump in her throat and tears adding spots to her freckles, Jenny wrapped her arms around her father's thick neck, hugging him tight. Only then did he allow his own tears to come, as they both cried together for his son and her brother, for the father that he barely remembered and the Grandfather that she'd never know, and for each other, for all that the other had lost or would never have the chance to find.

"Daddy," whispered Jenny, when her father finally broke their embrace, "I promise you, you'll never lose me. What I did last night was stupid, and I'll never leave the house that late again, without at least letting you know where I'm going and when I'll be back."

"I know, honey," said Paul, looking into his daughter's eyes, "and I *do* trust you, and, before you ask, I trust Shawn too."

"Dad…"

"Shush, honey, let me finish. I know you're getting older and it's probably time, maybe even past time, for you to be interested in a boy. And I know Shawn's a good kid. Hell, if he wasn't, he'd never have been Tanner's best friend. It's just hard for a daddy to let go of his little girl, even when she's not so little anymore."

This time it was Jenny who scrunched her eyes tight, holding back tears, as she once again hugged her father, saying, simply, "Thanks, Dad."

* * *

Sheriff Ruskin stood at the accident site, a light drizzle coming down around him. Dark clouds circled above, threatening to grow darker, mirroring his mood as he wondered just where in the blue hell his deputy was. He'd visited all the man's haunts and had come up empty, and so he'd returned to the scene of the crime, as it were, for any clues as to what might have happened to Alan Delacroix.

The deputy's car was long gone, of course, recovered by Sgt. Floyd at the Sheriff's behest and parked behind the station. Technically the man wouldn't be considered missing for 48 hours, but Ruskin had a sick feeling in his chest that he wouldn't be coming back anytime soon. Still, he decided, he wouldn't report Delacroix's disappearance until Tuesday, by which time he hoped to have some answers and avoid looking like a fool in front of the Mayor and the city council.

Surveying the scene, he noticed that while his team had taken the remains of the motorcycle they had managed to avoid dealing with the girl's broken pink Huffy. He didn't need to process it for evidence and so he hadn't implicitly ordered the bike's removal, but assumed that someone would have enough sense to dispose of the thing. Sighing, he felt an old hunger bubbling to the surface, and he knew he had to satisfy it or risk the migraines and shakes that had always come whenever he tried to kick the habit.

Looking around to make sure no one was watching, Ruskin slipped his silver flask of gin from his pocket and took a long, hungry swig, draining the contents in three deep swallows. The rain began coming down in earnest, soaking his clothes and running down his pants and into his boots.

Ignoring the rain and the chill that was slowly creeping into his bones, Ruskin lit a cigarette and walked over to the warped and burned fence. He knelt down and once again swept the ground for a sign of anything unusual. Nothing. No one – not the fire department, the Sheriff's department, nor he – could figure out how anyone could have driven the Kawasaki into the fence, survived the explosion, and walked away without leaving even a trace of evidence. Hell, they couldn't figure out how anyone could walk away from the accident, period, much less survive the explosion and the fire afterward.

And that probably meant that there hadn't actually been a rider, that whoever had stolen the bike had driven it straight at the fence and jumped off at the last second. Maybe the hippie had gypped someone on a dime bag of weed and this was their way of getting revenge. *Yes,* he thought, *it could have happened that way.* It would certainly make his job a whole lot easier if it had. Somehow, though, he couldn't shake the feeling that the McGee girl knew more than she was willing to say, and that the Spencer boy was somehow involved. He would have to pay him a visit later today or tomorrow and see if he could rattle his cage.

Thunder sounded suddenly in the distance, startling Ruskin, causing him to drop his cigarette just as the lightning that followed forked across the summer sky. Cursing, he reached for another but came up empty, the pack of Winstons he had bought just last night already exhausted. Muttering under his breath, he watched in dismay as the wind caught the cigarette, rolling it under the remains of the pink Huffy bicycle.

Kneeling down to retrieve the cigarette, he saw something out of the corner of his eye; a little glass bead, wedged between the frame of the bike and the ground, gleaming against the dim light of the burning Winston. Curious, forgetting the cigarette, he carefully reached for the tiny piece of glass, gently capturing it between his thumb and forefinger.

The little glass ball looked somehow familiar... and then he remembered that Delacroix was Catholic. And, like all good Catholics, he always carried his rosary. The deputy's rosary had been decorated with little glass beads, just like the one that he now held in his hands.

\* \* \*

"Hi Jenny, it's me," Shawn said into the phone, glad that for once that luck was with him and that it was Jenny who answered and not her father. It had taken him a full ten minutes to work up the nerve to pick up the phone, and if her father had answered he was almost certain he would have chickened out and just hung up.

"Hi, you," said Jenny, "I guess you're out of the hospital, huh? I've been wondering when you'd call."

"They finally let me go home just before noon. I would have called sooner, but Mom and Dad insisted on taking me out to lunch. We just got back a little while ago."

"Shawn, has the Sheriff been to talk to you?"

"What do you mean?"

"I mean the Sheriff. You know, the guy that runs the police force and arrests all the baddies," she joked, teasing him.

Embarrassed, he was glad that they were only talking on the phone and that she couldn't see his face. "Yeah, silly," he recovered, joking back, "I know what a Sheriff is. What I meant was, why would he come over here?"

"So you mean he hasn't?" she asked, letting out a sigh. "Well, he showed up on our doorstep about nine this morning, asking me all sorts of questions about last night, and about the motorcycle."

"What did you say?"

"The truth, of course, and nothing but the truth, so help me God," Jenny joked. "Well, okay, maybe not the whole truth. I just told him that I was on my way to see you and some madman ran me off the road and caused me to break my bike and lose my glasses, end of story."

"You're getting good at this lying stuff."

"Nothing fifteen or twenty good 'Hail Mary's' won't cure."

"So, did he believe you?"

"I think so, though he kept asking why it took me so long to hobble to the hospital. But I think he bought it."

"Good."

"I just want to put everything behind us, Shawn. I don't ever want to think about that horrible little creature ever again. But first I need to know something."

"Okay, shoot."

"Shawn, how did you know about my underwear?"

He told her about being able to see into the monster's memories of the night it had slipped into her window, and how he had finally been able to communicate with it through the bond that they had shared. Shawn left out the part about The Voice, about "hearing" someone inside the fetch's head telling it to kill Jenny and then to go after him.

He just didn't want to worry her, he rationalized, though closer to the truth was that he desperately wanted to forget being trapped in the confines of the monster's mind. More than anything, he wanted to forget experiencing the beast's absolute hatred for the two teenagers and its insatiable desire to feast on their bodies. If the creature had been that evil, that twisted, what did that say about whoever had been controlling it?

In the end, they had both agreed to put what happened behind them and to get on with their lives. And it was then that Shawn found his opening:

"Jenny, well, I've been thinking..." he stammered, "Would you like to have dinner with me tomorrow night and then maybe see a movie afterwards?"

"Sure, I'd like that," she responded, immediately adding, "as long as it's not a horror flick! I think I've had enough of that stuff to last me for the rest of my life."

"It's a deal," replied Shawn, suddenly wondering if *Jaws*, the new picture playing at the little Carthage movie house, was considered horror.

* * *

That night, as Shawn lay sleeping, he dreamt:

He was late for class again and couldn't find the room where he was supposed to be. He ran scattershot through the halls of the high school, opening doors, looking through windows, but nothing. Come to think of it, he wasn't even sure which class he was looking for, let alone its room number or how to find it.

"Shawnie has a girlfriend, Shawnie has a girlfriend!" mocked Mike Jackson and Rusty Boyer in unison as they loomed out at him from the boy's bathroom. "Shawn and Jenny sitting in a tree, k-i-s-s-i-n-g! First comes loves, second comes marriage, then comes Shawn and a baby carriage!" The old childhood taunt rang in his ears as he scrambled to get away from the two sneering boys.

"Shawn!" came a voice from just around the turn in the hall. "Shawn, I'm going to kick your ass!" It was Tanner! Shawn smiled as his best friend whipped around the corner, coming straight at him.

"Tanner, I thought you were dead," whispered Shawn, his smile fading as he remembered the funeral. "We buried you, Tanner. I put my two cents worth into your coffin, plus three cents more."

"Shawn, I'm going to punch you in the face for wanting to fuck my sister!"

"But… but," stuttered Shawn, backing up from his friend. "I didn't…I don't…"

"Shawnie has a girlfriend, Shawnie has a girlfriend," another voice taunted behind him. Turning around, he saw Jenny. Footprints of blood trailed behind her. His eyes dropped to her feet, and he gasped as he saw that she had no toes. And then she had no feet at all. She was disappearing. First her calves, then her knees, her thighs, her waist… before long there was nothing left of the girl save her mouth, which continued to chant, "Shawnie has a girlfriend, Shawnie has a girlfriend."

And then he was someplace else entirely. A cool mist swirled lazily about him, soaking through his clothes, chilling him to the bone. Looking down, he realized that he was only wearing his underwear, a red-and-black-checkered pair of Fruit of the Loom boxers, and that the rest of his clothing had melted from his body and disappeared into the ground at his feet.

Shaking the confusion from his thoughts, he closed his eyes tight. Upon opening them, he saw that he was standing in the center of a small pebbled path that wound this way and that through the heart of a dark forest. Huge, ancient oak trees loomed above him, their giant gray leaves blocking even the hint of sunlight from reaching the forest floor. Twisted and spiked branches reached out for him, moving, sweeping, quivering with anticipation, waiting for the moment when he dared step off the path.

Shawn stood absolutely still, though every nerve and every cell in his body urged him to run, run, run, to sprint from the path, tearing wildly through the woods until he reached safety. The path, his instincts screamed, led only to danger. But there he stood, not moving, a gentle breeze swirling about him. It started at his feet, brushed against his cheek, until finally coming in from all directions at once, growing both colder and stronger. It whipped savagely through the trees now, slapping his face, whistling a familiar tune that he just couldn't place.

"Where am I?" he called out, dropping to a crouch. His heart beat fast as he dug his fingers deep into the wet gravel at his feet, doing his best to prevent the wind from dislodging him into the hungry branches of the dancing trees. "What do you want?"

As if in response, he felt something cold and wet take hold of his wrist and begin to creep up his fingers, up his arms. His body grew frigid, cooler even than the wind and the mist swirling around him. The coldness sucked the breath from his lungs, enveloping him, entombing him, as he slowly began to sink into the ground.

And then he was elsewhere again, still in a forest but an altogether different one, one without threatening trees and winding, pebbly paths. And, this time, he knew where he was: he was at the Carthage Lake, about fifty yards into the woods, just past the overflow dam at the far end.

It was nighttime and yet, just as in the other forest, he could see without the aid of a flashlight. Taking a step forward, Shawn headed out of the forest and toward the lake. Each step he took, each foot he moved, seemed to inexplicably take him further and further from the edge of the forest, as if he were walking away rather than toward the rim of the woods.

Without warning, he found himself staring at the brown bark of a tall oak tree, his face only inches from the trunk. Bending down, the shovel from his father's woodshed suddenly in hand, he began to dig. Slowly at first and then with increasing anxiety, he threw mud and leaves up and over his shoulders. Finally, after digging for what seemed like hours, he found something. Reaching down, he grasped the taloned paw of the beast that had killed Tanner and had tried to kill both him and Jenny. He pulled it up from its grave, up through the leaves and mud, and finally to freedom.

"What do you want?" he asked the fetch. It now stood nearly six feet tall and held itself more like a man than the murderous creature that he had run over with his stolen motorcycle. "What are you looking for?"

"Freedom," it said, then added, "and the charm, of course."

"What charm?"

"The one that can set me free," the monster said. Its blood red eyes momentarily flickered to blue, mirroring Shawn's. "And the one that damned me." The beast began to shimmer, wavering in the dark, changing. In a rush of heat that scorched Shawn's eyebrows, the thick, spiky fur melted away from the beast's skin, and crimson claws fell from its hands. A slim teenager with blondish hair and wearing nothing but red-and-black-checkered boxer shorts stood in its place.

"Who… who are you?" whispered Shawn, recognizing himself as though he were looking in a body length mirror at Sears.

"I'm you," it said, shrugging. "The same blood pumps through our veins. For better or worse, I'm you."

# Chapter 17

LAST NIGHT hadn't been kind to Fred Ruskin. Frustrated by his inability to track down his missing deputy, he'd blown off interviewing Shawn Spencer and instead spent most of the night drinking scotch and sodas alone in his little second-story apartment on the edge of Carthage. An early morning phone call pulled Ruskin out of sleep and into the worst hangover he'd ever had in his life, and he had to struggle through the haze that filled his head as he spoke into the old black phone clutched in his right hand.

"Wha?" he mumbled, the taste of liquor and mucous lying heavy on his tongue. "Who is this?"

"Sheriff Ruskin, this is Bonnie at the switchboard," said a perky female voice in his ear, at least 300 decibels too loud for this time of morning, "and I wanted to let you know that we had a 415 – a disturbance report – come in Saturday night, from Mrs. Abignale at 768 Locus."

"So send someone…"

"Well," she interrupted, sounding irritated, "you are the Sheriff. And besides, Mrs. Abignale said it sounded like, and I quote, 'one of them motorcycle things.' That was around ten o'clock Saturday night, right before the accident at the school, and I thought it might have something to do with your case."

Ruskin sat straight up in bed, his hangover all but forgotten. "Could you repeat that?"

"I said, 'it might have something to do with your case.' There aren't that many motorcycles in Carthage, after all, and now I guess there's one less. I'm sorry I didn't let you know earlier. Sharon was manning the phones over the weekend, and you know how she is…"

Actually, he didn't, so he declined to comment on Sharon's competency. "Thanks Bonnie, I owe you one," he said, his large fingers dropping the receiver into its cradle before he'd even finished voicing the last word. Despite a pounding headache, the fifty-two-year-old Sheriff rolled out of bed and got to his feet with a spring in his step, ready to hit the shower and take a trip over to 768 Locust Street. Even after all these years, detective work still managed to energize him. It almost made him feel whole again. And then he realized he was still in his uniform from last night, save for his socks and boots, and that he reeked of scotch and cigarette smoke.

Shrugging to himself, thinking, the large bear of a man decided to skip the shower and went directly in search of his footwear. Looking under the bed, on top of the dining room table, and everywhere else in between, he quickly came up with his boots (they were in the refrigerator) but could find no sign of his socks. Not wanting to take the time to dig through the dryer where all his clothes seemed to stay until he was ready to wear them, Ruskin shivered as he slipped the cold, black police issue boots over his bare feet, then hurriedly made his way out the front door.

* * *

Talking to Mrs. Abignale didn't produce much in the way of leads; if anything, all it did was bring his hangover back to the forefront of his brain, with a vengeance. The white haired old lady was more than a little batty and barely remembered what she had eaten for breakfast much less anything from Saturday night. Still, he dutifully interviewed her, writing down every word that came from her toothless mouth. Frustrated, he thanked the woman and bid her farewell, for the third time in fifteen minutes turning down what was undoubtedly a week-old cup of coffee.

Ruskin stood outside the old woman's house, hoping that he'd learn more from the outside than he had inside. He'd noticed a long skid mark that weaved through the center of the street on his way inside, and now followed it to where it ended – approximately ten yards down the road, about half a mile before the intersection of Locust and Marion. He was pleased to find bits of red paint embedded into the asphalt all along the skid, though surprised that last night's rain hadn't completely washed away the evidence. Maybe luck was with him after all. The paint would more than likely match the paint that had once decorated the Kawasaki. Carefully collecting samples in a little sandwich baggie, he spied a broken wooden handle from the corner of his eye, sticking up from the drainage ditch opposite the old woman's house.

The Sheriff walked to the edge of the road, bent over, and, using a second sandwich bag, retrieved the handle from its resting place in the ditch. It was a plunger. The rubber end was still intact, but the handle had snapped clean in two. The other half was just a few feet away, sticking out of the mud that covered most of the rest of the drainage ditch. Why would the motorcycle thief have been carrying a plunger? Intrigued, knowing that the previous night's rain probably washed away any fingerprints, Ruskin nevertheless carefully picked up both pieces of the plunger and wrapped them with care in a blanket he'd found in the trunk of his car.

The old man who'd reported the accident claimed that there were two teenagers talking beside the swing set shortly after the motorcycle had crashed into the fence. And while normally he wouldn't hold much stock in anything that Jim Warner had to say, the man's statement made Ruskin wonder. Jenny McGee had been on her way to visit Shawn Spencer at Carthage Memorial. Was it possible that her friend had somehow snuck out of the hospital to meet her halfway? Or perhaps her story about the late night hospital visit had been just an excuse to meet up with some other boy, maybe even the person who stole the motorcycle?

His head spinning with theories – God, how he enjoyed working on something challenging for a change, like his old days in Chicago – the Sheriff decided to pay a visit to the hospital and hopefully talk to whoever had been Spencer's nurse on the night in question. If the boy had left the hospital, the nurse would know; and if Jenny McGee had been lying about going to see her sick friend, maybe someone would have picked up on that as well. Relishing the challenge of once again breaking a case, Ruskin crammed himself into his cruiser and headed for the hospital.

"Can you tell me who Shawn Spencer's nurse was Saturday night?" Ruskin asked the desk nurse, an attractive Asian woman in her early twenties. She sported long black hair tied up in a bun beneath her starched-white nursing hat.

"Let me see…" the pretty nurse trailed off, looking through a log book that she pulled from a shelf behind her desk. "Okay, it was Vanessa Wages - one of the night shift nurses. She just works weekends, mostly. She's getting her RN at Carl Sandberg. In fact, she's probably out there right now."

"Can you tell me her home address? It's important that I talk to her right away."

The pretty nurse rattled off a number and a street name, offering to write it down for Ruskin when his search for a pen came up empty.

"Sure, if you don't mind," he smiled, leaning on her desk.

Wang smiled, handing over a scrap of paper with Vanessa Wage's address and phone number.

"One more thing. Can you tell me who the desk nurse was during the time that Spencer was admitted?"

"This time, you're in luck: she was me. Or I am she, or something. Nurse Maya Wang, Sheriff, at your service," she smiled wanly. "I almost always work the night shift, and in fact I'm only here today because one of the other girls called in sick."

"Ms. Wang," he said, surprised at his good fortune, "it's a pleasure. Now do you remember a young girl by the name of Jenny McGee who came into the hospital Saturday night to visit Shawn Spencer?"

"Little red-haired teenager, cute as a button? Sure I do. Her right knee was banged up pretty bad. One of our attending physicians fixed her up, good as new, and then I let her sneak back to see her boyfriend. Please don't tell my supervisor, though!" she said, with a wink.

So Spencer was her boyfriend after all. *Well, there goes one theory,* thought Ruskin, ready to give up on the idea of a secret paramour for the redhead. "Don't worry," he bantered back, "your secret's safe with me."

"Was there anything else you needed, Sheriff?"

"That pretty much covers it, Ms. Wang. Thank you so much for your time, and have a great afternoon."

"Ditto," smiled Wang, as she turned back to a medical chart she'd been working on before he'd interrupted her.

"Actually, come to think of it, there is just one more thing," said the Sheriff, turning on his heels as he remembered the plunger. "Do you mind if I take a look at the room where Spencer spent the night?"

"Hey, Sheriff, knock yourself out," answered the nurse, looking up at him from her charts. "It's room 117, just down the hallway and around the corner. The room's vacant right now, so if the door's closed don't worry about knocking."

"Thanks, Maya," smiled Ruskin, marveling at the fact that foreign imports such as the pretty little Oriental nurse always managed to look so much better than their American counterparts. Sighing wistfully, he turned to walk down the hall and ran straight into Abby McGee.

"What're you doing here?" she questioned him, her hazel eyes betraying a challenge that her low and measured tone did not. The woman was dressed in a white nurse's uniform and carried a tray of syringes; he'd forgotten that she worked at the hospital and was the head nurse in the little collection of medical professionals that passed as an emergency room.

"Just following up some leads," he answered, doing his best to walk around her. Failing as she moved to match his steps, he ground to a halt, standing face-to-face with the mother of the girl that he was sure knew more than she was telling about the stolen motorcycle.

"Fred," she sighed, her face softening, "I know you're just doing your job. But my daughter's already told you everything she knows. She had nothing to do with what happened Saturday night other than being at the wrong place at the wrong time."

"I'm sure that'll turn out to be the case, Abby," he smiled, matching her tone of familiarity, "but I'll have to come to that conclusion myself. Now, if you'll excuse me..."

"Please... Jenny didn't do anything wrong, and I don't think Paul can take this right now."

"Abby, there was a crime committed, and I..."

"The only crime is that you've managed to keep your job for so long," she snapped, her demeanor shifting to that of a mother lioness protecting her cub. "I'm sorry, that was unkind. But haven't you already done enough to my husband's family? Please, just leave us alone and let us mourn." And with that she turned, brown hair flouncing around her shoulders, and disappeared into the recesses of Carthage Memorial.

Stung by her words, growing queasy, it was all that Ruskin could do not to make a run for his car and the little silver flask that he kept so carefully concealed within. Fighting down the urge to bolt, he instinctively fingered the pair of wedding rings that hung from his neck, drawing strength from a commitment made a lifetime ago. Breathing deeply,

Ruskin forced his legs to move beneath him as he ambled down the stark white hall toward room 117.

After leaving the hospital, it took him less than five minutes to drive across town to the address Wang had given him, and then another five to travel to the Carl Sandburg College campus when he discovered that the girl wasn't home.

Both Carl Sandburg College and the larger Robert Morris campus were both situated on the same lot off Highway 94, toward the east end of town. Despite being mere branches of the main schools in Galesburg and Chicago, they were probably the best selling points for the little city and the only reason that Carthage, aside from being the Hancock County seat and housing the Old Carthage Jail, remained as populated as it did. Parking in front of the little admissions building for the nursing school, Ruskin stood beside his car and tamped out the Winston he'd been smoking against his car's fender. He tucked the remaining half of the cigarette behind his ear for safe keeping. Taking a quick swig from his flask, coughing as it went down, he straightened himself and made his way inside. Pushing past a man in a light-colored trench coat, he immediately made a beeline for the first clerk he saw: a short, brown haired woman with her back to him, creating inky-smelling copies at a mimeograph machine.

"Excuse me, ma'am," he said, "can you help me? I need to get a class schedule for one of your students."

The matronly clerk spun around, clearly startled, sending her papers scattering to the floor. "Oh dear," said the woman, whose name tag proclaimed the words 'Hi, I'm Betty,' as she stooped to retrieve the documents. "Now I've gotten them all out of order."

"I'm sorry, ma'am," he apologized, leaning over to help gather up the mess, "I won't take up much of your time. I just need to find out Vanessa Wage's class schedule."

"Well, that shouldn't be a problem," said an ebullient voice from behind him, "I'm Vanessa Wages. I work in the office between classes, when I'm not working at the hospital."

"You're a very busy girl," joked Ruskin. Turning around, he let his eyes travel up the length of the woman's legs. In a contrast of styles, an old pair of white tennis shoes adorned her feet while black stockings covered a pair of legs that just wouldn't quit. Completing the ensemble, Wages sported a short brown skirt and a tight fitting red sweater that enhanced the contours beneath and left very little to the imagination. As his fictional hero Sam Spade might say, she was one hundred and twenty pounds of blonde hair, curves, and a radioactive smile that could melt icebergs. Aware that he'd been staring and feeling very much the dirty old man, Ruskin quickly lifted his gaze to find the blonde staring back at him, a knowing look dancing in her eyes.

"Sorry, ma'am," he continued, a red blush spreading across his jowly face, "I'm Sheriff Ruskin, and I just need to ask you a few quick questions about Shawn Spencer."

"Shawn Spencer?" asked the pretty blonde, kneeling to help 'Hi, I'm Betty' pick up and re-order the mimeograph sheets. "Oh, the kid from 117, right?"

"That's the one."

"What do you need to know?" she asked, rising to her feet. "He was only there overnight and he wasn't much trouble, and I tend not to remember much about the wheels that aren't squeaky, if you catch my drift."

"Well, for starters, was he there all night? Did he ever leave his room?"

"Oh, he was definitely there, all right. Aside from moaning about hospital food, though, he hardly made a peep."

"Are you sure?" he asked, feeling another theory about to be blown out of the water. "You're sure he was there the whole time?"

"Well, other than once when I went in to check on him and he was in the bathroom, sure."

"Are you positive that's where he was?"

"Well, I didn't open the door to check, if that's what you mean," said Wages, brushing back an errant layer of golden locks from her eyes, "but the door was closed, so I'm pretty sure he was in there. Besides, where else could he have been?"

Thinking back to his visit to the hospital and the plunger he'd found missing from the boy's room, he had a hunch that if Spencer had taken a leak last night that it hadn't been in the hospital.

"That's a good question," he finally said, the hint of a smile crossing his lips.

Thanking Wages for her time, Ruskin excused himself and quickly headed back to his car, not even taking the time for a lingering glimpse over his shoulder at the bewildered blonde nurse with the killer legs and body to match.

# Chapter 18

SHAWN AWOKE with a start, his brain jumbled with thoughts and images as the dream gradually faded from his memory. Something wasn't right in the room. Had the monster survived after all? And then it hit him; the room seemed wrong not because someone had entered but because Samson had never made his way to the foot of Shawn's bed, where the old tom had slept almost every night for the last seven years. The cat was still missing, and Shawn no longer believed that he was simply napping in one of his favorite hidey-holes.

Rising from bed, stifling a huge yawn, he realized with a start that it had actually been a full two days since he'd last seen Samson. With all that happened Saturday night, it seemed almost a lifetime ago. He felt guilty for not noticing the cat's absence until now.

Pulling on his jeans and an old blue t-shirt, he decided to take an early morning walk through the neighborhood in case the cat had somehow gotten out and was lost. Opening the bedroom door, Shawn ran straight into his father.

"Hey Dad, have you seen Samson?"

Half-asleep and still in his pajamas, Henry Spencer blinked, rubbing the sleep from his eyes before finally answering, "I'm not sure, Shawn. Come to think of it, I don't think I've seen him for a day or two. I guess with you in the hospital and all I wasn't really paying attention. Did you check his bowl to see if he'd eaten his food?"

He hadn't, but thought it was a good idea.

"I've got to be at work early today for a meeting or else I'd help you look for him. If he hasn't shown up by the time I get home tonight we'll make up some signs and post them around the neighborhood. He couldn't have gotten too far."

"Thanks Dad," he called over his shoulder as he raced to the kitchen to see whether the cat had been eating his Friskies; tellingly, the bowl was still full, as was the water dish that sat beside it.

Shawn walked up and down his street and through the surrounding neighborhood, but saw no sign of the cat. The streets were still wet after last night's storm, and he hoped that Samson hadn't sought shelter somewhere and accidentally gotten locked in someone's garage.

Somewhere in the distance a robin cawed, and he imagined Samson stalking the little bird, taking his time until finally, dramatically, he leapt in for the kill, ending the prey's life with one quick snap of his sharp feline teeth. Of course, despite trying on a least three separate occasions, the old tom had never even been able to land a mouse, much less something with wings. Samson was just too much of a gentleman, his mother liked to say, to go in for all that messy hunting stuff. Plus, his father had always added, he had all the Friskies and Meow Mix he could ever eat, so why bother?

"Samson!" the boy called over and over, disappointed each time when the orange and white house cat failed to appear. Defeated, Shawn decided to head back to the house for a late breakfast of Freakies cereal and milk.

Crossing the street, trying not to think about Samson, he jumped as the 'whoop whoop' noise of a siren blared behind him. Turning around, heart in his throat, he stared as a Hancock County Sheriff car slowly pulled up alongside him, a large, overweight man at the wheel. The sirens mercifully stopped, and Sheriff Ruskin pushed himself out of the car.

"Mr. Spencer," he smiled, leaning on the hood. "I've been looking everywhere for you."

Shawn's heart sank. Ruskin knew. "Why?" he blurted out, doing his best not to sprint from the scene. "What did I do?"

"Guilty conscience?" the Sheriff asked, his bloodshot eyes boring through Shawn. "Settle down, son. I just want to ask you a few questions, about the night you were in the hospital."

He was toying with him, like Samson with one of his toy mice. Shawn resigned himself to the worst. "Okay, what do you want to know?"

# Chapter 19

JENNY MCGEE sat alone at the park, perched on top of the very same bench where her brother and Shawn had sat just a little over a week ago. Because her parents couldn't afford to replace her bicycle she'd started riding Tanner's, which somehow made her feel ashamed. She didn't like the feeling. It wasn't because she no longer had her own bike, but because the bicycle belonged to her brother. It just didn't feel right.

Shaking her head, glancing first at the old Huffy and then back to the park, she watched with envy as a group of second graders ran and skipped with gleeful abandon, taking turns going down the big slide in the middle of the grounds. Jenny had grown up a lot in the last week, and she missed the days of carefree indifference personified by the idyllic scene of the giggling children playing out before her.

She had said her prayers every night for as long as she could remember, but since Tanner's death praying had been difficult at best. She believed in God, Jesus, and of course the blessed Mother Mary, and she still had faith, but it was harder. If God existed, why would He allow the creature that murdered Tanner to exist? Surely it wasn't one of God's creatures. But God saw everything, didn't He? How could He let something like that – something that had no right to exist in nature – destroy her brother? How could God take away the one person she always knew she could count on?

Like most siblings, Tanner and Jenny hadn't always gotten along. But she'd always known that, when it counted, he'd be there for her. Like the time when she was nine and was being bullied by a boy two grades ahead of her. Tanner, himself a grade behind her tormentor, had witnessed his little sister's attack one day during recess. He tackled the bully, knocking him to the ground and punching him into near unconsciousness. He'd been sent home from school and punished by their parents, but had refused to apologize to the bully, saying that no one was allowed to pick on his little sister but him.

God, how she missed him. It was so hard to accept that he was truly gone. It had been less than a week since his murder, but so much had happened since then that it felt so much longer. It was almost like she'd lived two lives during this last week, the first one ending with Tanner's death and the second one starting when Shawn killed the monster. The middle was a blur filled with mourning, anguish, and fear - something she didn't think she could ever go through again. The security and safety she'd felt as a child seemed a million miles and another lifetime away.

Hopping to the ground, waving to the kids on the slide, she made her way to the swing set across from the merry-go-round on the other side of the playground. Lowering herself onto the canvas seat, she almost felt like a little girl again. Maybe she could be a grown up and still keep a little of that carefree indifference after all. Thinking of Shawn and the promise that their date tonight held, she kicked high into the air, leaned back, and let her momentum take her, enjoying the warm summer breeze blowing through her hair and against her face.

\* \* \*

Less than two miles away, deep in the forest behind the lake, the fetch stirred. It thought of Jenny and of all the things it would do to her. Pushing up through the grass and leaves that had surrounded it for the last two days, the monster stretched its arms and yawned as if coming out of a deep slumber.

It was Big now, having mostly digested the meat it had eaten two nights ago, and it looked more like a huge gorilla than the rabid little raccoon it had resembled when it had snuck into the girl's bedroom.

The fetch had fed and healed, and was finally ready to hunt again. And, this time, it would feed at its leisure, enjoying the sweet marrow of the girl's bones before grinding them to bloody little bits of skin and hair in its gullet.

# Chapter 20

IT WAS JUST after six when Shawn showed up at Jenny's house, dressed in his best pair of blue jeans and sporting a yellow short-sleeved button-up shirt. They were just going to the Tastee Freez and then to the little movie theatre to see *Jaws*, but his mother insisted on him at least "dressing like a gentleman" and swore that she wouldn't let him out of the house in his usual outfit of cutoffs and a t-shirt.

His father had slipped him a crisp new twenty-dollar bill, telling him to take the girl out in style. He'd tried to tell him that he already had ten dollars in his wallet and that would easily be enough for dinner and the movie, but his Dad said he wouldn't take no for an answer and that after last week they both deserved to enjoy themselves. With thirty dollars burning a hole in his pocket, Shawn was starting to second-guess his decision to take Jenny to the Tastee Freez. He felt like a cheapskate.

Standing at Jenny's door, feeling nervous and sweaty from the walk over, he finally worked up the courage to knock just as the door opened. Mr. McGee stood at the door, dressed in his security officer outfit. A small black pistol and a nightstick hung sat on the entry table. He must have just gotten off work.

"Come on in, Shawn," he said, a weary smile crossing his lips when he followed Shawn's eyes to the gun. "Don't worry, I'm not going to use that – at least as long as you get Jenny home before eleven."

"You don't have to worry about that, sir," Shawn said, suddenly feeling very small, "I'll have her home by eleven for sure."

"Listen Shawn," he leaned into the teenager, putting his hand on his shoulder, "I'm sorry about the other morning. I just..." his words faltered. "Just watch out for Jenny, alright? She's all we have left now."

"For heaven's sake, Paul, invite the boy in," said a voice from inside the house. It was Jenny's mother, still dressed in her nurse whites from the hospital.

"Come on in, Shawn," she said, pushing past her husband to take the boy's arm, "and have a seat with us on the couch. Jenny will be ready in just a minute."

*Famous last words,* thought Shawn, stuck between Mr. and Mrs. McGee on the old worn brown couch that occupied the center of the living room. The little television in the corner was tuned to the local news, which, thankfully, Jenny's father seemed intent on watching. That left only Mrs. McGee to grill Shawn about the evening's planned activities, which she did admirably.

"Will you look at that?" interrupted Mr. McGee, gesturing at the television. "First that teacher goes missing in Hamilton, and now one of our local deputies. What's the world coming to?"

Shawn's attention was instantly drawn to the old Sylvania. They were watching channel 7, the CBS affiliate out of Quincy, and rarely did the broadcast mention anything that happened in Carthage.

"...Ruskin refused to comment on the late Saturday night disappearance of Deputy Alan Delacroix, insisting that the missing police officer and the disappearance of teacher Lisa Barnes of Hamilton, missing since last Tuesday, are not related. Ruskin did promise to keep reporters updated on both cases as progress was made..."

The camera cut to a shot of the Sheriff looking harried and agitated. He moved quickly away from the camera before ducking into his black-and-white police car and driving away. The scene rapidly shifted to a soft shot of the station's weather girl, a big-bosomed blonde wearing a clingy black dress, gesturing with a pointer at a screen filled with a miniature representation of a lightning storm behind her. "And now for the weather," intoned the same voice that had reported on the Sheriff seconds earlier, "presented to you by Quincy's favorite meteorologist, Melissa Rhoads."

"I've had to patch up Eloise Delacroix more than a few times after one of her husband's drunken rampages," Mrs. McGee said under her breath. "It wouldn't bother me if they never found him." She looked at Shawn, her hand flying to her mouth.

But he wasn't paying attention, a sick feeling settling into the pit of his stomach as he stared at the television. What if, against all odds, the fetch hadn't died after all? The woman in Hamilton had apparently vanished last Tuesday, but, according to the television, the deputy had gone missing Saturday night. What if the little monster survived the fire? Or, worse yet, what if there was more than one fetch?

"Remember those murders in Keokuk, about fifteen years ago?" Mr. McGee asked his wife, turning from the television. "That was right after we were first married, I think."

"I remember," nodded Mrs. McGee, with a shudder. She took her husband's hand, ignoring Shawn. "Those two waitresses. Christine something and Rose Bailey, I think. They never did catch that man. Do you think this might be related somehow?"

Shawn stopped listening the moment that Jenny stepped into the room, all thoughts of the fetch banished to the back of his mind. She was dressed in a yellow peasant blouse, Levis, and a pink pair of Keds. The sight of her took his breath away. She was the prettiest girl he had ever seen, including all the nurses at the hospital, the TWA stewardess on his flight home from Texas, and, yes, even Quincy's favorite meteorologist, Melissa Rhoads. Two delicate silver earrings partially hidden behind the redhead's long hair completed the ensemble, adding a subtle contrast that made her emerald eyes sparkle with fire. Looking down at his own clothing, Shawn knew in an instant that he had woefully underdressed.

"Hi, Shawn," she said from across the room. "Well, I'm ready if you are."

It took them less than ten minutes to bike from Jenny's house to the Tastee Freeze. It was Monday night and so they avoided the usual weekend crowd, but there were still a fair amount of customers at the ice cream stand. Shawn and Jenny parked their bikes in the rusting metal rack at the side of the building, then walked up to the sliding glass window to place their order.

"Can I help you?" asked a willowy brunette, a bubblegum-popping cheerleader they both recognized from high school.

"One cheeseburger, ketchup only, an order of onion rings, and a vanilla malt," said Shawn, conscious of at least six or seven of the kids he went to school with sitting at the tables around them, "and whatever she wants."

"I'll take a cheeseburger with everything but onions, an order of ta-ter tots, and a Frostie root beer, please," added Jenny, watching Shawn watch everyone else. "Come on," she said to her date, "let's sit down until our food comes up."

"Is this weird for you?" He asked her, as they settled on a little wooden picnic table covered in green peeling paint. It was one of a group of twelve mismatched tables, positioned haphazardly around the restaurant, added to over time as business increased.

"What do you mean?"

"Hey Shawnie!" cawed a familiar voice from behind their table. Feeling his shoulders tense at the interruption, Shawn turned around to see Mike Jackson, his tormentor from the pool, waving and smiling. As usual, Rusty Boyer sat beside the boy, sharing a table just a few feet from where they sat.

"Hey, Mike," added Boyer, grinning from ear to ear, "looks like Shawnie's got a girlfriend."

Shawn gritted his teeth, saying nothing. The two had bullied him since fourth grade and the only break he ever got from them was when Tanner happened to be around to scare them off. And now that Tanner was gone, he could just imagine the hell he'd go through when school started up again in September.

Misreading his silence, looking across the table trying to catch his eye, Jenny asked softly, "Shawn, are you embarrassed to be with me?" Shaking her head, she half-rose from the table as if to leave.

"No!" Shawn said, reaching out to take her hand. "No, please don't do that. I know I shouldn't let them get to me. It's just that... well, I'm just sick of them. That's all."

"Aww, Rusty, would you look at that?" taunted Jackson, rising from the table he shared with his partner in crime. "They're holding hands. Boy, Shawnie, you just couldn't wait, could you? Your best friend's been in the ground less than a week, and already you're going out with his sister."

"Bet he's doing more than going out with her," responded Boyer, with a dramatic wink aimed at Jackson but more for the benefit of the crowd surrounding them. "I bet they screwed right on her brother's grave, before the dirt was even settled."

Hearing the bullies' words, something broke in Shawn. Almost beyond his control, he felt himself stand up from the table and launch himself at Jackson, quickly punching the boy hard in the face, once, twice, sending him sprawling backward into his table. Fries and onion rings and soft drinks flew everywhere, mixing with the blood that was now flowing freely from the boy's broken nose.

"You can say what you want about me," shouted Shawn, towering over the bully, "but don't you *ever* talk about Tanner. He was worth more than the two of you put together, and so is his sister. And leave her alone, too. If you ever so much as look at her again, I swear to God I'll break more than your nose.

"And you!" he shouted down at Boyer, who looked as though he were about to cry. "The same goes for you. Leave us alone."

"Shawn," Jenny stood from the table, moving to lay a hand on the boy's shoulder. Her face was ashen. "Let it go, please. They're not worth it."

Ignoring her, shrugging her hand from his shoulder, Shawn's features contorted in a barely-controlled rage as he moved toward Boyer. " I know you're Jackson's lapdog and pretty much just do whatever he says, but if you so much as look in my girlfriend's direction…"

"Okay, okay!" whined Boyer, as a warm yellow puddle of urine pooled down around his shoes. "Okay, please just don't hit me, okay?"

"Hey, break it up!" yelled Mr. Patterson, the owner of the Tastee Freeze franchise, running out of the little building toward Shawn and the bleeding boy who lay sprawled across the table before him. "I don't know what this is about, but it better stop right now or I'll have to call the Sheriff."

With those words, Jenny, who had watched the impromptu fight with numbing shock, laid another tentative hand on Shawn's shoulder. This time, he didn't shrug it off. Taking his hand in hers, fingers intertwined, she pressed close to him, whispering, "Girlfriend?"

The disturbance ended almost as quickly as it had begun. Mr. Patterson managed to staunch Jackson's bleeding nose with a generous supply of napkins, and afterward Boyer helped him home. The owner of the Tastee Freeze had glared at Shawn and Jenny and threatened to ban them from the premises but, never one to turn down paying customers, had finally relented and served them their supper after extracting a promise that it would never, ever happen again, at least not at his restaurant.

Once Boyer and Jackson were out of earshot, several of Shawn's classmates came up to him and slapped him on the back or shook his hand. A few walked away in support of the bullies, but the majority of the crowd seemed happy to see Boyer and Jackson taken down a notch. Mr. Patterson, sensing that with happy customers came more sales, ended up giving Shawn and Jenny a pair of chocolate-dipped ice cream cones on the house.

And so it was that Jenny and Shawn found themselves standing in the bank parking lot where both their fathers worked, beneath the moon and the stars and across from the movie theatre, forty-five minutes early for the feature. Cicadas and tree frogs chirped and hummed incessantly in the grass and trees, creating a perfect symphony of nature to serve as a backdrop for their conversation.

"Jenny," Shawn whispered, not having spoken more than a handful of words since the incident at the Tastee Freeze, "I'm sorry for what happened back there. I'm not usually like that. I'm *never* like that. That is, of course, unless I'm busy running over monsters with stolen motorcycles." He smiled, hoping to break the tension between them.

"Girlfriend?" she repeated the question she'd asked him at the restaurant.

"Well, I'm sorry about that. I know we're not… Well, I'd like to… I mean, if you'd like to…"

"Yeah," she smiled, looking up at him. Her deep green eyes twinkled under the starlight. "I think I would." And then she kissed him. Just like that, her lips brushing softly against his, lingering for a moment, a promise of hope for the future.

"Wow," he said, after their lips parted. Her taste still haunted his mouth, and the smell of her perfume lingered in his nostrils. "I guess I'll have to get in fights more often."

Smiling, she punched him hard in the arm. "If you go to jail, you know, you'll never get to kiss me again."

"On second thought, maybe fighting isn't such a good career plan after all," he returned her smile. Taking her hand in his, they walked across the street to see the movie.

"So what did you think?" asked Shawn, after the film was over. The movie had let out at about half past nine and they still had an hour and a half before Jenny had to be home. Shawn enjoyed the movie immensely, though not half as much as he'd enjoyed seeing it with Jenny. The two had shared a giant tub of popcorn with extra butter and had each downed a package of Twizzlers and a large Pepsi, so maybe the feeling of euphoria was just a sugar high, but somehow he didn't think so.

"Scary," said Jenny, taking his hand as they walked down Wabash Street toward their bikes.

All around them people poured out of the theatre, talking to each other about how much they enjoyed the movie. Shawn thought he recognized a tall, blonde man in a trench coat walking against the crowd, heading into the theater for the second showing, but shrugged it off as the man silently passed into the building.

"Which part, the movie itself or seeing it with me?" Shawn teased, moving aside to avoid running into two twelfth-graders he recognized from school.

"Well, maybe a little of both," she laughed, squeezing his fingers. "After seeing that shark, I don't think I'll ever be able to bathe in peace again. And just forget about any more swimming lessons! Boy, if Tanner could see us now."

"But do you think he'd be okay with it? You know, with us going out?"

"I think so. But even if he wasn't at first, he would be eventually."

"How do you know?" Shawn asked, as they reached their bikes.

"Because he was my brother and your best friend, that's how. He loved you, you know, like the brother he never had. He loved us both. How could he *not* have been okay with it, at least once he thought it through?"

Shawn hoped that she was right. "So," he said, changing the subject, "Sheriff Ruskin caught up with me this morning."

"What did he say?"

"Asked me a bunch of questions about the hospital and stuff. I was a little nervous at first, but I just stuck to the story and he seemed to lose interest."

"Thank goodness for small favors," Jenny sighed.

"We have an hour and a half to kill," Shawn said, glancing at his watch, "assuming you don't want to go home until eleven. What do you want to do?"

"Well, how about the park?"

\* \* \*

The park always looked different at night to Jenny. Gone were the little children giggling and whirling around the merry-go-round and tee-ter-totters, replaced by older kids smoking or drinking or, occasionally, just hanging out. Officially, the Jaycee Park was open from eight in the morning until eight at night. Unofficially, however, it was open whenever anyone happened to be there. But the park was mercifully deserted tonight, almost as if the Jaycee's had reserved the plot of land exclusively for their date.

So much had happened in the last week. Losing her brother, almost losing Shawn to another drowning, nearly getting killed by the little monster... and yet, despite all of those terrible things, inexplicably she felt happy. She missed her brother with a terrible ache that might never go away, but right now, at this very moment, she was happy to be alive. Happy to be with the boy she'd had a crush on for as long as she could remember.

It was nearly ten now and the staggered street lamps combined with the light from the full moon and stars above served to fill the park with an eerie cerulean blue glow, at turns both intriguing and more than a little discomfiting. Parks, like most other public areas in any given city, even in a city the size of Carthage, were designed almost exclusively for daytime use. So much so, in fact, that Jenny often secretly wondered if they put in the lights and planted the trees at just the right angles to spook anyone from using it outside the range of the intended hours.

Still, there was something nice about being in the park at night. For Jenny, what tipped the scales toward the positive was the feeling of isolation. It was as if the act of being someplace where you weren't exactly supposed to be walled you off from the rest of the world, protecting you, keeping you safe.

"The last day that Tanner and I spent together started in this park," Shawn said, as he pushed Jenny in one of the swings.

Leaning back with each push in an attempt to go higher and higher, Jenny finally asked, "What did you do that day?"

"You remember the old house on Randolph, the one that was supposedly owned by my great-great grand uncle?"

"Of course I do. Tanner talked about that place all the time. I swear he thought someone had stashed gold in there or something."

A strange look passed over Shawn's face. "Maybe he was right."

"What do you mean?" she asked, touching her heels to the ground. Stopping her momentum, she turned to look at Shawn.

"It was that day that we finally decided to break into the house."

\* \* \*

"So did you ever find anything other than books?" Jenny asked, enjoying the tale of Shawn and her brother's exploits. "I saw the Abraham Lincoln book that Tanner took, but didn't know where it came from. For all Tanner talked about that place over the years, I'm not sure what I expected."

"If you quit interrupting, you'll find out," grinned Shawn, amused by Jenny's impatience. "Good things come to those who wait."

"Yeah, yeah," she returned his easy smile, playfully punching him in the arm. "I'll be a good girl from now on. Continue, please."

\* \* \*

Shawn and Tanner had just started searching the second floor of the huge three-story manor when they found the dumbwaiter. The big wooden panel enclosing the contraption proved more difficult to open than its counterpart downstairs but, with both teenagers tugging on the little wooden handle, they finally managed to pull it ajar.

Shawn immediately saw why the pulley on the first floor had failed to retrieve the cart. The desiccated remains of a brown rat lay wedged between the ropes that ran the gadget up and down the shaft, gumming up the works. No matter which line was pulled, the skeletal remains prevented the rope from moving through the little hole in the bottom.

"Disgusting," commented Tanner, poking at the rodent's remains with his crowbar. That was all it took to shatter the bones into dust, sending the chipped little fragments and the leftover bits of fur and teeth falling through the shaft and into the depths below.

"Well, at least it works now," said Shawn, slowly pulling the ropes. The dumbwaiter descended with a raspy creak, then rose again as the boy changed the direction in which he maneuvered the ropes.

Bored with the dumbwaiter, Tanner followed the musty hallway south, disappearing into a room off to the right. From Shawn's vantage point, the room looked to be filled wall-to-wall with books. Not wanting to miss out on any discoveries his friend might make, Shawn padded down the hard-wood floor after him.

The walls of the library were covered in big maple bookshelves that ran from floor to ceiling, sporting volumes on plumbing, weaponry, martial arts, religion, ancient civilizations, and dozens of other topics. A huge wooden ladder lay against one bookshelf, attached at the floor and the ceiling via rollers. The room also housed three leather wing-back chairs, another huge mildewed couch with clawed wooden feet, and even a radio that looked as though it might actually work were electricity still flowing through the grand old house. Everything was bathed in dust, and more than a few spiders, flies, cockroaches, and other assorted crawling creatures had decided to homestead the property. The entire second floor of the house was a virtual metropolis of bugs.

"Hey, do you see that?" Tanner asked, pointing his flashlight toward the ceiling.

Craning his neck, Shawn caught the gleam of something metallic near the top of the bookshelf, resting in front of a huge set of moldy encyclopedias.

"I'm going up," said Tanner, handing his flashlight to Shawn. He began to scale the big wooden ladder. No sooner had he reached the second rung did the ladder begin to creak, coming lose from its connection to the ceiling. The ladder swayed dangerously as though it might splinter and fall apart at any moment.

"Get down!" Shawn warned, yanking his friend backward by the pants.

Tanner landed with a thump on the library floor.

"What's the big idea?" Tanner yelped, just before the ladder toppled to the ground. Landing with full force on the nearest of the three wingback chairs, the ladder cleaved the chair in two with a thunderous, splintering crack.

Surrounded by dust and debris, Tanner sat on the ground, turning his head between the destruction behind him and the bookshelf. "Well, shit," he said, rising to his feet, "now how are we going to see what's up there?"

"Here," offered Shawn, handing both flashlights to the other boy. Retrieving his favorite green yo-yo from his pocket, he threw the toy at an arc in the direction of the metal object, hitting the books just behind it. The toy bounced off the books to bump a little silver box that fell into his waiting hands below. The yo-yo spun on the shelf, turning in lazy little circles, finally stopping less than a half an inch from the edge of the shelf.

"I'm sorry, Shawn," apologized the sixteen year old, taking the box from his friend's hand. Handing one of the flashlights back to Shawn, he pointed the other at the box, revealing intricate little patterns inlaid into the silver. Opening the box, he was happy to see that it wasn't empty. "Hey, I'm really sorry about the Yo-yo, but there's an old silver necklace in here with a star on the end. How about you keep it and I'll keep the box. Deal?"

"I guess so," answered Shawn, taking the proffered jewelry. He looked longingly up toward his lost yo-yo, the green edge just visible from below.

"Let's go check out the rest of the floor," said Tanner, moving toward the door.

"Hey, what time is it?"

Tanner glanced at his old Timex. "Shit, it's nearly five. How about we split up? We can cover more ground that way."

"Works for me," said Shawn, with a bravado he didn't feel. He was still nervous about being in the old house, but didn't want Tanner to rag on him. "I'll check out the studio."

"Hey, Shawn, come here!" yelled Tanner, from the opposite end of the hallway. Shawn had been searching a work studio and was amazed to find a plethora of old toys expertly carved from wood, including a big rocking horse painted with red and white stripes, a little truck that actually rolled, and a life-sized, bugged-eyed brown toy monkey that didn't look at all appropriate for a child. In fact, Shawn found it a little frightening. The monkey's eyes seemed to follow you around the room, no matter where it was or where you were. Everything, of course, was covered with the now-customary thick blanket of dust, including the empty canvas that hung from a large painter's easel that stood next to a window against the room's north wall. The floor was covered by a huge drop cloth that had once sheltered the wooden floor beneath from the mysterious artist's paint and wood chips but now just added to the disarray of the room.

Paintings in various states of completion adorned all four walls, including a water-color of a monstrously large gothic cathedral, the beginning of a study on a clearing in the woods, an almost-finished portrait of the very house in which they now stood, and a sketch of a man dressed in Renaissance clothing, his face caught in a silent scream, as strings stretched from his hands and feet to somewhere past the border created by the edge of the canvas. That last one made Shawn shudder. The hands that had painted the scene were obviously skilled, but there seemed to be such rage and fury emanating from the oils that the boy was hard-pressed to look at it for more than a few seconds without turning his head away in shame.

Beneath the east window stood a dusty old wooden bench which, upon further inspection, opened up to reveal a storage space beneath its seat. Ignoring his friend, Shawn searched through the cubby hole, finding various wood working tools and an old Shrade pocketknife.

"Come on, Shawn!" bellowed Tanner, sounding irritated now. "I'm in the master bedroom, and wait till you see what I found!"

"All right!" Shawn finally answered, dropping the little wooden truck he'd been holding to snatch the pocketknife from the bench. "Hold your britches, I'll be right there!"

Shawn walked down the hall and past the big marble staircase before reaching the master bedroom. Stepping through the threshold, the boy found Tanner kneeling beside a sturdy oak nightstand just to the right of a huge, rotting bed, his flashlight in one hand and a glass object of some sort in the other.

"Okay, already, what did you find?" Shawn asked.

"This," said the boy proudly, holding aloft an old mason jar filled with pennies.

"Cool," Shawn said, rolling his eyes. "Yippee, we're rich. Let's retire now, and we'll even hire Jenny her own personal swimming coach."

"Hey dweeb," Tanner grinned, tossing the jar of change at Shawn, "catch!"

Shawn grunted as he turned to leap over a mildewed leather ottoman at the foot of the giant old bed, just managing to catch the jar of pennies as he slammed into a huge chest of drawers. The boy crumpled to the ground, not moving.

"Oh fuck!" breathed Tanner, running around the side of the bed to his best friend. "Shawn, are you okay? I'm sorry, I didn't mean…"

Shawn's eyes opened and he grinned. "Gotcha, geek!" he said, shifting the jar of pennies from one hand to the other, "Now give me a hand, will you?"

Tanner politely applauded, trying to hide a smirk as he turned his back on Shawn to retrieve his flashlight.

"Hardy-har-har," said Shawn at the age-old joke, climbing quickly to his feet. "Sorry buddy, I just couldn't resist. Hey, what time is it? I'm supposed to be home before six."

"Just a little after five now," answered Tanner, looking down at his watch. "Let's finish looking through this floor and then come back tomorrow or something and check out the third floor."

They quickly searched the rest of the master bedroom, not finding anything worth salvaging. All of the drawers and cabinets held only mildewed clothing, most of it in a disarray as if someone had quickly went through the shirts and pants and took only what they absolutely needed.

The master bathroom looked lived in, just not for a very, very long time. An old, crusty tube of toothpaste and a rotting red toothbrush sat upon the marble counter, while a thread-bare towel lay draped over the side of the claw-footed bathtub. The medicine cabinet was completely empty save for an old, unused bottle of Bayer Aspirin and a rusted straight razor.

The balcony that led out from the master bedroom seemed to hold more promise, but ultimately proved to be empty save for a little planter that hung from a peg beside the balcony doors. Whatever plant once lived in the basket had long since rotted, leaving a thick slime only vaguely resembling dirt in its place. The best thing about the balcony was the view, which unfortunately was obscured by the huge oak that was the focal point of the yard below. The untrimmed branches came dangerously close to encroaching upon the marble railing that enclosed the little stone terrace from the open air beyond.

The rest of the floor held little to pique their interest, the other bedroom being completely devoid of anything of consequence save the now-obligatory cobwebs and dead bugs. As soon as they were finished, the pair agreed to head down the winding marble stairs and split up the booty.


"Well, hell," complained Tanner, as he tried in vain to twist the rusted lid from the old Mason jar. The two sat just outside the huge house, hidden by the tall grass and the old weathered garage. "I just can't get this thing open."

"Can I see your crowbar?" asked Shawn.

"Sure," he answered, dropping the jar to the ground as he sifted through his backpack to retrieve the metal rod. "What are you going to do?"

"This," said Shawn, grabbing the crowbar and swinging it down hard on top of the rusted metal lid. The old Mason jar exploded with a splintering crack, spraying pennies at both boys' feet.

"Shit, Shawn, I could've done that!" Tanner laughed, kneeling down to gather up the pennies. Perched on top of the flood of copper, in the middle of the pile, was a lone buffalo nickel. It caught the sunlight with a brilliant gleam.

"Mine!" Tanner called, snatching the nickel from the pile before Shawn could react.

"Hey, no fair!" complained Shawn, frowning down at the brown pile of pennies. "I opened the jar, I should get it!"

"But I found the jar," Tanner countered, looking intently at his prize. "Hey, it's from 1931. I bet it's worth a lot of money."

"At least five cents," Shawn retorted, bending down to pick up a handful of pennies. "My dad collects coins, so we can ask him. Hey, these are all wheat pennies. I bet they're worth more than the nickel. Dad has a lot of wheat pennies."

"You're just trying to get me to give up the nickel. Tell you what; you can have all the pennies. There must be at least a hundred here. I just want the nickel."

"How about we flip for it?" Shawn suggested, not ready to give up. "The winner gets the nickel, and the loser takes home the pennies."

"Okay, already," sighed Tanner, resigned to the game of chance. He tossed the nickel to his friend, who deftly caught it in the palm of his hand. "You broke the jar, so you get to flip."

"Fair enough," said Shawn. He flipped the nickel high into the air, squinting as he watched it arc toward the hot summer sun. "Call it!"

"Heads!" yelled Tanner, as the nickel spiraled down to land with a soft plop in Shawn's right palm.

Not looking at the coin, Shawn slapped the nickel down against the back of his left hand, only then moving his right away from the nickel. It showed tails, and so the nickel was Shawn's.

"Easy come, easy go," shrugged Tanner, as he began to gather up the copper coins lying at his feet. "I wish you hadn't broken the jar, though. How am I going to get all these pennies home?"

* * *

"…and then we went home," Shawn concluded the story of their foray into the house. "We'd meant to come back the next day and search the third story but got involved in a baseball game instead and before we knew it, it was time for my trip. So we never went back."

Laughing at the thought of Tanner counting all of those wheat pennies and carefully wrapping them in an old handkerchief before slipping them into his backpack, Shawn thought his friend had probably ended up getting the better deal: weirdly, there had been exactly 555 pennies in the jar, so, at the very least, he'd gained almost six dollars, while all Shawn had to show for the adventure was the first edition Tolkien, a rusty knife, a tarnished necklace holding a little pentagram, and an old Buffalo nickel. But then he remembered tossing the nickel into Tanner's coffin, and realized that he had one less item to show for his part in their quest after all. Still, he knew, he'd gladly give up every book and every nickel he'd ever had or ever would have for a chance to spend even just one more day with his best friend.

"You know, I'd wondered about all those pennies that Tanner lugged home, and the nickel that you put in his coffin. It all makes sense now. Thanks for telling me."

Taking his hand, she led him to the big slide in the middle of the park. They quickly climbed the stairs to stand atop the huge metal contraption, surveying the world around them. It was almost like a little playroom up there. There were wheels that children could turn and spin and little open windows they could look out from, all contained in a wooden tunnel that led to the metal slide.

"Let's sit down," Jenny said, joining him at the top. Dropping to sit with her legs tucked beneath her, she patted the platform beside her. Light from the overhead moon caught her emerald eyes, and Shawn wondered how he could ever resist anything she asked. Unsure of where this was heading but anxious to find out, he took a seat beside Jenny.

"I've always wanted to do this," she murmured, snuggling close to him. Removing her glasses, she sat them on the wooden floor. "To sit up here among the trees and stars, alone with my boyfriend..." she grinned, leaning into his arms, "...and kiss him," she pressed her lips softly to his for the second time that day, and the world seemed to fall away around them. The moon, the stars, the trees, the horror they destroyed two nights ago, and even Tanner's memory – everything took a back seat to the kiss shared by the two teenagers, enjoying each other's warmth and building desire.

"Jenny," he started, suddenly pulling away from her. An idea that had been subconsciously crawling around in the back of his head finally blossomed into something coherent. "You don't think they could have been after the jar, do you?"

"They?" she asked, opening her eyes as his lips moved away from hers. "Do you mean the monster?"

"Do you think the monster was after the jar?" he said quickly, trying to change the subject. "Maybe the money was worth more than we thought."

"Is there something else you're not telling me?" she asked, ignoring his explanation.

Mentally kicking himself for his choice of pronouns, forgetting for the moment what he had been about to say, Shawn sighed and admitted that there was. "Okay, but you're going to think I'm nuts."

"Join the club," she shot back, looking straight into his eyes as if to say, *why wouldn't I, of all people, believe you, you dolt?* But instead she said, "So tell me already."

"Okay," he took a deep breath, exhaled, and began, "When I was asleep in the hospital and had the vision of the fetch..."

"Fetch?" Jenny interrupted.

"That's just it. I heard someone else talking to it, in its mind. It called it a 'fetch.'"

"What do you mean that you *heard* someone? Is there more than one monster?"

"No. I mean maybe, I don't know. It wasn't there with it, I know that much at least. It was a voice inside its head, and I could sense that it didn't know I was listening. It told the fetch to…" he faltered, afraid to let the words pass his lips for fear that, though the fetch was dead, it might somehow come true.

"What, Shawn?" she said adamantly, grabbing his wrist, her green eyes betraying anger within. "I deserve to know this."

"I'm sorry I didn't tell you, okay? I just didn't want to worry you, and I thought I might have imagined the voice anyway."

"Kind of like I imagined my brother being drowned by a monster at the lake?" she said, voice trembling. Tears clouded her green eyes.

"Jenny, I'm sorry."

"What did it say?" she yelled at him, squeezing his wrist hard between her fingers. The kiss shared between them just moments ago was all but forgotten. "Just tell me what it said, Shawn."

"It told the fetch to find you, to find you and… and to kill you, and then to come to the hospital after me."

Shawn could feel Jenny tremble as she released his wrist, dropping her hands to the side of her body. He reached out a hand to comfort her, but she pulled away.

"I'm sorry, okay? I just didn't… I didn't think it was real. I didn't want it to be real. And I didn't want to scare you. I promise you, I'll never keep anything from you again."

"You better not!" She warned him as she rose to her knees, flinging herself into his arms, pulling him tight. His arms encircled her shoulders, returning the embrace. He felt warm tears flowing against his shoulder, soaking through the shirt and touching the skin beneath. Kissing her hair, he pulled her tighter, wishing for all he was worth that the fetch had never entered their lives and that Tanner was still alive.

\* \* \*

*Just watch them,* said the old man's voice inside the fetch's head. The monster, now standing just under six feet tall and nearly as big as a grizzly bear, stood behind a copse of trees at the edge of the woods that separated the park from the lake.

*Watch and follow them, but do not take them or make your presence known,* the voice repeated, further enforcing the command the monster had already been given. But how desperately it wanted to ignore its master's words and launch itself on all fours, loping quickly across the park grounds, throwing itself into the air and taking the two startled teenagers before they even had the chance to scream.

First it would disable the boy, cutting quickly behind the knees, throwing him from the top of the metal slide to the ground, abandoned for the time being but not forgotten. Then it would begin to dine on the succulent meat of the female that had escaped its hunger twice. And finally, after it finished, after every last sinewy muscle and fragment of bone had passed its lips and entered its stomach, it would slowly make its way down the slide to end the boy's suffering and drag away his body, hiding it in the woods for later.

But none of that would happen until its master allowed it, which in turn would not happen until the old man had the talisman firmly within his grasp. Silently seething, tasting the female meat's blood in its deformed and twisted mind, the fetch looked on through the trees.

\* \* \*

It was just thirty minutes before Jenny's curfew and Shawn didn't want to let her go. He feared that by keeping something from her he had damaged the trust that had slowly been building between them, not to mention the feelings of romance that had followed. He didn't know whether or not to be afraid of the voice, and without her he wasn't sure he cared.

"I think we'd better go," said Jenny, looking down at her watch. "I don't want my dad killing you or anything," she smiled at him, "at least, not yet."

"I really am sorry," he apologized for the tenth time in the last thirty minutes. "I should have told you about the voice. I'm still not sure why I didn't. I just didn't want to scare you."

"I know you're sorry, Shawn, but I'd rather be scared than dead." She pushed away from him to slide down the metal ramp, her long red hair catching the breeze as she sped toward the ground.

Following her lead, Shawn soon found himself standing beside her by the big elm tree where they'd parked their bicycles. "Jenny," he said cautiously, "I really enjoyed spending time with you tonight, and I don't want this to end…"

"Well, it has to, I'm afraid," she responded in a solemn voice before allowing a smile to break from her lips, "for tonight, anyway. I'm just mad, Shawn, and more than a little worried, but I'll get over it. Besides, you're not going to get away from me *that* easily." Removing her glasses once more, she leaned into the boy, brushing her lips across his in an all too brief kiss that left him wanting more.

"Remind me to lie to you more often," he slowly smiled, earning himself another hard punch on the arm.

"But if it happens again, there'll be no more kisses…"

"On second thought, maybe lying isn't such a good idea after all," he murmured, remembering their first kiss in the parking lot of the bank his dad managed, less than two hours ago. A warm shiver of excitement trailing up his spine, he took her hands in his, finally saying, "Come on, let's go home."

# Chapter 21

Fred Ruskin sat by himself at a table in the back of the Peacock, the seediest bar that Carthage had to offer. Tonight he didn't care who saw him drinking. The twang of Merle Haggard singing "Things Aren't Funny Anymore" drifted across the room from the old jukebox in the corner. "Ain't that the truth," mumbled Ruskin, raising his glass in a silent toast to the music.

Smoke filled the air, creating a foggy haze that hung over the entire room and stung his eyes. Blinking back tears, he thought over the events of the last several hours. The shit really hit the fan today. Someone on the force, apparently concerned about Delacroix's disappearance and the Sheriff's stonewalling, had gone over Ruskin's head and talked to someone on the city council who talked to the mayor. The Mayor, of course, sensed a chance to get Carthage some TV time, and had leaked the whole thing to the media. It was the second worst day of Ruskin's life.

The worst day, worse by far than this public embarrassment could ever be, had happened over fifteen years ago, back when he was young and had the world in the palm of his hand. It almost seemed like only yesterday, but also a lifetime ago.

Sheriff Frederick "Bear" Ruskin had been one of the most highly decorated officers to ever grace the 16th district of the Chicago Police Department. He had, in fact, just made First Grade Detective when life as he knew it suddenly came to an abrupt and screeching halt. He'd been working nonstop on a serial murder case and was closer than ever to finding the man who had murdered seven college coeds when the killer the media had dubbed "The Smiley-face Killer" decided to make things personal.

Knowing from the papers that Ruskin was the lead detective on the case, the serial killer began to correspond directly with him, first sending neatly typed letters in generic white envelopes and later the occasional package to him care of the squad. The letters contained cryptic clues to the whereabouts of the victim's bodies, about half of which Ruskin and the FBI had been able to figure out; the rest remained undeciphered to this very day. The packages contained bits of physical evidence from the killings – a necklace, a pair of stockings and, once, a woman's severed middle finger, effectively flipping the bird at the brilliant young detective who, along with the FBI, was in charge of bringing him down.

The seventh victim, found with help from the killer's letter, had helped spell the end to the murders. They'd found the woman's body – a 22 year old black girl named Sasha Reeves - in a shallow grave under a recently paved grocery store parking lot on the East side of Chicago. She had been beaten to death and raped postmortem, her face barely recognizable beneath the welts and bruises. One thing that was entirely too recognizable, however, was his trademark "smiley-face," a huge, gaping hole cut into the victim's throat in the shape of a smile. But Sasha would have the last laugh on her abductor: shoved into the man's trunk, she had managed to kick out one of the tail lights before being taken into the woods and murdered.

Three days later, when police pulled over a car missing a tail light, one of the traffic cops noticed blood on the rear fender. A search of the trunk revealed a silver pendant wedged beneath the spare tire, identified as belonging to the missing girl. The car belonged to David Lee Grainger, a foreman at a pet food factory in the lower side of Southwest Chicago. He managed to kill both police officers, both friends of Ruskin, before escaping, but not before one of the cops called in the car's license plate.

The killer's eighth and ninth victims would be his last. Exhausted and demoralized from the day's events, Ruskin left the station early, ordered by his Captain to get a good night's sleep and come back ready to join the hunt first thing in the morning.

Approaching the front door of his little bungalow in Wheaton, Ruskin immediately knew something was wrong. Everything looked normal, nothing was out of place and his wife's car was parked where it always was, but something didn't feel right. The detective's instincts had never let him down before and so he immediately flattened himself against the wall to the right of the door, drawing the Smith & Wesson snub nosed .38 from his shoulder holster, carefully reaching out with his left hand to turn the door knob. The door swung slowly open, and it was then that he felt his blood freeze. Molly always kept the house locked.

His weapon pointed down in front of him, Ruskin noiselessly stepped through the door and into the living room of the house. The room was empty as was the kitchen, den, and dining room. Just as he was thinking that, thank God, he'd been wrong after all, he heard a shrill gasp followed by a heavy grunt and the sound of a hand slapping against flesh coming from his twelve year old daughter Jessica's bedroom.

Racing to his daughter, all thoughts of stealth abandoned, he threw himself through the door, cracking it into splintered pieces, not even pausing to see whether or not it was locked. What he found beyond the door was a scene that would burn indelibly into his mind and haunt him for the rest of his life.

His daughter, naked, was lying spread-eagle across her bed, her wrists and ankles bound to the bed posts by an incredible amount of duct tape. And there, on top of her, between her legs, was David Lee Grainger, a low keening moan tumbling from his lips. "Just stop hitting me," he repeated, over and over, slamming his pelvis into hers.

Ruskin didn't hesitate. A loud crack vibrated through the air as the detective discharged his weapon, sending a bullet screaming into the back of the man's head, once, twice, and then a third time. Blood and gray matter slid through the back of Grainger's skull to roll down his hairy back and shoulders. He slumped down between the girl's legs without a sound, twitched once, and was dead.

"Sweet Mary, mother of Jesus…" mumbled Ruskin, his face going white. Throwing the dead serial killer from his daughter's bed, he stared down in agony into Jessica's lifeless eyes, her pretty young face a pasty pallor of gray. She was already dead. The killer had slit her throat from ear to ear before raping his daughter. Feeling the hot dog and onion rings he had for lunch rising up in his throat, he turned away from Jessica's body, dropped to his knees, and vomited the entire contents of his stomach into his daughter's Barbie doll trash can.

Ruskin untied his daughter's hands and legs and wrapped her in a sheet from the bed. He sat beside her, stroking her long red hair, saying her name over and over again as tears tumbled from his cheeks to land in her extinguished eyes. The Wheaton police arrived a short time later, a neighbor having heard and reported the three gunshots. They found the young detective sitting on the bed with his dead daughter's head in his lap, rocking back and forth, stroking her hair and whispering to her, "It'll be all right, honey. Daddy's home now and he's never going to go away again."

Wheaton's finest also discovered Molly Ruskin lying naked and alone in her own bed, just as dead as her daughter. Her wrists and ankles had also been bound, and she'd suffered severe blunt trauma to the head and body. She'd apparently put up a struggle before Grainger had finally managed to tape her hands and feet to the bed. She, too, had been raped post mortem, and shared the same signature slash across the throat that her daughter and seven other women had suffered.

Grainger, apparently, had suffered an awful childhood, abandoned by his father and repeatedly abused and beaten by his mother. Evelyn Grainger, the mother, had slit her wrists and drowned in the bath tub on Grainger's eighteenth birthday, while he was out drinking with friends. She had drawn a smiley-face on the tile with her own blood. Newspapers and pop psychologists all over the country had speculated that Grainger, in committing his horrible crimes, was killing his mother over and over, giving her the punishment that she had escaped in real life by killing herself.

Ruskin didn't care. He had lost his wife and daughter to the madman, that was all he knew, and he had never been the same after that. He was awarded the medal of valor for his part in the investigation, for finally putting an end to the "Smiley-face Killer," but without a family to share it with the accolades meant very little. He'd taken to drinking then, first before work, then during, and always after. Within a year, he had blown three major investigations and used up any slack he'd been given by his Captain. In the end, regrettably and without prejudice, the department had felt that it had no choice but to ask Ruskin to retire. He'd gone along with the retirement, of course, which had left his record, if not his life, unmarred.

He'd wandered around Chicago for five more years, picking up a hundred pounds and a three-pack-a-day cigarette addiction along the way. He worked security jobs when he could find them, accepting the couches of what few remaining friends he had when he couldn't. Finally his Captain had contacted him and told him about the Sheriff's job in Carthage. They would probably hire him based on his Medal of Valor alone, his Captain told him, and they certainly didn't need to know about his drinking or the reason he'd retired from the force.

Since his wife had been from Carthage and because she and their daughter were buried there, he'd considered the news of the job opening to be serendipitous and perhaps the change he needed. On the strength of the Captain's recommendation, he applied and had been accepted for the job. And there he'd been ever since. Nearly every day for ten years he'd wake up in the morning and decide his drinking days were over, but end up drowning his regrets in an endless line of whiskey shots or Scotch by nightfall.

"Can I get you another drink?" asked Candy, a pretty blonde waitress in her early-thirties. Just a few years ago, she had probably been considered beautiful and full of promise but now looked just this side of worn out and used up.

Happy to be torn away from his ruminations of the past, Ruskin grinned up at the hazel-eyed cocktail waitress and leered, "Well, I am thirsty, but not for alcohol…"

It was a line he'd used on all of the waitresses at one time or another, but he'd always had a soft spot in his heart for Candy. They'd had many cocktail-time conversations over the years, and he appreciated the woman's quick wit and optimism in the face of a life that had been much less than fair to her in return. As beaten down as she looked tonight, he could still see that inner spark that she'd once had, that intensity of confidence that could be so easily shattered, and it finally pushed him to whisper what he'd desperately been wanting to say to her ever since he began coming into the Peacock five years ago: "This time, I'm serious."

"Be careful, Sheriff, because one of these days I'm going to take you up on that, and you know I don't come cheap," she winked, used to the harmless patter and the occasional pinch that came with the territory. Ruskin figured she'd seen it all before, having worked at the Peacock since her early-twenties, after her husband abandoned her and a beautiful little one-year-old girl named Samantha to run away to St. Louis with another woman whom he'd met on his truck driving route.

That had been eleven years ago. She'd landed the job at the Peacock about two weeks after the breakup, and had supported herself and her daughter through the tips she earned at the bar ever since. Like most of the other waitresses, she was usually amenable to flirting if she thought it would earn her a bigger tip, but it never went beyond that. Maybe tonight would be different.

"How much?" he asked, past the point of being drunk and no longer caring what anyone in this town thought of him. By the end of the week he'd probably have lost his job anyway, so what did it matter?

"How much for what?" she asked distractedly, shrugging her bare shoulders. The move caused her little black and white cocktail dress to shimmy, and Ruskin's eyes fell on the delicate softness of her breasts as she moved closer.

"You said you didn't come cheap, so I'm asking how much."

"Seriously?" she asked, amusement dancing in her eyes along with a flicker of doubt. He'd acted this way with her before, but never had he pushed it beyond the little flirt he used with all the waitresses.

"Seriously," he said, reaching out a hand to slowly caress her hip, pulling her closer to the table.

"Sheriff, you know I don't..." her words faltered as she watched the drunken old man peel off ten twenties from a roll of money he produced from his back pocket. He counted the twenties in front of her, calling off dollar amounts, finally finishing at two hundred.

"Think this'll do?" he asked, as he pulled her down to within inches of his face and gently folded the money into her décolletage. "Candy, it's been nearly fifteen years since I've been with a woman, and..."

She slapped him hard across the face, and he recoiled like he'd been shot. "I am not a whore," she whispered through clenched teeth, as the entire bar shifted their attention to the altercation. "I may not be worth much, Fred Ruskin, but I'm worth more than that."

Bringing his hand to his face, gently fingering the angry red welt forming on his cheek, Ruskin numbly nodded his head in agreement. "I'm sorry, Candy. I don't know what I was thinking."

"Hush!" she scolded him. The Peacock's patrons went back to nursing their drinks, pretending that nothing had happened. She retrieved the handful of twenties from between her breasts, dropping them to the table in front of him. "Just go home, Sheriff, and let's forget this ever happened, okay?"

He nodded again, feeling ashamed. How much lower could he fall? Watching in silent resignation as Candy Martin hurriedly returned to her duties of flirting and taking drink orders from the other drunks in the tavern, he lit up another cigarette. Casually peering through the smoky haze at the big clock over the bar, having to squint to see the numbers, he was surprised to see that it wasn't even ten yet.

He peeled off another group of twenties – easily double the amount needed to cover his drinks – and laid them atop the money he had tried to use to buy Candy Martin. He stood up from the bar, ignoring the wave of nausea that made him feel like puking. Weaving through the room and the hallway beyond, he let the cool night air wash over him as he made his way out of the tavern and headed home.

# Chapter 22

FRED RUSKIN sat alone on the second-hand brown suede couch that occupied most of the floor space in the living room of his little two-room apartment, trying to sober up. Downing another cup of black coffee, he couldn't believe the audacity he'd shown at the tavern just three hours earlier. He felt like such an ass. Candy's job was a thankless one, and he'd made it even worse by doing what he did. He hoped that she at least wouldn't begrudge the tip he had left for her.

Once the news hit about Delacroix's disappearance and his phone began to ring, he'd more or less given up on everything. He should have reported the deputy's disappearance the morning that it happened instead of sitting on it for a day and a half. The man hadn't really been missing that long, but the mayor and the city council would have a field day over this. If he couldn't even keep his own deputy on the job, what use was he?

And then there was the whole motorcycle mess. He'd interviewed everyone and come up with nothing. Spencer seemed like he knew more than he was telling, but he couldn't prove anything. Sure, there was a plunger missing from the hospital room he had stayed in, and sure, he'd found a broken plunger next to a set of skid marks that may or may not have been from the Kawasaki, but it was all circumstantial evidence at best. Truth be told, he didn't have the slightest idea what had happened Saturday night.

Fighting the urge to reach for the last bottle of scotch, Ruskin instead removed the necklace that held his and Molly's wedding rings and crossed the room to the little desk where he kept his gun. He opened the drawer and pulled the little .38 from its drawer, cradling it in his massive hands, leaving the necklace in its place. One well placed shot and this sad excuse for a life would be over and done with. He knew he'd never see Molly and Jessica again, not where he was going, but at least he'd no longer miss them, no longer wake up in a cold sweat at four in the morning wondering for the thousandth time if he'd still have a wife and daughter if he had managed to get home just fifteen minutes earlier.

The police psychologist had told him that he couldn't be held responsible for other people's actions, and that he'd had no way of knowing that Grainger would track down his home address and turn his twisted attentions on Ruskin's family. On an intellectual level he knew all of that to be true, but it didn't stop the pain, and it sure as hell didn't stop his ever-growing desire to put a bullet in his brain, to finally – mercifully! – end the agony and self-recrimination that had wracked his soul every hour of every day since he walked into that house and found a serial killer raping his dead daughter.

Ruskin glanced at his watch, startled to see that it was nearly two in the morning. Might as well get this over with. Slowly, methodically, the Sheriff worked the muzzle of the handgun into his mouth, released the safety, and cocked back the hammer. Jesus forgive me, he thought, his finger tightening on the trigger, as he began to squeeze.

# Chapter 23

*I've been too careless,* thought the bald-headed old man in the white terrycloth robe, his hawkish face grimacing with distaste as he watched the children through his fetch's eyes. *I should never have allowed the child at the lake to be killed before I'd found what he'd stolen.* Everything was taking too long, but soon enough the fetch would be healed and he'd have the talisman back in his hands.

The old man surveyed his surroundings, his steel-gray eyes taking in everything. He shook his head. How far have I fallen? He was traveling by train, currently lying down in the small private quarters he'd rented for the trip. He remembered back to the days of great halls and temples, armies and priests, all at his disposal. Back then, first in South America, then later in Egypt, Greece, and Rome, he ruled with an iron fist, commanding respect and obedience from anyone who dared cross his path.

He'd been in Prague when he'd first felt the familiar thrum of the object resurfacing after all these years. He'd immediately used his powers to send the fetch to Carthage but, no longer having the strength to follow in the same fashion, had booked himself onto a train traveling to Hamburg. From there he had booked a ship to take him to New York, and then another train to Quincy, Illinois, where he planned to rent a car and drive the rest of the way to Carthage. All in all, the train out of Prague and the subsequent boat trip took a total of six days. He knew he could have arrived much sooner by flying, but in his three thousand years on this planet he had never trusted his life to an airship and didn't intend to start now.

The train route from New York to Quincy had several layovers and would take just under two days to reach his ultimate destination. By the time he arrived in the sleepy little town, the fetch should have found the object and all the power in the world would once again be his to wield.

The man rose up from the lumpy, unmade bed, balancing precariously on two shaky legs. With the help of his silver walking stick he made his way across the little room, the cheap, pea-green carpet looming up at him all the while, sending his surroundings spinning as he fought to right himself. Sighing, he shuffled out of his room intent on finding a turkey and Swiss sandwich for lunch.

He had been alive for centuries, but never had he felt so old – so tired – as he did today. And it was all because of Wainwright. Wainwright had been one of his disciples, and he'd made the mistake of trusting the man, of letting his guard down, of teaching him more than he'd ever had the right to learn. He gave the man the world, and Wainwright threw it back in his face.

Having finally made his way to the dining car aboard the train, the old man pulled his robe tight around his chest and limped to a dingy little table in the back of the room, carefully lowering himself down onto the wooden chair to read the menu. No Turkey and Swiss after all. Sighing, he waved at the waiter, settling on a Salisbury steak with a side of green beans and a cup of apple sauce for lunch.

\* \* \*

From another table across the room, a man with icy blue eyes and a long-flowing mane of blonde hair sat alone, intently watching the old man eat his lunch. Dressed in a tan trench coat and white tennis shoes, he didn't seem to mind as the waiter walked by his table, seemingly ignoring him, not even stopping long enough to take his order or bring him a simple glass of water.

# Chapter 24

IT WAS JUST after midnight and, though Shawn lay sprawled on his bed, he didn't feel anything remotely approaching sleepiness. Just a little over an hour ago, he had bicycled with Jenny back to her house, making the eleven o'clock curfew with mere minutes to spare. He could still taste the quick kiss goodnight she'd given him seconds before her mother opened the front door and good naturedly (albeit firmly) shooed him off. He hadn't been able to wipe the smile from his face since he'd left her driveway.

He wasn't exactly sure what love was – hell, he hadn't even turned sixteen yet, and there were a lot of things he didn't know – but he knew for sure that he wanted to find out. Already, his lips ached for her touch and his stomach clenched up whenever he thought back to the image of her face bathed in moonlight and the feeling of her hands in his. If that wasn't love, well, it was definitely *something*, and he looked forward to exploring that something with Jenny, and following it wherever it might lead.

Lost in thoughts of love and longing, Shawn carried the backpack he had retrieved from Jenny's house earlier in the evening to the closet when a strange odor wrinkled his nose. Puzzled, sniffing the air, he followed the odor to the back of the closet.

The smell grew stronger as he pushed through the clothes hanging from the metal bars just inside the closet. Moving a baseball mitt and an old pair of snow boots out of the way, he followed the rancid smell to the old blue toy box that was wedged between a boomerang and a pile of board games in the very back of the closet.

Tensing, his heart in his throat, he pulled open the lid to the toy chest, revealing nothing more than the scattered remains of a Hungry Hippo game, three beat up G.I. Joes, and a Johnny West action figure missing an arm. The smell still strong in his nostrils, he moved aside the action figures and began to sift deeper into the wooden box. There, poking out from between the purple jaws of the Hungry Hippo, was the tip of a furry orange tail. He dug frantically through the toys, throwing them aside as he raced toward the bottom.

Samson! The cat was lying on his side atop a folded checker board, his paws pointing to the back of the box, his head twisted completely around to face the front. His bloody tongue lolled out from the side of his mouth, and over each of Samson's eyes laid a red checker.

A wave of nausea rolled through Shawn and he breathlessly rasped the orange and white tabby's name over and over, dropping to his knees, choking and sobbing. Yanking the box out of the closet and to the floor beside him, he scooped the cat into his arms, sending the checkers flying, hugging him hard against his chest. He willed Samson to somehow be alive despite the broken bones in his neck, but the cat lay silent and unmoving within his embrace.

A scene immediately played itself out in Shawn's head, one he'd been trying to forget for over half his life; a little boy in Superman pajamas waking at half past three in the morning, knowing something was wrong but not yet understanding why. Swinging his legs down from the bed, padding slowly across the room, expectantly peering into the little wooden crib against the wall...

Anguished and alone, tears rolling down his cheeks, Shawn gently laid the cat back down into the faded blue box that had become his crypt. Gathering up the fallen checkers, he dropped them into the box and closed the lid. And then he collapsed to the floor, his body convulsing with wracking sobs and an ever-growing fire of anger.

Shawn buried the old tom outside, toy box and all, under the big willow tree beside his window. Even though it meant digging much deeper than had he buried the cat alone, he couldn't fathom ever again looking at the old toy box. Dazed and disoriented, shovel still in hand, he sat down beside the little grave and thought about life without Samson.

He received the tom as a gift for his seventh birthday and had learned the lesson of responsibility through feeding and taking care of him. He'd been an important part of Shawn's life and he couldn't imagine a night when Samson wouldn't share his bed. The cat's death marked the second best friend he'd lost in less than a week, both of them taken by the mysterious little monster.

Anger taking hold of his emotions, Shawn rose to his feet in a burst of wild energy, swinging the shovel hard against the old tree. It snapped in half with a loud crack, sending the shovel head tumbling end over end, where it finally landed in a patch of clover at the edge of the white picket fence that surrounded the house.

The rage that enveloped him left as quickly as it had arrived, and he once again felt numb. Tears welled up in his eyes but Shawn wiped the wetness away from his face with the back of his hand, willing himself not to cry. Before burying Samson he'd managed to hammer together a little cross from two mismatched pieces of lumber he'd found in the garage. Now he dropped to his knees, hammering the sharp end of the cross into the ground.

With a black felt tip marker, he wrote "Samson Spencer, 1966-1975, Rest in Peace" down the length of the vertical piece of wood. Saying a prayer for his cat, something he hadn't done since he was twelve, he made a vow to find whoever had been behind this and make them pay for all the destruction they had brought into his life.

"Shawn," yelled a voice from the front of the yard, interrupting his grief. He turned to see his father, dressed in blue flannel pajamas, pointing a flashlight at him.

"What're you doing out here?" his father asked, his face a mask of confusion. Turning the flashlight to his watch, he said, "It's almost one in the morning."

"Samson's dead," responded the boy, his voice a low monotone, the words spilling almost unbidden from his mouth. "My cat is dead, and I'm burying him."

# Chapter 25

THE OLD MAN lay on his bed in another little nondescript room, this time on the Amtrak passenger train heading from New York to Chicago. He had yet to fully recover from the seizure he had two nights before. At one time he could have healed himself with the merest of thoughts, but that time was past. Without the fifth talisman, there was much that he could not do. Actually, truth be told, he probably *could* do them, but he'd more than likely lose what already tenuous grasp he had on his own life force in the process. As it stood now, he'd almost rather be dead than go on living like this.

He examined himself in the mirror over the flimsy laminated dresser that stood against the wall opposite his bed and didn't like what he saw. He had lost all of the hair on his head, most of it seemingly transferred to his ears, and deep, craggy wrinkles surrounded his dark gray eyes. He looked a breath away from death.

Once, many generations ago, the jaguar's tooth alone could have restored both him and his fetch to full health. But he had used its power, coupled with the other four objects, to increase his natural lifespan many times over, and now it took the combined power of the four remaining talismans simply to keep him alive and maintain his link to the little black creature he had created as his servant some twenty years ago. Once he found the stolen charm all his strength would return and he would be young again.

He wouldn't have had to go through any of this had it not been for Colin Wainwright. He'd met Wainwright some two hundred years earlier, in England, and he had sensed a kindred spirit, someone with whom he could share his darkest and most dangerous secrets. His hubris had cost him, however, and he'd paid the price for his folly when the man had suddenly grown a conscience and had run off with one of the talismans. His empire had fallen apart within one year's time, and he'd had to switch bodies just to survive the maelstrom.

He had eventually tracked down and dealt with the man, but he'd never found the object that his disciple had stolen from him. The loss had taken its toll. The talisman was one of five that had been created by whatever came before man, when the world was fresh and young. They were never really meant to work together, much less used by human hands. But once the old man had traveled the globe and gathered them all, bent them to his will, they worked exactly the way he needed them to, how he had been told that they would work. But he needed all five of the charms to maintain the delicate balance that he had created when he merged them into the swastika that he now wore around his neck. Without all of the talismans working in conjunction, giving him unimaginable power and immortality, he would eventually wither and die. He'd been slowly dying ever since Wainwright's betrayal, and didn't have much time left.

As close as he was now to finally regaining all that he had lost, it never would have happened had someone else not done his dirty work for him. The charm that Wainwright stole all those many years ago had more than likely been hidden in the old Illinois house. Someone had managed to remove it, alerting him both to the building and to the talisman within. He liked to think it had been fate, but maybe it was all just coincidence. It didn't really matter as long as he regained what was rightfully his and made whoever now had the charm pay for their interference.

The house, apparently, had housed some sort of concealment ward, defeating all of his attempts to send out psychic feelers to search for the object. But the ward must have been broken when either Shawn Spencer or one of the McGee children had entered the house and removed the talisman, and he'd finally been able to sense it. Everything that Wainwright had set in motion was finally beginning to unravel. He still couldn't enter the house – not yet – but he could easily detect that the charm had been removed. He knew that Tanner McGee had once held it in his hand, as had Shawn Spencer. The girl he wasn't so sure about, but, according to the fetch, she had the scent about her as well. One of them had it, or at least knew where it was.

He fingered the four talismans, which he had melded into a large swastika that hung from a silver chain around his neck. He liked using the symbol that so many thought evil simply because it inspired fear in the less-knowledgeable. Before he'd used it in Germany, the symbol had been a Chinese good luck charm. Now, it inspired fear and loathing almost the world over.

Colin Wainwright had used the limited powers he had so foolishly granted him to separate the silver coin from the other four talismans, stealing it and corrupting his power, before running out of Germany like a thief in the night. But he had made the man pay. Oh, how he had made him pay!

\* \* \*

**Cologne, Germany, 1957**

It was the time of Kölner Karneval in Cologne, or, as many of the locals preferred to call it, *'die närrische Zeit'*, the fifth and foolish season. Once a year, just after winter had ended, the city would host a huge carnival filled with parades, performers, and vendors hawking various foods and desserts, all enjoying a full weekend of madness celebrating the year to come.

It was early spring and the harsh winter snow was still evident in the melting slush that met his every movement underfoot. After over a decade of fruitless searches, the old man had finally sensed Wainwright's presence in London and had followed him here, to Germany, to the land he had once ruled before his disciple had interfered and cost him everything.

Walking stick in hand, his body having aged rapidly in the last ten years but still not yet old in appearance, he hid behind a green-and-yellow potato fritter cart, watching as his adversary walked hurriedly toward the huge, thirteenth-century twin-spired gothic structure known as the Cologne Cathedral. A white-faced clown dressed in a garish combination of orange and blue clopped by on stilts, throwing little pieces of wrapped candy to all the children surrounding the stand, momentarily obscuring the old man's view of Wainwright.

*"Geh mir aus dem Weg, du idiot!"* the old man yelled, pushing his way past the clown. The jester teetered precariously on his stilts, the long poles attached to his feet dancing frantically against the cobblestone street. For a moment the clown regained his balance, but then one of his stilts came down on a piece of rock candy and the pole twisted out from under him, sending the stilt flying one way and him the other. He crashed headfirst into the brightly painted fritter cart in a cloud of wooden splinters and hot potatoes.

Pushing past the children who squealed with laughter at the sight of the clown covered in potatoes and sawdust, the old man turned his back on the chaos behind him but could no longer find his quarry in the crowd. Wainwright had disappeared from sight, but he could still feel the man's energy nearby. Muttering a quick incantation, he watched as a thin silver thread blinked into existence before him. The thread, invisible to anyone else who might happen to look his way, wound itself around trees, buildings, and vendor carts, until it finally settled on the huge wooden doors of the cathedral.

Moving quickly, working his way through the throng of people that celebrated in the streets, he found himself standing at the foot of the granite stairs that led up and into the huge gothic structure. Forcing his tired legs into motion with the help of his cane, the old man slowly, agonizingly put one foot in front of the other, climbing the stairs to the huge wooden doors that held sway before him. They were closed.

Frustrated, the man began to pound on the doors until he noticed the little sign that read: *"Wegen Reparatur zur Zeit geschlossen. Morgen Wiedereröffnung."* The damned thing was closed for remodeling! Cursing, the old man slammed his heavy wooden cane into the door and was rewarded when the wooden monstrosity unexpectedly creaked open to reveal a huge, darkened interior into which he couldn't quite see.

"Colin!"

Without warning, the heavy oak doors slammed shut behind him, leaving the man in absolute darkness. Stumbling, righting himself with his cane, he muttered an archaic incantation and fire suddenly blazed from his fingertips, lighting the way around him. The light exposed a long aisle that led to the center of the building. Grinding his teeth, clutching the silver walking stick tightly in his grasp, he focused on ignoring the pain that performing the magic had sent coursing through his body.

Once, when he'd had all of the talismans, such simple manipulation of the elements wouldn't have caused him even a drop of sweat. Once upon a time, the Jaguar's tooth had been the heart of his creation with the other four talismans serving as the four points of the swastika. Now, however, with the symbol broken, with one of the four points missing, any magic he did drained a little more of the already-dwindling life force from his body.

The spell had probably taken six months or more from his lifespan, but it would all be worth it if he could take the talisman from Wainwright and rejoin it to the other four, regaining his youth and the power that had been denied him since that fateful day in Berlin so many years ago. Once he'd done that, once he'd reclaimed the amulet, he'd once again have unlimited energy at his disposal, enough to raise a fire that could burn the towering cathedral to the ground.

"Wainwright!" he screamed, staring down the aisle leading into the heart of the cathedral, "Give me what's mine!"

"It was never yours, old man," said a handsome man with intense blue eyes and jet black hair, stepping out of the shadows to stand some twenty yards away. Dressed all in black and wearing a long, black duster, he presented a visage of Death himself, an image not spoiled by the long silver sword that hung from a belt draped across his hips. "The charms were never meant to be used the way that you used them. You corrupted them, made them into something they never should have been. All I did was right a wrong, one that should have been righted many years before."

"I am beyond right and wrong," said the old priest, quietly advancing down the aisle. "I am beyond your comprehension. I am your lord and master. I am your God!"

"You were many things to me, George, but you were never my God," Wainwright spat, removing the sword from its hilt. The sharp metal gleamed in the artificial light from the magician's fingertips, shining brightly as Wainwright walked toward his former master and one-time friend. "I serve only one God, and he..."

"Where is it, Colin?" the old man interrupted. The crackling fire from his fingertips threw shadows across the apex of the building, bringing to life strange and exotic silhouettes that danced to the beat of their conversation. "I meant it when I said that I would let you live if you gave me the coin. I loved you once; I have no interest in killing you."

"Then it's a pity that the reverse is not also true!" shouted Wainwright. He rushed the old man, sword high in the air, bringing it down in an arc toward his neck. "Die, demon!"

"I am not so easily killed, my friend," smiled the wizard, parrying the sword with his cane and sidestepping his opponent's rush. Wielding the walking stick like a staff, he brought it down hard on the other man's shoulder, a glancing blow that nevertheless knocked him off balance, sending him spinning into and over a row of pews.

Almost as quickly as he had fallen Colin Wainwright was on his feet, leaping over the pew, advancing once again on the old man with the stick. "I can feel your energies ebb like the tide in the ocean, growing weaker…"

"Ebb and flow, my friend, ebb and flow," interrupted the old man. Taking the offensive, swinging his cane up and over his head, he struck to the space that his opponent's skull had occupied just seconds earlier. "What tide goes out must come back in. Now give me the coin and be done with it."

"Do you sense it, George? Use your powers. Do I have it with me?"

And in an instant, he knew it was true. The old man could feel the psychic residue of the charm upon his old student, but he did not currently carry the artifact. "Where is it?" he screamed, throwing his walking stick to the floor. "What did you do with it? Answer me!"

"Would you believe me were I to tell you that I have absolutely no idea?"

The old wizard loosed the magic inside him, feeling it burn even as he did so, evoking an incantation he had learned centuries earlier. Reaching out with his mind to lift Wainwright into the air, he spun the man around and around in quick circles like a leaf caught in the wind.

"Tell… me… where it is!" screamed the old man, as his opponent whirled helplessly in the air before him. Wainwright's sword fell from his hand, clattering harmlessly to the stones below. "I will no longer let you live, Colin, but if you tell me where you hid my talisman I will make your death as painless as possible."

"Fuck you, George," Wainwright rasped, revealing a tiny dagger hidden in his palm. In one quick motion, before the old man had a chance to react, he buried the blade deep into his own neck. Blood sprayed in an arc across the room, staining the old man's suit in crimson. Colin Wainwright crumpled to the ground, dead.

* * *

Incredibly, the man had chosen to take his own life rather than give up the location of the artifact. It had always galled the old man that Wainwright had thought he could escape the wrath of his master through the simple act of dying. Of course, it hadn't worked, but regardless of whether he was spirit or flesh, Wainwright refused to give up the location of the artifact. He brought him back to life and killed him over and over again, each method of his demise more gruesome and painful than the last. Finally, in a fit of rage, he had simply made Wainwright disappear.

It was during his reign as the King of England when he first encountered Wainwright, a simple artist commissioned to paint a portrait of his royal majesty George the Second. Wainwright managed to not only perfectly capture the image of the King onto his canvas but also, inexplicably, the essence of the God within.

Entranced by the man's innate sight into his soul, as well as his long black hair and piercing blue eyes, he took the painter under his wing as an apprentice and invited him to join his inner circle. And because his tastes had always leaned toward the masculine (though he'd certainly had more than his fair share of beautiful women), he had taken the painter as his lover as well. The artist resisted his advances at first but eventually came around, as they always did, and finally agreed to share his bed. Perhaps it was mere loneliness, but they quickly proved to be kindred spirits. And slowly, bit by bit, the old man began to reveal secrets to his new companion, giving him power and immortality in exchange for sex and companionship.

For the first hundred years, everything had been perfect. After they had moved on from England to Russia and finally to Germany, however, the younger man began to pull away from him and began to ask questions. Why must we do these things? Why do we kill? He had tried to explain to his lover that one couldn't have power without using that power to rise above the masses, to control them, to eliminate where one saw fit, to change the course of history and to shape and mold it in their likeness. And if one happened to enjoy the pain in said elimination, to drink in the screams of the helpless, well, that wasn't so bad, was it?

Colin never understood that. Finally, just as he'd begun gassing the Jews and was poised to crush the allied forces and take control of the world, his lover had betrayed him, stealing the coin that had been the south point of the swastika, and, with it, destroying the largest empire he had ever created.

# Chapter 26

MORNING CAME early for Shawn and he woke to the realization that his cat was really gone. He and his father had stayed up until three in the morning, talking at the dining room table, sharing nine years of stories about Samson. He told his father the truth, at least about where he'd found the cat, if not the circumstances that he suspected had led to the tabby's death.

His father suggested that perhaps the cat had gotten out and fought with another cat or a dog and, mortally wounded, had managed to sneak back inside the house and crawl into the closet to die. That didn't explain how he wound up in the toy box, but Shawn had gone along with the story, knowing that he couldn't share his suspicions about the fetch.

Exhausted and cried out, the two had finally separated and retreated to the comfort of their own bedrooms. Shawn had hugged his father, wishing he could tell him what was really going on, but knowing that he couldn't risk putting his parents in danger.

Shawn awoke at just ten past seven, when the sun broke through the clouds outside his window to warm his face. He'd only managed to sleep four hours. His eyes burned from the tears he had shed the night before, and his head pounded with an ache that just seemed to get worse no matter how many aspirin he took. The excitement and wonder of his blossoming relationship with Jenny had all but receded while the pain of losing Samson was as sharp and as hot as a blue steel knife, cutting deep into his heart.

He needed answers, and the only place he could think to go to find them was the place he was sure this had all begun: the house on Randolph Street that he and Tanner had broken into just a little over a week ago. He was almost certain that somehow, something they had disturbed or taken from the house – the little silver box Tanner had taken, perhaps, or the necklace, one of the books, the jar of pennies, the nickel, or even the old pocketknife – had garnered the attraction of the fetch and its master, and they were more than willing to kill for it.

\* \* \*

The old house looked different - darker and more foreboding - without Tanner at his side. Shawn took a deep breath and rode straight up the overgrown gravel driveway, cutting through the grass across to the big redwood porch that surrounded the front half of the house. Leaning his bicycle against the great oak tree that crowded the rest of the yard and stretched forty feet into the air, he made his way up the steps and over the creaking porch, yanking open the little screen door only to find that the inner door was locked. Of course it was locked. He didn't want to depend on only one exit and then get trapped in the house, so he'd unlock it once he was inside.

Trudging around the building to the cellar door, he once again slipped inside. Nothing had changed in the ten days since he'd been in the house. His and Tanner's were still the only footprints visible in the layer of dust that covered the floor. Other than the spiders, cockroaches, and other assorted insects that had long ago laid claim to the property, it remained empty.

Pushing through the door that led to the kitchen, flashlight in hand, he heard the noise first: an ear-splitting screech, a mad cackle, as something dive bombed him. He threw himself to the floor, arms over his head, certain that he was about to die. But it was just a crow. A crow that had somehow gotten trapped in the house. Shawn lay huddled on the floor, heart pounding, as the large black bird careened against cabinets, feathers flying everywhere. It circled the room three times before finally rocketing past him and into the dining area.

Clambering to his feet, he followed the bird's trail through the house to the living room just in time to watch it fly into the fireplace and up the chimney. So that's how it had gained entrance into the old house. His heart still thudding hard in his chest, he couldn't help but laugh. If he was this spooked by a bird, how could he handle taking on the fetch again?

Flashlight in hand, he began to explore the house. Pausing this time to give the foyer more than just a cursory glance, he was startled to find another circled star adorning the area, this time cut deep into the warped wooden floor near the north end of the room. The pentagram was right side up, pointing north, so at least, according to the books he'd read, his ancestor hadn't been into devil worship or anything like that.

Shawn thought back to a report he'd written about Halloween in his freshman year of high school. He had become intrigued by the various symbols (the Jack 'o Lantern, the broom, the skeleton) associated with the holiday, and that in turn had led him to the library to research the use of symbology and the original meanings of all the various and sundry ancient symbols. Much like the swastika and other ancient signs, the pentagram had been claimed by various nefarious groups and subverted for their own gain over the years.

The pentagram, Shawn remembered, signified nothing more than a connection to the elements. The highest of the five points represented the spirit, while each of the other four represented the elements of earth, fire, air, and water. The number five, a prime number, also symbolized man because man had five fingers and five toes on each limb, as well as five senses – sight, hearing, smell, touch, and taste. There was also some connection to Phi, the golden ratio upon which everything in the universe was said to be based, but Shawn hadn't quite understood all of it and couldn't recall much now, nearly two years after the fact.

Of course, according to everything he read, the pentagram was also supposed to offer some sort of protection against evil. Despite his taste in literature, Shawn had never really believed in magic, but the last several days had given him pause to question the notion of dismissing anything out of hand. His research had been interesting and had taught him to always investigate everything for himself, never taking what the media at large presented at face value. Perhaps, he thought, that philosophy should be stretched to include things beyond the normal scope of human experience as well. Perhaps his relative had been using the pentagrams to guard the house or something in it against creatures such as the fetch, but whatever he and Tanner had done had somehow messed things up and thrown the whole thing into a mystical tailspin.

Shaking his head, he was glad that his parents weren't here to see him skulking through the house thinking about magic and creatures that shouldn't exist. If they could, they'd probably rent Shawn a room in the same loony bin that Jenny's parents had seemed intent on sending her to before she had finally decided to keep her mouth shut.

Marveling over everything that had happened over the last week, he sensed that the worst was yet to come. He clicked on the flashlight and moved deeper into the house, intent on checking and re-checking anything that he or Tanner had touched on their original treasure hunt.

He grunted in frustration as he reached the top of the staircase that led from the east side of the house to the living quarters above. The house seemed just as deserted as it had the last time he'd walked its halls, and he had found nothing else of value in any of the rooms below. If his theory was right and the fetch had been after something they'd taken from the house, why hadn't it simply retrieved the offending object? Until today he'd kept the necklace and pocketknife in his top dresser drawer, which was easy enough to find, and the Tolkien book in the little bookshelf that adorned one of the walls of his bedroom. And if it wanted any of the things that Tanner had taken from the house, finding them would probably have been just as easy.

Like a punch to the stomach, it hit him; the fetch didn't care about any of those things. What it cared about was the one thing that it hadn't been able to find because neither boy actually had it in their possession when they encountered the monster. The murderous little fetch had been after the nickel that Shawn had thrown into Tanner's coffin. That *had* to be it! It was the only thing that made sense.

And with that realization, another suddenly followed – the moment Shawn had boarded the TWA flight to Texas he had as much as killed his best friend. If Tanner had kept the nickel instead of Shawn, perhaps the monster would have been merciful enough to simply take the money and leave his friend unharmed. But, no, he knew that wasn't right – he had experienced the creature's rage through its own eyes. It would have killed him no matter what, regardless of whether or not he had what its master wanted.

He knew that it didn't do anyone any good to blame himself over something he couldn't have known, though it was tempting to do so, to just give in to depression that had been threatening to engulf him since he found Samson dead last night. But he couldn't do that. He owed that much to Tanner and Samson, and definitely to Jenny. If he wanted to be with her, and he realized just then that he did, he had to trust and protect her, and make sure that whatever horror he and Tanner had inadvertently brought into their lives could wreak no more havoc than it had already wrought.

Shawn soon found himself in the studio that he had visited ten days previous. He wasn't sure what he was looking for but hoped he'd know it when he found it. Searching the wood-working bench brought no new surprises, nor did looking behind the paintings. Perhaps he should just give up and go home. He kicked in frustration at the little toy horse that lay discarded in the middle of the room.

The toy bounced against the far wall of the studio, catching a bit of the old drop cloth that covered the floor on the rebound to expose a patch of hard wood floor beneath. The toy tumbled to a stop just inches from Shawn's feet. Thinking back to the foyer and the downstairs fireplace, a half-formed idea floated into Shawn's head. He hurried across the room to finish the job the toy had started. It was almost as if the two pentagrams downstairs were the two downward points of a bigger star... and there it was. He found a third pentagram, this one hidden under the cloth at the east end of the room, about ninety degrees diagonal from the one in the fireplace just a story below.

Shawn was staring to see a pattern. Puzzling it out in his head, he realized that, based on the positions of the pentacles that he'd already found, there should be two more. And, when taken as a whole, all five symbols would make one large pentagram that encompassed the whole of the house.

If he was right, one pentagram would be located at the west end of the library, while the other would be in the northernmost hallway of the old house or, perhaps, on the north wall of the still-unexplored third floor. Walking out of the studio and across the hall to the musty old library, he felt the world begin to give away around him and was suddenly somewhere else entirely...

He stood just outside the house, hidden in the shadows, under the shade of the huge oak that occupied most of the front yard. In an instant Shawn knew where he was: the fetch wasn't dead after all, and he was once again seeing the world through its monstrous eyes.

He felt its head turn to the right, then to the left, scanning the perimeter of the yard, wanting to make sure that it hadn't missed the meat leaving the house. But, no – his bicycle was still there, just inches from where it stood. Reaching out a huge hand, it raked a sharp gleaming claw over the bicycle's seat, splitting it in half and tumbling stuffing to the ground.

Shawn noticed two things that were different than the last vision he had of the beast; first, his vantage point. The creature was somehow taller than it had been before. Also, the connection between them seemed tenuous at best. Soon he knew it would be severed completely, almost as if whatever had bound the boy to the monster was breaking apart or wearing off. Could it be their blood? Jenny said she kicked the fetch in the mouth just before it bit him, so perhaps their blood had intermingled when they fought and somehow formed a bond.

His thoughts were interrupted by another's, undoubtedly the fetch's master, echoing through both their heads. *Just watch*, the voice told them together, *don't act. My train is just now arriving in Chicago, and I should be to Carthage by nightfall. Tomorrow morning, barring any more surprises, we shall end this little adventure once and for all.*

Shawn felt a surge of hot anger flame through his system at the words that came unbidden to his mind. *Hey, asshole*, thought Shawn at the fetch's mysterious master, willing his words through the conduit he shared with the monster, *how's this for a surprise?*

He could feel the fetch tense up with fear, ready to bolt, and only a harsh word from its master kept it in place. *Who is this*, asked the voice that he could not hear. *Colin?*

*Who's Colin?* Shawn thought to himself, the anger that had only moments ago flooded his body replaced by fear at the voice actually having answered. *Who are you?* He pushed at the beast, already feeling the connection beginning to fade.

*You're not Colin*, answered the voice, ignoring Shawn's question. *Ah, I see: the Spencer boy. Interesting. Just give me what's mine and no one else has to die, least of all your pretty little girlfriend.*

*What do you want?* asked Shawn, playing for more time. He needed to get whatever information he could from the voice vibrating inside his head.

*You know what I want. The talisman is mine, and if it is not in my hands by midnight tonight neither you nor Jenny McGee will live to see the morning's light.*

Shawn stumbled at the force of the man's words, momentarily finding himself back in reality. He knelt in the doorway of the library, one hand pressed against the dusty wall. And then he was once more in the mind of the beast, listening to a sentence already half completed.

*…whatever you want. I can give you wealth, power, women, anything, all for the return of something you probably don't even know how to use to begin with. It's either that or death, boy. Which do you choose?*

So the voice didn't know when he was connected to the beast and when that connection had broken. Knowing that the ominous voice echoing inside his head wasn't privy to his own thoughts gave him some small comfort, as he thought back, *Okay, it's yours. I'll meet you tomorrow at midnight, alone, here in the house. All I want in return is for you to leave us alone. You have to promise me that the fetch won't harm us in any way.* At those last words, the boy felt the monster whose brain he temporarily inhabited begin to boil with anger, wanting nothing more than to dine on his and Jenny's bones. *Then and only then can you have your talisman.*

*No, it cannot be the house. Choose another place.*

*Then meet me at the spot where your puppet killed my best friend,* Shawn sent back, anger echoing through his words.

*Agreed. Why tomorrow, though? Why not tonight?* Shawn felt a great frustration in the man's thoughts, as if time was the one thing that he didn't have at his disposal.

*Because I don't have it with me,* thought Shawn to the voice, doing his best to buy more time. *I've hidden it in a far away place.*

*…You are telling the truth. All right, you have your terms: tomorrow at midnight we shall meet at your lake and you will give me the talisman and I will spare both your lives. Betray me at your peril, human.*

*Human?* Shawn thought, before he could censure himself. *What are you?*

*I am your better, boy. For all intents and purposes, I am your God. You would do well to remember that.*

And just as quickly as it started, the vision ended. Shawn was back in his own body, curled up into a fetal position, covered in dust and lying on the floor of the library. Groaning, his head throbbing behind both temples, he gingerly made his way to his knees, groping in the dark for the flashlight. Finding it, he clicked it on and rose to his feet, dusting himself off.

Whoever this asshole was there were some things that he apparently didn't know and couldn't do. For instance, much like the fetch, he didn't think the master could enter the house, nor could he read Shawn's mind. In fact, the connection between him and the beast seemed to favor the boy over either of his two adversaries. Most importantly, the man didn't seem to know where or what the talisman was, for he had never asked for it by name. Shawn didn't understand why that might be, but he'd hoped he could somehow use it to his advantage when they met at the lake for the exchange.

But he wasn't a fool; he knew the chances of escaping the meeting were somewhere between slim and none, but he also knew that he had to do something to protect Jenny and his family. And then another thought hit him: if the fetch's master was, as he claimed, a god, then why did he need the nickel, and why couldn't he find it on his own?

Forgetting the other pentagrams and any notions he had of further searching the house, Shawn flew down the hallway to the staircase, taking the stairs two at a time, intent on reaching Jenny as quickly as possible. Screeching to a halt just inches from the front door, he was relieved to see his bike, ripped seat and all, standing alone against the great oak tree. The fetch was gone.

# Chapter 27

FRED RUSKIN woke to hear the shower running in his bathroom. Daylight streamed in through the window above his bed, past the brittle and browning Venetian blinds. He knew it must be morning, but beyond that he had no clue what time it was or why the water in the bathroom was running while he was still lying naked in a tangle of sheets.

Rubbing his eyes, he let out a long yawn followed by a low belch. A smile began to work its way across his face as he remembered the events of last night, slowly spreading to meet the big meaty ears that hung on either side of his 52-year old head. In a moment of melancholy-inspired stupidity, he had pressed his police-issue .38 deep into his mouth, ready to take his own life and any possibility of the future that, this morning, he so desperately wanted to have.

\* \* \*

A sharp knock rang without warning through the little apartment, vibrating against the hollow front door, nearly causing Ruskin to discharge his weapon as he jumped from the couch to his feet. Sweat pouring off his brow to meet and mix with the salty tears he hadn't even been aware were flowing from his eyes, the Sheriff slowly uncocked the firearm and flicked on the safety before returning it to the bottom left hand drawer of his desk, beside the necklace that held his and Molly's wedding rings.

Crossing the room, he peered through the peephole - it was Candy. Breathing deeply, trying to compose himself, Ruskin jumped again when the knock sounded for a second time, nearly falling over backwards. Unlatching the safety chain, he quickly swung open the door.

Candy Martin stood in his doorway, still in her waitress uniform, her eyes staring down at the dirty and worn 'Welcome' mat below her feet. "Can I come in, Sheriff," she asked, the tinge of a challenge in her voice, "or would you prefer me to just do you right here in the doorway?"

"Why, of course… I mean, please come in," Ruskin stuttered. He held the door open for the bedraggled waitress. He'd lived in the little apartment for nearly ten years, ever since he'd gotten the job of county sheriff, and this was the first time a female presence had ever graced the doorway to his apartment, much less his living room.

The woman walked into the house, pulling the door from his shaking hands. She gently shut it, turning the lock and then sliding the safety chain into place. "So where do you want to screw me, Sheriff?" She asked, turning to look him in the eyes. "How about the couch, or maybe even on the dining room table, if you actually have a dining room in this pit, that is. Or maybe, just maybe, you'd prefer to do it the old-fashioned way, on the bed. Just tell me, Sheriff, so I can start earning my two-hundred dollar tip."

"Candy, I'm so sorry," he mumbled, as the woman's eyes bore into his own. "I'm a drunken old man who's done a stupid, stupid thing. Please, you don't have to do this. Just keep the money, and you'll never have to see my face again."

"I don't need your charity, Sheriff!" she spat at him. Eyes full of anger, she slowly began to unbutton her blouse. "Never let it be said that Candace Martin doesn't deliver what she's been paid for."

"Please, Candy, I…"

"Shut up!" She pushed him hard in the chest, sending him stumbling backwards and onto the sofa. She continued to unbutton her blouse, giving a little flourish with her hands as she undid the last button. Slowly, tantalizingly, she let the blouse fall from her shoulders to the floor, revealing a black bra trimmed with lace ribbons. Dancing now to invisible music, her eyes closed, slowly swaying her hips, she gently caressed her breasts, cupping them in her hands.

"Do you like what you see, Sheriff?" she asked, moving her arms behind her back to unhook the bra. Letting the straps fall to the side, she slid her hands up and under her breasts, holding the satiny material in place as she slowly leaned forward, just inches from his face.

"Please," he choked, wanting her despite his embarrassment, "you don't have to do this." He felt the crotch of his trousers grow taut with pressure.

"Don't you want me, Sheriff?" she mocked, gradually letting her bra slip away and tumble to the floor. Moving her hands to the waistband of her skirt, she exposed her breasts to him.

"Don't you want to get what you paid for?" She let her skirt drop to the ground, revealing a pair of black panties that matched her bra. Kicking the high-heeled black pumps from her feet, she began to sway as she reached out to take his hand, bending down to tease the tip of his index finger with her tongue, slowly sucking it into her mouth.

"You don't have to do this!" he yelled, rising to her feet as he pulled his finger from her mouth. "You don't have to sell yourself to me, Candy. I'm pathetic! I'm damaged goods. You're worth more than this."

"Am I? Jack sure didn't seem to think so. Right after you left, he fired me. 'You can't slap the goddamned country Sheriff,' he said, 'no matter how much of an asshole he is.'"

Jesus, he'd gotten her fired? "It's okay, Candy. It's okay. I'll talk to Jack, we'll get you your job back."

"The thing is," she said, ignoring his promises, "I could really use the money." She reached out to take his wrists, pulling him toward her, putting the palms of his hands on her breasts. "I've sold myself so many times before, even if it wasn't for sex, so I might as well become your whore as anyone else's." Tears welled up in her pretty hazel eyes, and the Sheriff felt his heart break.

Ashamed, he carefully pulled his hands from her breasts, embracing her in his huge bear-like arms. She began to sob hysterically into his shoulder. "Candy, I'm so sorry. I'm so very sorry. Please, you're worth more than this, you're worth more than me, more than I could ever be."

Sniffling, tears running from her eyes, she peeled herself from his embrace and knelt to the ground before him. Riffling through the pockets of her skirt, she stood up with a wad of cash in her hand, pressing it into his. "I can't take your money," she whispered. The light from overhead bathed her in a dim yellow glow, accentuating the curves of her body and the lift of her breasts.

He held the money in his hand, ashamed at the way he had tried to buy her. Averting her gaze, he moved toward the couch, intending to snatch the red and white checkered quilt he always kept there so she could cover herself. Before he could reach it, however, something amazing happened. She took one step, then two, pressing herself against Ruskin's chest, pulling him down to her, kissing him deeply. Their tongues danced in rhythm to their desires as her hands found their way to his shirt, ripping it from his chest, buttons flying everywhere.

"Are you sure..." he started to ask, between kisses, but fell silent as her hands moved down his chest and began unbuckling his belt. The money fell from his hand, no longer important, as he was overcome with a desire he'd forgotten he could even feel.

Sliding his pants off, she whispered, "I want to do this," and then guided his hands to her panties. "Just not for your money, okay? It's been a long time for me too." She shivered as she felt his fingers move down the length of her legs, sliding the silky black material over her hips, past her thighs and to the floor to join the mix of clothing at their feet.

She lowered herself onto the couch, pulling him down on top of her. Bucking her hips to meet his, they began to make love. They moved slowly at first, tentatively, awkward and unsure, but their hunger soon took over, finally ending in a crescendo that left them both breathless and bathed in sweat. He felt more alive than he had in a very long time.

"That was... amazing," Ruskin said afterward, gazing into the eyes of the first woman he'd had sex with since his wife had been taken from him over fifteen years ago. "Thank you."

"Sometimes," she said, with just the hint of a smile, "it's the things that you *don't* have to pay for that brings you the most pleasure."

"The best things in life are indeed free," he agreed with a gleam in his eye, rolling away from her and to his feet. "And my bed happens to be free at the moment. Would you do me the honor of joining me there and spending the night with me?"

"I think I'd like that very much," said the waitress, reaching out to take the Sheriff's hand, allowing herself to be led into his bedroom.

* * *

"Hey there," smiled Candy Martin, standing in Ruskin's small shower, wearing nothing but a thick lather of soap as the hot water sprayed down across her legs. "Care to join me? I really think you could use it," she said, softening the comment by sticking her tongue out at him.

"You're probably right," he smiled, dropping his towel and stepping into the steam. She truly was the best thing to come into his life in a very, very long time, and it nauseated him to think that he'd almost avoided the entire experience by jacking a metal shell into his brain. "I hope I won't kick myself later for asking, but do you regret anything we did last night?"

"I was drunk then," she answered, looking deep into his eyes. "I'm sober now, and I wouldn't trade last night for anything." She reached out to him, pulling him close, running her soapy fingers through his hairy chest as she kissed him gently on the lips. "Nor would I trade the nights to come – that is, if you want there to be nights to come…" she trailed off, looking at him.

"I wouldn't miss it for the world," he answered, pulling her hard against his body, lifting her with ease from the tub and into his embrace. "Not for the world."

## Chapter 28

THE MAN IN THE trench coat walked through the gates of the Moss Ridge Cemetery, his coat rustling with the afternoon breeze. The sun beat down through the trees and gravestones, creating a crisscross pattern of light on the ground. Crows circled overhead, looking for the best trees to build their nests and hide their treasures. He smiled, brushing an errant strand of long blonde hair from his eyes to get a better look at the birds. It was a glorious day. He knew, though, that the night to come would be just as ugly as today was beautiful.

He wished there was another way, but if there was he couldn't quite see it. He'd need the woman's help to set things right; he just didn't like having to wake the dead. Once they finally fell asleep, they deserved to rest in peace.

He smiled again as he noticed a pair of children – they couldn't have been more than seven or eight – playing hide-and-seek among the tombstones. Just as the first child finished counting to a hundred, the second stepped inside a huge oak tree.

"That's cheating," he smiled, reaching through the tree to tousle the boy's hair. His playmate giggled, then ran to tag the boy and begin the game anew.

The spirits were everywhere; over a hundred strong roaming the graveyard, many times more asleep below it. He could see all the spirits, but not all of them could see him, and only a few could actually see each other. They were all trapped here, most unable to leave the confines of the cemetery, held back by the living or by their own tenuous grasp on what they remembered of their lives.

He was like a shining beacon of life to the spirits. All eyes turned to follow him, watching his progress as he walked purposefully down the path toward a twin set of gravestones.

Sitting on a stone bench, just to his right, two men were having an animated conversation about the weather, while an elderly couple – recently buried, he could tell – were arguing over whether or not the woman had forgotten to turn off the stove before driving to their Saturday night Bingo game. Spirits didn't drive, of course, and could rarely if ever leave the cemetery, but the couple hadn't yet fully realized they were dead. He dismissed them; they'd figure it out soon enough, and who was he to hurry along the process?

Finally, he found the plot he'd been looking for. With a sigh, he knelt close to the ground, laid one hand on the larger grave's marker and the other in the dirt surrounding it, then whispered, "Wake up, Margaret."

# Chapter 29

RUSKIN RECEIVED the call at eleven sharp, just minutes after Candy left his little apartment to pick up Samantha from a sleep-over at a friend's. It was the Mayor, and they were putting him on temporary suspension pending an investigation into the missing deputy. Apparently, someone had gotten it into their head that he might have had something to do with the disappearance, as he'd been the last person to see the Cajun alive. He was to report immediately to the little Sheriff's office across from the courthouse to surrender his badge and gun and submit to questioning by the new acting-Sheriff Jesse Floyd. Knowing Floyd's lust for the limelight, he was almost positive it had been the former sergeant who had reported him to the mayor in the first place.

Ruskin knew he should be angry, should be upset, but he just didn't care. After last night and then this morning, he wasn't about to let anyone terminate his new lease on life. He'd survive the interview down at the cop shop as well as the loss of his job that would surely follow. Hell, if he had to, he'd go back to security work, maybe even move to Macomb or Quincy if the position called for it. He'd come by his work in the police department honestly – both his father and his father before him had been cops – but it was no longer his life. He could do something else if he had to. He thought he might even prefer it that way.

Whistling Billy Joel's "Piano Man," he dressed in an old pair of black slacks and a ratty crew neck t-shirt, marveling to himself how good it felt to be getting ready for the day in something other than his customary Sheriff outfit. Slipping on another pair of dirty socks (he really needed to do laundry one of these days, and probably update his wardrobe as well) he quickly laced up his old pair of tennis shows and, badge and gun in hand, got in his cruiser and drove to the office for his meeting with Floyd.

\* \* \*

"What's up, Shawn?" smiled Jenny, opening the door. Her parents were both at work and she'd been re-reading one of her favorite books, *A Wrinkle in Time*, when she'd heard a sudden, frantic knocking at the door. Getting up from the couch to investigate, she was pleasantly surprised to see Shawn's deep blue eyes looking back at her through the window.

"Can I come in?" he asked, out of breath, as she swung open the door.

"Sure, Shawn, I mean, my parents wouldn't like it, but they're not here right now, so I guess so. What's up?"

Shawn pushed in past her, turning to lock the door behind him. "Jenny," he blurted out, looking hesitant but determined to go on anyway, "the fetch isn't dead. I just had another vision, and I spoke to the person who's behind all this."

"What are you talking about?" she exclaimed, a sinking feeling in her chest. The room began to spin. Fearing she might hyperventilate, Jenny walked into the living room and sat down on the big brown overstuffed couch that graced most of the south wall, patting the buttoned cushion beside her.

"Shawn, you killed it. We both saw it. I don't understand," the words came tumbling out in a rush. Shawn sat beside her, reaching out to take her hand.

"Jenny, it's back. Don't ask me how, because I don't know, but it's alive. And it's bigger than it was, just like when you saw it at the lake."

This was all too much for her to take in. Closing her eyes and breathing deeply, feeling as though her life were spinning out of control, Jenny asked Shawn to start at the beginning.

"God, Shawn, I'm so sorry about Samson!" she half-whispered as a lump caught in her throat, after he had told her everything. Tears rolling down her check, she reached out to hug Shawn. "Why didn't you call me?"

"I don't know. I don't know anything anymore."

"If what you said is true – no, I believe you, Shawn, I promise I do," she interrupted as the boy started to speak, "If magic is real, and after all we've seen I'm not sure we can doubt anything anymore, the fetch's master must need the nickel for a spell or something. Did he give you any clue why he wanted it?"

"He said that if we didn't give him the talisman - he just called it a talisman, and I don't think he knows what it looks like, that it's the nickel – he'll kill us. I'm pretty sure he will anyway, if he can. I know the fetch wants to, even if by some wild stretch of the imagination its master doesn't."

"But why did you tell him you'd take it to the lake? I mean, it's gone. It's buried with Tanner, and there's no way to get it back, unless... Oh no, Shawn, we cannot dig up my brother's grave! We can't!" Jenny's face turned pale and she looked as though she might throw up. With trembling hands, she took Shawn's face and pulled him close. "We cannot do this!"

"I may not have a choice," said Shawn, pulling away to look down at his feet. "They're going to kill us no matter what I do, but if I actually *have* the nickel, maybe I'll have a chance."

"Isn't there another way? There *has* to be another way."

"If there is, I don't know it. It's the only thing I can think to do…"

"You keep saying 'I' instead of 'We', Shawn. I'm going with you, no matter what you do, no matter where you go. Okay?"

"No, it's not okay! I've lost my best friend and I've lost my cat, and I'm not about to lose you too."

"But if we both die, how will you know?"

Shawn considered this for a moment. "Good point," he finally admitted, with the hint of a smile, "but you're still not going."

"Can we at least try something else first?" Jenny asked, ignoring Shawn's bravado and gesturing for him to follow her into Tanner's room. "If magic is real, then maybe Ouija boards are too."

* * *

The meeting had not gone well for Fred Ruskin. Acting Sheriff Floyd used the opportunity to berate and humiliate him in front of all of his officers and even the Mayor, who had shown up halfway through the process as if he were a shark following a trail of fresh blood through the ocean. Finally, after over an hour of questions to which he had no answers, they let him go, stripping him of his badge, gun, and his police car, not to mention what little honor and integrity he still had left.

Larry Joe Reynolds, a jovial, gray-haired man in his early sixties, offered to drive him home. But he knew if he accepted, Reynolds would be looked at with suspicion and distrust from the new Sheriff and the other Carthage cops, and he didn't want the man to have to go through that just to save him from walking. So he declined, instead deciding to hoof it down the square and the five blocks to his dingy little apartment on Walnut Lane.

His bravado of the morning had left him as surely as his badge had. What had last night really meant to Candy, anyway? A one-night stand with a man some fifteen years her senior. He'd been fooling himself into thinking he could have a life, when his peers and subordinates had both told him in no uncertain terms that was not to be the case. He was a drunk, they'd told him, just someone going through the motions of being a real cop, and once his suspension was permanent he'd never work in Hancock County again.

They didn't really suspect him of offing the Cajun, he knew, but used that possibility as an excuse to get the city council to agree to suspend him. And it had worked like the proverbial charm. Apparently, Floyd had been bucking for his job for years, and he'd been too stupid – too wrapped up in himself and his pain – to see it. And once Floyd had the Mayor on his side, it was only a matter of waiting for him to screw up, which he had most certainly done.

If only he'd reported Delacroix's disappearance the night that it happened, he might still have his job and whatever respect he'd managed to eke out from the community he had called home for the better part of a decade. He hadn't wanted to report the missing deputy because he feared being embarrassed over losing track of the Cajun, so instead had done his best to sweep the whole incident under the rug. In doing so, however, he let his own pride and fear blind him to the bigger picture – that a living, breathing human being had vanished, and that it was his job to find him. No matter what he felt about Delacroix's personal life, he had a responsibility to protect a fellow officer, and he had failed. The bliss he'd discovered this morning only served to make the disgust he felt with himself all the more sharp and raw.

Like a dying man crawling through the desert in search of an oasis, Ruskin slowly walked past his 1972 yellow Pacer – his "civilian" car – pausing to look at the severely dented and scraped fender. He'd been out drinking one night a couple of weeks ago and, drunk as a skunk, had managed to career into a big stone fence over on Randolph. The house had been abandoned a long time ago so he didn't feel too bad about the damage he'd caused, but he'd been embarrassed enough to put off bringing the Pacer into Mosely's to have it fixed. But none of that seemed to matter now.

He wound his way up to the apartment. The air conditioner was broken again, and it was a good ninety degrees in his little suite of rooms, just ten degrees cooler than it was outside. Already soaked in sweat from his walk under the hot summer sun, the suspended lawman quietly closed the door behind him. He kicked off his shoes and pulled his shirt over his head, dropping it to the ground. Clicking on the little oscillating fan that stood on top of an old barstool next to the front door, he padded past the dining table and into the kitchen on sock feet, in search of a drink much stronger and more potent than even an oasis could provide.

* * *

Candy Martin smiled as she allowed her thoughts to drift back to last night. She hadn't had sex in nearly five years and certainly hadn't planned on bedding anyone last night, let alone the Sheriff, but she was glad that she did. She'd gotten totally wasted after being fired, which was something she hadn't done since her days at Carthage high school.

The night had ended much better than it started. How she hated that man when he'd offered her the money, her emotions turning to a white hot anger that folded in on itself when Jack Darling fired her. But the hatred and self-loathing wasn't anything a few shots of gin wouldn't cure. Two hundred dollars richer and high as a kite, she'd finally made her way to Ruskin's house intending to become a prostitute, selling her soul to him, screwing the fat, smelly bastard for all she was worth.

He had surprised her with his reticence, and again with his insistence that she keep the money but leave with her dignity intact. Still inebriated, she had kept pushing, finally stripping for him, before he put a stop to her drunken dance. And then something exciting happened, something that hadn't happened in a very long time: sensing a kindred spirit somewhere inside the man, she realized that she'd actually been attracted to him for years, and could act upon it now that the money was no longer part of the equation. He'd apologized over and over again, berating himself, until she'd finally had to silence his self-recriminations with a kiss. One thing led to another, as things sometimes do, and she'd ended up making love to him right there on the couch, then twice more in bed, and once again in the shower the morning after.

She intended to take this new relationship one step at a time. She hadn't felt this way about a man since Steve, the snake who had left her and her daughter for another woman nearly a dozen years earlier. This time, she knew, she'd be careful. Though she'd had sex with many different men during her thirty-seven years, she'd only given her heart to one of them, and he had betrayed her. Worse still, he had abandoned their daughter. If she was going to risk falling in love a second time, she damn well better make sure it was going to stick before taking the plunge and putting not only her own heart on the line but the heart of her daughter as well.

With all of that in mind, the blonde waitress pulled her little blue Toyota into a space in front of the Black Hawk apartments. She had tried to call Ruskin at the police station but the man who answered, an Officer Reynolds, said he was home for the day. Not knowing the Sheriff's telephone number, she'd decided to pay him a visit in person, to invite him out for a late lunch. It was almost two in the afternoon, and Samantha was spending the day with a friend at the pool, so if a late lunch turned into a late something else…Well, she thought she could live with that. After all, five years was a long time, and who could blame a girl for wanting to feed an appetite she'd thought lost a long time ago?

Candy was struck by what a beautiful day it was as she locked her little Toyota. The sun was bright and she could hear cardinals chirping in the trees, perhaps trading stories about where the best worms were to be found or the best places to fly once winter came. She smiled to herself, wondering what this afternoon would bring. Candy realized that, though she'd driven by the little complex of maybe two dozen apartments probably at least a hundred times, she'd never really noticed it. It was actually quite pretty, for what it was. The owners kept the landscaped lawn well manicured, and a little group of peonies growing up around an outside light pole made her feel welcomed.

Walking down the concrete sidewalk and through the entrance to the building, she quickly made her way up the interior stairs to apartment 2-C. Knocking on the door once, then twice, seconds seemed to stretch into minutes, giving her pause to consider whether she had remembered the correct apartment number. Finally, a good two minutes after she'd first rapped on his door, she heard the sound of someone unlatching the security bolt from inside.

"I'm coming, I'm coming," said a gruff voice from within, as the door creaked open to reveal Fred Ruskin dressed only in a pair of brown slacks and white socks, holding a lit cigarette in one hand and a bottle of whiskey in the other. Smoke coalesced up around his face, giving the impression of a man on fire, being burned at the stake.

"Fred, what's wrong?" she asked, wincing as the stale smell of tobacco and alcohol hit her hot in the face. Coughing, waving her hand in front of her, she reached out to take his cigarette. She tamped it out on the doorframe, dropping it to the carpeted little welcome mat below.

"Wrong? Oh, nothing's wrong, everything's right as rain," he mumbled, stumbling against the doorframe. His eyes were bloodshot and unfocused. "Jus' lost my job, thas all, and the new Sheriff wants to arrest me for ob.. ob.. making is so justice isn't unobstructed, for lack of a better term. Oh, and my wife and daughter were raped and murdered, which is how I wound up here in this godforsaken town in the firs' place. Goddamn Grainger, it's all his fault, ruined my life…"

"Jesus, Fred, you're drunk!" she whispered, recoiling from him. She knew the story of his wife and daughter – he'd told it to her at least three times, though never when he was sober – and though her heart ached for him with each telling, she'd never expected to have to compete with a woman who'd been dead for over a decade. But what was this about being fired? She knew he'd lost his job as a detective on the Chicago police force over ten years ago, but as far as she knew he was still the county Sheriff.

"Fred," she continued, forcing herself to reach out to him, to steady his trembling arm, to guide him back into the apartment and to the little brown couch on which they'd made love less than twelve hours ago, "you need to tell me what's going on."

"My life ish shit, thas' whas' going on. Meet a nice girl, try to pay her to sleep with me, then get shitcanned the next day. And she wouldn't even take my money, like my money's not good enough for her or sumthin'..."

"I didn't take your money because I'm not a whore!" she yelled, her hazel eyes blazing with anger. "Damn it, Fred! Damn it! I thought… well, it doesn't matter what I thought, because I was obviously wrong. Last night was a stupid, stupid mistake, and I'm too old to make mistakes like this."

"Candy?" he slurred, seeming to see her for the first time. He reached out to her, only to have her pull away. "I'm sorry. Everything I touch turns to shit, just big, brown piles of steaming, stinking shit."

"You touched me last night," she half-whispered, her voice shaking, "does that mean I'm shit too?"

"No, I didn't mean it that way," Ruskin stuttered, trying to form more words, failing. Finally, he just shrugged, and said, "I told you, I'm jus' damaged goods. You're better off without me, thash for sure."

"You know, I think you're right," she said, turning on her heels to walk briskly down the stairs. Reaching the door to the outside, she turned around one last time, looking up the stairs at the sad, disheveled man standing above her. "I was so happy this morning, Fred, so happy… damn it all to hell, anyway!" She stepped through the door, the glass rattling behind her as she slammed it shut, walking out of his life just as quickly as she'd walked into it the night before.

* * *

"Aw, shit!" said Ruskin, some part of his inebriated brain knowing he had screwed up very badly. Gently closing his front door, he stumbled through the maze of heat and smoke that was his apartment, gulping down whiskey as he went. *If I only had my gun, I could do what I should have done last night and end this pathetic excuse for a life once and for all.* But his gun, along with his badge and his car, had been confiscated this morning.

Floyd and Grainger had joined forces to ruin his life. Hell, even Delacroix had been in on the fix, deciding to skip town at the worst possible time for no good reason other than to sabotage his then-boss' life. Everyone, it seemed, had conspired against him, including Molly, Jessica, the McGees, and now Candy Martin, who had the gall to come into his life, make him fall in love with her, and then leave the very next day. And the bitch wouldn't even take his two hundred dollars!

Taking another long swig of whiskey, he gagged and coughed as it burned down his throat. The once and former Sheriff of Hancock County picked up one of the big wooden chairs from his dining room and threw it full force across the living room into the television. The impact sent the little brown box tumbling backward from the flimsy wooden stand it had rested on, crashing to the floor in a splash of sparks and broken glass.

"Oh, God," he mumbled, bringing his hand to his mouth. He bent over in sudden agony, throwing up all over his slacks and socks, vomiting every last drop of whiskey from his stomach in a spray that arced and splashed halfway across the room. "Oh, God," he repeated, over and over, as he fell to his knees and then to his side, clutching his legs as close to his chest as his pot-bellied stomach would allow. "Oh, God, it's not them, it's not even Grainger. It's me, and it's been me all along... all along..."

# Chapter 30

THE OLD MAN sat alone in the little compartment he had rented, feeling the train chug beneath his feet as it moved away from Chicago and toward Quincy. He'd been alone for so long, even before Wainwright had left him. He'd had lovers, followers, even confidants, but he'd never been able to share the breadth of his life with any of them – they just couldn't understand. Power came with a price.

Sighing to himself, the old man focused his attention on the present. The train would arrive in about four hours, and it would take him another hour after that to reach Carthage. He was so close he could taste it.

Staring idly out the window, watching the world whip by as if he were viewing it through an old kinescope, he chuckled to himself, thinking how easy it had been to fool the boy. Their connection through the fetch had served him better than he could possibly have imagined. He now knew where the talisman was and, if not for the accursed hallowed ground protecting it, he would have ordered the fetch to dig it up and then dispose of the two teenagers. As it stood, he could not retrieve the nickel himself, nor could he have the fetch do it, but there were other ways…

Smiling to himself, he turned his thoughts away from the present and instead to the past, to better times, to the days before Wainwright had betrayed him, when he had controlled large armies and held the world in his sway. The old man allowed himself to revel in his memories, remembering past victories, past glories. It had all begun so very, very long ago.

He had lived several thousand years and was so old that he had long ago lost count of the many centuries he'd walked the Earth. He had worn many different faces over the years; he had been a priest, a Pharaoh, an Emperor, a King, a dictator, and once, in the beginning, even a god. He had had many names, many faces, and through each he had ruled empires and nations before moving on to a new people to enslave, a new civilization to conquer, a new life to mold. Once he had grown bored with the old, once the power he'd amassed had failed to amuse him and to keep his attention, or when the spirit moved him and he was called upon to find the next talisman in the set of five, he would move on to other challenges.

And, each time, he would change bodies with one of his disciples, giving each of them a gift beyond their wildest dreams, letting them have the coveted niche he had so artfully carved out for himself. He would leave them with the riches of an empire, taking only their face, and the artifacts, with him. And each time, without fail, the empire had collapsed behind him, wilting as though it were a delicate flower deprived of life-giving water. And somehow, this did not bother him. He had half come to expect it, and would have been surprised had it even once failed to happen.

The old man didn't remember his childhood, nor did he remember his original name, and only recalled bits and pieces of the first twenty or thirty years of his life. In fact, his first full memory was that of being a Mayan priest nearly five centuries before Christ was born. Before his awakening, he had lived on the continent of South America. One hot summer day, after a blood sacrifice designed to help the hunters and gatherers provide food for the rest of his tribe, a vision had mysteriously come to him. It had instructed him to seek out the first of five great talismans, one for each point of the star. He was to unite them, melding each of the properties they held together into one, making the whole of their parts far greater than the sum. He dared not question the thought, dared not give up the power that the voice inside his head offered. That night, after everyone had fallen asleep, he left his quarters and wound his way through the jungle, searching, waiting for the first talisman to call out to him.

The first object he found had been a simple jaguar's tooth, buried deep in the jungle, at the base of a great Monkey Puzzle tree. Directed by the vision, he had dug frantically in the mud and rocks, ripping away his fingernails, his hands awash in cuts and blood by the time he had pulled the tooth from the soil that surrounded the tree.

The tooth didn't look special, didn't even feel special. It was cracked and gray, and for a moment he thought his quest had been for nothing. And then he felt something open up inside him, questing, moving outward to meet the energy that he could suddenly feel emanating from the tooth. And in an instant, his wounds were gone, healed by the simple touch of the decaying remains of the Jaguar.

That first talisman had given him power over death, and, with it, the ability to truly live in the manner that he so richly deserved. He had immediately returned to his village, walked straight into the Chief's quarters, past his guards, and had broken the old man's neck with his bare hands. Afterwards, as the guards stood gaping, he had ripped the man's throat open with only his teeth, drinking deeply and freely of the blood that flowed from the chief's jugular.

After that, it was no hard task to declare himself the reincarnation of Ahpuc, the Mayan god of death, come to put down an unworthy Chief and rule the village in his stead. The entire settlement had cowered before him and his new-found ability to mete out life and death at the merest whims; all through the use of the jaguar's tooth.

He enjoyed his reign as a god, all the while knowing that it must come to an end; that he must seek out and find the other four talismans that sang through his blood. The power from the other artifacts called to him as a newborn calf might call to its mother. They needed him. He didn't know how he knew these things, and he didn't care. The power he had long craved was finally his for the taking.

Abandoning the village, he once again journeyed into the jungle, this time intent on crossing half the world on a quest that would take him into the heart of Egypt and to the hiding place of the second talisman. Less than a century later, he had gathered all of the objects together, taking what he wanted from anyone who dared to cross him.

Over the years, he had learned a lot about power. He had studied every ancient text he could find, learning how to use this great ability with which he had been blessed. The energy was everywhere, but few people had the ability to harness it, with fewer still able to wield it effectively. With the talismans, however, his ability to use the energy grew exponentially. The jaguar's tooth alone gave him perhaps a hundred times the strength of an ordinary magician, while adding another of the five talismans gave him the power of ten thousand. All five objects had given him the power of a god; no, it *made* him a god, and he craved that power again, had to have it, and would eventually die without it.

But soon, very soon, he would have it again. He would have everything he had ever wanted, everything he had lost and then some, and then the world would change, would be remade in his image. And that's when the fun would really begin.

# Chapter 31

"TANNER AND I tried to contact his grandfather once," said Shawn, looking at the Ouija board spread out over his best friend's bed, "but it didn't work. These things don't work, Jenny. It's just a game."

"And monsters weren't real until a few days ago," countered Jenny. She'd known that Tanner kept the Ouija board hidden in the back of his closet (their parents didn't approve of the game) and she intended to use it to contact her brother.

She hoped that he could tell them whether or not the nickel was the object the man was after. She prayed with all her heart that it wasn't, for she could think of nothing she wanted to do less than dig up her brother's body.

Jenny knelt down to examine the shiny wooden board upon which Parker Brothers had printed the alphabet, numbers from zero to nine, and the words yes, no, and goodbye.

"So how does this work? I knew where Tanner kept it hidden, but I never used it."

"Okay, when Tanner and I did this, we just concentrated on the name of the person we wanted to contact and then asked them questions." Shawn explained, kneeling beside Jenny to touch the planchette with both hands. "Just put your fingertips on the edge… yeah, like that. When we ask a question, the pointer's supposed to move around the board to spell out a word or answer yes or no."

Jenny touched the edge of the pointer with her fingers and felt an electric current slowly move up her hands, through her arms, and into her chest. Like the whisper of a slowly-falling feather, an unexpected name tickled Jenny's thoughts, causing her to blink in confusion. "Aunt Margaret," she whispered, unsure of why she had said it.

And why was it so cold in here? The hairs on Jenny's arms prickled and stood on end as the air around her dropped nearly ten degrees in half as many seconds.

"Huh?" asked Shawn, his breath creating a cloud of condensation on Jenny's glasses. He shivered, then asked, "Who's Aunt Margaret?"

Jenny started to reply, but before she could speak the pointer began to move beneath her fingers, touching first the letter "L," then "E," and finally "T".

"'Let'?" asked Shawn, his eyes growing larger as the planchette slid across the board. "Let what?"

"'Me in'," said Jenny, her eyes following the device. Finally, it stopped moving. "'Let me in.' Okay," she said, her eyes opened wide in wonder, "come in."

A pinprick of yellow light suddenly appeared a few inches above the middle of the board, hanging in the air, slowly rotating. It grew larger and, as the light expanded, also gained brightness as more and more colors appeared to weave together in a frantically spinning pattern. Finally, an image coalesced into view. It was a face much like Jenny's, though older, and with shorter hair. Like a badly-synced movie, words seemed to tumble from the woman's mouth seconds before she actually spoke them. "I don't have much time," she said, "It was difficult to cross over, so please listen to me."

"This can't be real," mumbled Shawn, staring open-mouthed at the spirit. "It just can't..."

"Shawn," the spirit interrupted, its words finally syncing with the mouth that spoke them, "Sarah wants me to tell you that she loves you very much and that she's sorry that she didn't have time to get to know you."

Shawn's face grew white and he looked weak in the knees, almost as if someone had punched him in the stomach. "How did you…"

"I told you, I don't have much time," warned the spirit. "I had to make you believe, before it was too late."

Jenny slowly turned her eyes back toward the vision. "Is it really you?" she whispered.

"Yes, it's really me," smiled Margaret, "and I've come a very long way because your life is in danger. The old man has to be stopped, and there's no one else left to do it."

"But why are you here?" asked Jenny, tears rolling down her cheeks. "We were trying to call Tanner, but…"

"That was my doing, honey. I needed you to invite me here before I could come."

"Can… can we defeat the old man?" asked Shawn, talking for the first time since Margaret had appeared. His face was white as a sheet, his eyes wide with wonder.

"In a matter of speaking, yes," Margaret said, beginning to fade, "though it might require a little luck."

"Wait," gasped Jenny, reaching for Margaret, watching helplessly as her hands passed through the spirit. "Can't you tell us anything else?"

"Don't believe everything you see," Margaret said, her face growing more translucent. "Faith is necessary," she glanced at Shawn, "but so is doubt."

And then she was gone.

"Well, that didn't happen when Tanner and I used the board," Shawn said, finally breaking the silence. He reached out to take Jenny's hand.

"My God…" said Jenny, still staring at the Ouija board, her fingers intertwining with Shawn's. "It actually worked."

"But what did we actually learn?"

"We learned that we can defeat him."

"Yeah, well, there is that, I guess."

"Shawn?" asked Jenny, turning to look into his eyes. "Who's Sarah?"

"She was… she was my sister," Shawn admitted, his face a mixed mask of pain and wonder. "She was born when I was seven, and she died less than three months later. We had to share a room because there weren't enough rooms in the house, but I didn't mind. I was thrilled to have a little sister… "

"Shawn," Jenny said, her mouth forming an 'o' in surprise. "I didn't know. I'm so sorry…"

"I remember saying my prayers the night before she died. I asked God to look over her, to keep her healthy and safe. Instead, I woke up in the middle of the night and found her dead in her crib. I'll never forget that. Her skin was so blue, and it wasn't quite as warm as it should have been…"

"Shawn…" she started, putting her hand on his shoulder.

"I haven't had much faith in anything ever since," he interrupted, a wistful smile forming on his lips. "But your dead aunt said my little sister loves me, and if I believe that was real, that any of this has been real, well… then maybe it'll all be okay. Maybe I do have a little faith left in me after all."

# Chapter 32

FRED RUSKIN lay tangled in sweaty sheets, awake, alone, and staring at the ceiling, just as he'd been doing for the last hour and a half. He was also very drunk, and had been since at least noon, maybe longer. He honestly couldn't remember. It was sweltering inside his apartment and he felt like he was going to puke again. Fighting down the urge to vomit, he forced himself to his feet, grabbing the bedpost for balance, and shuffled across his little apartment to the refrigerator to down another bottle of Pabst Blue Ribbon.

Having long ago exhausted all of the whiskey in his stash and being down to just the beer, the former Sheriff knew he would soon run out. And when he did, he'd finally do what he should have done last night, should have done a long time ago – end his pathetic excuse for an existence once and for all. Downing the beer in three quick gulps, he slammed the refrigerator door shut with a violence that punctuated his plans. It had finally come to this, just as he'd known it would all those many years ago when he'd cradled his daughter's lifeless form in his lap. He'd wanted to die then, too, and fear of the release that death would bring was the only thing that kept him from turning his gun on himself right then and there, joining his wife and daughter in eternal rest. But that fear had long ago faded, and now he would welcome the release that had once scared him and made him feel weak in the knees.

A thought kept trying to break through the morass of his drunken mind, and again he pushed it down, holding it, strangling it, not daring to examine it in the light of day. Candy Martin. For an instant, for the briefest of moments, he'd found hope. When they'd made love, the first time for him since his wife was murdered, he'd been fool enough to think that maybe he could find redemption in her warm embrace. But she'd seen the man he truly was, what he had become over the last fifteen years, and had been repulsed and sickened. She ran away, leaving him to wallow in his own filth.

He didn't blame her. Even as they'd made love that night and then again in the morning, something in the back of his head kept telling him that he couldn't have this, didn't deserve it, and sooner or later it would end, leaving him worse off than he'd been had it never happened in the first place. He hadn't known it would end practically before it had begun, though he should have. He was every much a ghost as his wife and daughter, and he knew from experience that you couldn't successfully love a ghost. Candy couldn't love him, not really, and it was better that it had ended when it did, before he'd really had the chance to hurt her.

Ruskin walked to the desk where last night he'd deposited the necklace that contained his and Molly's wedding rings. *I'll be with you soon, Molly,* echoed the words inside his head, as he fastened the chain around his neck.

Tracing his steps back to the bedroom, he stumbled to the closet in search of the 1955 Mossberg 16-gauge bolt-action shotgun his wife had given him for their tenth anniversary. He'd have to locate the box of shells that he knew lay unopened somewhere in the depths of his apartment, but as soon as he did he'd get in his car and travel the short distance to join his family in the welcoming shroud of death.

\* \* \*

It was nearly midnight and the clouds around the city blocked the light from the waxing gibbous moon and the stars shining down from the sky. Shawn was grateful for what little cover the clouds provided as walked down Fayette Street, toward Moss Ridge cemetery and the little plot of land where Tanner lay buried. The teenager was dressed all in black and had even worn his winter stocking cap in an attempt to blend in with the shadows. His skin and hair were already wet with perspiration from the humidity of the hot Illinois night, and the heat showed no sign of letting up anytime soon.

Shawn and Jenny had spent the better part of two hours arguing and strategizing over what to do next, doing their best to figure out everything before her father arrived home from work. The girl had finally relented and agreed to allow Shawn to dig up her brother's grave, though she had serious reservations about the whole thing. Both teenagers were sure that the mysterious man behind the fetch intended to see them dead, but all they could think to do was to get the talisman from Tanner's coffin and see what advantages might come from finally knowing what the fetch was after.

Jenny offered to come with him, but he knew it was something he needed to do alone – if for no other reason than to save her from having to see her brother's corpse. They'd eventually agreed to meet at three in the morning behind Jenny's house, well after her parents had gone to bed and Shawn had recovered the nickel.

Shawn brought along his father's hammer and chisel, an old shovel he and Jenny found in her dad's garage, the knife from the old house, and, of course, Tanner's infamous crowbar. Because it had a shoulder strap, he had wrapped everything in a big green canvas bag his parents used to carry their tent for camping trips. A flashlight and a Coleman lantern rounded out his gear.

He also brought the little silver pentagram Tanner had found in the box in the library of the Spencer manor. He'd polished it and the chain it hung from to a brilliant, glowing sheen, fastening it around his throat, just under the hooded sweater he wore to conceal his identity. If the symbol really did contain the power of protection against evil... well, he needed all the protection he could get to make it through this night alive.

The big canvas bag was already making his shoulder ache, and he'd trekked only ten blocks. He considered bicycling instead of walking, but finally decided that he would be more mobile on foot. Add that to the fact that he wasn't sure how to carry the bag full of tools on a bicycle and the decision ultimately made itself. Moving quickly across town, from tree to car to bush, he kept to the backyards and alleys when he could, attempting to avoid being seen in the light thrown down by the streetlamps that were placed every block or so down Fayette. Finally, already out of breath and feeling as if his shoulder would collapse at any moment, he reached the North County Road. The street intersected with Fayette as it wound around the town dump and followed the lake in a loop, where it came out on the other side of Carthage, near the park where all of this had begun.

His shoulder cramping and his body bathed in sweat, the teenager paused beneath a big fir tree to catch his breath. If he stopped moving for too long he'd lose what little resolve he had to do this terrible thing. He didn't want to see Tanner's dead face again; he wanted to remember his friend alive, swimming at the pool or playing Frisbee in the park. Switching the bag to his other shoulder, taking another deep breath, he steeled his nerves and began the steep climb up the hill that would take him to the cemetery's entrance.

"Great," mumbled Shawn to himself, as a light drizzle began, muddying his shoes as he tromped up the hill toward the cemetery gate. A bright flash of lightning sizzled across the sky to momentarily illuminate the whole of the graveyard, causing him to wince. Hunkering down, hoping no one had seen him, he quickly ran to the entrance, ducking past the stone columns that guarded the cemetery, hoping he could remember where they had buried Tanner.

Everything looked different at night. He clicked on the little green flashlight and swung it in an arc through the darkness, trying to remember where he had stood just four days ago as his best friend was being laid to rest. The rain began to fall harder and faster, splashing over the tombstones that surrounded him on all sides, leaving the granite markers with an eerie glistening sheen that somehow managed to look beautiful yet terrifying at the same time.

The smell of the rain did little to mask the pervasive scent of the graveyard - a peculiar mixture of freshly-tilled dirt, rotting flowers, and mown grass. The odor brought back memories of Tanner's funeral, and of Sarah's eight years earlier, which in turn conjured up cemetery scenes from some of the old monster movies he and Tanner had watched together. Pushing away all thoughts of skeletons popping up from the ground and werewolves baying at the moon, he shook his head, trudging onward, moving deeper into the graveyard.

He came across Sarah's little headstone. It had been ages since he'd last visited his dead sister, but, despite the rain, he had little trouble recognizing her grave. Pausing, momentarily forgetting his gruesome intentions, he dropped to a crouch beside the stone. *Sarah Louise Spencer, 1967, cherished daughter, beloved sister, we'll meet again in heaven*, read the marker, and for the first time Shawn dared to believe that it might be true. After all, his sister had told him that she loved him.

"I love you too, little sister," Shawn whispered through the torrent of water, his words lost amidst the rumble of thunder from the dark skies above. Switching the canvas bag to his other shoulder, he left his sister's grave to continue the search for Tanner's.

And, finally, he found it. The boy, his plot still unmarked, had been laid next to his grandparents on a little hill almost exactly in the middle of the cemetery, less than ten yards from Shawn's sister. Another grave caught his eye as lightning flashed overheard, illuminating the words on the ornately carved head stone that lay just to the left of Tanner's grave; *Margaret "Molly" McGee Ruskin, 1929-1960, beloved daughter, sister and wife, may she rest in peace*. Ruskin? Could Jenny be related to the gruff old Sheriff who had questioned her on Sunday morning? Why, it couldn't...

"What are you waiting for, Shawn?" asked a voice from behind. Startled, he spun around as the flashlight tumbled from his hand.

A tall, bald-headed man with pale white skin stepped out of the darkness, his face and eyes wrinkled with age. He wore a charcoal gray suit and walked with a long cane sporting a dull silver handle. Behind him, partially hidden in the shadows, stood something huge and black, its rain-matted fur melding into the darkness that surrounded it. Only its blood-red eyes were fully visible through the rain and under the midnight moon, but he was sure it was the fetch.

Lightning flashed, giving Shawn a better glimpse of the creature. It stood at least six feet tall, was covered in dark, wiry hair from head to toe, and glared with malevolent fury back and forth between the teenager and the old man, almost as if trying to decide which one it hated most. Stepping forward to stand beside the old man, he could see that there was someone else with them. Shaking and sobbing, Jenny stood next to the monster, clothed only in a pair of wet pajamas that clung tightly to her body. Her long red hair fell in drenched little ringlets around her face, giving the appearance that she had just stepped out of the shower. Her glasses were smeared with mud and rain, distorting her emerald eyes. Shawn wondered briefly why she didn't run away screaming, only then noticing the fetch's clawed hand clamped firmly across her throat. A small trickle of blood ran from between its fingers to stain the collar of her pajamas.

"Jenny!" he shouted, moving toward her. He stopped dead in his tracks as the old man thrust his cane out in front of the creature.

"Did you really think I trusted you?" smiled the old man, his voice *sotto voce* as he knelt into the boy's face. His fetid breath stung Shawn's nostrils. "The connection you share with my fetch goes both ways. I knew your plans almost before you did, and I know the talisman lies buried with the girl's brother. Ironic, isn't it? If he'd had it with him when we confronted him, none of this ever would have had to happen."

"You still would have killed him," uttered Shawn defiantly, unable or perhaps unwilling to believe otherwise. He didn't want to be – couldn't be - responsible for his friend's death.

"Oh, you're right, I would have," answered the old man. The rain splattered down around him, soaking his gray suit, turning the material almost as dark as the skin of the creature that stood beside him. "But you and your little girlfriend would have lived. Now I'm not so certain of that."

"You promised you'd leave her alone!"

"And you promised me the talisman. Start digging, and if you keep your promise I may yet keep mine. You live at my whim, boy; do not forget that."

His heart racing, Shawn slid the tools from the big canvas bag and dropped them to the ground.

"So, who's Colin?" he casually voiced the question he'd wanted to ask ever since their brief conversation earlier that morning. Picking up the shovel, shoving it deep into the wet soil, he began to dig.

"You still don't know? How fascinating! Colin Wainwright, my dear young friend, was the man who stole the talisman from me over thirty years ago and hid it in that dreadful house. He was also your ancestor, and a man I once loved very much."

Ancestor? And then it all began to make sense. Colin Wainwright and Charles Spencer had to be one and the same.

"Was he really my great-great uncle?" asked Shawn, as he shoveled piles of mud from his friend's grave. He threw each shovelful of soil up and over his shoulder as the rain and wind whipped through his hair, raising gooseflesh on his skin.

"Does it matter? Your blood won't save you this time, boy. Now dig."

Glancing over his shoulder and into Jenny's terrified eyes, Shawn began to dig faster. As he flung shovelful after shovelful of dirt behind him, his mind raced for a way out of this mess. *Your blood won't save you this time.* What did that mean? When had his blood saved him before? Not daring to ask or even to speak at all, he drew another pile of mud into his shovel and flung it out of the grave. His muscles began to cramp and his arms ached with fire. He wanted to just lie down in the grave and let the rain and the mud wash over him and pretend that none of this was real. But he kept digging, all the while trying to puzzle out the mystery that lay before him, hoping against all hope that there was something there that could save them.

Shawn was nearly five feet into the grave but had yet to hit anything more than dirt. His arms and legs were numb, and he was sure that if he could feel them that he'd have no choice other than to scream out in pain or simply collapse to the mud in a quivering heap. His fingers and palms were already covered in huge red blisters, and he bled from at least two of them, the shovel handle bloody with his fingerprints.

His arms worked automatically, digging, throwing, digging, as he allowed his mind to drift back to the day he and Tanner had become best friends. They had been in the same grade since Kindergarten, having grown up in Carthage, but hadn't really hit it off until fourth grade. It was November, right before Thanksgiving. They were attending school at Union Douglas, near the southeast edge of town, enjoying the first big snow of the season. It was recess time, and nearly all the boys in the fourth grade were involved in building forts out of snow and ice in preparation for a snowball fight.

Shawn was on one team while Tanner was on the other, both groups seemingly put together at random on the orders of the two team captains, both of whom were the school's worst bullies. Shawn would learn a lesson that day that he would never forget.

He'd thought the snowball fight just an excuse to get wet and have fun, but most of the fourth grade had other ideas. Less than two minutes into the competition, all of the members of Tanner's team began to pelt him with hard-packed snowballs, with most everyone on Shawn's team joining in to attack the husky boy. Taunts of "fatty, fatty, two-by-four" and "lard ass" could be heard echoing through the horse-shoe-shaped playground, and when Tanner tried to run inside he discovered to his horror that several of the boys who weren't playing had stayed inside the school to bar the doors. Howling in frustration and embarrassment, tears welling up in his eyes, the boy slammed his gloved fists over and over into door after door, but no one would help.

Finally the leader of Tanner's team, a tall, burly kid by the name of Mike Jackson, approached the boy with right hand extended, saying he was sorry, that it had all been nothing more than a practical joke that had gotten out of hand. Tanner was unsure of what to do and on the verge of nervously accepting the boy's apology when Shawn tackled Jackson from behind, sending the boy sprawling face first into the snow. Shawn had spotted something that Tanner hadn't: curled in Jackson's left hand and tucked safely behind his jacketed back was a huge ice ball, just waiting to be slammed into the overweight boy's face.

To this day, he really wasn't sure what prompted him to do what he did, why he tackled one boy to save another, earning a lifetime of harassment from Jackson and his sidekick Rusty Boyer as a result. But he knew he'd do it again in a heartbeat, for, even then, he'd hated liars and bullies, and Mike Jackson embodied the worst of both qualities. All Tanner wanted to do was join in the fun, something denied him until that moment, and all he got for trusting the other boys to play fairly were insults, ridicule and snowballs packed with ice.

The moment after Shawn tackled Jackson, Boyer jumped on Shawn, rolling the younger, smaller fourth grader over into the snow, rearing back to punch him in the face. The punch never landed. The next thing Shawn knew, Tanner was standing over Boyer, tears freezing on his cheeks, his hands balled up into fists. Taking hold of Boyer's hand with his left hand, at the same time swinging hard with his right, Tanner hit the boy square in the jaw, knocking him up and over Shawn to the snow-covered ground below. The boy was out like a light before he even hit the ground.

And then Tanner was standing above Mike Jackson, raining heavy blows down upon the huddled figure who lay with his back to the snow, arms and legs outstretched in defense, whining and begging the boy who had been his victim just minutes earlier to please stop hitting him. Tanner blackened both of the boy's eyes, knocked out a tooth, and opened up a big gash across his forehead before Mr. Landsbaum, the school principal, finally noticed the fray and ran out into the snow to pull a frenzied and flailing Tanner McGee from the body of his bloodied classmate.

All of the boys lost recess for the remainder of the year, and both Tanner and Jackson were suspended from school for a week. But it was all worth it, for in the moment that Shawn tackled Jackson, and in the instant when Tanner defended Shawn against the bullies' retribution, an unbreakable bond had been formed between the two misfits, and a great friendship and camaraderie was born. Tanner had naturally gravitated to the role of leader with Shawn gladly following, and they had rarely deviated from their roles in the seven years since. Shawn had never imagined having to go through life without his best friend at his side, and certainly it had never crossed his mind that someday he'd be digging up Tanner's grave.

Finally, after what seemed like days, Shawn's shovel rang with the sound of metal against concrete, bringing his thoughts back to the present. Soaked to the bone and shivering with cold, he had finally hit the concrete barrier that lay just above Tanner's coffin.

"I've hit something," Shawn mumbled in a shaky voice, his lips numb from the rain.

His hair and face glistened with sweat and water, and he felt feverish even though his teeth were chattering. Lightning flashed across the sky, a precursor to the shot of thunder that would follow, drowning out his words even as he said them. The big Coleman lantern hung from the chisel he had dug into the side of the pit, but he couldn't see much of anything other than the muddy concrete slab that he stood upon.

He was just a few inches from his friend's body and the talisman that lay disguised as a buffalo nickel, but it might as well have been a mile. Looking up and out of the grave, trying to see the old man through the darkness, he tried in vain to speak again. His voice failed him as a torrent of rain splashed him in the face, filling his nose, making him cough and gag as he struggled to find his breath.

Sucking in deep gulps of air, receiving no response to his words, he stood on his tiptoes, feeling around the wet soil above him for the crowbar. Finally his blood stained fingers gripped the curved end of the tool, pulling it down into the pit and into his grasp. Working the clawed end of the crowbar between the lip of the concrete barrier and the wall of dirt that surrounded it, he pulled, bracing his legs against the slab, trying to use his body as a fulcrum to snap the barrier in two. Stretching his muscles to the limit, pulling with all of his strength, he thought the concrete was about to give when a chunk from the end came loose, crumbling into dust, sending him stumbling back full force into the dirt wall behind him.

"I can't do this!" he cried into the howling rain.

He threw down the crowbar with a loud clang, anger and frustration drowning his spirit as sure as the heavy rain drenched his body. On the verge of tears, his eyes stinging from rain and dirt, he started in disbelief as a small crack appeared in the concrete at his feet. He forced himself to haltingly kneel to the ground to retrieve the metal tool, wedging the curved end into the crack. Stomping on the metal curve with the heel of his shoe until he could no longer stand the fiery ache that shot through his tendons, he picked up the shovel in his hands, swinging it in a wide arc, bringing it down hard against the crowbar, over and over, the crack opening up and growing wider with each ringing hit.

"Almost finished?" asked a voice from above. Turning, he could see the old man's bald head peering down at him through the darkness, a wry smile spread across his face.

"Getting there," he grunted, swinging the steel shovel down against the crowbar, imagining that it was the old man's face.

"You're better hurry. Your girlfriend's getting cold, and my fetch is getting hungry," he smiled, showing two rows of perfect white teeth, "and you know how he gets when he's hungry." And then the man stepped away from the rim, leaving Shawn alone again, wet, cold, and angry, standing alone in his best friend's grave.

Slamming the shovel down hard against the crowbar, he was surprised to see the slab finally give away, snapping in two, one side crumbling into pieces. The other side slid away from the coffin, sending Shawn's feet flying out from under him. The boy's hip and back slapped hard against the top of the casket, shooting sharp streaks of pain up through his body to the base of his neck. Struggling to his knees, pulling the crowbar from the bits of wet concrete and dirt, he maneuvered to find the seam in the coffin where the lid met the base and slowly started to work the heavy iron bar into the crack. Pulling back hard, he heard a satisfying snap as the lid flew upon, exposing Tanner's body to the muddy water splashing down from above.

"Hey, Shawn, what took you so long?" whispered a voice from within the coffin. "Boy, have we got a lot to talk about."

Shawn gasped as he felt his heart explode in his chest. He jerked away from the coffin, pressing his back as far against the side of the pit as he could, covering himself in mud as he tried to climb out.

"Shh!" commanded the voice. "Be quiet, we're only going to have one shot at this."

"But…" he squeaked, his heart ballooning in his chest. He blinked twice in an effort to focus his eyes and force himself to look into the coffin. Tanner's body lay there with its eyes closed and arms crossed over its chest, still dead, as unmoving as the stone that had sealed the casket from view. Pulling the flashlight from his pocket, clicking it on, he slowly swept the length of the coffin with the beam as he tried to tell himself that none of this was happening, that the entire last week had been nothing but a dream.

"Turn off the light!" whispered the little toy knight, crouched just under Tanner's elbow. One hand held the tiny plastic sword it had been buried with, while the other held the nickel Shawn had thrown into the casket before it had been interred. The doll's little blue and white shield lay at its feet, resting beside Tanner's hip. "If Ahpuc sees me, then we'll all die."

Ahpuc? Shawn clicked off the beam, slipping the flashlight back into his pocket. "What are you?" whispered Shawn, finally finding his voice. "This isn't possible! This isn't real!"

"It was your blood that saved me, I think, and this," he gestured with the nickel, "but we can talk about all of that later."

My blood? This was the second time tonight that someone had mentioned something about his blood, and he still didn't understand. He started to ask the toy, but stopped short as it made a shushing noise, once more warning him not to talk.

"Shawn, you've got to trust me. Lean over and pick me up, and I'll tell you what we need to do…"

\* \* \*

Jenny McGee stood soaking wet in her pink pajamas. The cotton material plastered against her chest and legs, while her long red hair fell down around her eyes like a mask. She knew for certain she was going to die. Mere hours ago (days? weeks? She wasn't really sure anymore) the fetch had crashed through her bedroom window while she lay in bed reading, all pretense of stealth abandoned, taking her thrashing and screaming from her bed. Her father, sleep still in his eyes, had burst through her door seconds later, recoiling at the sight of the monster.

Tossing Jenny back to her bed, the beast advanced on her father. Paul McGee swung a beefy fist at the monster's nose, only to be swatted aside like an annoying fly at a picnic. The man flew backwards into Jenny's little wooden bookcase, smashing it to splinters, sending records and books flying.

As the fetch turned its attention back to Jenny, her father forced himself to his feet, flinging himself at the monster, grabbing deep hanks of wiry fur and attaching himself to its back. He rained down blows upon the creature's face, punching it over and over, as the girl watched from the bed in horror. Unhurt, the monster reached up with its clawed hand and grabbed the man by the hair, flinging him screaming across the room as though he were nothing more than a rag doll. He hit the wall with a sickening thud, bounced once, and then remained silent.

"Jenny? Oh my God, Paul!" screamed her mother, standing in the doorway with the phone in her hand. "Hello, oh God, there's something in my house! This is Abby McGee, and I'm at 176 Main. Please hurry! My husband and daughter are hurt, and there's this huge… thing in my daughter's room!"

The creature turned to stare at the woman, revealing a long row of glistening razor-like teeth. It took a step forward, hissing, then snorted in laughter as the woman jumped back to hit her head on the door frame. She stumbled to the floor, sobbing and hysterical, dropping the phone as she fell.

Turning to Jenny once again, watching as the girl struggled to her feet, the monster picked her up and flung her over its shoulder. It growled once, and then passed her through the shattered window to a pair of old, withered hands that waited on the other side.

"Shh, girl!" hushed an old, bald man with steel gray eyes, his grip hard and cruel as his fingers encircled her wrist. She heard the purr of an engine close by, looking up to see a large black Cadillac idling in her driveway.

"Get in," the old man insisted, pushing her toward the open passenger door. Scared and in shock, she did as she was told, glancing back to see the fetch climb out the window and join the man beside the car. "My fetch will ride in back with you in case you get any silly ideas. I know you're already well acquainted, so I'm sure you'll have all the world to talk about."

The old man leaned down to her in an illusion of kindness, and she could see that he wore a charcoal gray suit and a matching tie as wide as the spread of her hand. "Do as I say, my dear, and you may yet live to see tomorrow," he whispered, winking at her as he moved aside to let the fetch slide in beside her. "Don't, and you won't; it's as simple as that."

She recoiled in fear and disgust as the beast sat just inches away from her, its dark black fur shining in the light from the overhead dome. Turning to her, it smiled once again, baring its teeth, snaking a long, wet tongue out to slap her across the face.

*"Jenn-eeey meat,"* it rasped, licking its scaly lips as it reached out a clawed hand to touch her cheek, *"Jenn-eeey...Jen-eeeeeey."*

She didn't remember much of the ride in the Cadillac. They arrived at the cemetery to the flash of lightning and the sounds of thunder, just as the storm began in full earnest. The old man and the fetch dragged her from the car in silence, watching Shawn from the shadows, the beast's clamped hand over her mouth. It was almost as if they were somehow afraid of the boy and wanted to make sure that he hadn't yet retrieved the nickel before approaching him. If she could only figure out a way to tell to him that the talisman might somehow be used as a weapon, or to stall while he thought it through for himself...

"I've got it," Shawn's voice echoed from her brother's grave, and it was in that moment that she knew for certain that all was lost. Despite the old man's assurances to the contrary, she knew that neither she nor Shawn would live to see the end of tonight's rainstorm, let alone tomorrow morning's light.

* * *

"I've got it," Shawn yelled, scrabbling halfway up the side of the pit before sliding back in again. He repeated the process, sliding back a second time. "Help me, damn it, I can't get out!"

"Throw me the nickel, boy," called the old man down to Shawn, raising his voice against the noise of the storm. "We'll haul you out after we have it."

"Do you think I'm stupid? No way! If you want the nickel, let Jenny go and pull me out and then you can have it."

"You presume too much, Spencer," the old man spat in anger. "What's to stop me from killing her right now and sending my fetch down to retrieve the talisman? But fine – we'll do it your way, for now. My fetch will help you out of the grave."

"No, you have to do it," Shawn countered, frustration in his voice. "I don't want to touch that thing."

"Boy, you try my patience. My fetch is coming for you. If you want out of that grave, reach out your arms and he'll haul you up."

Shawn shot a nervous glance down to his right hand, thinking, it's now or never. Tightening his grip on the crowbar, he waited for the fetch at the edge of the pit, all the while hoping and praying that Tanner's plan would work.

The fetch's dark face suddenly appeared above him, a look of absolute hatred glowing in its malevolent red eyes. For the first time he could see the creature clearly; its face was flat as an owls, with a small, protruding snout to break the curve. Its wiry fur was black as obsidian, seemingly drawing in the light around it, suffocating it, destroying it and leaving nothing but darkness in its wake. Its mouth, filled with what looked like dozens of razor-sharp knives, opened wide to greet Shawn in a mocking smile.

He flicked the flashlight he'd been hiding in his left hand across the beast's eyes, while swinging the crowbar in a wide arc up and over his head with his right. He brought the metal tool down hard into the beast's skull, splitting bone, sending blood everywhere. The fetch stumbled backward, reeling away from the pit, as Shawn shouted, "Jenny, run!" hoping that the knight had done his job and that they at least had a chance to escape the night unharmed.

\* \* \*

Jenny tensed under the grip of the old man's hand on her arm as she heard Shawn's voice yelling up from the pit, telling her to run. The fetch tumbled back from the edge of the grave, landing with a splash in the mud. Legs frozen in momentary panic, the girl felt something skitter across her foot, glanced down to see the little toy Galahad she had put into Tanner's coffin holding Shawn's pocketknife. She gasped, jerking back, throwing the man off balance just as the toy buried the knife deep into his ankle.

She yanked her arm from his grasp as he howled in pain, then shoved him hard in the chest. Arms wind milling out to his sides, fighting hard to keep purchase, he finally lost his balance and tumbled to the ground, landing flat on his back in the dirt from Tanner's grave.

"Run, Jenny!" yelled Shawn again. Scrambling out of the grave to plant his feet on solid ground, his face grew ashen as the fetch began to stir less than a yard away.

Jenny scooped up the plastic knight and sprinted across the dirt to Shawn's side. Taking his hand, she jumped with him over the length of the grave, running through the rain and mud, avoiding headstones, looking for a way out of the cemetery.

"Faster!" Shawn shouted, pulling her along with him, ducking branches and leaping over graves. They shot toward the barbed wire fence that separated the back of the graveyard from the field surrounding it.

She could hear the creature's growls behind them, getting closer, imagining its hot, fetid breath on her neck. And then a giant BOOM cracked through the air behind them, and Jenny felt something sting her right thigh, sending her stumbling to the ground. Shawn's hand grabbed hers as she almost fell and dragged her back to her feet, continuing the long sprint to the fence. Another boom and then a thunderous crack of lightning lit the graveyard behind them and Jenny thought that they were caught just as they reached the boundary of the fence.

"How...?" she asked, staring down at the doll. She quickly turned to search the darkness behind her, but could see nothing more than shapes moving in the distance.

"Give me your foot!" yelled Shawn, his eyes pleading with her to hurry. "Please, Jenny, we'll talk about the doll later." He dropped to one knee and entwined his fingers, looking up into her face. "We've got to go!"

"Okay!" Snapping out of her trance, she placed one bare foot in his hand, reaching out with her own hands to grab hold of the fence, and immediately found herself flying up and over the barbed wire. She landed with a splat face down in the grass and mud on the other side, winded and covered in dirt but, for the moment, alive.

# Chapter 33

DISTRAUGHT AND finally ready to end his life, Fred Ruskin pulled his Pacer into the small parking space outside Moss Ridge cemetery. Rain roared down in bucketfuls, splattering his windshield, making it difficult to see anything past the front gate. His shotgun in one hand and the box of shells in the other, he pushed open the door, squeezed past the steering wheel, and let himself outside.

Flicking open the small black umbrella he always kept in the car, he was curious to see another vehicle, a large black Cadillac, parked just a few yards from where he stood. What would anyone be doing out in this weather at this time of night? He had heard sirens earlier in the evening but had thought little of it, assuming it to be an accident or perhaps another stolen motorcycle. Could someone have boosted the Cadillac and deposited it at the cemetery? Momentarily forgetting his midnight intentions, the cop in him took over and he jogged to the big open gate to see if the graveyard had any other visitors. Lightning flashed over the middle of the cemetery and he could have sworn he saw a huge, hairy ape standing next to his wife's grave.

Rattled and disoriented, he crab-walked away from the main path that led to the center of the cemetery, circling around the south end instead, to approach whatever he had just seen from a different angle. Feeling the hairs on his arms stand up and salute, he pried a shell from the box of ammunition in his pocket, slid the bolt back on his 1955 Mossberg, and loaded it into the chamber. Shotgun in hand and his heart beating heavy in his chest, he slowly advanced through the storm toward the plot of land where he had buried his wife and daughter so many years ago.

Ruskin lowered the umbrella to his side and squeezed his eyes shut and open again, trying in vain to focus through the darkness and the rain. Squinting, he could just make out the gorilla; it looked like it was holding someone, and beside them stood a man wearing an old-fashioned gray suit at least fifteen or twenty years out of style. Something strange was definitely going on here, though he had no idea what it could be. He did know, however, that whatever was going on was taking place beside his family's graves. That thought sparked the always-smoldering ember of anger that rested within his breast, the one that blamed him for what had happened to his wife and daughter. He wasn't able to protect them while they were alive, but he sure as hell would make sure that they weren't disturbed in death.

Dropping the umbrella, he skulked to a huge stone cross that rose up from the cemetery ground. He peered around the marker just as he heard a voice scream, "Jenny, run!" Jenny McGee? Without thought, he sprinted past the cross and through a garden of gravestones, toward the voice that had called out the warning.

What he saw when he got there would stick in his mind forever. The gorilla lay motionless on its back, sprawled before Tanner McGee's open grave, while a sandy-haired teenager crawled up and out of it, yelling for Jenny to run. Turning, he saw the man in the suit suddenly tumble backward, reaching down for his ankle, howling in pain. And there was Jenny McGee, his dead wife's niece, dressed in wet pink pajamas and carrying something small in her hand, running for all she was worth to the boy's side. He watched in amazement as the gorilla stirred and swatted a big, hairy hand toward the girl's ankle, narrowly missing as she and the boy leapt over the grave and hit the other side running.

"What the fuck?" he mumbled, watching in wonder as the gorilla climbed to its feet. But it wasn't a gorilla after all. The thing stood well over five feet tall and sported a little forked tail and huge claws that spread out from its hands. It turned toward him, toward the old man, and Ruskin saw the face of a demon. Rattled, he backed away, thumping into his daughter's headstone, nearly falling over as the monster issued the most blood curdling howl he had ever heard.

"Kill them!" screeched the old man, his leg bleeding profusely, snapping his neck around to meet the former sheriff's eyes in the same breath.

"No!" screamed Ruskin, bringing the shotgun up to his shoulder, firing it point blank into the wiry muscles of the demon's back. The monster pitched forward as the little lead pellets drove into its skin, burrowing deep enough to splatter blood in several places. But the monster did not fall. Instead it turned around to glare in his direction, flashing a set of perfect white teeth, loosing a low, guttural growl from its throat. Quickly ejecting the spent cartridge from the shotgun and loading another, he shot again at the monster, hitting it square in the face; this time it did go down, falling to its knees, as it glared up again at the man who had shot it.

"Leave him alone!" shouted the old man, pushing himself to his feet with the aid of a large, silver-handled cane. "This is none of your concern!"

"It's my concern if you're trying to hurt people on my watch!" shouted Ruskin, searching through his pocket for the box of shells. "Just stay where you are. You're under arrest. You have the right to remain silent..."

His words were interrupted by a ripping belch from the creature that he had just shot. Risking a glance back toward the demon, he backed away in shock as he saw the creature's jaw dislocate itself as it began retching, excreting something from its mouth. First he saw a half-digested hand missing a thumb, then a black shoe followed by an ankle bone, until finally the monster disgorged the remains of Alan Delacroix's head. The back of his skull was missing but his eyes were wide open and staring ahead as though sitting at the four-way-stop in Carthage waiting for someone to run the stop sign. The head bounced once on the wet and muddy ground before rolling away and tumbling down into Tanner McGee's open grave.

The creature had changed. It was suddenly smaller, maybe the size of a small dog or a large cat, but just as dark and deadly as it had been three feet ago. It looked up at Ruskin, let loose with a rattling laugh, then turned tail and ran after the escaping teenagers.

"What the fuck is that?" gasped Ruskin, his face an ashen white as he fumbled for the shotgun shells. Finally pulling one from the box, he ejected another empty cartridge and began to load the shotgun. But turning from the old man to stare at the transforming demon had been a mistake.

He heard a strange crackling in the air, popping and sizzling like a fallen telephone line or a ruined microwave. He barely managed to turn back to stare at the old man before a crooked bolt of lightning shot from his fingertips, coming straight at Ruskin.

The bluish-red stream of energy struck Ruskin square in the chest, knocking him back against his wife's tombstone. The stench of singed flesh and charred clothing was strong in his nostrils as everything went dark around him. His limp body, bereft of breath, slid down the marble to sink and settle into the grass and mud below.

# Chapter 34

SHAWN AND JENNY burst through the copse of old pine trees that separated the graveyard from the field, splashing through the silt and mud, running for their lives. Shawn could almost feel the fetch behind them, pushing him to run faster, as they cut across the field of grass for the sidewalk. Feet slapping against earth and then pavement, he risked a look over his shoulder but could see nothing through the storm.

"We're going to die!" Jenny sobbed.

"We have to get to the house," he rasped, his heart thudding hard against his ribcage. "We'll be safe if we get to the house."

"What do you mean?"

"Just trust me!" he gasped, as they ran toward the highway that cut through Carthage. If they could make it that far, Randolph was just a little west from the intersection, and the house just a few blocks further.

*"Jenn-eeey!"* called a mocking voice from somewhere behind them, probably no more than forty or fifty yards away. *"Jenn-eeey...Jen-eeeeeey!"*

"Oh God, oh God, oh God," she screamed, stumbling against him. "It's going to get us!"

"Be quiet!" He pulled her along with him as he shot across the highway, not turning toward Randolph but instead heading straight, toward Walnut Street. "Just keep running!"

"We're going the wrong way!"

"Please just trust me," he pleaded, "and run like hell!"

"*Jenn-eeey!*" called the voice, closer.

"Leave us alone!" Shawn screamed into the night, his voice shaking with rage, "or I swear to God I'm going to kill you!"

A manic cackle rose up through the night in response, perhaps less than twenty yards behind them and closing.

"There it is!" Shawn gasped, gulping down mouthfuls of air as he ran. "The old Carthage Jail."

Constructed in 1839, the old jail had once housed Mormon founder Joseph Smith, who was murdered there by an angry mob just five years after the jail was built. The little building was now owned by the Mormon Church, which considered the jail a monument to the martyrdom of their leader. Shawn knew the history of the jail by rote, for he and Tanner had spent two long weeks several years ago taking the guided tour during a miserably hot summer in an effort to escape the heat and enjoy the air conditioning that the building provided.

Crossing Walnut Street, Shawn ran at a sprint toward the tall iron fence that surrounded the jail, praying that the gate wasn't locked. Pulling the gate open, he thanked whatever invisible god or universal force had answered his prayers. Slamming it shut behind them, he ignored the little visitor's center that stood adjacent to the jail and ran straight for the jail itself. Closing his eyes, he released Jenny's hand just seconds before throwing his shoulder hard against the old wooden door he had stepped through with Tanner countless times before. The door buckled under his weight, splintering and giving way as he tumbled through the entrance in a shower of ancient wood, landing hard on the old and worn oak floor inside.

"Shawn!" Jenny screamed, falling to her knees beside him. "Shawn, are you okay?"

"Up the stairs!" he croaked, pointing through the darkness to a set of steps barely visible from the hallway. "Leave me here. Run! There's a door at the top of the steps that leads to the jailor's bedroom. Close it and barricade yourself inside."

"Shawn, be careful," she said, her eyes finding his through the darkness. She turned to sprint up the old wooden stairs, leaving the boy alone in the dark.

"*Aww,*" rasped the fetch as it climbed through the broken doorway. "*Jenn-eeey so sweet.*" The monster was small again, looking more like a rabid dog than the Kodiak bear he had hit with the shovel.

"Shawn!" shouted Jenny's voice from the top of the stairs.

The fetch looked into Shawn's eyes, held his gaze for a second, and then launched itself over Shawn's head. Landing halfway up the stairs in a single leap, it reached the landing in another and burst through the open door and into the room where Jenny hid on its third.

"No!" Why hadn't she closed the door? Struggling to his feet, Shawn grabbed hold of the railing to steady his shaking legs and then began his ascent up the staircase, to kill the fetch or, more than likely, die trying.

* * *

Jenny stood up from the crouch she'd been holding at the edge of the L-shaped landing. Running to the door, she grabbed the handle and slammed it shut behind the murderous little monster, trapping it on the other side. The fetch was small again and had no way of reaching the door knob to open the door, though she knew that wouldn't stop it for long. But at least they had a chance.

"Shawn!" she shouted, watching him run up the stairs toward her. His face was pale and his eyes were filled with tears. "I'm okay, but we've got to go!"

"I thought…" he trailed off, stunned as he looked past her shoulder to the closed door above them.

"I'd never leave you." Taking his hand, she pulled him toward the bottom of the stairs. "It's trapped inside, but probably not for long. Let's get out of here."

"Let me go!" commanded the Galahad doll, wrenching itself free from her hand, jumping down to land on its feet on the wooden floor in front of the door. "I'll take care of the fetch once it gets out, and then I'll meet you at the house."

"Oh my God!" gasped Jenny, backing away from the doll, falling into Shawn as she recognized the voice. "Tanner?"

"You can't stay here!" Shawn argued with the doll, finally finding his voice as he reached out for the toy. He pricked his thumb on the little sword as the knight danced away from his grasp.

"Sharper than it looks, isn't it?" the toy grinned. "Yeah, sis, it's me, at least kinda. I'll tell you everything I know once we get to the house. Now go!"

On the edge of hysteria, Jenny fought the ever-increasing urge to just close her eyes and shut down. How could Tanner be alive inside the doll? How could any of this be happening? Torn between staying to find answers or running away to safety, Jenny looked back and forth between the toy and Shawn, unsure of what to do.

"Come on," said Shawn. "He knows what he's doing. We have to go."

The two teenagers sprinted down the stairs, past the ruined remains of the door, and into the storm.

\* \* \*

"Here kitty, kitty, kitty" called Tanner, standing outside the jailor's door. A loud scratching noise came from the other side, growing louder as the monster dug through the wood with its razor-sharp claws. Tanner readied his toy sword and shield, hoping that he truly could make good on his promise to meet Shawn and Jenny at the house.

And then the beast was free. Tearing through the entryway, the fetch issued a gurgled, guttural scream as Tanner buried the little plastic sword deep into the monster's throat, drawing first blood, pulling the weapon free in the same motion. He danced backward to avoid the fetch's claws, parrying with the sword.

"Aww, what's the matter, kitty got a boo-boo?" taunted Tanner, moving in to thrust with the sword. He quickly backed away, narrowly avoiding the creature's lunge.

Tanner swung again, just missing the monster's nose as it moved toward the edge of the landing. The sword was metal now instead of plastic; changed, he supposed, by the same force that had granted him his second life inside the doll. Being careful to avoid falling through the wooden slats, Tanner lunged at the fetch. He blocked its claws with the shield, doing his best to distract the monster so that Shawn and Jenny could put as much distance between themselves and the creature as possible.

The fetch went suddenly still, cocking its head as if listening to some unheard voice. Turning from its adversary without so much as a hiss or a glare, the beast sprang from the landing to land with a soft thump at the foot of the stairs, quickly scurrying out and into the storm.

"Shit!" cursed the little toy knight. He hoped he had at least bought them enough time to make it to the house. Running as fast as his little plastic legs would carry him, he followed the fetch's steps, climbing down the stairs and out the door into the darkness beyond.

\* \* \*

"It's not much further now," Shawn shivered, brushing wet hair back from his eyes as they ran the last block toward the house. Jenny's hand in his, he risked a look back over his shoulder, seeing nothing but rain and shadows from the streetlamps around them.

"My feet…," panted Jenny, out of breath, her steps leaving bloody footprints in her wake.

"There!" he pointed, as the house came into view. "The front door's unlocked, and once we get in, they can't…" Shawn's steps faltered, as he noticed a black Cadillac pulling into the driveway of the old manor.

"No," he whispered, gesturing toward the vehicle.

"Shawn, that's his car!"

As if on cue, Ahpuc, with the help of his cane, stepped from the confines of the vehicle. His eyes met Shawn's from less than twenty yards away.

"Good show!" the old man shouted through the night, lifting his cane in mock salute as he started toward the teenagers. "You've nowhere to run. My fetch is just minutes behind you and closing in fast. Give me the nickel."

"Come on," whispered Shawn, running for the broken gate that guarded the yard from the outside world.

The old man thrust his arms into the sky, bringing them down to point at the gate. Thunder rumbled as lightning crackled down from the clouds, striking the entrance with an explosion of ferocious intensity. Twisted metal and burning stone scattered across the yard, leaving the old man's path unobstructed.

"You can't win this little game," he rasped, stumbling a little. "Just give me what is mine and be done with it!"

Shawn ignored the old man's words, running straight for the front door with Jenny in tow. They veered off to the right at the last second as a bolt of lightning struck the ground just a few feet from where they'd been standing. Pushing his body beyond the point of exhaustion, knowing Jenny was doing the same, he raced around the corner of the house.

"Is there a back entrance?" whispered Jenny, squeezing his fingers as they neared a huge, decaying redwood porch built on to the back of the house.

"Probably, but that's not where we're going," he answered, ducking down to scurry under the porch. Pulling Jenny with him, he wormed his way through the mud to the opposite end of the veranda. "Follow me and run when I say run. There's a cellar entrance on the west side of the house, and that's where we're going."

"But why not…" Jenny wiggled alongside him, her words dying away as she heard footfalls fast approaching just a few feet in front of them. The steps grew silent for a moment, then louder as they echoed on the wood.

"Damn it, where are they?" cursed a frustrated Ahpuc.

"Now!" whispered Shawn, throwing the hammer he'd slipped from his pocket toward the end of the porch. It bounced off one of the rotting beams that held the structure in place and skittered out into the yard.

Squirming through the mud, the two teenagers burst from under the porch just as the old man had reached the opposite end. Rising to a crouch, they carefully slipped past the edge of the house before turning the corner and breaking into a full-fledged run.

"Here," Shawn cried. They stood before an old, weather-worn cellar door, just a few steps from the safety they so desperately needed. "Come on," he whispered, pulling the door back, letting it fall heavy to the wet ground. A dark entrance revealed itself, promising sanctuary.

"Shawn, I can't," said Jenny, her eyes suddenly glazing over. She looked as if she were going to throw up. "I can't go in there."

"What do you mean? Come on!" He grabbed her wrist, pulling her through the doorway. She screamed in pain as her hand breached the perimeter of the entrance, blue sparks blazing in the air between them. She fell back to the muddy ground, as though struck by some unseen force, and remained still.

Shawn climbed back up the stairs just in time to see the old man rounding the corner, his eyes on something off to the right. Craning his neck, the blood nearly froze in his veins at the sight of the fetch loping down the driveway.

"It looks like Colin's wards were stronger than I'd realized," mused the old man, hobbling toward the two teens. "If you want to flee to safety, boy, then go right ahead. I promise you we'll take very good care of your girlfriend. You'll give up the nickel before we're through with her, that I also promise."

The fetch giggled in response, a shrill, high-pitched noise rising from its throat. *"Meat,"* it said, crouching low to the ground, ready to pounce.

Why could Shawn enter the house while Jenny couldn't? If it was because he was related to the owner, then why had Tanner been able to enter? Thinking back to his first journey into the manor he remembered Tanner's hesitance when first approaching the cellar, which had all but vanished the instant they stepped over the threshold. So what was different about this time?

*It was your blood that saved me,* Tanner told him in the pit, and the old man had said, *your blood won't save you this time.* But what did it mean? *Think, Shawn,* he urged himself, knowing there was something there that he wasn't quite getting.

His heart racing in his chest as time closed in around him, he suddenly remembered the dream he had the night after coming home from the hospital. *The same blood pumps through our veins,* the nightmare fetch had told him. Blood again. And in an instant he knew that Colin Wainwright hadn't simply disappeared, at least not in the way that everyone seemed to think. He also knew how to get Jenny through the ward.

"Jenny," he screamed, yanking the barely conscious girl to her feet, "you have to drink my blood!"

He squeezed his thumb, milking it despite the pain, fresh blood welling up from the little wound that he'd suffered at the jail. Blinking in confusion, Jenny's eyes met his as she slowly began to suck the blood from his thumb, the plasma mingling with her saliva as it traveled down her throat and into her stomach, finally entering her bloodstream.

The look on the old man's face spoke volumes as he watched the swaying girl drink from Shawn's cut. Pulling his thumb from Jenny's mouth, wrapping his arms around her, he threw himself backward and through the cellar entrance just as the fetch lunged, raking a sharp claw down the length of Jenny's foot as she and Shawn disappeared into the dark asylum below.

Gasping for breath, the wind knocked from his lungs in the fall, Shawn's neck and back ached with a fiery intensity from landing on the rough hewn surface of the cellar floor. He groaned, thankful to still be able to feel his fingers and toes, risking a glance up toward the looming face of the old man peering down into the cellar. Unable to enter, Ahpuc slammed his fists against the invisible barrier in an angry rage, the ward sending electric blue sparks flying into the air.

"Jenny?" he mumbled, moving his neck from side to side. He finally spotted her to his right, blinking and trying to sit up.

"Shawn?" asked Jenny, studying him from the dark. "What happened? Are we safe?"

"We're safe," Shawn reassured her as he struggled to pull the flashlight free from his soaked and tangled pants pocket, finally wrenching it from the material with a rip.

Switching on the flashlight, he pointed it up the stairs into the wrinkled and faded eyes of the man who had only moments earlier tried to kill them. His head hurting and his back on fire, he managed to raise himself to one elbow before straightening out his other arm to extend his middle finger up at Ahpuc.

"Are you sure?"

"We're safe," he repeated, as much for his own benefit as for hers. They were safe in the house, but how long could they stay? They had no food, no water, and their clothes were in tatters. And what about Tanner or, god forbid, their parents?

He knew the old man wanted the nickel with such an all-encompassing desire that he would do anything to get it, the least of which would be to take another life. They needed to find some answers to the many questions he had floating around inside his head, and he knew that if those answers existed anywhere, they were more than likely inside the house.

"Let's go," Shawn grunted, pushing himself to his feet. His body ached in places he didn't even know could hurt.

"Go where? And why didn't the just follow us?"

"We need to get up there," he pointed toward the stairs that led to the kitchen, "and then we'll talk."

* * *

The man in the trench coat stood beneath a weeping willow on the opposite side of the street from the old Spencer House, patiently watching as the night unfolded before him. The storm raged on, yet his hair was perfectly coifed, not a strand out of place, and the tan trench coat he wore was as warm and dry as the day he had first put it on. He watched the two teenagers through the front window, and then slowly turned his head to follow Ahpuc and his demon as they investigated the house.

Sighing heavily, he settled back against the tree. He folded his arms in front of his chest, enjoying the sound of rain falling around him. He didn't see much rain where he was from. Settling in, gauging his vantage point, the man cocked his head to the right, listening for the roar of a car engine that he knew would soon come. This was going to be a long night, he knew, but at least it would finally be over, for better or worse. And then he'd have to pick up the pieces.

* * *

Shawn and Jenny stood in the middle of the second floor library. They'd stayed away from the windows at first, skulking from wall to wall like two scared field mice, fearing Ahpuc and his minion might spot them. After a while, though, they decided that it didn't actually matter. Try as he might, it didn't seem as if the old man could penetrate the house's wards. They knew, however, that eventually their stalker would find his way inside, and then all hell would break loose.

Searching the library, Shawn immediately noticed something he'd failed to see before; there, beneath the cracked and broken old ladder, was another pentagram carved into the wooden floor. That made four, and, based on the location of this one as well as the other three pentagrams, he had a feeling that they would find a fifth at the far end of the third floor. But that could wait; now that he understood that the pentagrams were magical wards that were keeping the old man and his monster at bay, he had no great desire to disturb them.

"There has to be something somewhere in the house that will give us a clue," shouted Shawn, frustrated and exhausted, as he dug through the books that lined the shelves of the room. He had stripped off the mud-caked sweatshirt downstairs in the kitchen to reveal only the silver pentagram that hung from a chain around his neck. He still felt filthy. His pants and shoes were covered in wet slime, dead leaves, and whatever else he had managed to pick up between Tanner's grave and the house.

He and Jenny exchanged stories about what had happened before their meeting in the cemetery. Both teenagers decided that with the police more than likely out looking for her, Ahpuc was unlikely to call attention to himself by going after their parents. Still, they knew they couldn't stay in the house forever. The old man could simply outwait them, picking them off when they inevitably left the protection of the wards.

"If your blood let you into the house and, by extension, Tanner and me," Jenny asked, trying to puzzle out the riddle that lay before them, "then why can't the fetch enter, since you and it swapped blood? And will Tanner be able to come inside, assuming the fetch didn't kill him all over again?"

Shawn shrugged. "You've got me," he said, instinctively reaching into his pocket for his yo-yo. He had always been able to think through problems more effectively if he had something to occupy his hands, but of course the yo-yo was no longer there, resting instead on top of the bookshelf that loomed over their heads. Instead he pulled the pentacle out from beneath his shirt, turning it over and over with his fingers.

"What is that?"

"This necklace? Tanner and I found it when we broke into the house." Tanner. That's what he was most worried about. Through some miracle, Tanner had returned to them in the form of the doll Jenny left in his coffin. They'd barely had the chance to speak when circumstances tore him away from them again. They should never have left Tanner to fight the fetch, but what choice did they have? Tanner seemed to know more about what was going on than either of them did.

"Maybe it does something."

"The necklace?" He slipped it over his neck and handed it to her. "Well, it's supposed to be a protection against evil, but it wasn't been doing much for me so far."

"You know," Jenny said, eyeing the necklace with more than a little distrust, "magic seemed more inviting when it was on the other side of the television screen or safely locked away in a book."

"What did you say?"

"Magic seemed more inviting…" she started to repeat, her words cut off as he moved forward to snatch the necklace from her fingers.

"Come on!" He urged, rushing out the door and down the stairs to the floor below.

"It'd be nice if you occasionally told me where we were going before we got there," she sighed, trudging down the creaking staircase after him.

"What's that?" she asked, after they had reached the living room, watching as he plucked a little book from the cushion of an old and molding couch.

"It's a blank journal that Tanner and I found, but…" he trailed off, flipping the pages. "Well, it's still blank."

"Let me see," she asked, snatching the book from his hands without waiting for a response.

"Yep, it's blank alright. What were you expecting?"

"I don't know. It just doesn't make sense. Who leaves a blank journal behind? I thought maybe the pentagram was the key."

"Let me see the necklace again," she asked, snatching it from his outstretched palm. She laid it atop the cover, but nothing happened. Undaunted, she flipped upon the book and pressed the medallion against the first page of the diary, but it remained unchanged.

"I just hoped…" started Shawn, at a loss for words. "I don't know what to do. Why didn't he leave us something, some clue?"

"He who?"

"My great-great-uncle Charles Spencer, aka Colin Wainwright. He had to have known this would happen."

Jenny rubbed her chin, lost in thought for a moment. "Let me see your thumb."

"Okay," he said, giving her a thumbs up, "but why?"

"This is why," she explained, gently taking his thumb in her hands and pressing it against the first page of the book. He pulled back his hand, leaving a bloody thumbprint upon the paper.

And then the diary began to change. Where once there had been only blank pages, writing now swam across the journal, red ink quickly filling the space. The cover had changed as well, the title reading: *My*

*Journal,* much like the cheap little diaries she'd seen for sale in Ben Franklin and other five and dime stores.

"Voila," she said, handing him the little journal with a flourish. Curtsying low to the ground, she bowed her head before him. "At your service, milord."

"You're brilliant," he said, as he watched the words dancing on the page before him. "How did you know?"

"Blood seems to be the key to a lot of this," she shrugged. "It got me into the house, I thought maybe it could get us into the diary. Now, what does it say?"

"You can see for yourself," he said, settling down to the dusty ground. Flashlight in hand, he patted the floor beside him.

The girl dropped to the ground, sitting Indian-style in an attempt to avoid the painful cuts and bruises on her feet. Snuggling close to Shawn, she wrapped her arm in his as they began to read.

# Chapter 35

January 4<sup>th</sup>, 1954

MY STORY starts over two hundred years ago, in Great Britain, where I worked as an artist, painting portraits to put food on my family's table and to earn my keep. I was a man of reasonable, if not exceptional, talent, though perhaps I am being too hard on myself. It was, after all, my eye for capturing the spirit within that drew me into this web from which I am only now beginning to extricate myself.

The year was 1743, and I had just been commissioned to paint the portrait of His Royal Majesty, King George the Second. I was ecstatic. If I could capture his noble visage on canvas, the sky would be the limit on the commissions I might receive. To paint the King of England…why, it was my dream! But the dream quickly turned into a nightmare.

George, as it turned out, had been living for well over 2,500 years, though of course I didn't know that then. Pleased with my painting, he offered me a room in the castle. I quickly accepted, not once even considering the consequence. I never saw my family again. Sometime later, he revealed to me his supernatural past, and then seduced me into his bed, taking me at his will. It's not something I am proud of, but it's what happened, and I must at least be honest with myself through my writing even if I cannot be honest with those around me.

George (even he doesn't remember his original name, though he's had dozens over his lifetime: Ahpuc, Artaxerxes, Vlad, and Hannibal, to name but a few) had many disciples at the time, all lovers of both sexes, though I quickly became his favorite. He revealed many things to me, including that he had been a Mayan priest when he'd received what he referred to as "the calling." He had been given a mission to recover five talismans of great power hidden throughout the world. By the time I met him, it had been 1,700 years since he'd collected the last, a piece of silver paid to him by the high priests of Judaea to betray Jesus Christ himself.

George not only had all five items, but, by using forbidden magic, had successfully melded them together, further increasing their power. This gave him near-limitless control over the world around him. For George, at the height of his strength, moving a mountain would require no more energy than it would to simply imagine the mountain moving. At any time, he could have destroyed the world without as much as a shrug. Instead, he used his powers to make himself immortal, choosing to explore the intricacies of pain and suffering, and the brutality of war and politics.

I knew the man was corrupt but, God forgive me, I was blinded by his powers and my own ambition. I turned a blind eye to his orchestrations, always choosing to believe that the awful things – the murder, the genocide, the slaughter – that happened around him would have happened anyway had he not been there to nudge things along. But always, deep down, I knew.

It wasn't until Germany, however, just before the Second World War, when my eyes were truly opened. George was using the name Rudolf Hess, manipulating political situations behind the scenes in Germany. He befriended another aspiring young painter named Adolf Hitler and helped to turn him into one of the most hated and feared men in history.

Oblivious as I was, I could not quite manage to turn a blind eye toward the senseless slaughter of hundreds of thousands of Jews. It was then, during the days of the Auschwitz death camp, that I made my decision. Thanks to the power of George's talismans, I had lived to be over two hundred years old yet barely looked twenty-five. My time on earth should have been over many years previous. And so, knowing that I had nothing to lose, I used the tricks my master had taught me to separate one of the items from the necklace – the silver coin, the charm that formed the lowest point on the swastika – and ran away to America.

If he hadn't forced the objects to merge, he would simply have had the power of four talismans instead of five. In other words, in terms of what magics he could perform, it wouldn't have mattered that much. But because he had altered them, the four talismans would no longer work together exponentially. In effect, he went from having the power of a god to the power of an amazingly gifted magician, still much stronger than anyone else using magic, four times that of the coin that I now had, but nearly crippled compared to what he had been before. For all intents and purposes, he became mortal.

Weakened by the loss and distracted by his search for me, the Third Reich that George had created through Hitler quickly fell. He abandoned Hitler and the Hess identity so that he could carry on his work elsewhere, work that now included finding and punishing me.

George almost caught me several times. I was always on the run, moving here, going there, in an attempt to keep him from tracking me down. I soon grew tired of running. After the war ended, I used the coin to seek out any distant relatives I might have in America; to my surprise, I had quite a few. I'd eventually settled on Carthage, simply because it was the furthest I could get from George. Once again using the power of the coin, I convinced Hiram Spencer that I was Charles, his younger brother whom he and his family had long thought died in the war. Through my deception, the Spencer's accepted me as one of their own. Once I was established in the community, I used some of the money I had squirreled away during my many years as George's disciple to purchase the first house I could find on the market. I hoped to eventually meet a young woman and settle down, living the rest of my days in peace and safety with my family. but it was not to be.

I'd only been in Carthage for a year when I felt the psychic tendrils of George's mind reaching out for me, searching, demanding that I return what I'd stolen. He had found me because I had carried the coin with me for so long, and its energies had mingled with my own, making me the perfect target for his searches. It was then that I set up the wards; one pentagram for each of the five positions in a larger pentagram, two each on the first and second floors, and one on the third. Infused with energy from the coin, the wards would keep anyone from entering the house. I also created charms outside that would keep anyone from breaching the security of the fence. Moreover, no one would even want to enter; thanks to a particularly inspired spell, interlopers would be greeted by a strange compulsion to run away as far and as fast as they could, forgetting all about the house.

But still, I felt his presence; weaker now but growing stronger by the day. And it was then that I knew I could not have the life that I so desperately wanted, that for once in my life I needed to serve the greater good. I tried destroying the coin, but to no avail; it could not be harmed. Instead, I used its own magic to transform it into a coin more suited to the realm: a common American nickel. I then hid the nickel in plain sight, surrounded by copper, which I knew from experience had the strange ability to block most of the supernatural vibrations that the talisman gave off. That, combined with my wards, should have keep the coin hidden forever.

My last act before leaving the house will be two-fold. First, I'll attune the wards to my blood, hoping that Hiram or one of his children or one of their children's children will act in my place to defend the coin if ever it becomes necessary. Though they still can't get past the wards outside, anyone who shared my blood could easily gain entrance to the house itself once the wards I'd placed on the fence were destroyed. I've conjured a failsafe psychic beacon that would call out to my descendants until one of them heeded the summons and walked through the wards and into my former home.

My second act will be to spell myself to prevent me from ever again, under any circumstances, stepping foot into the house. What I plan to do after I leave Illinois is dangerous and I didn't want George to turn my own blood against me, or all my preparations will have been for naught. Finally, I'll cast a spell that will wipe all thoughts of the wards and the hidden coin from my memory the moment I leave the safety of my home. If George does find me, my memories will be useless to him.

If you have found this journal and deciphered the key to reading it, my preparations have failed and you no doubt already know much of what I have written. What you may not know is that there is no way in heaven or on earth to defeat George. I leave now for London and if my former master finds me, I am fully prepared to defend myself against him. In the end, however, I know I will die, if not by his hand then by my own. I will not let him corrupt me any more than he already has. The best that I can hope for is that you will hide the coin so that he does not find it, and then run away to the farthest corners of the earth. I pray to God and all that is holy that he does not deem it worth his time to pursue you.

# Chapter 36

"WELL, THAT explains some of this," said Shawn, closing the book. "But if this guy's, what, nearly three thousand years old, what can we possibly do to stop him?"

"Maybe we can't," Jenny whispered in a hushed voice, "but we have to try. We owe Tanner at least that much."

"I know. I'm just… scared."

"Me too," she breathed, collapsing into his arms. "But at least we're safe in here, for a while."

"For a while," he agreed, "but they'll get in here eventually."

"It would be so easy just to give up," she murmured, her gaze not quite meeting his, "to let him have the damned nickel and hope he goes away."

"Hey, whoa," said Shawn, pulling away, "we can't do that, and you know it. It wouldn't make any difference, anyway. We'd still wind up dead, and so would a lot of other people."

"I know," she replied, leaning into him, resting her head on his shoulder. "I just…I want to have a normal life, I guess. I want to do normal things, like go to the movies with my boyfriend. I don't want to fight monsters."

"I've thought about you almost constantly since Saturday morning," he said, looking into her eyes. That earned him a tentative smile, though her eyes still betrayed fear.

"I wondered when you'd notice me," she grinned, her eyes glowing in the beam of the flashlight.

"I noticed you a long time ago," he admitted, "but you were a grade behind me, not to mention my best friend's sister."

"Hey, cut it out," a voice came from behind them, echoing through the fireplace. "I don't need to see this stuff, especially since I'll never have a girl of my own. It's going to be pretty difficult now that I'm an action figure, for crying out loud. Who wants to date a hunk of plastic? And this is a weird conversation to be having with my sister, even if I am dead, so somebody say something, okay?"

"Tanner!" Jenny screamed, rising to her feet and rushing toward the fireplace. "My God, Tanner, we thought you…"

"We thought you were dead. Well, dead again, at any rate," Shawn finished for her, staring at the toy. "How did you get away? And how in the hell are you even alive?"

"I was fighting the fetch when it suddenly ran away. I figured Ahpuc called him to get you two. I would have been here sooner, but," he paused, gesturing down to his legs, "these can only carry a guy so fast, you know?"

"How did you get into the house?" asked Jenny, finding her voice.

"I climbed the big oak out in the yard and jumped on the balcony, then climbed up to the chimney. I wasn't sure whether or not I'd be able to get past the house's wards, and at first I couldn't, but then I lowered myself down into the top of the chimney and just sort of …went away, for a while, I guess. And then I was at the bottom, my armor cracked but none too much the worse for wear."

That made a strange kind of sense. The rats, bugs, even the crow - they weren't really sentient beings. The wards kept out humans and even things like the fetch, because people and apparently little monsters had consciousness, whereas bugs and birds didn't. But he still wasn't convinced that the animated Mego was telling the truth.

"How do you know all this stuff?" asked Shawn, "Tanner didn't know about the wards. How do we even know you're really Tanner?"

"First of all, I'm not sure I am Tanner, at least not completely. I have all of his memories and feelings, but I also...I know a lot of stuff now, Shawn, things I never even dreamed of before I died. I don't know how I do, I just do. I know about Ahpuc, the fetch, and even about you two," he grinned up at them, "though even if I didn't, I would have the moment I stepped through that fireplace. And, if you're wondering, and I know you are, I approve. My best friend and my favorite sister – well, okay, my *only* sister... how could I be anything but happy?"

Jenny blushed, brightened by her brother's approval - even if it was posthumous. "I knew you'd think it was okay."

Shawn, however, still wasn't convinced that the doll was actually Tanner. "Where's my yo-yo?" The real Tanner would know what happened to the toy, and how it had gotten lost.

"You mean the green one up on the top shelf of the library," the doll asked, "that you lost trying to get that box down for me, or maybe the blue one or the red one or one of the other colors you have at home? Shawn, it really is me. I'm back. I don't know why or for how long, but I'm back, and we need to stop Ahpuc. If he gets hold of the nickel... he'll be a hundred times worse than he was before. He'll destroy us, our parents, this town, maybe even the whole world. He thrives on pain and suffering, and he's missed out on a lot of it over the past thirty years, and he'll need to make up for lost time. And that's exactly what he'll do if we can't stop him."

"How do you know this?" demanded Shawn.

"I don't know!" the knight yelled, "How can a toy sword turn to steel when I hold it? How can I even exist in this body? You'll just have to accept it on faith, Shawn, at least until we get out of this mess"

"Faith isn't something I have a lot of confidence in," muttered Shawn, "and even if I did..."

"He's telling the truth," interrupted Jenny, her eyes pleading with Shawn. "It has to be true. He's Tanner."

"Okay, okay," shrugged Shawn, prepared for the moment to believe that the little doll truly was his best friend brought back from the grave. "But what can we do about the old man? He's killed Tanner once and he's almost killed you and me three times just since Saturday!"

"Do you have the nickel?"

"No, but it's somewhere safe. I knew it was important, and I didn't want to bring it with me in case the fetch caught us."

"So, where is it?" the doll asked, looking from Shawn to Jenny and back again.

"Well, I guess you don't know everything after all, do you?"

"Tanner," Jenny interrupted, "what else do you know? Is Dad okay?"

"He's fine. A little bruised up after his fight with the fetch, but fine. He and Mom have half the town out looking for you."

"How do you know all this stuff?" interjected Shawn, repeating the question he had asked earlier.

"I told you, I don't know. It's like… well, like after a while you don't know how you know how to ride a bike, if that makes sense. You just do it. I woke up in that coffin screaming for my life, Shawn. I didn't know where I was or what was going on, I just knew that some monster had risen up out of the lake, screamed at me, and then pushed my head under the water. And that was it."

"Tanner, I'm so sorry I didn't save you," started Jenny, looking down at her feet. "And then no one believed me, not even Shawn, at first. It was awful."

It was Shawn's turn to look embarrassed. Turning to Jenny, he said, "I promise, I'll never doubt your word again." And then to Tanner: "How did you figure out where you were?"

"I didn't, not at first. After a while, I just started crying, yelling, cursing, anything I could think to do to get someone's attention. But no one came. And a little while later, maybe hours, maybe days, I fell asleep. And then it was like I was drifting up through the ground, over my grave, and I just knew. I saw the other graves in our plot and I saw one new grave, and I knew it was mine. And then, once I accepted that, I knew other things as well. I knew what had killed me, and why. I knew the house was the only safe haven from my killers. And I knew that you, Shawn, would ultimately have to be responsible for saving us all, and that you'd need to use the nickel to do it."

"But why me?" Shawn asked, feeling very small and powerless. He wanted nothing more at the moment than to crawl away somewhere and hide under a rock.

"Blood," Tanner said. "It didn't have to be you; it could have been anyone on your father's side of your family; your father or his father, or your son or your daughter, for that matter, if you ever have children," he glanced sideways at Jenny, about to say something but thinking better of it. "But at this point, Shawn, there's just no choice; it's you or it's no one. I can't do it and Jenny can't do it. It's got to be you."

"Boy, talk about pressure," Shawn tried to laugh, but the sound came out like a choke. "Okay, so what do we do next?"

# Chapter 37

THE FETCH stood motionless behind the old man, watching as he poured eldritch energy into the wards that protected the house. No single attack did the trick, but the sum of the assault was having a cumulative effect, slowly weakening the house's defenses. But the attack took a toll on the old man as well; he had aged at least ten years in the last thirty minutes, his skin wrinkled and hanging loose from his skeletal frame, looking as though he might collapse at any moment. Once the coin was recovered, however, he would regain the strength that had once been his before it was stolen. And, finally, he would make good on his promise to let the fetch go to live and hunt as it desired.

It longed for freedom, a concept that had somehow never even occurred to it until recently. The fetch had been changing ever since it swapped blood with the meat named Shawn Spencer. Before, it had never dared question its master's orders; now, all it longed to do was rip Ahpuc's beating heart from his chest. And then it would be free. But for now it stood beside its master, as always, waiting to do his bidding; to kill the meat in the house, to gorge itself on their bodies, to feast on their bones.

But once the deed was done, it – no, HE, not "it", he – would betray his master. He had learned to hide these feelings from the old man, even when their minds were connected. He was becoming more than just Ahpuc's plaything. Perhaps he would eventually remember what came before…

"Fetch, climb up on the roof. I just felt something enter the house through the chimney. Perhaps we can follow," ordered Ahpuc, his eyes never once leaving the house's front door.

The creature stared at his master, unmoving, ignoring his command. For the first time it dawned on him that he had a choice, that he didn't have to wait. He took one step away from the house, then another, feeling whatever bound him to the priest begin to weaken with every step. Freedom. He could smell it on the wind, taste it in his mouth.

"Do you defy me?" asked Ahpuc, turning to meet the creature's eyes. Sweat poured from his brow to meet the rain drizzling from above, rolling off his skin in great waves of liquid rage. "Do you dare?"

The old man curled his hand into a fist, and he felt an invisible leash begin to close around his throat. The promise of freedom was gone, coalescing into the air as if it had never been. The fetch couldn't breathe, couldn't even move. Pain crawled through his body, traveling every nerve, like he was rolling in a field of broken glass.

He thought he was dying, but in an instant he could move again and the pain was completely gone. He bowed his head, gazing at the ground. He'd been punished, and dared not cross the old man again.

Defeated, doing as he'd been ordered, the little monster quickly scaled the side of the house, climbing all three stories in a matter of seconds. Pausing to survey the area, he scurried over the old shingles of the dilapidated roof to investigate the chimney.

He caught the scent of the thing he'd battled in the old jail, but it disappeared down the chimney. The fetch stretched a tentative paw past the brick that made up the fireplace exit, paralyzed with pain as blue sparks danced over his fur. He tumbled back, nearly rolling off the roof before sinking his claws into the shingles. The old priest sensed the fetch's failure through the link they shared, ordering the creature back to his side as he prepared to unleash yet another torrent of energy at the dwelling's defenses.

\* \* \*

The house rocked on its foundation as though hit by an earthquake. Dust shook from the ceiling and wood creaked, straining against beams. Shawn and Jenny stumbled against the staircase railing as they neared the second floor landing, nearly falling down the stairs.

"What was that?" yelped Jenny, holding the warped wooden railing. She pulled herself past the last few stairs to the temporary safety of the landing.

"Ahpuc," said Tanner's muffled voice from inside Shawn's pocket. "He's expending his energy trying to get past the defenses of the house. If he uses too much he'll eventually destroy himself, but that won't matter if he manages to get in here and kill us first."

"Come on, before this place falls down around us!" shouted Shawn, joining Jenny on the landing. Together they sprinted through the hall toward the back of the house, past the open doors of library and the studio, toward the stairs that would take them to the third floor of the mansion.

Their feet echoing through the empty halls, the teenagers traversed the creaking flight of wooden steps to find themselves in the middle of a huge, empty room. Shining the flashlight all around, Shawn was disappointed to find it empty.

"Let me down," pleaded Tanner from Shawn's pocket.

Shawn dropped him to the floor. "Okay, I'm stumped. There's nothing here."

"Hey, what's that?" interrupted Jenny. Another pentagram, this one made from sculpted marble and inlaid into the dark cherry floor, gleamed in the light made from Shawn's beam. "That must be the fifth pentagram."

"It could be," agreed Shawn, moving closer. "But the position isn't right. This is right in the middle of the other two on the second floor and doesn't form the giant pentagram that I thought it would."

"Maybe you're wrong about the positioning," offered Tanner. Moving to the pentagram, the action figure kicked at it with a little plastic foot, creating a tiny cloud of dust that rose a few inches into the air before settling back down across the floor.

Curious, Shawn dropped to a squat, reaching out to trace the lines of the star that shined up at them from the floor. As his fingers met the marble contours of the pentacle, he felt a searing heat burn deep into his chest, just above his heart. The floor almost seemed to open up beneath him, revealing darkness so cold and vast that it chilled him to the bone and made his head spin. One moment he was there, his fingers brushing dust from the marble, and in the next he wasn't. There was no puff of magician's smoke, no dazzling array of lights. He was simply gone, leaving nothing in his wake.

Shawn blinked, readjusting his eyesight to the light that flooded his senses. Clicking off his flashlight, he squinted through the brightness to find himself in a small room, the absence of any doors or windows making his heart skip a beat. He immediately realized he was standing in the center of another pentagram, this one created through the use of wax and chalk, five blazing candles lighting the room from each of its points.

A shimmering curtain of light stood at the far end of the room, pulsating through a range of colors - blue, silver, magenta, gold, red, pink, green, orange – in a pattern that seemed to make no sense. He walked to the end of the room, reaching out an unsure hand to touch the wavering air before him. His fingers passed through the curtain as though it wasn't there, feeling nothing but bitter cold on the other side. Jerking his hand back, his fingers momentarily numb, he backed away from the curtain. Turning around, he felt his eyes settle once again on the little circled star at the opposite end of the room.

*Am I still in the house?* Jenny and Tanner were alone and – glancing down at the flashlight in his hand, he realized – in the dark, while he was... where? Like an episode of *Star Trek*, he had apparently been teleported from one pentagram to another.

"Scotty, beam me up," he murmured, his mind reeling.

In a moment of inspiration, he suddenly knew where he was. Based on the pentagrams he'd found in the house, he'd determined that the top most point of the symbol should be on the third floor in the very back of the house, right above the turn in the stairs. Of course, there had been nothing there. But what if the pentagram was located in a hidden alcove buried within the walls? That would mean he was still inside the house.

Moving to one wall and then another, pressing his ear against each in turn, he finally heard something. Pushing his ear tighter against the wood, concentrating, he could barely make out his name being called over and over, just on the other side of the wall.

"Jenny!" he shouted back, pressing his lips against the wall, "Jenny, I'm okay! I don't know where I am, but I'm okay!"

Another earthquake rolled through the ground, nearly causing him to lose his footing. The candles, however, didn't even move, nor did their flames as much as flicker. Curious, he reached out to within inches of the closest candle, fanning his hand before the flame. Another quake suddenly hit the house, this one worse than the last, sending him stumbling toward the pentagram. His hand brushed against the candle, singing his skin. He watched in horror as the tapered pole of wax began to wobble, its flame dancing crazily in his vision. The fire cast moving shadows on all four walls before it struck the ground, immediately going out.

"Oh shit," Shawn whispered, as one by one, almost like a group of mystical dominoes, the other four candles followed suit, toppling to the ground and flaming out the moment they hit the floor. And for the second time in five minutes, Shawn was once again, unceremoniously and without preparation, thrust into a pit of swirling darkness that leapt up to meet him from below.

* * *

"Tanner, I can't see a thing," Shawn heard Jenny's worried voice call out. Her steps circled the room, echoing through the darkness.

Quickly rising to his feet, Shawn's hands fumbled as he moved to activate the flashlight. His thumb finally clicking the button into place, he was rewarded with an arc of light lancing out to reveal Jenny's tear-stained face staring at his in amazement. She held the little knight in one hand, the other hovering next to the wall opposite the staircase, poised as though about to knock.

"Shawn!" she gasped, turning from the wall to run into his arms. "God, Shawn, what happened? You were here one moment and then you were gone. We thought we heard your voice, but…"

"Hey, let go!" Tanner said, crushed between his sister's and best friend's embrace. "Is it too late to change my mind about you two?"

"I was in a hidden room, just over the staircase. I think this," he fingered the still-warm pentagram that hung from around his neck, "was responsible. There was another pentagram there, this one with candles, and when that last quake hit…well, I knocked the candles over. If that's what was keeping the wards in place, there's nothing between us and Ahpuc now."

As if to confirm his worst fears, he heard a low rumble coming from beneath them, and then the sound of doors slamming open.

"Saint Michael the Archangel," Jenny began to whisper, recalling one of the prayers she had learned in church, "Defend us in battle. Be our protection against the wickedness and snares of the devil; may God rebuke him; we humbly pray; and do thou O Prince of the heavenly host, by the power of God, thrust into hell Satan and all evil spirits who wander through the world for the ruin of souls. Amen."

"I'm not sure it's Satan we have to worry about," muttered Shawn.

"He's inside," interrupted Tanner, his rubber eyes going wide. "Shawn, where's the nickel? We need the nickel!"

"It's back in the graveyard! It seemed safer to hide it there, in case the fetch ran us down. Don't worry, it's protected."

"Shawn, pick me up and don't drop me until I say so," the doll commanded. Then he went stiff, the life going out of his plastic frame like an extinguished pilot light. And the doll was just a doll again.

Shawn scooped up Galahad with one hand while pushing the flashlight toward Jenny with the other. "Take this," he hissed, pressing the light into her unresponsive fingers. "If we get separated, take the back stairs and leave through the cellar. Then just run as far and as fast as you can, and don't stop until you're somewhere safe."

"Shawn, I'm not going to leave you."

"She's right," said Tanner, once again inhabiting the knight, "you two shouldn't split up. But we have to get moving now, because they're definitely in the house, just inside the foyer and coming fast."

"What can we do?" asked Shawn, almost wishing he'd abandoned his plan and brought the nickel after all. With it, at least they'd have something with which to bargain; without it, they were as good as dead.

"We can be ready for them," said the doll, pointing across the big open room toward the set of stairs that led down the back half of the house. "There's only one way up here, so once they reach the staircase we're trapped. We need to get down to the second floor."

"Come on!" Shawn shouted, grabbing Jenny's hand and yanking her toward the stairs.

The pair took the steps two at a time, Tanner carried along in Shawn's hand. They reached the landing just in time to see Ahpuc, walking stick in hand, round the corner at the far end of the hall.

"Stop where you are!" wheezed the old man, leaning against his cane for support. His breathing grew more labored with every passing second.

But where was the fetch? A guttural growl answered Shawn's question, and he watched with horror as the little monster flew up at them from the stairs below. Jenny's flashlight arced across the demon in mid-jump, gleaming against its outstretched claws and deadly fangs.

"Get down!" Shawn cried, pushing Jenny to the floor. The flashlight tumbled from her hands as she fell to the landing, clattering down the stairs and out of sight, leaving the house in darkness.

Shawn felt the beast slam into him, knocking him hard against the bathroom door, its claws tightening around his throat as they fell through the doorway. He heard the old man shout something and felt Tanner scramble from his hand, and then…

…he was looking through the eyes of the fetch, sharing the monster's vantage point as it dug its claws deep into Shawn's shoulders, pulling a dark paw back in preparation for the killing blow. He saw himself as an orange blotch in the darkness, wilting under the grasp of the beast.

Then he was tumbling off his own body, as Tanner drove his little sword into the creature's flank, wounding it, sending it scurrying away deeper into the bathroom.

"Shawn, run!" he heard Tanner yell as he advanced on the monster. "Get Jenny and get out of here!"

*I can't,* Shawn thought, but then he realized that he could, after all. He was back in his own body, sucking air into deprived lungs, his body aching and bruised but otherwise unharmed. Visually, he was still connected to the fetch, but he realized he could still feel his own body.

Stumbling to his feet, he blinked in an effort to restore his vision but all he saw was his own back – a big splotch of moving red energy – just as the monster saw him. And then he was rocked back on his heels – not him, he realized, the fetch – as Tanner launched another attack, tackling the little monster, pushing it against the wall.

"Shawn?" questioned a voice just a few feet away. Jenny! "Where are you?"

"Buddy…" gasped Tanner's voice from the bathroom. "I can't hold it back much longer. Get out!"

"Tanner?" whispered Jenny's voice. "Where's Tanner?"

"We've got to get out of here!" Shawn urged, reaching out blindly to take her hand, pulling her toward where he thought the stairs should be. He concentrated on remembering the layout of the house. If he could manage to not fall down the stairwell… there!

"You're not going anywhere, boy!" Ahpuc's voice echoed through the darkness. And then the connection was broken, and he was completely himself again, blind as a bat but free from the fetch's link to the old man who wanted them dead.

A glowing orb of reddish-orange energy suddenly appeared at the end of the hallway, burning Shawn's eyes as it pulled back the curtain of darkness before them. The ball hovered in front of the old man, bobbing up and down like an apple in a barrel. It slowly began to move away from the wizard, picking up speed. Within seconds it was rushing through the air, its flames scorching the walls of the corridor, coming straight at them.

"Come on!" Shawn yelled, pulling Jenny through the hallway and around the corner just as the ball of flame crashed into the wall. Flames licked their heels, burning flesh, but then it was over as quickly as it had started and they were in the dark again.

Panting, his heart in his throat, Shawn felt along the wall. It had to be there. And then he found it; a hole in the wall, with ropes running down the center – the dumbwaiter. Thank god he had left it open.

"Follow me," he whispered to Jenny. Climbing into the little space, he contorted his body to squeeze into the three foot by two foot opening. Jenny climbed in after him, her legs straddling his, her head pressed against his shoulder.

"Are you in?" Shawn asked.

"I think so," she responded, pulling her legs tighter around him. "Where are we?"

Shawn's response was drowned out by a deep, guttural growl moving down the hallway, fast approaching their hiding spot. He knew it was now or never. Wrapping his arms around Jenny, his bruised and bloodied fingers found the pull rope, and he began to work the pulley. And, slowly, the dumbwaiter began to move.

Light flashed before them in the form of a small globe of flowing yellow energy held aloft by the old man's hand. He rounded the corner of the hallway, just a few steps behind the fetch.

"Kill them," he panted, pointing a gnarled finger at the pair of frightened teenagers. "Kill them now."

The fetch launched itself into the air, screaming, claws flashing, narrowly missing Shawn and Jenny just as the dumbwaiter slid past the edge of the wall.

"We're going to make it!" Shawn breathed, maneuvering the pulley down through the walls of the house.

"What's that noise?" whispered Jenny, her face pressed tight against Shawn's cheek.

Shawn heard it too; the sound of sawing coming from above their heads, like a knife scraping against sandpaper…

"Hold on!" he shouted, the ropes growing limp beneath his hands. The fetch had clawed or chewed through the ropes and the dumbwaiter was suddenly in free fall, the teenagers weightless, plummeting through the air toward the kitchen.

He felt as though he were floating in water without being wet. The fall seemed to go on forever, and then they were crashing into and *through* the floor of the shaft, past the kitchen, and into someplace else entirely.

The dumbwaiter began to slow, teetering awkwardly like a car with bad brakes, finally screeching to a halt just seconds after it had all start-

Small Things | 271

ed. A lit room appeared before them like a beacon of hope, just outside the dumbwaiter's exit.

"We're alive," whispered Shawn, his face white as a sheet in the glow of the light beyond the dumbwaiter's walls.

"Come on," Jenny choked. Rolling to her feet, she reached out for the wall to steady her shaking legs.

They found themselves standing in a small rock cavern somewhere below the house. The light, it seemed, came from a torch attached to a bracket on the far wall. More sorcery? From the dust and bug carcasses lining the floor, he knew that they were the first people to enter the cavern in a very long time.

Blinking, Shawn turned around to find a heavy steel door standing to the left side of the dumbwaiter. The door had wheels above and below its frame and rested on a pair of rusty tracks that ran from the floor to the ceiling.

Thinking only of the fetch, Shawn immediately moved to the door, grunting as he pushed at the huge piece of metal. Jenny moved to help him, and together they slowly began to move the door, first a few inches, then a foot, until finally the door blocked the entrance.

Backs to the door, they let themselves slide to the ground. They were both physically exhausted and mentally spent, wanting nothing more than to rest. But less than a minute later, they heard an angry howl from the other side of the door, quickly followed by the sound of razor-sharp claws and teeth grinding against metal. The fetch was in the shaft, and if it hadn't been for the door they'd be as good as dead.

Shawn was the first to speak. "I guess Colin set this up to escape in case something happened." Something had definitely happened.

"What about Tanner?" Jenny asked. Removing her streaked and dirty glasses, she made a half-hearted effort to clean the lenses with the bottom of her pajama top but quickly gave up.

"He saved our lives, you know."

"I know," she whispered, reliving her brother's death for the second time in a week.

Finding Shawn's hand beside her, she clutched it tight, bringing it to rest against her cheek. She held it there for a moment, enjoying the warmth of his skin, before finally pressing her lips to his palm.

The noise from behind them began to slow and, finally, ceased altogether, leaving the room in silence. Had the fetch given up?

Shawn rose on shaky legs to survey the room. There seemed to be only one exit from the cavern, and that was through a natural opening in the rock on the wall opposite the dumbwaiter. An escape route, to be sure. But to where? Taking the torch from the wall, Shawn began to edge toward the tunnel.

"You're not leaving me here," Jenny's voice quavered.

An enormous explosion sounded behind them, like a stick of dynamite dropped into a vat of nitroglycerin, and the ground shook violently beneath their feet. The force of the concussion sent them sprawling to the ground, bits of rock and dirt falling from the walls all around them.

Shawn recovered first, his ears ringing from the blast. He turned his head to see a huge, angry bulge in the metal door. The barrier had withstood the blast, but it didn't look like it could withstand a second. The door had been pushed out a good three inches from the face of the wall. Bright blue licks of flame curled around the corner, a huge rush of superheated air escaping from beyond the gap. Shawn gasped as he felt a boiling wave of heat rush through the cavern, pulling moisture from his body, his bare back releasing a torrent of perspiration as he cried out in pain.

Then they were crawling frantically on hands and knees through the dark tunnel. From what little they could see, the tunnel looked as though it dead-ended some fifty feet ahead. As the tunnel grew larger they were finally able to rise to their feet, sprinting the rest of the way to the end.

A shiver ran down Shawn's spine and he momentarily hesitated, unsure of what to do. Jenny's voice brought him back to the present, yelling at him, urging him to run, and he grasped her outstretched hand and moved one foot in front of the other, quickening to join her pace as they ran with breakneck speed towards the end of the tunnel.

Another explosion rocked the tunnel, and they knew that Ahpuc had breached the heavy steel door. The fetch would be hot on their trail in a matter of minutes. Taking in gasping gulps of oxygen, they pushed their already-drained bodies to the limit, running for their lives.

They found themselves at the end of the tunnel, which, amazingly, wasn't a dead end after all. A smaller passageway, just as tall but only half as wide, opened out from the right wall, sloping downward. Fueled by a mind-numbing fear, their bodies moved almost of their own accord. They quickly rounded the corner, hurtling themselves down the slanted passage and deeper into the earth.

They abruptly reached the end of the tunnel, finding only a rusted metal ladder leading down from a hole in the roof of the cave. The ladder ended in a small wooden door, barely large enough for one person to fit through at a time. Shawn just hoped it wasn't locked.

"Go on," he breathed, trying to catch his wind. "I'll hold it steady."

Ignoring her aching muscles, Jenny began to climb the rusty ladder. Putting one foot after another, she moved one rung at a time, until she stood just inches from the door above her head.

Pushing the door open with a thud, Jenny scrambled through the trap door, disappearing from sight.

"Shawn, hurry," she pleaded from overhead, her eyes gleaming down at Shawn through the flickering light of the torch.

"*Jenn*-eeey!" rasped a guttural voice from just beyond the bend in the tunnel, moving Shawn to action.

And then the world around him seemed to waver again.

"Please, not now!" he choked, his vision clouding. "Jenny, go on…" he managed to get out before stumbling to the ground, falling face first into the middle of the dusty tunnel just inches from the bottom rung of the ladder.

* * *

Shawn found himself standing in the middle of a snowy clearing, surrounded by tall, willowy aspens that swayed in the harsh winter wind that raged at him from all directions. The moon shone down through the branches and leaves, illuminating a spot in the center of the forest floor. A naked man lay there shivering, wrapped in a fetal position, his dark matted hair dirty with gray ice and blood.

"Where am I?" Shawn shivered.

"Impossible!" said a voice from behind him. "You should not be here."

"But where is here?" Shawn asked, turning to meet the steel gray eyes of Ahpuc.

"It doesn't matter. Tell me where the talisman is and your death will be quick."

For an instant Shawn's thoughts flickered to Tanner's coffin, to the coin's hiding place, and immediately he knew it was a mistake.

"Right you are, boy," Ahpuc answered, reading his adversary's thoughts. "I did, however, underestimate you. Like your kin before you, you've proven to be quite a challenge. But you can't stop me now. The coin is my destiny."

Kin? Shawn felt his life start to slip away as the frigid forest around him began to dim. And then he remembered.

"Colin!" he screamed with what little strength he had left. He turned back to the naked, shivering man in the middle of the clearing. "You're Colin Wainwright, and you're not a monster. You're a painter. Ahpuc… no, George! George did this to you, and you have to fight him!"

He thought he saw the man twitch a finger, but then he grew still again, huddling against himself in the cold white snow.

"Shut up!" shouted the old man, advancing toward Shawn. He raised his fingers toward the heavens as if to summon another lightning bolt.

"Colin Wainwright!" screamed Shawn, running to the man, dropping to his knees beside him. "Wake up!"

The form before him begin to stir, seemingly confused and uncertain as he fought to take in the information he'd just been given.

"Colin?" he finally mumbled, his voice dry and cracking. His eyes found Shawn's and he blinked as though he wasn't sure if any of this was real. "My before name is Colin?"

"Kill him!" hissed the old man, his eyes wide with fear. "Kill him, you wretched monster!"

"I am not a monster," Colin Wainwright rasped. He slowly clambered to his knees, shaking off twenty years of ice and snow and dirt. "I am a man, and I finally remember what you did to me. I remember everything. I remember it all."

Shawn held out a hand to the naked, shivering man before him, amazed and awed by the transformation he was witnessing.

He figured out some time ago that Colin Wainwright had been twisted and changed into the murderous little fetch through the use of Ahpuc's corrupting magic. What he hadn't been so sure about was whether anything remained of the man inside. Now he had his answer.

Wainwright took his hand, grasping it tight within his own, and the instant their skin made contact the mental connection between the two was broken…

\* \* \*

…And Shawn found himself once again in the dusty tunnel, Jenny by his side. She was tugging at him, doing her best to drag him up the ladder.

"Jenny," he said, meeting her emerald green eyes. He rose to his feet on trembling legs, using the ladder for balance, "Why didn't you escape?"

"Because," she panted, releasing the boy's arm, "no one tells me what to do, not even you. And, besides, if you didn't catch it before, I'm awfully fond of you." She smiled back at him, then turned her attention toward the tunnel.

Shawn started to reply, but his words were drowned out by a bloodcurdling scream that echoed through the tunnel behind them. A shiver ran down his spine, making the fine hairs on the back of his neck grow rigid; the voice sounded almost human.

"Come on!" pleaded Jenny, looking frantically toward the turn in the tunnel.

"Hand me the torch."

"I'm coming with you, then," she said, climbing down the ladder.

Shawn took the torch from Jenny, sprinting down the tunnel and around the corner to the source of the noise.

A creature that looked something like a cross between a man and a grizzly bear lay huddled in a ball before him. The creature was covered from head to toe in a smattering of dark, wiry hair, and its open snout showed needle-sharp teeth surrounding the pink tongue of a man. The beast continued to scream at the top of its lungs as its body began to undulate, its crystal blue eyes focused on some non-existent point somewhere past the walls that housed the tunnel.

"What is that... thing?" whispered Jenny, her fingers slowly reaching out to entangle Shawn's.

A fiery explosion of pain suddenly rocked Shawn's skull, and he dropped to his knees beside the creature. His head felt like it was on fire, and colors danced wildly before his eyes. He arched his back in pain, mirroring the movements of the creature writhing upon the floor.

"Shawn, what's happening?"

He heard more screams, not just Jenny's, and it took him a full minute to realize that they were coming from him. The pain was so unbearable that he thought he might pass out. And then the attack ended as quickly as it had begun. He felt a great and powerful rage leave his body, a fury he hadn't even realized was there.

In perfect synchronicity to Shawn, the beast grew stock still as its fur began to disappear into its skin, receding inches at a time until all that was left was a fine sheen of body hair. The snout melted away to reveal the anguished features of a human face beneath. Where one moment laid a monster the next lay a man, naked and shivering, covered in scratches and bruises, tears streaming from his eyes.

An unearthly red glow rose from the man's chest, a perfect circle of energy, bobbing in the air as it fully disengaged from his body. It circled the room, almost as if looking for something, before suddenly shooting toward the shaft at the end of the tunnel like a fish caught on a hook. It bounced against one wall and then the other, before disappearing into the dumbwaiter shaft and vanishing from sight.

"What was that?" asked Jenny, staring after it.

"God..." Shawn breathed, ignoring the red ball of energy. "The anger...I think the monster's bite affected me more than I realized."

"Thank you," rasped the man on the floor, his voice cracking and hoarse. He started to cough and sputter, finally throwing up bile as he rolled on to his stomach, doing his best to get his arms and legs under him. "My God... thank you."

"Colin?" Shawn asked, his voice shaking as he took in the sight of the six foot naked man with long black hair lying on the ground in front of them. "What just happened to me?"

"I think... whatever caused us to share the link also did much more than that. It helped me to be a little more human, somehow, but in turn caused you to..."

"To be a little more monster," Shawn finished for him, realizing that it was true. The fight at the Tastee Freeze, his father's shovel, even running over the fetch… he'd been changing and hadn't even realized it. The rage had served him well, had perhaps even saved their lives, but he was happy to let it go.

"Who is he?" asked Jenny, pointing at the naked man still lying sprawled across the floor.

"Colin Wainwright…" looking down at his state of undress, Wainwright grimaced, "That name has not passed my lips in so long… and I have done so many things, murdered so many innocents. I'm not sure I still deserve the name, though I think it might suit me better than being called a fetch.

"Jenny, I am so sorry about your brother. I was not myself when I took his life, but I have full memories of the event – and hundreds more like it – and to say that I'd gladly and willingly trade my life for his in an instant is a gross understatement."

"The fetch…" Jenny mumbled, grabbing hold of Shawn's forearm, "is… was… Colin Wainwright?"

"I suspected it, but I was never sure," admitted Shawn, hand on his still-aching head. His eyes flickered between Wainwright and the red-headed girl in the stained and ripped pink pajamas beside him. "We …connected again, just after you reached the top of the ladder, and I found myself deeper in his mind than I'd ever been before. I called his name, and I guess it worked."

"It did indeed. We shared blood when I bit you and, because we were related, that opened up the connection between us. And once you called me by my true name, George's hold over me was broken. I owe you a debt of gratitude much deeper than I could ever repay. But for now, we need to get out of this tunnel and stop George, before it's too late."

# Chapter 38

FRED RUSKIN coughed once, tried to roll to his side, failed, and then lay still. Thunder rolled overhead in time to the lightning that streaked across the sky, illuminating the landscape of tombstones and trees. Rain poured down on him, filling his eyes and his nostrils, soaking through his clothes. Still he could not move. He knew he was dying.

He missed his wife and his daughter with an ache so intense that he thought his heart would split apart, spilling blood from his chest to soak through his clothes and into the graveyard dirt beneath him. He had loved them with everything, every fiber of his being, and they were gone. Gone forever. There was no more room for anything but memories and pain in that shell inside his chest that had stopped beating a lifetime ago. Perhaps he would see them now, joining them in death in a way that he never could while stumbling through life these past fifteen years.

Death was the release he had been seeking for the last decade and a half, or at least it was until the grim reaper had actually come for him. Strangely, despite the thoughts that echoed in his head to the contrary, there was someone else in his heart after all. As much as he wanted to die for Molly and Jessica, he wanted to live for her, maybe even more. And, most of all, he wanted to live for himself. Candy Martin was a beautiful and sensitive woman who had shown him a rare and special kindness in the face of his insults and bravado. He could see now that she had wanted nothing more than a chance, a chance with him, of all people, to love again, and maybe, just maybe, a chance to live again as well. But he hadn't been able to give her that, and regret burned deep in his heart alongside the memory of his murdered wife and daughter.

Why was it that you never really saw the world around you until you were ready to leave it? His chance at redemption, the one he hadn't even known he so desperately longed for until this very moment, was slipping away.

Ruskin coughed raggedly, hacking and wheezing, spitting up blood to mix with the rainwater that continued to pool around his body, to wash him of his sins, leaving no trace that he had ever been anything more than a thought or a memory. Sighing, he breathed once, and then no more.

And then something funny happened, something he'd never be able to explain in a million years. He was standing over himself, whole again, looking down at his ruined and bloodied body. Before him was a circle of light, expanding through the darkness, a blazing, brilliant light, so bright that it almost hurt to look. There in the light, standing and waving, was Molly and their beautiful daughter Jessica. Both were dressed all in white, and Jessica was smiling, mouthing the words, "I love you, daddy," as she blew him a kiss. There were other people there as well, inside the light. His parents, his oldest brother Sam, and even Alan Delacroix, who winked at him before smiling as if to say, *don't worry, I'm okay now.*

Molly, however, was not smiling as she glided toward Ruskin, her beautiful green eyes shining even brighter than the luminescence that surrounded her. "Fred," she said, the words tumbling from her mouth as if heard from a great distance. Like a gentle breeze flitting over the ocean, she whispered, "I'll always love you, but this has got to stop."

Her words hit him like a slap in the face. "What do you mean, Molly?" he asked, tears running down his craggy cheeks. "I've missed you for so long, you and Jessie, I'm so sorry…"

"That's just it, Fred," she finally smiled, moving closer to him. "You are sorry, and you should be, but not for the reasons you think."

"Molly, I don't understand."

"Did you really think that throwing away your life on alcohol and self-recrimination was the best way to honor our memory? You haven't honored us, Fred. Instead you've shamed us, and more importantly you've shamed yourself, and it has to stop now, before it's too late."

"But Molly, I just want to be with you. I need to be with you, I need to see my little girl grow up…"

"But you never will," she interrupted, shrugging her shoulders. "It's sad and it's tragic and it certainly isn't fair, but it's true nevertheless. But just because we died didn't mean you had to stop living. We never wanted that."

"Molly, I…"

"Hush, Fred," she said. She came forward to pull him into an embrace, her breath on his skin just as warm as the day they first made love so many years ago. "Marrying you and having your child was the best thing I ever did with my life and I'd give anything for what happened not to have, but… it just wasn't that way, Fred. It just wasn't. My life is over, but yours is just beginning."

"But I don't want…"

"Yes, my love, you do. And that's okay. It's better than okay, it's wonderful. And, if you need this to move on, I'll say it just this once: I like Candy Martin. She's good for you, and you're good for her. Or you will be if you don't die tonight…"

Looking into his dead wife's eyes, he felt something inside him burst. Tears flowed down his face like rivulets rushing to meet the river and he felt as if he might float away, swept out to sea by the strength of his emotions. Shielding his eyes from the light that shadowed Molly, he reached out to take her hand, kissed it, whispering into her ear, "I do want to live, Molly. God help me, I want to live."

"All you had to do was ask," she smiled, kissing him gently on the lips. "Promise me you'll help my niece and her friend. They're in trouble and may not live to see tomorrow. Bring the jar from my nephew's grave and protect it and the children as best you can. After that, your life is yours to live as you wish. Make it a good one."

He saw an image, just then, of a bald-headed old man. A huge black creature stood beside him, its razor-sharp teeth glistening with blood. The image slowly faded, changing to that of the old Spencer house on Randolph. Shawn Spencer and Jenny McGee were frantically running for their lives, furtively looking over their shoulders, sprinting toward the side of the house, to the sanctuary that lay inside.

"I promise," he whispered, shaking his head as the vision faded. Pulling her close, looking over her shoulder at the beautiful little girl who stood in the center of the circle of light, his heart swelled with a love that would never, could never, die. But, for the first time in many, many years, he knew he had room in his heart for another, an endless supply of love from which to draw, and that love could only strengthen and would never demean the feelings he'd always hold for the wife and daughter he had lost fifteen years ago. "Honey," he said to Jessie, as she began to waver before him, "you're always in my heart."

"I know, Daddy," she whispered, her words echoing in his ears like a secret joke shared across a canyon. "Make us proud." And with that, they were gone, and with them the light, and the emptiness that had once filled his heart. In an instant he was back in his body, wracked with pain, yet somehow feeling better than he had in years.

Ruskin sat up from the mud and sticks with a gasp, sucking in water and air, coughing, spitting, finally breathing deeply. Breathing had never felt so good. Rolling to his side, pushing up to his knees, he gingerly laid a shaking hand on his chest where the lightning had struck him. There was no charred flesh, nor was there blood; just a jagged hole in his shirt where he had been hit, singed around the edges, and beneath that the melted remains of the gold chain he used to hold his and his wife's wedding rings. Molly? Had he imagined the whole thing?

But he knew it really didn't matter, and, with that, he also knew what he had to do.

Rising to his feet, scanning the ground for his shotgun, he swore he wouldn't let his wife and daughter down. Weapon in hand, he loaded one of the remaining shells into the chamber, cocked it, then waded through the flooded graveyard to Tanner's grave, to make good on the promise he'd made to Molly, to save the lives of her niece – no, *their* niece – and Shawn Spencer, as well as his own.

# Chapter 39

SHAWN, JENNY, and Colin found themselves inside the old, weather-beaten garage just to the side of the house. The ladder from the tunnel led up through the ground and to the garage, the trapdoor opening up behind the remains of a rusty 1950 Ford Crestliner.

Wainwright pulled a cache of clothing tightly wrapped in wax paper from a hidden niche in the north side of the building, stored for decades behind a rotting water hose and a box of rusted tools. The clothes, miraculously, had survived the years, though they smelled strongly of mildew and dust.

"Let me see that," he asked Jenny as he dressed, gesturing for the torch. "The light is good enough in here and this will only attract attention." He waved his hand over the torch, causing the flames to waver and wink out like a candle in a breeze.

"More magic?" asked Shawn, intrigued.

Dressed in a pair of blue jeans, a white cotton t-shirt, and a pair of canvas shoes, Wainwright shrugged, then passed the torch back to Jenny as he began to talk, "I can still feel him in my head, though our connection is fading fast. He knows what's happened, and he's angry, and when George is angry, he's very, very dangerous. You kids have done enough. You need to get out of here and let me handle this."

"Just like you did the last time?" Jenny asked the man who killed her brother, eyes bright with anger. "We can't risk you being turned into a monster again. I don't have any brothers left for you to kill."

"I'm so sorry for that," Wainwright whispered, staring down at his feet, "I'd give anything to…"

"Jenny's right," Shawn interrupted, reaching out to touch the girl's shaking hand, "You're weak and God only knows what…"

Shawn never had the chance to finish his sentence. The entire garage rose inexplicably into the air, beams pulling apart, nails squeaking from boards. The building hovered some ten yards above their heads to reveal Ahpuc, his eyes blazing with fire, arms raised high into the air, standing between the little building and the fence that surrounded the house.

"Run!" Wainwright yelled, meeting Shawn and Jenny's eyes for an instant before turning to rush the priest.

* * *

Ahpuc smiled as he released his hold on the garage, sending it hurtling back toward the ground. It hit the foundation with a thundering crash, narrowly missing Wainwright. Bits of wood, metal, and glass flew everywhere and the little building stood still for a moment, perched precariously upon the now-cracked concrete foundation, before finally collapsing inward, imploding in a hazy cloud of dust.

Wainwright tackled the old man around the waist, knocking the wind out of him as they fell to the cold, wet ground, two mortal enemies rolling in furious combat, scrambling for purchase. Despite spending the last twenty years in a body not his own, the younger man had the advantage in strength and quickness, quickly surprising and overpowering his former master.

"Let me up!" Ahpuc yelled, finding his enemy's eyes. Wainwright had him pinned to the ground, fingers wrapped around the old man's wrinkled throat.

"You deserve to die," Wainwright screamed, squeezing for all he was worth. "You should have died years ago."

"Perhaps," rasped Ahpuc, a smile slowly spreading across his face, "but not by your hands, and not today. But you will."

Wainwright stared down at the old man with a mixture of hatred and confusion, his expression slowly contorting into terror as he locked eyes with Ahpuc. He felt the psychic tendrils of the magician's mind begin to weave their way through his thoughts and consciousness, pulling at him, twisting, changing.

"Not again," he whispered, choking harder. The old man's face began to turn purple. "You won't change me again. You *can't*."

"I don't…intend to…"

"Then what…"

Wainwright felt his eyes grow weak, fluttering, closing of their own accord, and when he managed to force them open he was staring up at himself. His breath caught in his throat and he realized that he could no longer breathe.

"I should have done this a long time ago," smiled the face staring down at him. His face. "This shell suits me much better."

"But…" Wainwright choked out as spots began to dance in his vision, but he never had the chance to finish. His new body was dead, and he was dead with it. Ahpuc had won after all.

\* \* \*

Colin Wainwright was dead. His eyes looked on lifelessly, staring from the wrinkled face he'd only worn for the last few seconds of his life. Blood trickled from the corner of his mouth and down his chin to collect in an ever-expanding pool beneath him.

Ahpuc carefully pulled the chain that contained the four talismans from his old, wrinkled body. "You had the world at your fingertips," he whispered, feeling strong and alive for the first time in many years. "But now you're dead and I have your body, and soon I'll have the coin you stole from me. All will be as it should, and you'll have died for *nothing*."

There was no doubt about it – the old man's body, and with it the consciousness of Colin Wainwright, was dead. And the two teenagers had joined him in death, having been crushed when the garage folded in on itself. Ahpuc let his - Wainwright's - head drop back to the ground with a dull thud.

He couldn't exchange bodies with someone without their permission, but Wainwright had essentially given his leave when he slit his own throat in Germany all those many years ago. He gave up his life and Ahpuc had taken it, and it was his there ever after to do with as he pleased. Despite the small victory Wainwright had won earlier, he had never truly been free from his master.

The old man had traded bodies with many deserving souls – all disciples – over the last thirty years, but, because of the missing talisman, whenever he worked even the smallest of spells, the bodies would rapidly age. He'd last traded shells less than two weeks ago, but already his body was used up. He suspected Wainwright's would fare no better. But soon, after he'd regained the coin, he'd be young again. More importantly, he'd be able to *stay* young. But, before that could happen, there was still work to do.

Rising to his feet, he immediately stumbled as a sharp pain shooting up his leg took his breath away. Wainwright had apparently twisted his ankle in the fight or the leap from the garage. He slipped the necklace up and over his head, letting it fall around his neck. Smiling to himself, he touched the swastika, feeling the power course through his veins. This body wasn't used up, wasn't near death, and he could use it with greater abandon than he'd been able to use the body before it. With a thought he healed his ankle, making it whole again, making it stronger.

Ahpuc strode toward the rented Cadillac, his heart singing with the knowledge that he would once again soon hold Judas' thirtieth piece of silver. He patted the necklace that hung from his new neck, knowing that soon the circle would once again be complete.

\* \* \*

Fred Ruskin barreled through the rain down Buchanan Street in his battered Pacer, the jar his dead wife had directed him to retrieve from his nephew's coffin bouncing in the seat beside him.

He saw four or five black-and-whites out and about – more than the county had, so probably they had called in help from the state – but managed to avoid them. His cop's instinct yelled out for him to bring in the police, but he knew that by the time he explained everything to Floyd and his crew, Jenny and Shawn would probably be dead – if they even believed him in the first place. And so he'd driven with his lights off, using the light from the moon and the streetlamps to navigate; it was slow going, but he managed to make it across town undetected.

The old Spencer house finally in sight, he hung a left on Randolph and parked by the curb. He recognized the fence in front of the house as the same one he'd run into two weeks ago. Shrugging off the coincidence, he was about to get out when he noticed the large black Cadillac from the cemetery backing out of the narrow driveway.

He pulled his Pacer in behind the other car, blocking access to the street. Killing the motor, he gathered up his shotgun and the jar, leaving the car in a sprint as he spied a young, dark-haired man dressed in a t-shirt and jeans climb out of the Cadillac to stare in his direction.

"Who are you?" Ruskin asked, his hand tightening around the shotgun's grip.

"You should be dead," the man spat, his eyes glowing with malevolence. "How are you still walking?"

"Just lucky, I guess," Ruskin lied, bringing the shotgun up to his shoulder. He pointed it at the dark-haired man, all the while advancing toward the Cadillac. "Where's the old man?"

"You wouldn't believe me if I told you."

"I guess we'll find out down at the station. You're under arrest," Ruskin began, as his eyes fell on the body of the old man beside the destroyed garage. Jesus, what was going on here? "You have the right to remain silent…"

"Shut up," the man dismissed him, waving his hand toward the sheriff. The air in front of Ruskin wavered and the shotgun flew from his fingers, spun twice in the air, and fell harmlessly to the ground.

"Well, shit," muttered Ruskin, "This just isn't my day after all."

# Chapter 40

"ARE YOU OKAY?" whispered Shawn, looking up at the ladder they had scrambled down just moments before. They barely had time to dive through the trapdoor before the garage came crashing down all around them. The noise from the imploding building still rang in their ears, and dust filtered down from above, covering both of them in a brown grainy powder.

"I think so," offered Jenny, sitting on the dirt floor of the tunnel. "Just a few more bruises to add to the bunch." She passed a hand over the torch, her eyes widening as it flamed to life.

"Colin must be dead."

"He killed my brother, Shawn."

"He was forced, he didn't know what he was doing," Shawn countered, rising to his feet. "I was in his head. The pain Ahpuc put him through… it was unbelievable. He was naked, trapped in the freezing snow, and covered in blood. I think…"

"I know," she cut him off. "I'm sorry, Shawn. And I'm sorry if he's dead. I just..." Jenny paused, angling her head up toward the trap door. "Do you hear that?"

Shawn did. The ceiling of the tunnel was shifting, creaking, as though it were about to fall in on them. Large chunks of dirt and rock began to separate from the top and side of the tunnel, tumbling to the ground at their feet, one particularly large sliver nearly knocking the boy in the head.

"We've got to get out of here!" Jenny screamed as the ceiling began to give way.

Everything seemed to move in slow motion as the two teenagers ran for safety, narrowly making the turn just as the remains of the garage caved in above them. The old Ford came crashing through the ceiling in a huge explosion of metal, flattening the rusted ladder with an enormous metallic snap. Debris slid in around the car to fill the void left by the crumbling ceiling, filling the hole with wood and rocks and twisted car parts.

"My god…" Shawn mumbled in shock, gesturing mutely at the wreckage before him. "There's no way Colin could have survived that."

"If we don't hurry, we'll be next. Come on!"

The teenagers sprinted down the tunnel toward the dumbwaiter.

"I bet the old man thinks we're dead, too," Jenny whispered, stopping before the charred and ruined metal door that had once guarded the tunnel from access through the dumbwaiter shaft. "If we can get to wherever the nickel is, then maybe we can surprise him, use it against him. You said you hid it in the graveyard."

"It's in Tanner's grave," he admitted, staring at the mangled door. "I didn't want to take it with me in case they caught up to us, and it just seemed safer to leave it there. I guess that was stupid."

Jenny ignored his self-recriminations, peering past the door and up through the shaft to the first floor. "I think we can make it up there. And you're not stupid."

"Thanks," he smiled. "Okay, let's do it. But let me go first, okay?"

"You're such a man," she returned the smile, moving aside to gesture toward the shaft. "Too bad the ladder didn't survive the cave in."

"We won't need it," Shawn said, stepping through the opening and into the shaft. "There are hand- and foot-holds carved into the wood. Just be careful, and hand me the torch once I'm up."

* * *

The jar held tightly in his hand, Ruskin broke into a run through the crumbling gate and toward the house as a clap of thunder rocked the street. He was nearly to the front door when the t-shirted man's words literally stopped him cold; his feet were rooted fast to the ground and he couldn't move a muscle, nor could he speak or even breathe. He was completely paralyzed.

"I told you to leave," the man growled from behind him. "Why won't anyone listen?"

Ruskin couldn't move, couldn't even speak. He knew his body couldn't survive long like this. He found it ironic that, now that death seemed imminent, he no longer wanted to die. There were so many things left undone, starting with his niece and Candy Martin.

"What is this?" the old man stood in front of him, looking down at the Mason jar full of loose change. "Ah, I see. You've just made this a lot easier for me. But you're still going to die."

\* \* \*

"Colin's alive!" Shawn whispered, staring out a window near the front of the house. He and Jenny had managed the climb through the shaft to the kitchen without incident, and had snuck through the house thinking that the front door would be the last exit Ahpuc would expect them to use. "And Sheriff Ruskin's with him. What's he doing here?"

"Why is he just standing there, like a statue?" Jenny asked. "And what's he holding?"

Shawn's face went white as he noticed the jar. "Colin," he screamed, pushing past Jenny, flinging the front door open to stand in the doorway. "The Sheriff's got the nickel!"

"Spencer?" asked Wainwright, looking confused at Shawn's sudden appearance. "How did you..."

Shawn's eyes moved to Ahpuc's lifeless body lying beside the garage. Finally, the old man was dead. But how had Colin killed him without the nickel?

"Sheriff Ruskin, we're okay. This is Colin Wainwright, and…" He walked toward Wainwright and the Sheriff but stopped short when he noticed that the younger man now wore a necklace around his neck: a huge swastica, just like the old man had worn. "What's going on? Why are you wearing Ahpuc's necklace?"

Jenny's eyes moved back and forth between the frozen Sheriff and Wainwright, and it dawned on her that all was not as it seemed. The way Wainwright held himself, the way he moved, was nothing like the man she'd seen earlier in the caves, and the way he'd addressed Shawn by his last name… and then it hit her. "Shawn, that's not Colin!"

"The girl's right," Ahpuc gestured toward the boy, "I am most definitely not Colin Wainwright."

Shawn gasped as he was pulled forward by some unseen force. He rose into the air, spinning, unable to move as his muscles grew taut and precious oxygen was forced from his lungs.

"Shawn!" screamed Jenny, running from the house. She leapt through the air to grab hold of his ankles, her glasses tumbling from her face, landing somewhere in the wet grass below.

"Stupid girl," Ahpuc laughed. Gesturing toward Jenny, his magic levitated her into the air beside Shawn. Twisting and turning, the two teenagers danced above the ground like marionettes in a deranged puppet show.

"What did you do to Colin?" demanded Shawn, even as he felt the life draining from his body.

"I took his body, boy, what do you think I did? He's dead, and you're about to join him."

"Let my niece go. Let them both go!" Ruskin shouted, suddenly able to move. He took one step toward Ahpuc, and then another, before once again freezing in his tracks.

It was raining but Shawn could swear he saw a bead of sweat roll down Ahpuc's forehead. Perhaps, not yet used to the body he had stolen, controlling three people was too much for him; or maybe the fact that he didn't yet have all of the talismans continued to affect him. Whatever the reason, he had to find a way to use Ahpuc's weakness to his advantage.

Shawn fought with everything in him but he couldn't move, couldn't speak, and pinpricks of light danced before his eyes as he fought to remain conscious. And then from a distance, as though in a dream, he heard the tinkle of breaking glass somewhere above, and the sound of little feet running across shingles.

"Geronimo!" yelled Tanner's voice. The little plastic action figure – missing an arm and most of one shoulder – flung itself from the roof of the house, speeding down through the drizzling rain toward Ahpuc.

"What?" screeched the man, looking up just in time to see Tanner plummeting toward him. The sword tore deep into the wizard's cheek, spurting an arc of blood through the darkness to create a Rorschach pattern in the grass.

Ahpuc stumbled backward, startled and in pain, grabbing at his face, swatting at Tanner. His strong fingers circled around the knight's waist, and in an instant his hands were blazing with fire, engulfing the toy in flames. And then Tanner was gone, nothing left but charred bits of dust and the stink of burning plastic.

"Tanner!" screamed Jenny, as she and Shawn fell. She was moving before she hit the ground, running at her brother's killer, throwing herself at him. The element of surprise in her favor, she knocked him to the ground, pummeling him with fists, her hands wet and slick with the priest's blood.

"Shawn," yelled Ruskin, suddenly able to move. He lurched awkwardly across the lawn, throwing the jar high into the air, "catch!"

The jar of change flew through the rainy night, spinning in the air, sparkling as it caught light from the streetlamps. Shawn, for the moment free of Ahpuc's magic, ignored the shooting pain between his shoulder blades and jumped for all he was worth. His fingertips caught the edge of the jar as he tumbled backward, tripping on Jenny's glasses to land flat on his back. The jar lay safe and unbroken, cradled in the boy's outstretched hands.

"Get off me!" screamed Ahpuc, grabbing Jenny's hands just as Ruskin reached the pair. He released the girl's left arm to gesture behind him, and one of the iron spokes snapped off from the ruined fence to fly through the air, impaling the Sheriff through the chest, sending him stumbling backward through the rain to land with a sickening crunch on the ground. He twitched once, then lay still.

Shawn frantically worked to unscrew the jar, his cut and blistered fingers fighting to get a grip on the lid. Finally, it was open. Pennies tumbled to the glistening grass, revealing a gleam of silver in the center of the pile. Plunging his hands into the pile of copper, the boy plucked a nickel from the sea of brown, preparing to do battle with the three thousand year old man who had murdered his best friend.

"The game is over, Shawn. Give me the coin and I'll let the girl go."

He spun around to see Ahpuc on his feet, one hand wrapped around Jenny's throat, the other pressed against her forehead. The girl stood stock still, defiant, determined not to give the man the satisfaction of showing fear.

"Okay," whispered Shawn, defeated. "Okay, just don't hurt her."

"Bring me the coin, boy – now!"

"Get it yourself," Shawn yelled, flipping the nickel high into the air.

All eyes snapped to the coin as it spun through the night, first heads, then tails, then heads again, arcing toward Ahpuc's expectant hand.

Slamming a heel down against the man's foot, Jenny used the distraction to pull free, scrambling through the grass to Shawn's side.

"Finally!" moaned Ahpuc, reaching out to snatch the coin from the air. Immediately pressing the nickel to the amulet that hung from his neck, he smiled in ecstasy as magic coursed through the coin, changing it, merging it with the other four talismans, power lost years ago finally regained and...

Something was wrong. Ahpuc's lips parted to release a strangled cry of anguish as his hand spasmed open to reveal a mass of glowing melted metal. His hand began to bleed, bone exploding through skin, flesh shredding as his cry turned to a full-fledged scream.

"You... you... you," he rasped, shaking his head, pointing his undamaged hand at Shawn. "It felt like the coin, but it was not. How did you do this?

"I saw into your mind," gasped the magician as he fell to the ground in shock, smearing wet grass stains on the knees of his Levis. His hand was nothing but bone now, and the necklace slipped from between his skeletal fingers to fall to the blood-stained grass at his feet. Whatever magic he had unloosed was eating him alive. "How did you..."

"I didn't," Shawn admitted, pulling Jenny close. "My dad collects coins, and I borrowed a buffalo nickel from his collection. After I dug up Tanner's grave, I put both of the nickels into the jar of pennies that Jenny's family put in the coffin." He reached down to scoop up a handful of pennies, letting them fall into the palm of his hand to reveal a nickel at its center, "I didn't even know which one I'd given you. Just lucky, I guess."

"Shawn," Jenny whispered, "what are you talking about? We didn't put a jar in the casket."

Shawn raised his eyebrows in response but said nothing, his attention drawn back to the dying man.

*"You were careless, Pacal,"* whispered a voice through all of their heads, causing the wizard to wince with pain, *"and now you pay the price."*

"Pacal?" asked the dying man, his teeth gritting with pain and his eyes clouding over with memories. "My name was Pacal. I remember now. I remember everything. I remember what you made me do..."

"Pacal – you of all people should know that you cannot tempt one who cannot be tempted."

"What's happening?" whispered Jenny. "Where's that voice coming from? Shawn, my glasses… I can't see anything."

Shawn remained speechless, watching in horror as the priest's skin fell from his body, all the while listening to a conversation held between a dying man and a voice whose owner he could not see.

"I… Colin, I'm so sorry… all the pain, all the death… I never meant…" and then he fell forward, his words lost in the splatter of rain. His head turned to a skull, and then to dust. He was gone, as if he'd never been.

A brightly glowing ball of energy shot from the steaming metal slag that had once been Ahpuc's necklace to explode in a sonic wave of thunder, shaking the earth and knocking Jenny and Shawn to the ground. And then the energy redoubled on itself, changing colors, growing smaller but brighter, cycling faster and faster through the colored spectrum of a rainbow. It flamed through the air, sizzling, crackling, searching, moving this way and that, finally heading straight for Shawn.

"Oh shit," Shawn whispered. His eyes moved between the smoldering remains of the old man to the downed Sheriff and then to Jenny, backing away. And then it was upon him, the ball of energy enveloping him, and everything went dark.

# Chapter 41

SHAWN KNEW that something important had just happened, but for the life of him he couldn't remember what. He found himself upright again, watching the rain come down around him, feeling unbelievable power coursing through his body. The nickel, still in his hand, glowed with an unearthly bright blue light. Slowly, he tightened his fingers around the coin, holding it tight within his grasp. It felt *good*.

"Shawn?" said a tentative voice beside him, "What's going on? I can't see anything without my glasses."

Almost as an afterthought, the boy flicked a finger in Jenny's direction and a thin stream of light arced out from his fist. It wrapped itself around her face, hanging there for a moment, shimmering, sliding slowly down her body, finally fading from view as if it had never been.

"Oh!" the girl gasped, rising to her feet, moving a hand to adjust glasses that weren't there. "Oh! I can see, Shawn, I can see without my glasses! And..." she quickly examined the cuts and bruises that had accumulated all over her body during the last several hours; they were gone. "Shawn, what's happening? Are you okay?"

*Okay?* he wanted to scream at her, *of course I'm okay!* He was better than okay. With the merest of thoughts, he healed his own body, feeling an energy unlike any he'd ever experienced wash over him, mending, healing, making him whole. Making him better than whole, better perhaps than he'd ever been before.

Walking purposefully to the downed Sheriff, he bent over and pulled the bloody metal spike from the man's shoulder. Ruskin opened his eyes in pain but then passed out again. The wound bled freely, running down his arm to the wet summer grass beneath him.

"I'm tired of this rain," Shawn smiled, gesturing toward the sky. And then it stopped, just like that. The clouds parted to reveal the three-quarters moon behind, lighting the yard of the old Spencer house before which Shawn stood.

"Be healed," he smiled again, snapping his fingers. Ruskin's wound vanished, leaving no evidence that it had ever existed save for a ragged hole in the man's shirt, showing bright pink skin underneath.

Ruskin struggled to his knees. Shaking his head in confusion, he looked up at Shawn. "Son, you're... glowing. What's going on?"

Shawn realized the man was right; he was enveloped in a bright blue flame, the power within his palm barely contained by his own skin. He levitated into the air, spinning in lazy little circles, laughing with the sheer delight of it all as he sensed the fear of the two humans on the ground below.

The girl was saying something to him, but he couldn't quite make out what it was. He dropped back down to the ground, landing before her, but he still couldn't understand her words; it was almost like she was speaking another language.

Who was this girl anyway? This... human? And then she was touching him – how dare she touch *him* – wrapping her arms around his neck, her lips moving to brush against his. And, finally, he understood her words;

"Shawn, please come back to me. I love you!"

But who was Shawn? And then he remembered...

In the instant that the energy struck the nickel and flowed into him, he knew that he was lost. The power sang through his soul, calling to him, and he wasn't sure he could resist it. He wasn't even sure that he wanted to. He... opened up, was the only word he could think to describe the sensation, and the world was suddenly his for the taking.

*"All you need to do is to accept this gift,"* the voice whispered inside his head.

"And wind up like Ahpuc?" Shawn replied, his voice echoing through space and time as he held a conversation with a ghost.

*"Power, Shawn. To do with as you will. Think of the lives you could save. Think of the lives you might bring back."*

"Bring... back?"

*"Tanner, if you so desire. Alive and in the flesh, his body restored to him. Your sister. Your cat. The possibilities are endless, for one such as you…"*

Bring back Tanner? Such temptation…

…but now, looking into Jenny's eyes, he knew that it was wrong. Tanner had come back to life to save them, and by using the magic that he had fought against to bring him back a second time he'd be denying his friend's sacrifice. Tanner had made his choice, and now Shawn had to make his.

Floating to the ground, Shawn stared at his closed fist, concentrating. A flash of light escaped from between his fingers, and then it was done. He opened his hand to reveal not only the nickel but also a long, pointed animal's tooth, a shining green gem, a brown twig, and a tiny geode. Sighing, he let the objects tumble from his fingers to land at his feet.

A part of him ached for the power he had just given up, but another, larger part knew that were he to accept it that he would be giving up so much more. It just wasn't meant to be. In the end, the decision was surprisingly simple.

"I love you, too, Jenny," he said, leaning in to kiss away the girl's tears, his arms around her, knowing that he did indeed love her and that he never wanted to let her go.

# Chapter 42

"AZAZEL!" CALLED an angry voice from behind them, nearly causing Shawn to jump out of his skin.

He turned to see a man in a tan trench coat walking toward them from across the yard. His blue eyes were deeper than all the world's oceans and his flowing blonde hair remained perfectly dry despite the downpour that had ended just seconds earlier. It was the man from Tanner's funeral, the same one he'd seen outside the movie theatre. But what was he doing here?

"Who is that?" whispered Jenny, her hand finding his. "He looks familiar."

"No clue," Shawn replied under his breath, "but I think we're about to find out."

"Michael!" said a voice from somewhere in the shadows, "You should not be here. You have sworn not to interfere…"

"And I didn't, Azazel, not until the boy refused you," said Michael, stopping just a few feet from where Shawn stood, "and now I am finally free to act. I bind you, Azazel, by speaking your true name thrice. Now show yourself."

The air shimmered in front of Shawn to reveal a muscular, dark-skinned man with jet black hair and wild dark eyes to match. He wore a trench coat identical to the man the voice had called Michael, save that his was so black that it almost seemed a part of the night around him. He wore a pair of silver manacles around his wrists, and didn't look too happy about it.

"It's not too late, boy," Azazel argued, turning to Shawn. "Think! Immortality, unlimited wealth, unequaled power... all at your fingertips! Just bend over and pick up the talismans..."

"Enough!" roared Michael, moving between Shawn and the demon. "He has already turned you down. Look into his heart and you'll see that no matter what you offer him, the results will always be the same."

"...as you wish, Michael," the demon smiled, his eyes blazing with hatred as he winked at the man who had bound him. "But there will be other days, other possibilities. You know this to be true."

"Perhaps," said Michael. "But not on this day. Now be gone!"

The air shimmered once more and it was as if the man had been yanked off some unearthly stage; one moment he was there and the next he simply wasn't, banished to some unknown place.

"I think I need a drink," the Sheriff mumbled, rising to his feet to stare open-mouthed at the man in the trench coat.

"No, you don't," Michael said, turning to look into the man's eyes, "and you never really did. But you know that now, don't you?" He reached out to grasp Ruskin's hand.

"You know," answered Ruskin, shaking his head in wonder, "I think I do." He let his arm fall to the side as Michael finally released his grip.

"Michael," whispered Jenny, moving toward the man in the trench coat, "are you an angel?"

An angel? Shawn had stopped believing in such things a long time ago. But whatever he was the man wasn't of this earth, that was for sure.

"I am what you need me to be," Michael whispered, leaning in to kiss the girl on the cheek. "You have had such pain, Jenny McGee, losing your brother twice in one lifetime. But he is so proud of you, and he loves you so much. Always know that."

"Thank you," she whispered, tears rolling down her cheeks, "Thank you so much."

"Wait a minute," interrupted Shawn, laying a trembling hand upon the man's wrist. "If Jenny's parents didn't put the jar in Tanner's coffin... you did, didn't you? It had to be you."

Michael smiled and shrugged his shoulders. "Perhaps," he said, "but then again, as Azazel so eloquently reminded me, I'm sworn not to interfere. So it couldn't have been me, now could it?"

Shawn returned his smile, saying nothing. Maybe he didn't need to know after all. He hadn't seen the man reach to the ground, yet he now held the five talismans in his outstretched hand. He transferred all of them but the nickel to a pocket in his trench coat, then presented the coin to Shawn.

"The other four talismans will be dispersed around the world, where capable hands will guard them. As for the coin," he nodded at his hand, "you will be the guardian of the wild magic that was put into this so very long ago." It wasn't a question, and Michael didn't look as though he required an answer.

"Um, no, I won't," replied Shawn, holding his hands up before him. "I don't want to end up like Ahpuc. Hell, I can't even drive or vote yet, how would the coin be safe with me? I'm just a kid!"

"You are more than that, Shawn Spencer, and I wouldn't ask this of you if I didn't know you could handle it. I believe it was Uncle Ben in *Amazing Fantasy* # 15 who said to Peter Parker, 'with great power comes great responsibility.' You've held the power of all five talismans in your hand, and you rejected it. Who else but someone who has triumphed against such temptation could guard the coin against those less scrupulous?"

Michael was right. Along with Tanner, Jenny, and Ruskin, he had worked to defeat Ahpuc, and they had won. And with that victory came the responsibility to keep the nickel safe, to see that no one like Ahpuc could ever again claim the mantle that he had created for himself by corrupting the five talismans. Besides, after the Spider-Man reference, how could he say no?

"All right," he said, in a small voice, reaching out to take the coin from the man's hand. "I'll do it."

"Michael," Jenny interrupted, her gaze shifting back and forth between Shawn and the angel, "will we ever see Tanner again?"

"Anything is possible, but, if not, he'll always be in your heart," the man said, as he began to fade from view, "And now I must go. Be well, all of you. And whatever you choose to have faith in, remember to first have faith in yourself; if you have that, all else will follow."

And then, like the demon before him, Michael vanished. There was no puff of smoke or flash of lightning; it was as if he stepped sideways through a door that none of them could see, leaving nothing behind to prove that he had ever stepped foot on the lawn outside of 1771 Randolph Street.

Shawn stared at the buffalo nickel that he and Tanner had found in the old house just over a week – or maybe a lifetime – ago. He smiled. Okay, so maybe he could handle the responsibility after all. It didn't look like he had much of a choice, though he knew that he really did; there were always choices, and several had been made tonight, on both sides of the cosmic fence.

He heard sirens in the distance, the shrill whine of the police cars growing closer with every passing second. The cavalry was coming, late as usual.

"I think that's my cue," said Ruskin, indicating the sirens. "I don't understand most of what went on here tonight, but I think a good thing just happened."

"A very good thing," Jenny agreed, reaching out to squeeze the burly Sheriff's hand. "So you're my uncle, huh? I knew my aunt Margaret had been married before she died, but…Wow, I just never knew. I even asked my dad once, but he said that the 'Ruskin' who married

Aunt Margaret wasn't the same man who was the sheriff…" she stopped in mid-sentence, finally understanding her father's words.

"In a way," Ruskin said, looking wistfully at the young girl, "he was right. But maybe, just maybe, he was wrong too."

Ruskin smiled, looking as though he wanted to embrace the girl but didn't know if he should. So Jenny decided for him, throwing her arms around his neck, hugging him tight.

"We're family," Ruskin whispered as he returned the hug, his eyes glistening under the light of the moon, "I forgot that for a while, but I never will again."

As soon as Jenny released him, the big Sheriff surprised Shawn by clapping him on the shoulder and giving him a gentle squeeze as if to say, we're family now, too.

Turning from the two teenagers, the burly ex-cop waved down the approaching police cars, moving toward them to bring them up to speed on everything that had happened – or at least the parts that they would believe.

"Come on," said Shawn, reaching out to take Jenny's hand. He pulled her fingers to his lips, kissing her palm just as the police pulled into the driveway behind the black Cadillac. "Let's go home."

With one hand holding tight to Jenny's, Shawn fingered the nickel with the other, turning it over and over with his thumb and his forefinger, wondering how something so small could wield so much power. Then he thought of Tanner, of the love that he and Jenny had discovered for each other, and of the unbreakable bond that had been formed here tonight between the three of them. Perhaps the only real power in the world came from the small things, after all.

# Epilogue

## Six Months Later

*IT'S NOW OR NEVER,* Fred Ruskin thought to himself, his fist poised to knock on Candy Martin's door. He'd just received his six-month chip from the little Alcoholics Anonymous group he'd joined, and had finally finished the paperwork required to purchase the Morgan Oil restaurant across from the college at the east end of town.

For years, he had resisted using the money – nearly $250,000 – he'd received from the insurance company and the police department when his wife and child had been taken from him. He was surprised to learn that the money, left in the hands of his accountant, had ballooned to nearly double that amount. He'd taken the original insurance settlement and used it to open the Molly Ruskin and Tanner McGee Memorial Fund, a charity that would help the families of victims of violent crimes cope with their losses, both monetary and emotional.

He used $50,000 of the remaining money to buy the restaurant, choosing to leave the rest in his account for a rainy day. Even if the venture went belly-up, he could easily live on the combined pensions from the Chicago Police Detective Squad and the Hancock County Sheriff's Department.

He was sober and smoke-free now, had lost thirty pounds, and for the first time in years was bathed, clean shaven, and didn't reek of alcohol and cigarettes. He regretted how things had ended with Candy and hope that she would give him another chance to prove to her that he could be the kind of man that she needed. With a bouquet of roses in one hand, he finally worked up the nerve to knock with the other, his heart thumping in his chest. Finally, the door opened.

"Fred?" asked Candy Martin, standing just inside the doorway. She was dressed in a white blouse and a green skirt, and her dark blonde hair dangled from a ponytail behind her. "Well, this is a surprise. Come on in."

Ruskin smiled sheepishly, both unsure of himself and of what the future would bring. But for the first time in years, he knew that there *was* a future, and that thought gave him hope that things could work out for the two of them after all. Besides, he was only fifty-two; he had the rest of his life ahead of him, and he didn't intend to waste one more minute of it.

Roses in hand and hope in his heart, Fred Ruskin stepped through the door, over the threshold, and into the rest of his life.

Coming in fall of 2013

# Threads

The sequel to Small Things, and book two in
the Small Things trilogy

Please turn the page for a preview chapter

# Threads
## by Joe DeRouen
## Coming fall 2013

KATY RUSKIN awoke tangled in covers, bathed in sweat, breathing hard and on the verge of screaming. She'd had another one of the dreams, this one worse than the last. She was in the house again, the house that Henry Spencer had turned into apartments before she was even born, and was running, running, running for her life. Running from some unseen force, constantly looking over her shoulder, hiding in the shadows, scurrying away from God only knows what.

She'd been having the dreams since she was thirteen and, though they varied from time to time, the theme was always the same. Something she couldn't see – had never managed to see, despite her abilities – was chasing her, mocking her, calling to her, wanting her dead. She'd been having the dreams for over half her life, usually at least once a week, sometimes more but rarely less, and she wanted them to stop. She needed them to stop. But instead of stopping, they seemed to be getting worse.

Rarely did she have the dreams two nights in a row, but last night was the third time in as many days that she'd found herself trapped in the house. She'd been terrified out of her mind, unable to escape, with whatever chased her hot on her heels and closing in fast. And it was getting closer.

The dreams started when she was thirteen, two days after she had her first period. At first, she'd just had the sense that something dangerous was following her. Later, she heard fragments of a voice, and lately she'd almost been able to see the thing. The dreams were progressing, and she felt powerless to do anything about it. Worse still, she feared what would happen when her pursuer finally caught her.

The house in her nightmares was different than the real house, but, apparently, that hadn't always been the case. She'd surreptitiously asked questions about the building and had long ago confirmed that, without the partitions and remodeling that had turned it into an apartment building in the late seventies, it had once looked exactly like the house that she so feared.

Sighing, shaking her head, Katy rose from her bed and padded to the bathroom. Running a brush through the tangles in her straight brown hair, she blanched as she caught her reflection in the mirror. The night had not been kind to her. Puffy bags hung from under her deep brown eyes and she looked as if she hadn't slept in days. In fact, if she didn't know better, she'd almost think she had aged a good ten years overnight. Katy was only twenty-four, but, this morning at least, she looked to be in her mid-thirties, if not older. This definitely did not bode well for her date tonight.

"Are you okay?" asked a tentative voice from outside the bathroom. "The way you ran in there…"

"I'm fine, Mel. Just a bad dream, that's all. Give me a sec and I'll be right out."

"No rush. Go ahead and take a shower, my first class today isn't until ten."

"Cool," Katy answered, picking up her toothbrush with one hand and a half-used tube of Crest with the other. "Ten minutes and the bathroom's all yours."

Melissa Fleming was Katy's best friend and roommate. They'd been paired up in their first year of college at Western Illinois University in Macomb, and, discovering to their amazement that they had a lot more in common than their incredibly good fashion sense, had quickly become friends. After earning their bachelor degrees - Mel's in journalism, Katy's in art history - they decided to move to Chicago, where Mel was from, to pursue their Master's and find their fortunes. That was nearly two years ago, and they'd remained roommates ever since.

They'd been close since that first year of college, but Mel had really become her touchstone when Katy's father died shortly after graduation. Sure, she was close to her mother, but her Mom had been too torn up by the loss of her husband to even breathe. And she and Sam, who was eighteen years her senior and the product of her mother's first marriage, had never really been as close as she would have liked. But Mel had really come through for her, even going so far as to drive with her to Carthage for the funeral. That, more than anything, had cemented their friendship.

Katy stripped off her faded WIU nightshirt, finally ready to shower before schlepping off for another day of work at the gallery. She chanced a second look in the mirror and frowned at her disheveled appearance. She'd never been what anyone would call beautiful, but at five-seven and one-hundred-thirty-five pounds she wasn't ugly either. Her B-cup size breasts had yet to start their inevitable journey southward, and she had reasonably firm, muscular legs with an ass to match, honed to perfection -or at least as close to perfection as she was going to get - by years of track in high school and college. She had pale, porcelain-like skin, and her straight brown hair was cut in a classic page boy bob. She was definitely presentable.

She was intelligent, had a good sense of humor, and knew a lot about a wide variety of subjects. And while she wasn't a knockout, she knew that she was definitely cute, maybe even approaching pretty in an abstract sort of way. Her brown eyes matched her hair, both inherited from her father, while her delicate features and bone structure she had managed to acquire from her mother. All in all, not a bad package: so why weren't more guys interested in her?

Mel had told her on more than one occasion that she was simply unapproachable. Guys were interested, Mel insisted, but they couldn't get past the barriers she had built. She had to be more open, more willing to give people a chance.

"You'd have barriers, too, if you spent your nights running from monsters," Katy muttered to herself, stepping through the steam and into the shower.

**For more news about Threads and the Small Things trilogy, be sure to visit www.JoeDeRouen.com.**

Made in the USA
Charleston, SC
09 December 2012